The man of her dream.

Destitute and without friends, Violet Carlton is forced to seek employment at the House of Pleasure in London. She steels herself for her first customer and is shocked when the man rescues her instead of ravishing her. A grateful Violet cannot help but admire the handsome Viscount Trevor. But she must curb her desire for the dashing nobleman she can never have because he is already betrothed to another . . .

Tristan had gone to the House of Pleasure for a last bit of fun before he became a faithful married man. But when he recognizes the woman in his bed, he becomes determined to save her instead. Now, his heart wars with his head as he falls for the vulnerable courtesan. Unable to break his betrothal without a scandal, Tris resolves to find Violet proper employment or a husband of her own. Still, his arms ache for Violet, urging him to abandon propriety and sacrifice everything to be with the woman he loves. . . .

Books by AUTHOR

House of Pleasure Series
Only Scandal Will Do
Only Marriage Will Do
Only A Mistress Will Do

Published by Kensington Publishing Corporation

Only A Mistress Will Do
House of Pleasure Series

Jenna Jaxon

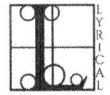

LYRICAL PRESS
Kensington Publishing Corp.
www.kensingtonbooks.com

Lyrical Press books are published by
Kensington Publishing Corp. 119 West 40th Street New York, NY 10018

Copyright © 2017 by Jenna Jaxon

All rights reserved. No part of this book may be reproduced in any form or by any means without the prior written consent of the Publisher, excepting brief quotes used in reviews.

All Kensington titles, imprints, and distributed lines are available at special quantity discounts for bulk purchases for sales promotion, premiums, fund-raising, and educational or institutional use.

To the extent that the image or images on the cover of this book depict a person or persons, such person or persons are merely models, and are not intended to portray any character or characters featured in the book.

Special book excerpts or customized printings can also be created to fit specific needs. For details, write or phone the office of the Kensington Special Sales Manager:
Kensington Publishing Corp.
119 West 40th Street
New York, NY 10018
Attn. Special Sales Department. Phone: 1-800-221-2647.

Kensington and the K logo Reg. U.S. Pat. & TM Off.
LYRICAL PRESS Reg. U.S. Pat. & TM Off.
Lyrical Press and the L logo are trademarks of Kensington Publishing Corp.

First Electronic Edition: April 2017
eISBN-13: 978-1-5161-0282-2
eISBN-10: 1-5161-0282-7

First Print Edition: April 2017
ISBN-13: 978-1-5161-0284-6
ISBN-10: 1-5161-0284-3

Printed in the United States of America

This book is dedicated in memory of beloved romance author Jo Beverley whose works gave me so much pleasure and were the inspiration for this series.

Acknowledgements

I would like to acknowledge, as always, the wonderful people who have helped and supported me during the writing of this book: my family, who suffered through my first oral recitation of the plot while we were on vacation;, my beta readers, Ella Quinn, Alexandra Christle, and Patricia Green, who kept me on the straight and narrow(ladies you are awesome); and my wonderful editor, Penny Barber, without whom this work, and my writing, would be much the poorer. Thank you all from the bottom of my heart.

Chapter 1

London, November 1761

Shivering in the brisk wind cutting straight through her thin gown, Violet Carlton trudged across the small dirt-packed backyard, littered with tufts of dead grass and scattered brown and red leaves. Teeth clenched to stop their chattering, she mounted the short three steps of the back stoop, straightened her shoulders, and rapped three times on the dull gray door of the silvery clapboard house. Beyond the weathered board fence of the house next door a dog barked, but no one stirred. No prying eyes to witness her shame.

The door opened a crack, and a lad of about twelve stuck his head out. "What you doin' 'ere this time o' day?"

"I would like to speak with Madame Vestry, please." Perhaps she should have waited until later in the morning. Such an establishment would obviously keep late hours. But the ache in her belly had forced her here as soon as the sun had risen.

"She's still sleep. Come back later today." He started to push the door closed but Violet rammed her boot between it and the jamb. The boy kept shoving, squeezing her foot until she winced in pain, but she gritted her teeth, put her shoulder to the door and pushed back. If she didn't do this now, she wouldn't have the courage, or the strength, to come back.

"I need to see her now." She raised her voice, and threw her weight against the rough boards. Despite her small stature, she was stronger. He staggered back and she fell into a narrow back foyer with a row of coat hooks and the devastating yeasty smell of baking bread. Her mouth watered and her stomach rumbled. She hadn't eaten for days.

Blond hair straggling from under a mobcap, a girl, maybe fourteen, rushed into the room. "What the hell's going on in here Willie?" She wiped her hands on her apron, streaked with flour and grease. Warily, her gaze shifted from Willie to Violet. "Who are you?"

"I've come to see Madame Vestry." Violet focused on the girl's narrowed eyes. "I need to talk to her, please." Her heart gave a sickening lurch.

In one practiced glance, the girl took in her appearance, from what used to be her second-best hat to the rumpled and stained deep-purple dress to her scuffed black boots, and sniffed. "I see you do."

The appraisal stung, but was probably fair. She'd come down fast in the months since her grandmother's death. Her possessions long gone, her wardrobe—reduced to two dresses and a well-worn cloak—had been sold, leaving her with only the dress she stood up in. These clothes wouldn't fetch a shilling in a secondhand shop now.

The servant girl nodded to Willie. "Close the door before we freeze to death, jingle-brains. Come on." She led Violet out of the foyer. "I'll ask if Madame will see you. But she won't be happy being woke up this early, you can bet your dippers on that."

The last thing she wanted was to antagonize her future employer. Still, she couldn't risk waiting until later.

Taking a firm grip on herself, she followed the girl down a shadowy hallway until she motioned her into an equally dim reception room. "Wait here." The girl turned on her heel and left.

Violet let out the breath she'd been holding. She hadn't fainted yet, though her empty stomach had tied itself in knots. The pain meant she was alive and by God she intended to stay that way. She strode farther into the room and perched on the red cushioned sofa. Let the woman arrive swiftly to get this over with.

Sitting rigidly, she stared at her hands clenched in her lap, then shook herself. She had better be stronger than this. Determined, she sat straighter. A classical-style painting in a large gilt frame across from her caught her interest. A naked woman lay on a chaise, her legs spread. Oh, good Lord. Her womanly parts were exposed and a swan lay with its beak pressed between her thighs.

Her face heated and she had to look somewhere else, anywhere else but at that painting. The fireplace on her right held two candlesticks, shaped like naked women. Wax had dripped onto the figures, drops hanging from the nipples. Was there nowhere in the room without a lewd image? Violet gripped the end of the sofa. The plush red carpet seemed safe to study. The smooth, polished wood under her fingers had been carved in an oval with folds in the middle. She traced the pattern absently, still unable to get the image of the painting out of her mind. The swan's long neck lying at the apex of the woman's open legs. Her forefinger stroked the wooden oval, so similar to the—

"Dear God!" She snatched her hand away and rubbed it against her gown.

"Miss Carlton?" A small, dark-haired woman in an exotic scarlet silk robe seemed to fill the room.

Violet jumped to her feet, her heart thudding wildly.

"My maid said you wished to see me?" Madame Vestry's dark eyes took in every detail of Violet's appearance. She raised an eyebrow.

On the tip of her tongue to retort of course, she did not wish to see the owner of a brothel, she instead swallowed back her anger. She could ill afford to provoke Madame Vestry. "Yes, ma'am. My brother told me if things went very badly for me I should…" Words stuck in her throat like a fish bone.

"Come to my establishment?"

Face flushing, Violet nodded. "Yes."

"Who is your brother, Miss Carlton?" A narrowing of the woman's eyes echoed the suspicion in her voice.

"James Carlton, ma'am."

Vestry's head rose slightly and she relaxed. "Ah, yes, Jamie. You are his sister? Then I am sorry for your loss, Miss Carlton."

"Thank you, Madame Vestry." Thankfully, her voice held steady, the months since her brother's death easing the grief to the point she did not weep instantly at the thought. Her current plight was enough to do that.

"And you have now come to that desperate point where you seek employment with me?" The business-like tone, neither condoning nor condemning, stiffened Violet's resolve.

"Yes, ma'am. As of today, I have nowhere else to go, no one to turn to." A sickening churn of her stomach that had nothing to do with hunger sent tension through her. "Nothing else of value."

Except herself.

"You are how old, Miss Carlton?"

"Nineteen, ma'am. Almost twenty."

"Let me see you walk, please." With a crisp snap, Vestry pulled the curtains open and nodded to the path between the sofa and fireplace.

Violet straightened her skirts as best she could. Suddenly stiff and self-conscious, she concentrated on putting one foot before the other until she came face to face with another obscene painting. She clenched her hands and averted her eyes.

"Turn please."

Feeling more and more like a horse or a cow at Smithfield market, she did as she was told, hopefully with a bit more grace.

In reward, Vestry gave her a slight nod. "You speak and move as befit your station, Miss Carlton. With a little training, I suspect you will be quite popular with our patrons. I should be able to command a high price for your virginity."

Violet's feet tangled in the plush carpet.

The scant approval vanished as Vestry glared at her. "I assume you are intact?"

Oh, the shame. How could this woman suggest she had already lain with a man? Bitterness flooded her mouth and her chest ached with mortification. Finally, she managed a curt nod.

"Lie down on the sofa please."

"What? Why?"

"I am not fool enough to take your word, Miss Carlton." Vestry smiled mirthlessly. "A brief inspection will allow me to assure your buyer he is indeed purchasing a virgin."

Her cheeks heated at the humiliation this woman suggested. The cold inevitability of her situation rolled over her, engulfing her as though she was drowning beneath a relentless sea. Madame Vestry demanded almost nothing compared to the real horror awaiting her at the hands of her buyer. Still, she had chosen to live. She could no longer afford the luxury of respectability.

Vestry stood immobile, a flicker in her eyes the only hint of interest.

Steeling herself, without word or plea, Violet lay down on the disgusting sofa, raised her knees and turned her head toward the garish red satin cushion. Cool air rushed past her thighs. Hot tears slipped down her cheeks. She hadn't wanted to cry. The time for weakness had passed.

"You may sit up now."

Indignant, Violet sat up and raised her chin. "Are you satisfied as to my honesty now?"

"I always was, Miss Carlton." Madame Vestry stared into Violet's eyes, her gaze seeming to penetrate to her soul.

"Then why—"

"I needed to test your mettle."

Rising, Violet scowled. Simply coming to this place should have shown her determination.

"Respectable women often believe they can eschew respectability to save their lives, only to find, in the end, starvation far pleasanter than immorality," Vestry continued matter-of-factly. "You, however, I believe will do, Cassandra. Come with me." Motioning her to follow, she headed out of the room.

"Cassandra?" Violet hurried to keep up.

"All of my girls have false names, false identities." At the end of the hallway, they headed up a flight of stairs. "The life they lead in the House of Pleasure is just as fraudulent. Cassandra is the mask you will wear to protect a vestige of your self-respect." When they reached the landing, Madame twitched her silky robe out of the way and turned to her. "Think of it as a role, very like one an actress might take upon the stage. It is not who you are, unless you allow it be." The vehemence of the last sentence rang in the cramped stairwell.

Violet stumbled back a step. "Why Cassandra?" It was a classical reference she couldn't quite place.

A peculiar smile curled Madame Vestry's red lips. "She was a prophet and a spoil of war. A woman men used but dismissed because they could not understand her prophecies, although they came true with a vengeance." A fire glowed in her cunning eyes as she scrutinized Violet's body.

More than her earlier examination, Vestry's calculating perusal made Violet uncomfortable.

"What prophecy will you reveal to your customers, I wonder, Miss Carlton? A promise of pleasure or one of pain?" The light extinguished as quickly as it had come. "This way." She started down a corridor to the right. "You will have a room of your own on the second floor. Depending on circumstances, you will entertain your clients either there or in one of the ground-floor rooms."

Violet followed, each step hardening her heart.

"I will see to your training during the next week." Passion drained from her voice. The businesswoman had returned.

A shiver shot down Violet's spine.

"I will also inform certain special clients I have an item of interest for them."

No going back now. She had become a whore. Tears threatened, but she beat them back.

"You can only sell your virtue once and I will make sure you receive the highest price, my dear. Half of those proceeds are yours."

Violet wavered between fainting and nausea, then steadied. Perhaps thinking of the encounter as a business deal might make the situation tolerable.

Madame Vestry showed her into a small, clean room boasting no lewd artwork, only a wide oak bed, a chest on chest, an armchair and table.

"This room is yours as long as you work for me, though should you receive a better offer, I'd advise you take it."

"A better offer?" Who on earth would want her after this?

"Many of my girls have gone on to become exclusive mistresses to the noblemen who take a fancy to them. Such arrangements are often quite lucrative. With judicious saving one might have enough to start their life over after four or five years." A mischievous smile flitted across Madame Vestry's face. "One of the girls who passed through here briefly—very briefly, mind you—ended up marrying a marquess. That smacks more of fairytale than reality. Still the tale is true."

The animation drained from her face as the brusque woman of business returned. "I will leave you to settle in, although I'll expect you ready for your first lesson this afternoon. We serve late luncheon at four and supper after midnight. The house opens for clients at dusk." She looked Violet up and down once more, lingering on her face. "You might want to stay in your room tonight. Just ignore anything you may hear. You'll get used to the noise rather quickly." Abruptly, she shut the door.

Violet dropped into the chair as her legs finally gave out, praying to God she could get through this nightmare, if only one moment at a time.

Chapter 2

"What pleasure may I give you this evening, my lord?" No matter how many times Violet had practiced it in the past five days, she still doubted she would be able to ask the question when the time came. She sat before the fire in the green room downstairs in the House of Pleasure, staring into the dying embers, repeating the words of her first lesson. A question all Vestry's girls were supposed to ask their clients before complying with their demands for the night.

Swift footsteps clacked on the wooden floor outside the door.

Violet clutched her arms, disregarding the pain as her nails dug through the thin fabric of her purple dress. The steps continued past and she sagged in the dark green velvet armchair. Five days of training, in which she had learned acts she never imagined went on between men and women, had shredded her nerves. Still, she'd made her choice. She'd have to see it through. Her employer had already housed, clothed and fed her. She wouldn't take losing such a valuable commission lightly.

"What pleasure may I give you this evening, my lord?" Violet forced the words out over and over. Wild laughter in the hallway, faint strains of a pianoforte, and the lewd grunts from the room next door twisted her stomach, yet she kept repeating the phrase. The raucous sounds of the brothel had become more familiar during the week, but still set her on edge.

Footsteps approached once more, slowed, stopped.

Violet's heart pounded, her rapid breathing keeping pace. The huge bed to her right drew her attention for perhaps the hundredth time. Was this the moment? She seized the arms of the velvet chair, fighting to hold herself in place. Her nails sank into the soft fabric as she struggled to slow her breaths.

The handle lowered.

Her head came up, back straight, forced smile plastered on her face as the door opened wide and she caught a glimpse of the man who had bought her for the night. Madame Vestry had informed her this morning that one of her regular customers had responded favorably to her invitation—she'd actually called it an invitation—and for Violet to make herself available in the green room at eight o'clock tonight.

She'd not been told who he was and somehow it mattered little to her that she did not know the name of the man about to ruin her. One of the house rules forbade her to ask. If the gentleman offered his name, that was his business. The other girls had told her if she needed to put a name to the face, to think of customers as "Lord John."

This Lord John entered the small room in a swirl of black fur and sandalwood, the spicy scent tickling Violet's nose, making it twitch.

She tipped her head back and looked up into the swarthy face. Dark hair and piercing blue eyes, a strong jaw, and a long, straight nose. Too tall, though. He was too tall for her. The ridiculousness of the irrational thought broke through her lethargy. She forced herself up out of the chair as he strode toward her.

The smile curling his full lips would have been charming had not the gleam in his eyes betrayed his lustful intent.

"Good evening, Cassandra." His deep baritone voice sent a frisson of dread through her. "Such a lovely name for a lovely temptress."

"What pleasure may I give you this evening, my lord?" The words came out flat, but by God, she'd gotten them out. Now to remain standing and not faint. One small goal at a time. She stared at the wide expanse of blue velvet jacket barely two inches from her face.

He ran the back of his hand along her cheek and goose flesh pimpled her whole body. "I do hope the pleasure will be mutual, my dear."

Violet jerked back from his caress. Her gaze, firmly fixed on the gold buttons of his jacket, now shot to his face, expecting a leer. How could he suggest she might enjoy being debauched?

His dark brows had puckered into a surprised frown, almost reproachful. He lowered his hand.

Dear God. She couldn't refuse him anything. Lord John owned her for the night. Whatever he wanted to do to her, be it lewd touch or soft caress, she had to submit. No matter she wanted to scream, or cry, or pummel his chest. Curse him for being a depraved wretch who reveled in her misfortunes.

That wasn't fair. She returned her gaze to his chest. Despite her misery, she couldn't blame him for her misfortunes or her decision to come here. He was a man bent on the usual pleasures of men, and she needed the patronage of such men to survive. If he wanted her to be pleased, then she would convince him of her pleasure. A leaden weight settled over her, grounding her. She tipped back her head and smiled at him, the practiced false smile that showed her teeth. "Then I am certain we shall both be pleased, my lord."

A broad grin spread across his swarthy face. "Amorina has taught you well, little one. You will go far here, I believe." He untied his cloak and tossed it carelessly onto a chair.

Violet gawked at his body—perfectly proportioned shoulders, waist, and hips, well-muscled legs—and her bravado slipped a notch. He was gorgeous, with a face like a cherub bent on mischief and a body made for sin. Somehow a devilishly handsome, virile man made the situation worse. She had assumed whoever ruined her would be old, ugly, evil. Like the deed he performed.

He touched her cheek.

She started then forced herself to remain still this time. Despite the heat of the blazing logs, uncontrollable shivers wracked her body. Twisting the fabric of her skirt helped.

Slowly, Lord John leaned down, bringing the scent of sandalwood to swirl around her head. He scattered kisses along the side of her neck. "Don't worry, *ma petite*. I don't bite, unless instructed."

His caresses sent chills down her arms. When she turned her head and rubbed her arms, he laughed and pulled her against him. Don't fight. Just submit. She made herself relax, lean on his taut body. As if given permission, his mouth descended, tickling the sensitive flesh of neck, making her whole body glow as though a fire had been lit within. Her heartbeat pounded a staccato rhythm. Did he hear that? Did he feel her getting warmer? Pressed together as they were, he must.

He slid his mouth down her throat, and cupped her derriere through her thin lavender striped petticoat.

Her bottom tensed. More heat rushed to her face and she burrowed her head into his chest, grateful he couldn't see her.

A low humming vibrated the skin of her neck, and his full-throated growl ensued. He gripped her buttocks, surprising a gasp out of her. With strong fingers, he kneaded them before he traveled up her backside, across her back to her waist. Lord John raised his head, his eyes bright with desire. He moved her away from him and continued up to stroke her breasts.

Smiling all the while, Violet closed her eyes and gritted her teeth. So that was why Madame Vestry had given strict instructions to remove her stays beforehand.

He circled her nipples with his thumbs, making them tingle and ache. She bit her lip to stifle a moan. He couldn't be right, could he? She shouldn't enjoy being ruined.

But he had awakened sensations Violet couldn't deny. Her nipples swelled as he stroked them, tightening to rock-hard points. When he gave them a playful pinch, the pain shot through her and lodged an unfamiliar throbbing at the apex of her thighs. She couldn't stop her moan that time.

A sensual smile touched his lips. "We should get you out of these clothes now, my dear. It's so much better skin to skin." In two swift motions, he had her garments in a pool on the floor.

Violet stared at her naked body, the pink of a body blush spreading downward like a wave. She clasped one arm across her breasts, the other across her body to shield her sex.

A chuckle brought her head up to stare into appreciative blue eyes. "I must say, Amorina has got quite the little gem in you, my dear." The renewed hunger in those bright eyes leapt at her. He grasped the hand clamped to her breasts, drew it over her head, and then led the other one up to join it, so her breasts jutted toward him in invitation.

Shame clogged her throat, making it hard to breathe.

He raked her nakedness with his hot gaze, and sighed deeply. "If I were free, I might have to spirit you away from here. Keep you all to myself." Some of the hunger died and his voice softened as he released her. "Why don't you climb up onto the bed, now? I'll just take care of my clothing and we'll continue."

Violet scurried toward the tall, four-poster mahogany bed, covers and sheets turned down as per Madame's instructions. Two steps up and she collapsed onto the mattress, her skin pebbling from the cold sheets. If she could make it through the ordeal this once, the next time would not be so bad perhaps. She steeled herself and turned toward him.

Divested of all attire save his breeches, Lord John stood near the fireplace. The flickering glow gave his skin a golden sheen, the muscles of his chest rippling as he worked the buttons at his waist. Light danced along the blue velvet encasing his thighs, until with a twitch of his fingers the fabric came loose. He bent swiftly, peeled the tight garment down his legs. When he stood again, all of him gleamed in the firelight.

Violet's breath rushed out with a hiss. She'd never seen a naked man before, save in statuary. The shaft jutting toward her in the flesh was much larger. Her stomach fluttered. She dragged her gaze away. Better not to look.

He strode toward the bed, his smug grin fading into a puckered frown. She scooted away from him, barely registering the new chill of the untouched sheets on the far side of the bed.

"You look pale, my dear. Are you not well?" The concern in his voice sounded genuine.

Still, all she could do was shake her head.

He cocked his head then shrugged, climbed the steps and sat in the middle of the bed. His hip brushed hers, scalding her skin and setting her to trembling again.

"Just cold, perhaps?" He ran a finger along her arm and the shivers increased of their own accord.

Like a mouse fascinated by a snake, Violet couldn't take her eyes off of him.

"I believe I can take away the chill." His voice deepened, softened like spun silk. He leaned closer and clasped her hands, their fingers intertwining as he drew them up over her head once more. Levering himself over her, he straddled her thighs, using them as a cushion, his long, hard shaft lying atop her mass of dark brown curls.

If she watched him any longer she would surely cry, which she had sworn not to do, so she closed her eyes. Warm, wet lips latched on to her nipple, startling her, and she arched it into his mouth. Bounding up, he pressed his knee between her thighs and her whole body tensed, waiting for the pain. Tears slid down her cheeks as she tried to stifle a sob.

"Did I hurt you?" His kind voice held a desolation all its own.

How could she rail against such kindness? Even that bit of comfort was denied her.

"No, my lord." She fought the tears, but they choked her voice even worse when she held them back. Instead, she concentrated on controlling her breathing, hoping that would calm her. In just a few minutes it would be over.

"I know you haven't had a man before." He brushed her hair back from her forehead, a soft touch that devastated her with its gentleness. "It will hurt, but not very much, and not for very long."

No, not for very long. Only for the rest of her life. She buried her head in the pillow and sobbed.

Suddenly, her hands were free and his weight eased off her.

"Look at me." Lord John grasped her chin and her eyes popped open. He wiped his thumb over her cheek, collecting the tears she could not stop. "Is Madame Vestry forcing you to do this?"

Violet blinked rapidly and shook her head. "No, my lord. I came to her of my own free will."

He scowled and moved back on the bed.

"Why?"

Odd he would be interested in her woes. "I have no one and nothing, my lord." Despite the heat stinging her face, she forced herself to continue. "Except for my body."

"No one at all you might turn to?"

Madame Vestry had questioned her thoroughly about her connections.

"My brother was killed in a duel over a year ago. What money and possessions I had left, I lived on. Until last week when there was no more."

He searched her face as if trying to catch her out in a lie. "Your brother was killed in a duel? Then he was obviously a gentleman. Have you no family or friends who might take pity on you?"

"Our family had dwindled in our generation, though there may yet be a cousin in the colonies. But here in England it was just Jamie and Kit and I. After my brother died, the way he died, most of our friends shunned me."

"Jamie and Kit?"

Resigned, she stared at the glowing embers in the grate. What was that shame compared to this? "James Carlton. In his cups one night, our cousin insulted a nobleman's family and was challenged to a duel. Jamie agreed to be his second. I begged him not to, but he said he had to look after Kit."

With a grim-set mouth that alarmed her, Lord John studied her face.

"Our cousin was killed in the duel and Jamie—" She still hated admitting this to anyone, but forced the words out. "Jamie then attacked the nobleman and was killed himself."

Harshly, he seized her legs through the sheet and pinned her with an intense stare. "Do you know who the nobleman was? Who killed your brother?"

"No, my lord." She dug in her heels, trying to shrink away from him. "The men who brought his body home wouldn't tell me anything. Except what he had done was a most dishonorable thing."

He slid off the bed, and to her amazement, padded over to the heap of his clothing and began dressing, all the while cursing lightly under his breath.

Violet's heart pounded. He was leaving. What she had said to anger the man? Was he too disgusted by her brother's dishonorable behavior? Whatever it was, it must have been horrific if it had deadened the rampant lust he had shown for her.

The man pulled on his shirt, shook his hair back and glared at her.

She reached down and pulled up the covers, shielding herself as best she could from the eyes that still smoldered, with anger now rather than lust. Should she be relieved by her reprieve, or despair that her inevitable ruin was merely postponed? What Madame Vestry would have to say about the turn of events she had no idea, save it would not be pleasant.

"Let me help you dress, my dear." The soft-spoken words exploded in the quiet room.

Violet jumped.

The man tugged the sleeves of his coat before adjusting his cloak over it.

She rose on her elbow, keeping the covers tight over her shoulder. "Thank you, my lord, but I will manage. I would not want to put you to any trouble." If only he would leave, she could go back to her room upstairs and perhaps stop shaking enough to get some sleep.

"It's no trouble." He stooped, grabbed her purple dress then approached the bed. "Here…" He stopped, a light flush suffusing his face. "I am sorry. Miss Carlton."

Violet shook her head, regretting she had given him that piece of information about her identity. "I'm Cassandra."

"No, you are Miss Carlton. Miss…" He waited expectantly, with a raised eyebrow that brooked no nonsense.

"Violet," she whispered, her shame complete that he now knew her name. She cringed and slid further under the covers. Madame Vestry was right. Only anonymity made survival possible at the House of Pleasure.

"Well, Miss Violet Carlton, I have a proposition for you." His bright blue eyes glittered.

"What do you mean, my lord?" She clutched the cover tighter.

"I want you to become my mistress."

Oh, God. She slid all the way beneath the covers. He still wanted her. So why hadn't he taken her just now?

"Miss Carlton?" There was a tap on her shoulder. "It would be a temporary arrangement, and in name only. I would like to help you."

Inch by inch, Violet poked her head out. "You want to help me? But why, my lord? I have no claim on you. I don't know you." God knew she should be grateful, but she had seen the look in his eyes. This might be a mistake. Here, at the House of Pleasure, if he hurt her at least she could scream and help would come. Madame Vestry did not tolerate her girls being physically harmed.

"I knew your brother, Miss Carlton." He sounded grim and impatient. "And therein lies the claim. I insist you allow me to help you. I would not have you end up in this house because of the untimely death of your brother."

"You knew Jamie?" Her brother had known all manner of men, but none of them had had the decency to attend his funeral. His shameful death had tainted all his family.

"We were not well acquainted. However, I feel the obligation."

Fear, stress, and shame of the past hours must have taken their toll. Her overtaxed brain could not make the connection. Simply knowing a man did not obligate one toward his sister. "But how—"

"None of that really matters, does it, Miss Carlton? I offer my assistance to keep you from a life of prostitution." Hard lines scored his face. "Will you insist on bandying words about it, or will you accept my offer?"

"But you asked me to be your mistress!" She sat up in bed, careful to swath herself in the sheets. "How is that different?"

"As I said, you will be so in name only. The woman I employed as such for the past six months went home last week. I gave her a large settlement and sent her off. But the house I rent for her residence still has three months left on the lease." Lord John approached the bed and she shrank back. Startled, he put up a hand and retreated. "If you live there, no one will know your identity. You will be thought to be Serena if we are careful. We will have time to find you a place, respectable employment." His eyes beseeched her. "Is that not better than living in this house?"

Madame Vestry's admonition about accepting an offer of protection resounded in her head. Madame would think her a fool if she did not accept Lord John's proposal.

Violet nodded. "I won't really be your mistress?" Hope crept back into her heart. With the help of this lord, surely she could find a place somewhere.

"No, my dear." His kind smile touched her heart. "I would not so dishonor you, although after our interlude this evening I should, by rights, marry you."

Appalled at the thought, she shook her head. "Oh, no, my lord. This was not your fault. I lost claim to gentility the moment I set foot in this house." She drew the sheets tighter around her. Thank God for sending this man to her. "If you can help me find a respectable position, anything at all, you will earn my eternal gratitude."

His quick smile relieved her of some of the embarrassment of the situation.

"But if you will excuse me, my lord, it will only take me a moment to dress and get my things." She paused and looked pointedly at the door.

Averting his eyes, he nodded and left.

Violet tossed back the covers and threw on her clothes. Madame Vestry had instructed her in the art of swiftly disrobing and enrobing. At least one part of her training would be put to good use tonight.

After joining Lord John outside the green room, Violet led the way upstairs. Five minutes saw her things gathered, and with her thin cloak over her shoulders, she followed her rescuer down the shadowy staircase, once again trying to ignore the bawdy noises swirling around her. Whoever Lord John was, he could not lead her into a worse hell than this one.

They arrived outside Madame Vestry's office door, and he ushered her in.

Tonight Madame was dressed for a party in the guise of Aphrodite, goddess of love, draped in layers of sheer fabric. The woman's ebony eyebrows rose as they entered, but her self-satisfied smile made Violet suspect she was not surprised to see them.

"Your business is concluded so swiftly, my lord? Did Cassandra not please you?" She turned her enigmatic face from the tall man to Violet.

Lord John laughed, harsh as a cawing crow. "I think the business you sent me to see to has been accomplished." He nodded curtly toward Violet, but kept his gaze on Madame Vestry. "In fact, Miss Carlton has pleased me so well I have persuaded her to take Serena's place."

"Excellent." A gleam appeared in Madame Vestry's eyes as she stroked the small plaster dove sitting on her desk, Aphrodite's symbol. "I will, of course, require my usual finder's fee."

"I expected nothing less, Amorina. I am especially grateful you found Miss Carlton for me. Such a rare flower needs special tending." He glared candidly at the Madame. "Tending I will oversee personally."

"I never had any doubt about that, my lord." Vestry turned to Violet, the smug look vanished. "You have been given this opportunity to improve your situation, Miss Carlton. I trust you will take every advantage it offers."

"I will, Madame Vestry." Violet felt too weary to speak more.

Lord John placed a protective hand at the small of her back, a gesture that sent a frisson of warmth through her. As they reached the threshold, her protector looked over his shoulder, his face softening as he smiled at the goddess of love. "Thank you, Madame Vestry."

"No, it is I who thank you, Lord Trevor. *Bon chance.*"

Not Lord John, but Lord Trevor. Violet did not recognize the true name of her new protector, but she didn't care. If he was willing to help her escape this brothel and keep her safe, she didn't care if he was the devil himself.

Chapter 3

"Send my carriage around, Will." Tristan, Viscount Trevor, tossed a coin to the little urchin stationed in a corner of the front foyer.

"Yes, m'lord." The lad scurried out the door.

An awkward silence ensued, punctuated by raucous calls from the main public room where one of the House of Pleasure's infamous masquerades was in full swing.

"It shouldn't be long," he said, eyeing the small woman at his side. Lord, her head barely reached his chest. No bigger than a child, really. Except she was very definitely a woman. The memory of her beautiful naked body had him turning away and cursing the slowness of his carriage. Perhaps he should stand out on the porch where the chill night air might cool his ardor.

The door opened and Tris stepped back as several men entered, all in classical costumes, ranging from Zeus clutching a quiver of lightning bolts to a scantily clad shepherd.

"Trevor! Don't tell me you're for home already?" Zeus clapped him on the shoulder. "Never known you not to close the place down." His gaze fell on Miss Carlton. "Oh, ho. Found you a giggler already? I can see why you'd make it an early night here. Long night elsewhere, though." He elbowed Tris and leered at Violet. "Where's Vestry been keeping you, dearie?"

"By special order, just for me, Feldon." Tris stepped in front of her, and raised his chin. Damn, what was keeping that carriage?

Feldon raised his hands. "No offense, Trevor. There's more where she came from." Another lecherous grin. "Enjoy your strapping, now." He turned and headed into the main room, his cohorts right behind him.

Tris made sure they were well away, then turned back to his charge. "I am sorry for that, Miss Carlton. Let us wait outside. I don't know what the devil is keeping the carriage."

The woman pulled the hood of her cloak well over her head.

Good. Less chance she'd be noticed. He yanked the door open and pulled Will, clinging to the latch, into the room.

"Carriage's here, m'lord." The boy let go and bounded past Tris back into the house.

"About time, scamp." Tris took the woman's arm and guided her out, praying they met no one else.

"Weldon Street, please, Stokes," he called to his coachman as he helped Miss Carlton into the carriage, then climbed in behind her and took the back-facing seat. At last a moment to take stock. He'd had no time for more than a minimal plan since discovering her identity. Silently, he cursed fate. What were the odds a mere night's entertainment would turn out to be James Carlton's sister?

"Are you warm enough, Miss Carlton?" A moment rummaging underneath the seat and he drew out a dark red carriage blanket. Not waiting for an answer, he leaned forward and tucked it around her, tensing at the whiff of her soft, feminine scent. Fortunately, his cape hid the evidence of his continued arousal.

"I am fine, my lord." Clutching her reticule, she kept her head down.

Well, that made one of them. He struggled to relax. The woman's presence put him on edge and not only for the obvious reason. James Carlton. He'd tried to forget that name. Tried to forget all the duels during that bleak time last year as second to the Marquess of Dalbury. 'Sblood but it had come back to haunt him...them, with a vengeance. What the devil was he to do with this woman?

She looked up at him oddly.

Had he spoken the question aloud?

Settling further into the seat, she returned her gaze to her lap.

Perhaps not, then. He sighed and his shoulders slumped. Thank Christ he'd gone no further with her in bed tonight. Had he actually violated her and found out her identity afterwards, he might well have put a pistol to his head. He'd never considered the far-reaching effects of the deaths of the men they had killed last year. Nor to the repercussions it might mean for their families. To have a gently born woman come to this pass because of...well, if one wanted to lay blame it would rest ultimately with Tommy Redmond and his treachery toward Duncan. However, he and the marquess bore the actual responsibility for the deaths of those three men.

The carriage hit a bump. He blinked and looked out the window. They were leaving the Covent Garden area, heading into more respectable territory.

So what must he do with Miss Carlton? His plan to move her to his mistress's house would do for a while, but he couldn't keep her there indefinitely. If recognized, she'd be assumed to be his latest bit of skirt and her reputation would be just as ruined as if she'd been discovered at Vestry's establishment.

"Is it very far, Lord Trevor?" Miss Carlton spoke, pulling him out of his reverie.

"Not very, Miss Carlton. We'll have you there and in bed in no time." She jerked her head up, her eyes wide. "What?"

Tris wanted to cut out his tongue. "I beg your pardon, but you seem fatigued after the trials of tonight. I believe a good long rest will put you to rights."

She pulled the blanket closer and stared out the window at the inky night.

Tris leaned back in his seat, the creak of the well-oiled leather loud in the now dead silence of the carriage. He would have a word with Madame Vestry as soon as possible. Had bringing him in to debauch Miss Carlton been a master touch in getting revenge on the marquess? Or had she gambled he'd question the girl before he ruined her? The woman had a penchant for playing games, so Duncan had told him. Tris had patronized her house for years—three of his mistresses had come from the House of Pleasure, all well trained in the ways of pleasing a man. He'd certainly never had a complaint with his treatment there. Until tonight.

The woman across from him sat with her head bowed so only her dark hair showed. In his mind's eye it lay spread out over the white pillowcase, her face turned to the side in a profile reminiscent of the head on a Greek coin. Beauty and grace fanning his desire. Her soft skin beneath his hand, her tantalizing nipples, dark hued like her hair, both above and below—

The carriage hit another rut, jolting him out of his daydream. Damn, but this must stop. He could not have erotic fantasies about the woman he intended to save.

"I beg your pardon, my lord?" She had raised her head to look at him.

God's bones, *had* he spoken aloud? Tris froze, hoping to Christ he wasn't blushing. He swallowed, although his mouth had dried as if he'd eaten sand. "Are you quite all right, Miss Carlton? That was a nasty bump. I wanted to make sure you hadn't come to grief."

A warm flash of red lips and white teeth, her smile did nothing to cool his ardor. The happiest he'd seen her tonight, though.

"No, my lord, I am not hurt. Although the road is quite rough in places." The smile left as quickly as it appeared, replaced with a sober look in her big whiskey-colored eyes. "I have yet to thank you properly, my lord, Trevor, is it?"

"Yes, I am sorry, Miss Carlton. We haven't been properly introduced. I am Viscount Trevor, Tristan to my friends."

Immediately, she returned her attention to the darkness of the London night. "I am truly grateful, Lord Trevor, for your kindness earlier." The robe had fallen to her lap and she pulled it up to her shoulders. "Few men would have cared enough to listen to my story. I believe most would have seen to their own pleasure first and asked questions later if at all." She sought his eyes at last, their frankness piercing him. "You are a true gentleman, my lord. Thank you for rescuing me."

At a sudden loss for words in the face of her honest gratitude, Tris clenched his fist. Cad described him earlier in the evening, not rescuer. He cleared his throat, incredibly aware of his state of arousal and his recent thoughts about the luscious woman seated before him. Damn, but he must get himself under control.

"I fear your rescue is far from complete, Miss Carlton. I have yet to discover a way to remove you permanently from the threat of a life at The House of Pleasure." How the deuce he was to accomplish it remained to be seen. Perhaps Duncan would have an idea. "We must find some means of respectable employment for you, which for a gentlewoman means either as a companion to a woman of good reputation or a governess in a good household."

"Thank you, my lord." Her eyes lit up, eagerness in her face. "I will be happy to take any decent position you find for me. I can sew a fine seam, if that helps at all." She shook her head, the light fading from her eyes. "Although that skill helped me not at all when I asked for a position at the mantua makers in the more fashionable section."

Tris cocked his head. "If you sew as well as you claim, why would they not take you on?" The modistes he'd always patronized when furnishing his *amours* were usually dreadfully understaffed. It had taken him ten days to get Serena completely outfitted.

The woman laced her fingers together and pressed back in her seat. "Because I would not admit my situation to be as dire as it was until too late." With a little shake, she settled back into the seat. "When my brother's estate was settled, our home had to be sold, and though it brought a decent amount, half of it had to go for the funeral expenses and to pay off Jamie's debts." She stared not at him, but spoke to the corner of the carriage beside him. "He had expected me to marry well, you see, therefore his money had flowed rather freely. Then he died in May, so of course, I was in mourning throughout the season. My grandmother insisted I return to society before I should, for we knew the only way to secure our future was through a decent marriage."

"But you were unsuccessful?"

The scornful gaze she turned on him made his stomach churn. "With the handicaps of no dowry and a disgraced brother, I'm surprised I received any invitations, much less proposals. I did attend some functions, but it was to no avail. We spent the winter quietly, outside of London in less expensive lodgings and prayed for the spring." Again she drew into herself. "Then this past March, my grandmother died."

Tris grasped her hands as she tried to blink back tears. "My dear, I am so terribly sorry." Her hands, bare and smooth to the touch, sent a current of warmth up his arm.

She fought for control, at last looking him in the face. "Thank you, my lord."

He nodded and released her, sorry to let her go.

"I mourned her loss deeply, but could not afford to lose that season as well. Her final words were a prayer I would find a kind man to take care of me." A catch in her voice, Miss Carlton dashed a hand across her eyes. "I finally had the great good luck to make the acquaintance of a Miss Forsythe, who had just arrived from Ireland."

"Miss Alethea Forsythe? Lady Braeton's cousin?"

"Yes."

"I have met her. She seems sweet." A rather brash young woman, also.

"She befriended me and so I was invited to all manner of events from her connection alone. I was sure I would find someone, but my lack of dowry evidently proved insurmountable." Lips pressed into a stark line, Miss Carlton shook her head. "At that point, my lord, I should have given up and applied to a mantua-maker. It was late August. I still looked respectable. I could perhaps have gotten a position. But I convinced myself a man could fall in love with me and take me without a dowry."

"I believe he could." Tris's words slipped out before he thought. She embodied all the womanly traits a man would wish in a wife. Beauty, charm, poise, passion. And a tenacity for life he would match against any man's. Had he met her this summer, perhaps he would not have taken the path he had chosen.

"Unfortunately, none did." She lowered her gaze to the carriage robe, worrying the fringe. "I came back from a week-long party at the Braeton's in Kent to find my landlady had seized all my belongings as payment for my room. Her actions left me three outfits to sell for food. So I started eating only every other day, sleeping where I could. That is when I sought a position as a seamstress. But by then I looked less than respectable and they wouldn't even speak to me. I ate less, sold everything I had but the dress I stood up in. Three days without food and I knocked on Madame Vestry's door." The raised chin and narrowed eyes issued an unmistakable challenge. "I decided to choose life rather than death. Society will surely condemn me for that, although I highly doubt any of them has ever missed a single meal."

"I rather doubt that myself." Tris wanted to put his arms around her, to comfort her, to let her know he did not judge her. He suspected she already knew. Still, he grasped her hands again, reveling in their touch. "You are past that now, my dear. I will not rest until you are safely taken care of either through employment or marriage."

"Thank you, my lord. You are truly kind." She squeezed his hand.

A sizzle of heat shot straight to his groin and he bit back a groan. "As I said earlier, by right, having ruined you, I should marry you." He raised a hand as she opened her mouth to protest as before. "I regret, however, that I am encumbered. I am betrothed to another lady and cannot break my word to her." A heartfelt sigh escaped him and he wondered at it. Would he prefer marriage to a penniless woman, no matter the temptress she might be? Or the daughter of a wealthy and powerful man whose dowry would be a piece of land his family had coveted for generations?

"You are generous even to think of such a thing, my lord." Something—regret or relief—flitted over Miss Carlton's face. "Are we stopping?"

The shadowy lapboard front of Lammas House came into view. His gaze, as always, went immediately to the upper room in the right corner of the house. Serena's bedroom, filled with delights. But now no lights showed in the rooms, either below or above. Of course not, fool. No one was there. Serena had left last week. The house had been closed, the servants sent away.

"Damn." He took in Miss Carlton's startled gaze, and chuckled. "I seem to have misplaced my wits for the moment. The sight of great beauty will do that, you know."

Her wan face and a pinched attempt at a smile told him the poor woman was nearing the end of her endurance. Life had been an unholy hell for her recently. Let him not add to it.

"My mistress left and the servants were dismissed. Hence, no lights. Fortunately, I still have my key. Stokes." Tris opened the door and called to the coachman. "Tell Thomas to find Mrs. Parker and Susan, and send

John to Mr. Gates. Tell them to return to their posts at once and I will be very generous. Come, Miss Carlton." He offered his hand and it swallowed her petite one as he assisted her to the ground.

She picked her way to the gate, then turned and looked back at him hesitantly.

"Hand me her satchel, Stokes. I will send to Madame Vestry tomorrow for the rest of your things, Miss Carlton." He hefted the bag, so light it might be empty. Why had the woman not packed more of her things?

"That won't be necessary, my lord. Those are all my possessions."

Tris stopped and stared. "Madame Vestry didn't outfit you—"

"No, my lord. She wanted to wait until...until she knew if I would work out or not." She bowed her head and whispered, "Apparently, one woman, after her first time, went and drowned herself in the Thames. Madame did not want to spend money on additional clothes for me if they would not be put to use."

Gripping the valise, a sudden disgust with the whole business gnawing his insides, Tris took Miss Carlton's arm and escorted her inside. Immediately, he lit a lamp beside the door and conducted the woman into the parlor on the right. He indicated a large wingback chair in gold and burgundy stripes, and proceeded to light the lamps in the room. Damn, he forgot to send for another footman to light a fire here and upstairs. Had Mrs. Parker left any bed linens or covers? Why hadn't he thought of this before Stokes had gone?

He smiled at Miss Carlton, a false one to be sure. His had always been a life of pleasure organized by other people to accommodate him. How the hell did they think of all these things? What would he do if there were no linen? No fire? No servants? They might have already taken other positions. He couldn't leave Miss Carlton here alone. Neither could he take her to an inn without a maid or companion. How the devil would he produce either of those at this time of night? Well, he'd have to take charge and hope for the best.

"If you will stay here, please, I'll just check upstairs to see what's available." He frowned and apologized. "I'm afraid you may have rough quarters for tonight."

She laughed, and her shoulders slumped beneath her cloak. "I assure you, Lord Trevor, this is a palace compared to the places I have had to sleep in recently." Gingerly at first, she eased onto the chair, then settled quickly into its depths. "I'm so comfortable, I would be quite content to curl up right here."

What a delightful damsel in distress. With a nod he headed upstairs.

Automatically, his feet turned toward what had been Serena's bedchamber. Well, it would still have to serve. The house had been fitted out with only one bed. The light of his candle revealed a clean-swept room, orderly if severe. All of the former occupant's frilly and colorful decor had been stripped away, leaving a chest of drawers, a full-length mirror, washstand, and of course the massive bed where he'd so often frolicked.

No sheets or covers. Where would they be kept? He shook his head. The efficient Mrs. Parker would have left nothing that did not come with the furnished house. Tris sighed and left. Miss Carlton would have to make do until he could remedy the situation tomorrow.

"I'm afraid you will find the chamber—" Tris stopped as he crossed the threshold.

Miss Carlton sat curled in the chair, asleep. The exhausted lines in her face had gone, smoothed out in her peaceful slumber. She reminded him of an innocent child. A very beautiful child, with delicately arched eyebrows, high cheekbones, and creamy skin that begged for him to touch it.

He set the candle on the mantelpiece and approached her quietly, uncertain whether to wake her or let her sleep. She would be stiff and sore if he allowed her to remain cramped in the chair. Still he hated to waken that cherubic face. Could he move her without awakening her? Even the nearby sofa would be better for her to stretch out on.

Gently, he eased his arm around her shoulders and rolled her toward him. She stirred briefly, then lay still, her head on his shoulder.

He stifled a groan as her touch sent a new wave of anguish to his groin. Damn, but he must take care of that as soon as possible. If he was going to help this woman, he couldn't have an erection every time she touched him. Tris slid his other arm under her legs and lifted her.

She nestled into his chest, which wreaked further havoc with his cock.

Carefully, he climbed the dark stairs, praying he did not waken her. His face brushed against her hair and her womanly scent, sweet and clean, furthered his agony. He wanted to bury himself in that smell, in her, so badly he almost shook. What was it about this woman that undid him so? He'd lusted after women from an early age, and had been gratified with their attentions most of his life. Yet his yearning for Miss Carlton surpassed anything he'd ever experienced before. Forbidden fruit, perhaps? That made about as much sense as anything. Not that the explanation would ease his need at all.

At last, he entered the bedchamber once again and laid his burden on the bare mattress. She touched the cold fabric, shivered, and drew her legs up, making herself into a compact ball, but did not wake. The room was chilled as well. She would be freezing until the servants arrived and made up the fire.

Tris untied his black wool cloak and spread it over his sleeping charge, tucking it around her as he had the carriage robe earlier.

She sighed in her sleep and her body relaxed further into the mattress.

The room's cold proved a welcome damper to his hot blood and he backed away from the bed. He'd return to the parlor and await the servants. So much to be done.

He sped down the steps, making plans as he went. A call on Duncan was the first order of business tomorrow. If his normal cadre of servants wasn't available, he'd have to find others, including a maid for Miss Carlton. And of course, he must begin inquiries about a position for her. He'd need to concoct a story to account for his relationship to her. The truth certainly wouldn't do. A distant relation who had sought his help? It might serve. As long as his sister, Theodora, didn't get wind of it.

As he rounded the doorway into the parlor, his foot hit a soft object and sent it flying. He reached over and snagged Miss Carlton's satchel. It weighed almost nothing, and when he shook it, the muffled sound of small items rattling around in it suggested the woman truly had little to her name.

Tris smiled into the empty room. That, at least, he could remedy.

Chapter 4

Sunshine streaming into Violet's face pulled her out of a delicious dream of having tea with her grandmother. She groaned and grabbed the pillow from under her head and dragged it across her face. The almost real dream-smell of fresh baked scones with clotted cream and hot, fragrant tea urged her to return to slumber.

"Good morning, miss."

She bolted up, fully awake. A strange woman in an unfamiliar room held a tray containing a teapot and cup. Who was that? Where was she? What was she doing here? Her gaze came to rest on the black cloak covering her. Memory of the past night came flooding back and she clutched the material as her face burned. Dear Lord, had that really happened?

"Are you all right, miss?" The young maid, dressed soberly in gray, smiled tentatively, a small frown creasing her forehead.

"Yes, I'm fine thank you." Violet rubbed her face, trying to remove the final cobwebs of sleep. "I'm sorry, but I don't know your name."

"Susan." She bustled forward, put the tray on the bedside table, and poured a cup. "Sugar and milk?"

"Yes, please." The steam tickled Violet's nose with the familiar, earthy smell. She sipped, and relaxed against the headboard.

"Lord Trevor asked for you to come breakfast with him downstairs, when you're ready."

Violet clutched the delicate teacup, then carefully released it. There seemed no need to be afraid of the viscount. He'd been kindness itself last night after finding out who she was. Still, he'd seen her naked and taken outrageous liberties. How could she talk to him, or even look at him, without dying of shame, wondering if he was remembering her that way? Nevertheless, she'd have to put it out of her mind, because as long as he assisted her, she would have to see him. She nodded, gulped another mouthful of tea, and threw off the cloak.

"Do you know where your clothes were put last night? This is all I could find this morning." Susan produced Violet's satchel.

"I'm afraid these are the only clothes I have at the moment." Suddenly aware of her dishabille, Violet brushed at the sadly wrinkled petticoat. She certainly looked like a fugitive from a brothel this morning.

Susan frowned, then shrugged. "Then we will make you as presentable as possible, Miss Carlton."

Violet jerked violently. Lord Trevor had given the servant her real name. She needed to remain anonymous, although what other name could he have given? "Thank you, but you don't need to bother about the clothes. I'm really no one special." Despite her words, she continued to fluff and straighten her outfit. Best look as presentable as possible.

"Somehow I doubt that, miss. Lord Trevor's very particular." The girl eyed the gown critically. "Let me pop down and fan it with some steaming water and see if that will take out the worst of the wrinkles. Here, I'll help with that." In seconds, Susan had expertly stripped off the rumpled garment, leaving Violet once again naked.

Her face heated, yet the maid didn't even raise an eyebrow.

Instead, she laid the dress on the bed and opened the satchel. "Ah, good. These stays are a little worn but will do nicely for the time being. I'll assist you when I return." She nodded to a screen, painted with a huge peacock to which real feathers had been attached. "I brought water for washing there. When I get back, we'll see how well I can turn you out for the day." With a toss of her head, she snatched the gown off the bed and left.

Violet leaned back against the bed. Her life had become a whirlwind, ever since Lord Trevor had intervened in it. She'd best get used to his routine and expectations. Perhaps she could question Susan when she returned. In the meantime, a wash was well in order.

By the time she had finished and stood before the fire to stay warm, Susan had reappeared, the purple dress looking miraculously refreshed as well. Given the original state of the garment, the maid had done wonders.

Taking over completely, Susan cinched, fluffed, combed and curled Violet until she couldn't believe the woman who stared back at her from the small mirror atop the dresser. Her hair had been swept up and pinned cleverly to allow little tendrils of chestnut to emerge from the knot at the back of her head. Her gown, second best and worn to begin with, had been transformed into a serviceable outfit. The width of the skirt had been reduced slightly, the frayed panel at the side gone. The already low neckline of the bodice had been lowered even more to disguise a tear in the fabric, but a fichu had been added to give a demurer look, fitting for a breakfast rather than a ball.

"You are pleased, miss?" Susan beamed with satisfaction.

"I cannot believe it is the same dress. The same me." Violet couldn't take her eyes off the image in the mirror.

"Lord Trevor has always been pleased with my efforts for his mistresses." Violet froze, the smile still on her lips.

"His last one, Miss Starke, was delighted as well. She wished for me to go with her when she left, but unfortunately could not afford to employ me." Pinning up a final curl, Susan gave a nod of approval to Violet's coiffure. "So I was happy to receive his lordship's summons last night."

Violet's mouth had dried. The roaring in her ears kept her standing, staring at the image in the mirror. Mistress.

"Shall I draw a bath for you for after breakfast? Do you know if Lord Trevor will require you today?" The maid had bundled up the cloak and put her satchel in the wardrobe. "I will take this down and bring up fresh linens before you have done." She looked pointedly at the door.

Still unable to form a word, Violet made herself turn from the mirror and walk stiffly down the stairs. Mistress. He had said she would be that, but in name only. Had it been true? She'd believed him last night, but now.... Taking hold of herself, she continued toward the murmur of voices at the bottom of the stairs. The room to the left seemed a parlor, empty save for a sofa, end tables, and the chair she remembered sitting in last night. Apparently, she'd fallen asleep. Then how had she awakened upstairs?

She turned toward the right hand room, and away from all thoughts of that question.

"Well, if Gates has taken another position, I cannot blame the man." Seated at the small dining table, Lord Trevor, impeccably groomed and dressed in an elegant suit of dark blue wool, raised a cup to his lips. Coffee to judge by the savory aroma. He spoke to a footman who nodded at regular intervals. "However, I must have a butler nonetheless. Put your ear to the ground, Thomas, and come up with some sort of solution. There must be one butler in London currently without a position."

When she entered, the quiet young man stood even straighter.

Lord Trevor marked the man's movement, noted her, and rose. "Miss Carlton." He stopped, his mouth still slightly open, but wordless.

What was wrong? A thousand possibilities bloomed in Violet's imagination. Fearful her dress had suddenly popped open at the site of the repair, she glanced down. When she raised her head, Lord Trevor had managed to close his mouth, but that hungry look still smoldered in his eyes.

"Miss Carlton, excuse me." He cleared his throat, sipped the coffee, and tried again. "Please be seated." He pulled out the chair next to him. "Another plate, Thomas."

With a lurching bow, the footman hurried out of the room.

"I trust you slept well? I apologize for the lack of creature comforts. However, you look as though the night's adversities never happened." His sapphire gaze hadn't left her face since she entered the room. "You are a most beautiful woman."

Heat rose in her cheeks. "Susan is a very skilled ladies' maid, my lord. She believes me to be your current mistress and insisted on turning me out for your satisfaction." The words were a challenge. Let him deny what he would.

"I beg your pardon, Miss Carlton. I wasn't exactly sure how to proceed." Lord Trevor sat back in his chair, shoulders sagging. "I'm in two minds about the situation, you see." He folded his napkin and laid it neatly on the table before looking at her. "What we do not wish to happen is for anyone to discover I'm keeping you here. You'd be as ruined as if you were found at Madame Vestry's, no matter the true circumstances. Last night I had no choice but to bring you here, since you had no companion or maid and could scarcely be left alone. It may be that in several days I can move you to more suitable lodgings. With Susan accompanying you it may serve."

"Thank you, my lord."

Thomas entered with a plate filled with sausage, smoked herring, grilled kidneys, potatoes, and hot rolls. Enough food to feed her for a week.

She inhaled and the rich scent of the kidneys mingled with the yeasty smell of the rolls made her sway. A quick indulgence before she shook off the delicious distraction. "That is most kind of you. However, why did you tell her I am your mistress?" Violet forced herself to remain calm. Lord Trevor seemed to trust the maid to remain silent, so she must as well.

He shrugged and sipped his coffee again. "I told her only that I wished to employ her services again, immediately, for a guest at Lammas House. She assumed our relationship based on past occupants."

"Then you don't intend to make me your mistress, Lord Trevor?" Her voice came out harder than she had intended, but she was coiled like a spring inside.

"Would you like to be, Miss Carlton?"

Her throat closed as if she'd swallowed a peach pit. Worse, her entire face flamed.

He eyed her coolly. "I believe we covered that subject last night, however, if you have reconsidered, I'd be delighted to discuss the terms."

"Terms?" Her squeak startled her. What terms would a woman be able to dictate to a man?

"Yes, the terms of your employment as my mistress. Do you think such arrangements are done on the fly?" His boisterous laugh made her shrink back in her seat. "I've heard of marriage settlements that were less advantageous to a bride-to-be. Mistresses, if they are canny and the protector generous, can negotiate everything from amounts, times and places, to how many trips to the opera or the numbers of pieces of jewelry she can expect to receive each year of the arrangement."

That such dealings involved detailed contracts had never crossed Violet's mind. She gawked at Lord Trevor as he sipped his coffee, watching her every move. Of course, she'd never had cause to wonder about anything like this at all, until now. Still, it sounded almost like a settlement. With a kind and handsome man like Lord Trevor, such an agreement might almost seem like a marriage.

Lord Trevor sat up, the lascivious twist to his mouth replaced by a sober line. "I beg your pardon, Miss Carlton. Such information is not within the purview of genteel ladies. And at any rate, as I informed you, I am no longer inclined to take a mistress, due to my impending nuptials."

Of course. He'd told her last night he couldn't make her as his mistress because he would shortly marry. Unaccountably disappointed, Violet raised a forkful of kidneys to her mouth. The brief temptation had been absurd. Lord Trevor had promised to find a respectable position for her. That was the next goal.

"If you do not mind," Trevor said, "it may be best for the servants to think you are my mistress. They have been discreet in the past. I have no reason to believe they will be any less so now."

Trying to mask her disappointment, Violet sipped her tea and said brightly, "Then I will not disabuse Susan of my true status, my lord."

Trevor set his cup back in its saucer, then ran a finger around the delicate rim. "I suppose Susan may be let in on the secret. You will spend more time with her than the other servants, at any rate." He left off playing with the cup. "If I can indeed manage to get a butler for you. You may have to make do with Thomas."

"I'm sure Thomas would do admirably, my lord."

"You've not been used to having servants I take it, Miss Carlton?" Lord Trevor shook his head, his jaw rigid. "I'll arrange something." He peered at her, one eyebrow shooting upward. "Would you object to my calling you by your given name? It has been my custom in the past with my previous mistresses. The servants will expect it." His voice had softened, giving a little wrench to her heart.

"Of course, my lord." She ducked her head. The familiarity such address implied would take getting used to.

"And you must call me Tristan or Tris." He smiled and his eyes darkened. "My closest friends do and I believe we have reached that level of intimacy, my dear. If you are to have my protection in all ways, you must give me my name as well."

"Yes, Tristan." The sound of his name on her tongue sent a flurry of chill bumps down her arms.

"Delightful." His gaze lingered on her mouth a second too long, and then he rose. "I am off to appointments for the rest of the morning and afternoon, but if you are willing, I would like to have supper with you this evening. See how you are progressing."

"Of course, my—"

"Uh-huh." He wagged a finger at her, trying to pull a stern face. "Not my lord, Violet."

"Tristan." As she had suspected, her protector had a playful streak. "I would be honored to have supper with you, although I fear my conversation will be dull in the extreme. I will have to ask Susan for suggestions of something to keep me employed."

Tris opened his lips, closed them, then quirked the corner of his mouth in a smile. "I believe she will be able to find something to keep you well occupied." He rose and bowed. "Good morning." With a jaunty step, he disappeared out the doorway as Thomas scurried forward to clear the dishes.

Her life had changed so much in such a short time she kept expecting to wake up on the hard church bench at St. Anne's. Or worse in her room at The House of Pleasure. But as long as the dream continued, she'd be glad to share whatever she could with the handsome Lord Trevor.

Chapter 5

Tris left Lammas House whistling an airy tune. As soon as Mrs. Parker had arrived at dawn, he'd gone home, bathed, changed clothes, and returned to see to Violet's settling in. Having to replace Gates would be tiresome, but necessary since he'd taken on the new duties regarding his charge. She'd been adapting well so far, better than he'd expected, in fact. The only thing still upsetting her was the faux title of mistress.

He chuckled at the memory of her face, bright red when he suggested she'd like to be his mistress. Not that he'd mind at all if she did. His cock stirred and he adjusted his breeches. If not for his betrothal…. Well, it was done, or as good as, this afternoon. And of course, Miss Carlton was a gentlewoman. Hopefully she could play her part long enough for him to find her a position or an offer of marriage. Then she could relax and put this whole episode behind her.

He mounted Lucifer, his bay stallion, and headed him for Dunham House. The Marquess of Dalbury would be very interested in his trip to Madame Vestry's last night. The horse sped along the streets of Mayfair, bustling this time of morning with smart carriages, ladies shopping, and nursemaids walking with their charges despite the chilly day. Tris breathed deeply, the crisp air enhanced by the earthy scents of dirt and manure, the mélange of London.

Too soon, however, he pulled his horse to a stop before the imposing townhome belonging to his friend. Whistling again, he tossed the reins to a groom, and strode up the short, wide stairs and knocked. His news about Miss Carlton would draw animated comment, no doubt. The door opened and Grayson greeted him.

"Lord Trevor. Good morning, my lord."

"Good morning, Grayson. Is the marquess stirring yet?" Tris entered the house, untying his cloak and handing it to the butler.

"I am sorry, my lord, but Lord Dalbury has just ridden out."

"The devil you say." Snatching back his cloak, Tris swirled it around his shoulders in one fluid movement. "Which way was he headed?"

"Hyde Park, I believe, your lordship," Grayson called after him as Tris rushed back out the door.

In a mad dash, he rounded the side of the house to snare his horse, but he was up and on his way before the saddle had cooled. A touch to Lucifer's side and they set off at a fast trot, restrained by the gathering traffic. The park was mostly deserted as the fashionable hours for carriages or strolling were much later. Thank God for that. Duncan would be easier to spot. Tris stood up in the stirrups for a better vantage point. Only two gentlemen walking fat geldings to his right. Grass and the pale dust of the bridle path greeted him to his left. Where could the man have gotten so quickly?

About to take off across the manicured lawn, Tris pulled back on the reins and sat. Straight ahead, about halfway down the Serpentine, he spied Duncan going along at a spirited trot. Tris touched Lucifer and the bay leaped forward, as eager as his master to overtake the other horse.

"Ho, Duncan." Tris reined Lucifer in as they galloped up beside his friend.

"Tris! This is a pleasant surprise." Lord Dalbury pulled up his horse and beamed at him.

They'd been fast friends since they were boys, attending Winchester for several very harrowing years, followed by a Grand Tour together. A spate of scandals had surrounded Duncan almost a year and a half ago, when their friendship had been tested in the extreme.

"Not as pleasant as you may think."

"Indeed." Though the marquess sat his horse easily, tension hummed in every line of him. "Have you heard news of that bastard St. Cyr?"

"Should I have? Didn't you tell me he's now claiming to be married to Juliet?"

"Yes. We are attempting to prove otherwise." Dalbury straightened his reins meticulously. "Her current husband would like to be sure the child she carries will bear his name."

Tris whistled. "Quite a little *contretemps*, I'd say."

"If only we could find the blighter and prove his marriage invalid, we'd all rest a deal easier." Restless fingers on the reins, lips pursed, Duncan studied the bright lake.

"And here I come with less than welcome news on another front." Tristan settled uneasily in his saddle. His friend needed no more worries this morning it seemed.

"Have you managed to finally lose your substantial wealth at Charbury's?" The marquess flashed a quick grin. Tris's exploits at the most disreputable gaming hell in London were a constant source of amusement to his friend.

"Sadly no." Tris glanced around, a sudden need for caution filling him. "James Carlton."

A mask of indifference slammed down on Duncan's face. "An unsavory name from the past. What unwelcome news might a long-dead corpse have to offer?"

"I bought his sister at Madame Vestry's last night."

"The devil you say." The scars on Duncan's left cheek stood out vividly as his skin paled.

"Yes. My reaction was a bit more colorful." Tris clenched his teeth. The memory of what he'd almost done still sickened him.

Hoof beats approaching on his right drew his attention. A rider in gray bore down on them.

"We are about to have company." Tris frowned at the unfamiliar figure.

"No worries." Duncan assumed a wry smile. "Here's my brother-in-law now, Tris. At least the one I claim. Lord Trevor, I make known Mr. Amiable Morley."

The tall, straight figure nodded pleasantly.

Military bearing, if he didn't miss his guess. Tris returned the nod. Morley. The name had a familiar sound.

The man cut his eyes toward Duncan. "I didn't know you were riding this morning."

"Weather's too good to stay inside, wouldn't you say?"

"Indeed. Although it seems few have had the same thought." Something about the easy way Morley sat his horse stirred an echo from the past.

"I say, were you related to Pax Morley, by any chance?"

"My elder brother."

"Ah, you are the prodigal." He remembered tales of the younger brother running away to join the military. "Army, wasn't it? In the colonies?"

"Yes. Until I heard news of my brother in April. You knew him?" Morley's jaw tightened.

"Quite well, in fact. My condolences. Devilishly sorry." Pax had been something of a hero to Tris. "Great fellow, Pax. One of my older sisters was mad for him for a while until her current husband leaped in and offered for her. Must have been almost ten years ago. Awful shame." Damn, but the good did die young.

"Want to come back to lunch, Tris?" Dalbury asked. "It's early, but you may make your bow to the ladies and entertain them for a bit. They will want to hear about your prospective bride."

"Congratulations are in order then, Lord Trevor?" A smile broke out on Morley's face.

"Yes. I have just offered for Miss Dora Harper, Lord Downing's youngest daughter. It will be announced in a day or two." Tris gripped the reins, although the horse had been placidly standing the whole time. His mind filled not with the sweet oval face of his betrothed, but with the arresting one of Miss Carlton. Unsure if he'd revealed too much, he looked away.

"Thanks, Duncan. I believe I will renew my acquaintance with both lovely ladies. Has your wife not managed to skewer you yet?" Tris laughed and all three started their horses toward the south entrance to the park. Best put Miss Harper and Miss Carlton out of his mind.

The southern gate was within sight when Morley's head snapped up. A rider galloped toward them as if the demons of hell were on his heels. Blue and gold was the livery of Dalbury's household. Had something gone amiss at Dunham House?

Before the man could get closer, Morley spurred his horse and bounded away toward the newcomer.

"What's the stir this early?" Tris gazed after the man, who had shot down the pathway, engaged the servant, then kicked his horse into a gallop and headed for the gate.

"S'blood. It must be Juliet. Nothing else could make him push for that kind of speed." Duncan clutched his reins and squeezed his knees against his horse for all he was worth. The animal leaped forward, leaving Tris coughing at the dust he kicked up.

A touched of his heel and Lucifer sped after the others. What else would happen before noon? He really didn't want to contemplate that question at all.

* * * *

"If I'd found them together, I'd have shot the bastard without a second thought." Duncan poured a tumbler of brandy and handed it to Tris. "Morley showed considerable restraint in my opinion."

The quiet of Duncan's study was a blessed relief after the morning's excitement.

They'd reached the house to find it in an uproar. Viscount St. Cyr, claiming to be Juliet's husband, had boldly entered and attempted to seduce her. Morley had discovered them and threatened to put a bullet in the viscount's brain. After he fled, Juliet had fainted. Tris and Duncan had arrived just as she regained consciousness.

"If anything good has come of St. Cyr's treachery today, I suspect it's a reconciliation between Juliet and Morley." Hovering near the polished sideboard, Duncan downed three fingers of the fiery amber liquid and poured another. A familiar tic appeared in his right eye, which meant the marquess was damn well angry at someone.

"A reconciliation? Morley and Juliet have been estranged?" The scene Tris had just witnessed upstairs had hardly seemed between two people disinterested in one another. He'd hurried from the room, afraid the couple would forget themselves and indulge in a passionate moment before witnesses. "I'd never believe it."

"Oh, Morley's been the disenchanted one, to be sure." A moment of drumming of his fingers on the sideboard then Duncan set the decanter down and stoppered it. "I won't bore you with the details, but suffice it to say, Juliet's been damned unpleasant company for the past month. I'm just glad it's over." He eyed Tris and took a pull at the brandy. "You came to tell me about Carlton's sister."

Avoiding his friend's scrutiny, Tris took a gulp and set the tumbler on a nearby table. "Yes. Hell of shock, that. I'd no more idea Carlton had a family than the man in the moon. And to find the woman had been reduced to employment in a brothel made me damned uncomfortable."

"No business of ours." Duncan shrugged. "The code puts no onus on us to inquire about a combatant's associations. One would hope going into a duel a gentleman, even one acting as a second, had put his affairs in order in case the worst happened."

"It would seem not in the case of Mr. Carlton. He appears to have been undisciplined in all respects." Tris ground his teeth. The man should have known what might happen to his sister in the case of his demise. Of course, seconds rarely dueled these days. Still, he should have accounted for all contingencies.

Duncan stared over his glass. "Did you find out before or after you bedded her?"

"During."

"Gads." That seemed to shake the marquess. "Had she been there long?"

Tris gripped the glass, then chuckled. "I was to have been her first customer."

"What?" The scowl that darkened Duncan's face said he didn't find it a laughing matter. "You went to deflower a virgin?"

Throwing up a hand to ward off the recriminations that would surely follow, Tris stepped back, hoping to avoid a disagreement. Bad enough guilt over his part in this debacle nagged at him. He didn't need his friend castigating him as well. "Amorina has always looked out for the type of girl I like. This one, she said, was 'something special,' and a virgin." He could see the note this instant, the sweeping loops of Vestry's beautiful handwriting creating a brand across his mind. "She intimated I might hone my skills with this girl, as I was soon to marry."

"That indeed sounds like some of Amorina's machinations." Duncan gestured to a leather chair in front of the great mahogany desk, then took his seat in the tall chair behind it. "So you took her at her word?"

"It may sound callous, but I did." Tris dropped into the chair, suddenly disgusted with himself. "The idea made sense at the time. I'd done it before, but it had been a while. I didn't want Miss Harper hurt or frightened any more than necessary on our wedding night. So I thought since the woman was willing, it would be to both our advantages. You've heard what some women go through with men who fancy a virgin. I'd at least have tried to be gentle the first time."

"Wait." Duncan leaned across the desk, his head cocked. "You sound as if it didn't happen. You said she told you who she was while you were—"

"I stopped. Before I ruined her completely."

"Indeed." A smirk on his lips, Duncan leaned back in the tall leather chair. "I commend you on your control."

"She was crying, damn it." Her sobs still echoed in his mind. "And I thought...I thought she might have been brought there like your wife was."

"Christ." Duncan half rose out of his chair, his face pale. "Was that what happened to her?"

Tris waved him back. "No. She assured me she was there of her own free will, but only because she had no other means of making a living. It happens, even to gently born women." Thoughts of what almost happened to Miss Carlton made Tris gulp the contents of his glass. "I'm relieved my sisters are all well married. Miss Carlton's plight has touched a deep chord in me."

"Did you give her money? Is there anything I can do?" Duncan opened a drawer and took out a bag of coins.

"I got her out of there as quickly and anonymously as I could. She's currently at the Weldon Street house."

"With Serena?" The marquess looked scandalized.

"She's gone." Tris waved her away. His last mistress had been an amusing distraction at best.

"What happened to her?"

"I sent her home with a large settlement last week." He stared at Duncan, who had his stern face on. "I'd planned to give up my mistresses once I was married and Serena's family needed her. Her mother had taken ill. It seemed a good time."

Rubbing a hand over his face, his friend asked, "So what do you intend to do with Miss Carlton? She cannot stay at Weldon Street indefinitely. It will become known no matter how careful you are."

"After what I did last night I should marry her." Tris dropped his gaze to his lap.

"Not a good idea, even if it were possible." An edge had crept into his friend's voice.

That hadn't been unexpected. Still, Tris studied his hands, placed carefully on the chair arms, avoiding his friend's gaze.

"You do see the danger, Tristan." The tone sharpened. "She could bring all the ugliness of the scandal down on our heads again with only a word or two in the right places."

"I suppose I see that." He fixed his stare on the marquess. "You offered to help her, however. Do you have a position somewhere, anywhere we could be assured of her continued welfare? A companion to Juliet, perhaps?" That possibility had lurked in the back of his mind when he'd decided to approach Duncan with the information about Miss Carlton.

"Good God, no." Duncan shot up and headed to the decanter once more. "You have run mad. We are the last people who should employ her." He stopped and looked at Tris. "You haven't told her what happened the day her brother died, have you?"

"It didn't seem necessary as we were putting our clothes back on." Tris rose and took the tumbler to the sideboard, waving away Duncan's offer of another. He needed some wits left for his next interview. "Very well, I'll find her a position far from London. She's bright and forthright. She'd make an excellent companion." To him or to any other gentleman. "Or she could be a governess. She also professed to me that she can sew a fine seam." He shrugged and prepared to leave. He damn well couldn't be late.

"As long as she stays far away from us. She still could marry, you know. She'd have no dowry, but there are men who don't seek marriage just for wealth." Duncan contemplated the swirling contents of his glass.

"Then I need to somehow get her back into society." He grimaced. He'd thought those tedious days were done. "Not much going on at the moment, although I suspect there will be a spate of Christmas parties and balls shortly." His sister always gave one such ball the week before Christmas Day. Perhaps he should confide in Theodora, at least about

Miss Carlton, while leaving details of exactly how he met her pleasantly hazy. It might serve.

"Be careful, Tris." Duncan gripped his shoulder. "Send her as far away as possible."

The warning sent a frisson of alarm through him and he shrugged off Duncan's hand. "I'll keep that in mind." He gathered the cloak he'd dropped on a chair near the door.

"Off again? I'd thought you were staying to luncheon." Duncan beamed with one of the few true smiles he'd seen today. "Cook is so ecstatic to have Katarina breeding, she makes twice the quantity we'd ever need. Twice what Morley's old regiment could eat in a day, much less at a single sitting."

"Thank you, but I am engaged." The irony of his words struck him as funny, though he hardly felt like laughing. "Indeed, the very reason I'm rushing off. I'm for Lord Downing's to sign the settlement agreements for Miss Harper. Adding the estate in northern Yorkshire to my family's holdings has been an uphill battle, but I will seal the deal at last." Then why did he feel so despondent at the prospect?

"Miss Harper is an exemplary choice for a wife on many fronts. Young, sweet, likely fertile. You'll have an heir in your nursery inside a year." Duncan slapped him on the back. "Even if you haven't had any practice, I'll lay a wager you find your mark and introduce Lady Trevor to the pleasures of the bed with little fuss."

"Is that what has turned your marriage around, Duncan? You and Kat were less than cordial when I first met her. Did you manage to win her in the bedroom after you wed?" Tris fought to keep the despair out of his voice. "For I fear Miss Harper's charms for me lie in the fertile fields of Yorkshire, not the one I'll plow and sow on my wedding night." Try as he might to banish it, Violet's lovely face and naked body, sprawled and beckoning on the crisp sheets, appeared whenever he thought about a wedding night.

Shaking his head, Duncan steered him to the doorway. "Katarina and I had perhaps the most uncertain first few weeks of married life in the history of England. Yet we weathered it and now are the most content couple in Christendom. I suggest you woo Miss Harper, find something you have in common, and let nature take its course. If it doesn't," Duncan gave him a lecherous grin, "you can always return to your mistresses once she gives you an heir."

Tris gave his farewell automatically and left for Lord Downing's. That last bit of advice sat ill with him, even though he longed to take it. Trouble was, the mistress he wanted to keep was the woman he'd sworn to protect from such a life.

No one had said rescuing a damsel in distress would be easy.

Chapter 6

After breakfast, Violet let Susan coax her upstairs and into a steaming bath. As she soaked, the tensions of the past days slipped easily away and she let her mind drift as she breathed in the soothing scented steam. At first she assumed the maid had added lavender oil, but the smell was less sweet, more astringent. Unusual. She breathed deeper, trying to puzzle it out.

"Violet."

She jumped and water sloshed out of the tub.

Susan had entered the room with a pale blue silk comforter. "The scent is violet. A bit different, but it was in my box of oils and I thought you might like it, as it is your namesake." She smiled and began to make up the bed. "I've been known to have a touch of whimsy."

"Thank you, Susan." Violet returned the smile and sank lower in the water. It had been so long since she'd had the luxury of a maid. A lifetime ago it seemed. And this woman was good at her job. Apparently, Lord Trevor spared no expense for his paramours.

She'd enjoy her services while they lasted. Once she became a companion or governess or seamstress, she'd have to fend for herself again.

Unless she became Lord Trevor's mistress in earnest.

Her face blazed like a furnace. How could she think of such a thing? Although whenever the memory of his heavy body pressing her into the mattress returned, as it did with an alarming frequency, it didn't fill her with fear or disgust as before. Thought of his hands on her, his fingers circling her nipples, his palms hot against her thighs, filled her instead with a strange longing deep within. Oh, but she was turning into a wicked woman. The House of Pleasure had changed her despite her brief residency.

"Are you ready for me to wash your hair, miss?"

Violet snapped out of her indecent reverie and sat up quickly. "That would be lovely, thank you."

Susan lathered and rinsed her hair, then squeezed it in a thick piece of toweling. "We need to have you ready just after luncheon."

"Ready for what?" Violet jerked her head up. Tristan had put her fears to rest, or so she'd thought. Still she was living here under his protection in the guise of his mistress. How easy it would be for him to make the arrangement a true one.

"Lord Trevor's sent for Madame Angelique, the mantua maker, to outfit you, miss. She'll be here at two o'clock sharp." Alternating between cloth and brush, Susan worked methodically to dry and untangle her hair.

"Madame Angelique?" Dear Lord, the premiere dressmaker in all of London coming to outfit her?

"You have heard of Madame Angelique, haven't you?" Susan's eyebrows swooped up like startled birds.

"Of course I have heard of her." But she scarcely dared to dream of having one of the woman's legendary creations. "I just had no idea Lord Trevor would choose to outfit me so grandly."

"Why ever not?" The maid's words were muffled through a mouthful of hairpins as she brushed and twisted and pinned her hair up. "Lord Trevor is most particular that his mistresses be as fashionable as possible. He is a long-time customer of Madame."

Was this more proof he intended to make her his mistress? What other explanation could there be? She had no claim on him, save for a passing acquaintance with her brother. So why would he take such pains to dress her well if not for his own enjoyment? The more Violet thought of it, the angrier she became. Why didn't he just come out and tell her that's what he wanted from her? Why keep denying it? Did he think after giving her the clothes, the food, and the servants, she wouldn't be able to say no when he finally asked her?

Finished with the coiffure, Susan darted into the dressing room and emerged with a simple *robe de chambre* in green silk damask. She held it out to Violet and the lovely garment slid smoothly over her skin, soft and soothing as the bathwater.

"Wherever did this come from?" Violet asked, rubbing her cheek against the sleek fabric. She hadn't enjoyed the luxury of silk for over a year.

"His lordship sent to Madame Angelique for it first thing this morning. He said he believed you would like to wear something other than your one gown." Susan tied the sash for her then sat her down in front of the mirror on the *toilette* table.

"Lord Trevor is a very thoughtful man." Reveling in the richness of the garment, Violet trailed her fingers slowly down the arms of the robe. She'd been dreading putting the lavender gown on again. Somehow she didn't feel clean in it any more.

"He knows how to treat women, I can tell you that." Susan gave a quick nod, then hurried into the dressing room again, this time returning with a pair of pale green satin mules, embroidered with pink rosebuds. "Here, try these on."

Violet stared at the shoes then cut her eyes over at Susan. "I suppose Madame Angelique happened to have a pair of shoes in her shop as well?"

"No, miss." The woman laughed. "These are mine. Miss Starke gave them to me when she left. When Lord Trevor sent me for the robe, I stopped back at home and got them." Susan laid her hand on Violet's shoulder. "I thought you'd like to have new shoes as well."

Violet put her hand over Susan's. "Thank you. I don't know what I would have done if it hadn't been for Lord Trevor and you." A tear slid down her cheek and she wiped it away. No reason to start the waterworks now.

"Let me go down and get Mrs. Parker to make you some tea." A swift squeeze of her hand, and Susan left.

Violet sighed. She scarcely recognized the woman staring back at her from the mirror. Oh, of course the clothes were different and her hair had been coiled on her head and a lace handkerchief pinned over its shiny chestnut mass. But the eyes that looked back at her weren't those of the woman she had been a week before. Before the House of Pleasure and Madame Vestry. Before Lord Trevor had opened the door of the green room and showed her a glimpse of what men and women did in the night together. This new woman must decide if that glimpse was enough for her or if she had changed into a woman who would give more if only he would ask.

* * * *

Tris rapped on the door of Lord Downing's study. The viscount had kept him waiting for the better part of half an hour. Their appointment had been made for one o'clock, which should have given him plenty of time to take care of the settlements and return to the Weldon Street house in time for Madame Angelique's visit. He did so enjoy watching as Madame plied her trade so skillfully. Not that Angelique held any charms for him. However, watching women take off and put on clothes was one of the pleasures in which he always indulged himself. He loved women dressed in the first stare of fashion. He loved them undressed as well. And watching Violet try on all the outfits he had suggested to the mantua maker would be incredibly fun and arousing. Of course, today's appointment would be primarily measurements, although his note to Angelique had specified at least two gowns to be made up to the point they could be fitted, finished, and returned completed by first thing in the morning. Violet couldn't sit around in her one purple gown.

"Come."

Tris pressed the latch and entered the dim study.

His future father-in-law stood behind his desk, bent over, making notations on various papers strewed over the surface. He didn't look up.

"Good afternoon, Lord Downing." Tris bowed and approached the desk.

Nothing resembling marriage settlements occupied the untidy surface. The largest piece of paper, embellished with a pair of cherubs holding a shield, bore the words, *A Map of the Manor and Haven of Bromley in Yorkshire*. Ah, Downing was contemplating the settlement.

The Bromley estate, five hundred acres and a large manor house, abutted Tris's family lands in Northern Yorkshire. Several generations of Marshalls had lusted after the piece of property. The Harper family, however, had a tendency to produce mostly male children. Dora Harper was the first female in three generations suitable in age to be a bride for a Trevor. Tris's father had impressed it upon him for years to do his duty and marry the girl to secure the land. His father hadn't lived to see the union. Still, Tris could imagine the old man rubbing his hands together and gloating over his triumph. Tris had been waiting most of his life for the girl to grow up so he could marry her. Well, finally the day was at hand.

"I finished the settlements this morning, Trevor. The original agreement, between your father and I, has now been codified with specific instructions for the transfer of the property upon your marriage to my daughter. Sign here." The shrewd little man with a slight paunch and a knife-edged nose handed him the quill.

Forcing himself to think only of his duty, Tris signed the document with a flourish of pure bravado. Damn, he wished he hadn't promised his father. But he couldn't go back on his word. He stared at the map. So this was how it felt to sell your soul to the devil.

"Now for her jointure." Lord Downing drew forth another piece of parchment. His quill scratched busily over the yellowish surface. "We must see to Dora's welfare, should you pre-decease her."

The sinking feeling in his stomach would pass, he hoped. He'd given his word, now doubly so. Stand firm. Show no emotion. Yet, despair at the thought of Violet Carlton's exquisite amber-colored eyes washed over him. Damn. Let him get on with it and be done. Tris took the proffered pen and dipped the point in the inkwell one more time.

* * * *

Tristan closed the door and let his shoulders slump. Lord Downing had droned on and on about the impeccable bloodlines his daughter came from. The man must breed horses. He was so obsessed with his lineage. Dora was a sweet girl, undoubtedly docile from her reactions both times he'd met her. He should probably speak to her before he left, let her know the betrothal had been officially arranged.

He looked at the clock in the main hall. Almost three o'clock. Damn, he'd missed Violet's fitting. He headed for the front reception hall to ask Pratt, the butler, to tell Miss Harper he wished to speak to her. Well, he'd get Violet to show him the gowns tomorrow.

Tris stopped dead, heat rushing into his face. What the hell was he thinking? He was betrothed to an innocent of eighteen and contemplating the enjoyment of watching another innocent woman under his protection disrobe. Had he become so truly depraved? Of course, he could not watch Violet try on her gowns. She was not Serena. Not his mistress. She would be nothing to him as soon as he could find her a position. Duncan had been right. Best for all their sakes to get rid of Miss Carlton as quickly as possible and forget their heated interlude.

He continued down the corridor, determined to control this ungodly appetite for the woman. Concentrate instead on igniting passion in his bride-to-be. Fortunately, he found Pratt outside the reception room and sent him to fetch Miss Harper. Her father had suggested waiting a mere three weeks before the wedding, although Tris found no need for such haste. Still, perhaps given his current preoccupation, it would be best for them to marry swiftly and begin a new life for the New Year.

Miss Harper entered the room, a pleasant smile pasted on her face, though her gaze darted nervously around the room. When she discovered they were alone, her eyes widened and she retreated a step.

"How good of you to call, Lord Trevor. Would you like for me to fetch my father?" In two steps she had reached the door, but Tris was determined to make the most of this encounter. If they only had three weeks until they wed, they would need to get used to one another.

"No, Miss Harper, please stay. I have already been in conference with Lord Downing this afternoon."

Escape cut off, she tensed and closed her eyes, as if expecting a blow.

"We have agreed on the settlements and as soon as I have the traditional family sapphire fetched from my estate in Yorkshire, we shall be formally betrothed." He'd thought she'd be happier at the news, although it could be no surprise to her.

"Indeed, my lord." Her face had drained of color, until her cream-colored gown stood out starkly against her skin. "I had no idea Father intended to move forward with his plans so soon. I thought I would have at least until the spring." The wistful timbre dropped her voice almost to a whisper.

It smote his heart. He wished to force this girl as little as he had Violet. Yet arranged marriages still occurred with great frequency. How did a gentleman proceed without frightening his bride? A speedy courtship then, with lesson number one immediately.

"I'm certain this is sudden, my dear, yet I hope we may be better acquainted before the wedding in three weeks." Forward into the breach.

"Three weeks!" She swayed and Tris grasped her arm, taking the opportunity to draw her closer.

"Soon, yes, however," he gathered her hands into his, "we will spend much of the time in conversation, getting to know one another. Would you like that, Dora?"

She jerked her head up at the familiar use of her name, then hesitated, her mouth open.

Would she protest? He had the right now, although it was the first time he'd ever used it with her.

"Yes, I would like that, Lord Trevor." The assent had come out almost too low to hear, but she'd accepted his proposal. That was something, surely.

"You may call me Tristan or Tris when we are private. In public, of course, simply Trevor will do." He kissed her hands and she shivered. They would need to further their acquaintance a bit more rapidly. "Have you never been kissed before, Dora?"

She turned her head to the side and shook it, then tried to slip her hands out of his.

"No need to be afraid, my dear. I won't hurt you." Slowly, sensually, he brushed the back of her hand with his lips, then turned it over and grazed her palm as well. "Kisses are a normal part of married life."

"I know." Her voice was stronger than a whisper, but still low. "I've seen my brother Simon kissing his wife Judith."

"Would you like for me to kiss you?" He stared into her clear blue eyes and cupped her cheek.

An almost imperceptible nod.

Good.

Tris angled her face toward him and pressed his lips against hers, gently at first, then more insistently. He slid his other hand around her back and pulled her even closer, until he could feel her small breasts against his chest. Carefully, he opened his mouth and ran the tip of his tongue along the seam of her tightly clamped lips.

She gasped and stumbled away. "My lord."

He let her go. Her stricken stare told him this would be an uphill battle, near impossible to win in such a short time. Still, he smiled at her. "Did you enjoy your first kiss, Dora?"

Raising her fingers to her lips, she rubbed them lightly, as if she could feel the kiss better that way. "I don't know, my lord."

"Tristan, please."

A brief nod. "Tristan."

"Then we will have to try again, when next I come." He smiled gently, trying to reassure her as he would a skittish colt. "Perhaps then you will know."

"Did...did you enjoy it, my...Tristan?" The big blue eyes held out the hope of his approval.

"I did, Dora, very much. Soon I hope you will feel the same."

Her smile stretched the width of her face, banishing her uneasiness and lightening her eyes to a dazzling azure. "Oh, I am sure I will, Tristan." She bobbed her head and scurried out.

Tris collected his cloak from Pratt and sent for his horse. What a damnable mess. He hated to lie, but the hesitant hope in Dora's face when she asked if he enjoyed the kiss had squeezed his conscience into that pathetic admission. Perhaps it would be better next time. The girl was sweet, too sweet for his tastes if truth be told. So he should not be surprised she stirred not one iota of passion in him, even pressed firmly against his cock. There hadn't been so much as an inkling of a stirring down below.

That might concern him except for the immediate response when he thought of kissing Violet. If he had been engaged even in this light a dalliance with her, his ride home would have become damned uncomfortable. In fact, if he didn't stop thinking of her right this minute he might regret it, though he doubted that.

Stepping out onto the portico in the brisk wind, his ardor abated somewhat. Still, it didn't matter. He'd be tortured by thoughts of Violet in his arms long after her departure and his wedding were things of the past.

Chapter 7

"Hold your arms straight out, *mademoiselle*. Do not move." Madame Angelique's voice was firm as she passed a measuring tape around Violet's chest and pulled it tight across her breasts. The mantua maker had arrived promptly at two o'clock. Once she had been ushered to Violet's chamber, she set to work immediately. With quick, sure movements, the petite woman in the fashionable ecru gown plied her tape and recorded measurements for chest, waist, and hips, then lengths for her arms and legs.

Violet's head whirled. The swiftness with which Angelique worked astounded her. She had planned to ask the woman about possible employment, however she feared now her sewing skills might be found lacking by the energetic French woman.

"Now for the 'at hand' gowns *le seigneur* requested. Here, let us try this one." From a huge box, she produced a half-finished gown and dropped it over Violet's head.

"But—"

"Ah, that shade of blue suits you perfectly. *Bon.* Marie, pin the waist to mark it. Estelle, you do the same to the hem. Not too low. It must not drag the ground." Stepping back, Angelique surveyed Violet, mounted precariously on a chair, while the assistants bustled about in a flurry of work. Madame Angelique was a hard taskmaster, it seemed.

"It will need trimming. Gold braid with pearls, I think. Make note of that, Estelle." Angelique beamed at Violet. "I understand you will need complete outfitting, *mademoiselle*. *Seigneur* Trevor is a most generous man. Remove that one, Marie. There are still the cream print and the coral red jacquard to try." She turned back to her box.

"I don't think I need so many gowns, Madame." Violet ran her fingers over the expensive blue silk before the servant unfastened it. How could she repay Lord Trevor for even one such gown, much less two or three?

"Nonsense, *petite*. *Le seigneur* informed me you had no suitable clothes." Dipping into the box again, Angelique produced a beautiful cream-colored gown, figured with medallions of red and blue flowers. "He is a man who enjoys a well-dressed woman, *non*? I have worked for him several times in the past to outfit his mistresses."

Violet froze. Of course he had told the seamstress she was his mistress. Her cheeks flamed. What must Madame Angelique think of her? She longed to tell the woman it wasn't true. But she couldn't let the secret out yet. And niggling at the back of her mind was the question: Would he ask her to be his mistress in truth? Perhaps it was wrong to be so suspicious of his motives. Still, why else would he go to such expense for her?

Angelique helped coax her arms into sleeves frothy with costly lace at the edges. "He expects me to provide one or two simple gowns today. After these fittings, we will sit with the sketches and fashion dolls I have brought and plan what you need, down to chemises, stays, panniers, stockings, and shoes."

"But this is too much, Madame." Violet couldn't breathe. She would never have been able to afford such luxury.

"Of course it is not. You please *Seigneur* Trevor, he rewards you. *C'est trés facile.*" Catching her look, Madame frowned. "Do you not like this one, *petite*? You look as though you have swallowed a fly. I assure you, the gown is quite becoming with your coloring." She turned Violet so she could see herself in the mirror.

The beautiful gown did make her skin glow. It was so soft she scarcely knew she had anything on. How she would love to wear it out shopping, or to church, or to pay a call. All the normal things a lady did. She longed to be ordinary again, although an ordinary woman could scarcely afford such gowns. Unless…

"Madame Angelique. I could not help but notice your two seamstresses have been extremely busy all during my fitting."

"They are slower than a slug in a spring garden, *mademoiselle*. Marie, this hem will not do. It is more crooked than an old man's back." The seamstress bounded up and finished pinning it, glaring at her assistant as her fingers flew. "They come to me as refugees from France. I take them in, teach them valuable skills, and what repayment do I get? Crooked hems and huge stitches. Look at this. Such stitches you can put your finger through." She shook her head and glared at Marie, who lowered her gaze and continued with the alterations.

"Perhaps you would be in the market for an additional seamstress?" Violet tried not to reveal her eagerness, but it was very hard. If she could get the mantua maker to agree to take her on, she would have an income, and access to materials to make clothes for herself at a fraction of the cost of fine ladies' wardrobes.

"Oh, oui! *Absolutement.* Do you know such a person? If they do the work quickly and well, I can be very generous." She stripped the gown off Violet, leaving her in a very short chemise. "Was this *mademoiselle*'s previous maid? Tell her to come to my shop, *immediatement*."

"No, it's not my maid, Madame Angelique. It's...me."

"You?" The mantua maker stared at her as if she had grown two heads. "You wish me to employ you? *C'est incroyable.*" Then she shook her head and laughed. "You have had the little joke with me, eh, *mademoiselle*? Another talent to amuse *Seigneur* Trevor, *oui*? But you should not suggest I would take his lordship's mistress from him. My custom would be ruined, not only with *Seigneur* Trevor, but with all of his friends as well." With a shiver she crossed herself. "No, *cherie*," she said, patting Violet's arm, "do not jest about such things."

Violet closed her eyes and sighed. Another avenue closed to her.

"Come, we have much to do, *damoiselle*." She drew Violet to the chairs before the fire. "Here, these are sketches using some of the fabrics I have in my shop. We must choose six more dresses and two ball gowns."

"Ball gowns?" Her high-pitched squeak sounded loud in her own ears.

"*Mais oui*, his lordship insisted." Angelique smiled, and Violet's spirits sank at the predatory gleam in the seamstress's eyes. "I have just the thing at my shop, the perfect fabric to bring the gold in your eyes leaping straight to *Seigneur* Trevor's heart. It is a heavy silk with a lace pattern woven into the fabric. It is beige and rust on a dark brown, all shot through with golden threads. It will be an exquisite ball gown for you, my dear. His lordship will not be able to take his eyes off you, especially after I lower the neckline several inches."

Dear Lord. If the woman lowered the necklines of the ones she'd just tried on, she'd be showing her bosom down to her navel. They needed a fichu now. Still, the designs were entrancing. She could imagine herself dancing at a ball in the one Madame Angelique held before her, a *robe à la française* in lavender and green stripes over a lavender petticoat with scrollwork edged in rust around the jacket front. Oh, but she hungered for the feel of such a gown.

"*Mademoiselle* Cassandra, you must choose, my dear."

Violet jumped, startled as much by the voice as by the name.

"*Seigneur* Trevor insists all the gowns must be completed no later than next week. I must begin this afternoon." Angelique cocked her head like an expectant bird. "Your choices, *mademoiselle*?"

Desire to appear once again as she had before Jamie's death coursed through her. She should take Lord Trevor at his word. Surely, he wished her nothing but well. In order for her to appear as a member of good standing in Society of course she must look her best. Even a companion needed different gowns. And he had spoken of perhaps a marriage. In order to attract a gentleman of the nobility she would have to be outfitted splendidly, according to her station. This was what Tristan had had in mind by giving these instructions to Madame Angelique.

Heartbeat pounding, she pointed to the lavender and green stripe. "This one, Madame. Along with the one in beige and brown you described for the two ball gowns." Violet picked up the other sketches and smiled at the mantua maker. This would be exciting and fun. Life as a faux mistress had distinct advantages. "For the day gowns, I think I prefer the *robe à la anglaise*, in this salmon print and in this light blue brocade. Then I believe the cream-colored one with the embroidered stomacher will do nicely as well. And do you have any others in lavender or violet? Those are my favorite colors."

* * * *

Attired in the two-piece cream print gown, Violet spun in her room, laughing in sheer delight at having a new and fashionable gown. While she and Madame Angelique had finalized her selection of gowns, the two assistants had stitched and tucked and hemmed like fiends to ready the gown before they left. The result was an outfit that made Violet hold her head high, ready to meet the world head on. Her lack of clothing had compromised her self-esteem. Now armed with this new gown, Susan's expert hairstyle, a pinner cap, and the silk mules, Violet marched down the staircase confident for the first time in weeks that life would work out to her satisfaction.

She stuck her head in the kitchen and was greeted with the deliciously sweet aroma of baking breads. "Mrs. Parker, could you please arrange a tea for me?"

"Of course, miss. Shall I serve it in the parlor or the music room?" The kind woman looked up from the dough she was rolling out and smiled.

"There is a music room?" The day kept getting brighter and brighter.

"Yes, miss. Just across the hall from the parlor." The cook nodded toward the door where Violet stood. "We've been so busy putting the rest of the house to rights, and without Mr. Gates to oversee the work—the man knew everything about running a household—we've not been as swift to have the house just so for you."

"Well, I think everything here is wonderful, Mrs. Parker. Thank you so very much for taking such good care of me." The closed door at the end of the hallway beckoned. Excitement raced through her veins. "Could you please serve tea in the music room? I would like a little time to explore now that I am more settled." She smoothed the skirt of her new dress. Amazing how a fresh, handsome gown had made the whole day seem better. What wonders were in store for her in the music room?

"Of course, miss. Would you like to wait until this batch of shortbread comes out of the oven?" She gestured to the dough lying thick, sparkling with a dusting of sugar on the butcher block table. "I'll have it in the oven in a twink."

"Oh, yes, please." Violet's mouth watered. "That would be lovely." She backed out of the kitchen and strode down the corridor, noting the Turkey carpet and the tasteful landscapes on the walls. Tristan certainly seemed to enjoy the arts. Painting, carpets, furniture, fashionable gowns. Did he also attend the theatre? Perhaps he was an artist himself. That would certainly make sense. He seemed a very sensitive man, much different than her brother and their cousin, who had been loud and boisterous. More like overgrown boys than men. Tristan was most definitely a man—a very handsome and charitable one.

She pressed down the latch and opened the door on a room similar in size and elegant furnishings to the parlor across the hall, save for the beautiful cherry wood spinet that sat before the bay window looking out onto the street. Very carefully she walked forward, ran her shaking fingers across the gleaming surface. Lovingly, she stroked the exquisite instrument, played a C, then an F. In tune, and with a lovely tone. She sat on the stool and rested her hands on the keyboard.

Their harpsichord at home had been the first thing sold, her harp the last before she and her grandmother had been forced to move to London. She had sorely missed playing every day. The few times she'd been asked to entertain at a party with a song she'd been forced to choose easier pieces because of a lack of means to practice. Her exhibitions had thus not shown off her talents to their best ability. Perhaps that had been a factor in not attracting a husband.

Where might they keep sheet music? A lacquered cabinet beneath a picture of Venus and Cupid seemed a likely place. A search of it turned up a case with several pieces she did not know, and one sonata by Scarlatti that she did. She clapped her hands and took it back to the harpsichord. After laying out the music sheet by sheet, she settled onto the bench and ran her fingers over the keys. It was like coming home. Scales as always to warm up. They came automatically, even after all this time. That done, so much more palatable now she'd actually missed them, she set about re-familiarizing herself with the Scarlatti.

The concerto K1 hadn't been one of her favorites, still she'd learned it once and could certainly do so again. She began slowly, stopping and starting, then found remembered passages where the music flowed effortlessly from her fingertips. After one such passage, however, she faltered, her fingers losing the thread of the keystrokes, and she jangled to a discordant end. She stretched her hands, then flexed them, and smiled. With daily practice she could master the piece once more.

Enthusiastic clapping from the doorway behind her sent her hurtling to her feet. Her hand knocked the music to the floor and Tristan darted forward, scooping up the sheets almost before they hit the polished planks.

"I beg your pardon, Violet. I didn't mean to startle you." He smiled and her heart stuttered. "But I always acknowledge a rare talent when I hear one. Brava!"

"You heard me playing?" She didn't know whether to be excited or terrified.

"I came in about halfway through. Just before you broke free." Straightening, he handed her the sheets of parchment. "It was like watching a bird leave the ground and soar." His fingers brushed her palm as he passed the music to her.

The spark that leaped from him to her sent her reeling. She stumbled back and he caught her wrist, scalding her, making her tremble inside.

"I do beg pardon. I shouldn't have startled you so. Come, sit down here." He escorted her to a chair before the fire. "Let me get Mrs. Parker. She had brought the tea tray while you were playing, but I selfishly sent it back." His eyes were warm and dark. "I didn't want you to stop." He disappeared into the passageway, calling for the cook.

Torn between the elation of playing music again and the shock of Tristan's touch, Violet sat in the chair, allowing the warmth of the fire to soothe her for a moment or two, until he reappeared. At least he had liked her playing, although she was mortified he'd heard her stumble so badly at the end. She would practice hard so when he heard her again he would be even more pleased. And she did want to please him. A small repayment for his numerous kindnesses, but something within her power to do.

Tristan entered bearing the tea tray himself and she rose, holding out her hands to take it from him.

"No, my dear. Please sit." He nodded to her chair and she sank down again. "You've given me a treat after a long and taxing day, so indulge me by allowing me to serve you." Once he had settled the tray on the music chest, he pulled a small flute-edged table in front of her. "Mrs. Parker assures me the shortbread came out of the oven not ten minutes ago."

Violet inhaled aromas of fragrant tea and sweet pastry and her stomach gave a growl. She clamped her hands over the offending organ as heat rushed to her face. Curse it. Just when she might have become comfortable with him.

"You are ready for tea, I see." He grinned, taking some of the embarrassment out of the moment. "Well, I could tell you have worked hard for it. That is why you are so accomplished."

"Not very accomplished now," she said, accepting a napkin from him.

"Nonsense. I've no musical ability myself, but I recognize true talent when I hear it. Sugar? Milk?" He poured a cup, then hovered over the bowl of sugar with a pair of tongs.

"One lump and a splash of milk, please. I have not played for a very long time. And even longer since I had the opportunity to practice regularly." She sipped the tea, deliciously hot and sweet, and took a bite of the still warm petticoat tail. "Ummm." Violet couldn't hold back the sigh of contentment. The confection all but melted on her tongue.

"Mrs. Parker's shortbread would rival Mrs. McLintock's I'm sure." He leaned back in his chair opposite her and crunched into a wedge. It disappeared in two bites and he reached for another one.

"Who is Mrs. McLintock?"

"The Scottish woman who apparently invented shortbread about thirty years ago." When he laughed, his face turned boyish. "At least she gets the credit for writing it down in a recipe book before anyone else. Mrs. Parker told me the first time she baked them for me." His laughter died as he looked at her, his gaze traveling from her head to her feet. "I see you met with Madame Angelique."

"Yes, I did. It was quite a surprise." Completely aware of his scrutiny, Violet sat straighter and smoothed out her skirt. "I cannot thank you enough, my lord."

He glared at her over the shortbread. "My lord?"

"Tristan. Tris." She blushed and could do absolutely nothing about it. "You have been more than generous to me. I cannot think how I shall ever repay you." There. She had given him the opportunity to issue the suggestion she still half expected. Better to get it out in the open and be done with it.

He raised his eyebrows as he lifted his teacup to his lips.

Those very full, very sensual lips she could still feel kissing her body.

"Can you not, my dear? Perhaps I can think of a way you could repay me that will be to our mutual satisfaction." Tris set his cup down and took her hands.

Her pulse raced and her mouth dried to dust.

"Will you become my mistress?"

Chapter 8

Tris waited for Violet's outraged explosion, biting the inside of his cheek to keep from smiling. Despite their conversation this morning, he knew she expected him to issue the indecent proposal. She'd given him the opening deliberately and he'd taken it. He stared longingly into her eyes. He loved to tease and suspected she'd be a fun target.

Violet bit her lip. Her face paled a trifle, but she squeezed his hands and said quite calmly, "Yes, I will."

"What?" Tris jerked his hands away from her and pushed himself back in the chair, setting the cups and saucers to rattling. If he could have gotten farther away he would have. "What do you mean, 'yes'? You should have said absolutely not."

A puzzled frown ruffled her brows. "But you said I could repay you—"

"Christ in Heaven, I was teasing you, Violet." He pounded his fist against his forehead. Idiot. "You seemed to expect such an offer, despite my words this morning. I thought you'd turn me down with a large flea in my ear." 'Sblood, he had to make this right. Poor Violet looked as though she was about to cry. "I do beg your pardon, my dear. It was a very ungentlemanly thing to do."

"It's just you have been so kind and generous to me, Tris." She sniffed and wiped a tear from her eye. "I kept thinking of all the gowns I ordered from Madame Angelique. They must be terribly expensive. And the house, the servants, Susan. I simply wanted to do something to show how grateful I am." She bent her head. "I thought you wanted me…like that."

The last words were spoken so low Tris had to lean in to hear them. Damn. If only she knew the truth. He put his finger under her chin and lifted her face until she looked him in the eyes.

"Violet, you are correct. I do want you like that. You knew that last night, I believe."

Slowly, she nodded, trying to turn her head, but he held her so she would have to see him. She needed to hear his story and understand why any relationship between them was impossible.

"I also told you I am betrothed. I signed the settlement papers today. Once I have given my word, I will not go back on it. That would be unfair to my betrothed."

With a jerk that reverberated up his arm, she pulled her chin out of his hands and sat back, clutching the napkin. "I know how society works, Tris. Such things are expected of an honorable man." Her unwavering stare unnerved him. "I also know, married or not, many men keep mistresses. When you ordered so much for me, were so particular about my clothing, I thought you had changed your mind." She bit her bottom lip and twisted the napkin. "I have no other way to repay your kindnesses."

"I do not seek repayment, Violet." He'd be angry with her, if she didn't look so forlorn. Her eyes were downcast again, her mouth taut, without a glimmer of a smile. He wanted nothing so much as to take her in his arms and stroke her hair, tell her everything would be all right. But that was impossible. "And much as I might desire you, I will not dishonor you. You should not dishonor yourself by agreeing to such a scheme with me or any other man. Especially not a married man." The melancholy mood she had created touched him as well. "A bachelor may sow his wild oats, but once a man marries, he is duty-bound to cherish his wife. No matter where his heart may lie."

"More men should think as you do." She picked up her teacup, sipped, then grimaced and set it hastily down.

"It is not always easy." He should ring for fresh tea, but had the idea she wanted it as little as he.

"Yet you are choosing the more difficult path. That is commendable."

"I have seen first-hand the devastation such actions produce. A whole family could be destroyed." His had been.

She cocked her head, but wouldn't ask.

Then he'd tell her. Lay it to rest once and for all.

"My father had a mistress. I didn't find out about her for years, but he kept her from the first year of his marriage to my mother."

"Oh, Tris." Violet's eyes became sadder. "Then why did he marry her?"

"An arranged marriage, very common in their generation. They liked one another well enough and there was respect in the beginning. At least my mother professed there was. But they didn't fall in love." Why hadn't he poured himself some brandy before beginning his tale? "While she was increasing with my eldest sister, my father hired a woman to take care of his 'needs' because my mother was indisposed. It was regarded as being considerate of a woman in a delicate condition."

"Indeed." She snorted and Tris couldn't help but laugh. Violet had a fiery streak in her to be sure.

"I never met this woman, but Father loved her desperately. She wasn't of the nobility of course, but her family was genteel and had fallen on hard times."

Violet gasped.

She'd likely agree to a brandy now as well. Why the hell not? He rose and headed for the writing desk that held a decanter and glasses. Bless Mrs. Parker for replenishing it today.

"A remarkably familiar story, isn't it, my dear? Would you like some?" He held the bottle up and she stared at it so long he thought she meant to refuse. But at last she nodded and he poured two fingers of the smooth cognac into each tumbler. If she didn't want it all, he'd be happy to finish hers off. "What is sad is that it's not in the least a remarkable occurrence. It happens all the time, even now." He handed her the glass.

She sniffed it and wrinkled her nose.

Charming in a completely devastating way.

Cautiously, she took a sip. Her eyes widened and she struggled to swallow.

He wanted to laugh. She surprised him in so many ways.

Then she recovered, gulped, and cradled the glass in her hands. "And did your mother learn of the mistress?"

"Not at first. My father strove hard to keep it from her. As I said, he did respect her and wanted to keep her from any unnecessary pain." Especially while she might be carrying his heir. Tris downed his drink. "She found out just before I was born. It was fortunate I was the hoped-for heir, because afterward she wouldn't let him into her bed." He shook his head. His home life had been hell growing up. "I've always suspected my name had something to do with the old legend of Tristan, Iseult, and King Mark. A lovers' triangle from before the Round Table." He poured another two fingers for himself.

"Did your father send your mother away?" Violet took a sip and puckered her lips. At last she swallowed. She still had a good bit left.

"He tried, but she refused to go. She was Viscountess Trevor and would let no one forget it, least of all my father. She begged, pleaded, even berated him to give the woman up, but he refused. He'd fallen in love with her, you see." Tris stared at Violet, his heart beating with little jerks. He gripped the goblet then reminded himself not to break the stem. "In all those years, he never let her go. He and my mother lived estranged under one roof for more than twenty years before she died. Two years later Father's mistress died as well. He was inconsolable. Her death broke him inside and he followed her to the grave within two months." Tris tossed back the remainder of his cognac. He wanted to smash the glass into the fireplace, but what good would that do? "I've vowed not to repeat my father's mistake. So you can best repay my kindness, Violet, by being happy in your life, no matter if it's work, music, or marriage. Just be happy."

Her eyes fixed firmly on the glass, she toyed with it, swirling the contents to and fro. "Then you are in love with your betrothed? I didn't understand that." When she raised her head, her gaze was cool. "I supposed since you had come to the House of Pleasure, to me, you did not love her."

Tris bit his tongue and clenched his fist. Violet was damned intelligent, even when somewhat foxed. The drink had freed her tongue. She wouldn't have asked such a question had she been sober. "It is a typical arranged marriage."

Incredibly, her eyes filled with pain. "Why in the name of God would you agree to such a thing, Tris? Knowing what your parents' lives had been like?"

"I never meant it to happen like this, Violet." Seen from her point of view his actions must seem those of a lunatic. Perhaps they were. "My father's dying wish was for me to marry Miss Harper in order to bring a valuable piece of property back into the family."

"A piece of property?" She gazed at him, as though he had indeed lost his mind. "You've sacrificed your happiness for a piece of land?"

He drew himself up. She didn't understand. "My family has waited generations to reacquire it. My father made me promise and I will not go back on my word."

"He should never have asked that of you if he loved you."

"I am not quite sure he did." Tris set his glass down on the desk, then strode across the room to stand beside her. "Nevertheless, he begged me and I agreed. Do not let it distress you, my dear. I have made my peace with it."

"I beg your pardon." The wooden response smote him. "It is not my place to pry into your personal affairs."

"It will always be your place, as my friend, to keep me from harm, as it will be mine to do the same with you."

"Ever the protector, Tris?"

"Guilty, I'm afraid." He offered his hand. "If I do not love the lady now, perhaps it will come in time. She is sweet and accomplished, worthy of any man's love. I will endeavor to make myself worthy of her. It will be my life's aim to protect her from any unkindness." Though it hurt like the devil, he smiled and helped her to her feet. Her warm hand was a knife in his heart. "Come. You must rest and refresh yourself before dinner."

"Thank you. I do feel a bit fatigued." She twined her hand in the crook of his elbow.

"You will need all of your strength, for I intend to find out all about your gown selection." He nodded at the stylish cream print dress. "And I am sure you have much to tell me about your meeting with Madame Angelique."

A smile lit her face. "Yes, it was the most enjoyable afternoon." She pulled the skirt out a little.

"How very lovely, my dear. It becomes you." A good color choice for her. It also showed off her figure nicely. His gaze had continually strayed to her breasts, pushed up by her stays and, without the covering of a fichu, very much on display.

"This was only one of the selections." When she arched her neck, her breasts swelled even more. "Wait until you hear about the ball gowns."

"I am breathless with anticipation." He kissed her hand and led her to the staircase. "Rest well." The gentle sway of her hips as she mounted the steps set his blood to pounding. Damn, but he must stop ogling her. Turning on his heel, he strode back to the music room. Another libation might help dull the ache in his groin—and his heart.

She'd been right, of course. How had he managed to put himself in the same intolerable position as his father? Odd, but the thought of an arranged marriage hadn't seemed odious when he'd made the promise to marry Miss Harper. The girl was pretty enough and sweet, although painfully shy. He'd believed he could coax her out of her shell, a challenge to his charm and talents of seduction. A good possibility had existed they might develop an affection for one another that would grow, especially after he introduced her to the pleasures of the marriage bed. That would have satisfied him, even if it had not inflamed his passions.

Little hope of that now.

Tris drained another glass of the cognac, relishing the burn that erupted in his stomach. Nothing for it, he must find suitable employment for Miss Carlton immediately. Strict reminders to himself that that particular avenue was closed to him would only work for so long if the tempting woman remained practically under his nose. Violet was a woman meant for passion and love. She'd revealed that much while playing the spinet. She had poured her heart, her longings into every note. Such a passionate nature should not be denied.

He didn't want to deny it or himself.

Christ, he'd best focus on wooing his bride. He needed to find a way to put her at ease with him, to encourage an affection, to make her stir his soul like the woman who had, too late, captured his heart.

Chapter 9

Violet finished the last measure of the Scarlatti sonata with a flourish and sat back, smiling. The final chords rang a moment longer in the deserted music room. She wished Tris had been here to hear it. Still, excitement bubbled up, causing gooseflesh to appear on her arms. In a single week, with diligent practice morning and afternoon, she had mastered the piece, surpassing even her previous efforts when she'd lived with her grandmother in Surrey.

Of course, there had been precious little else to occupy her time this past week. The delivery of the "at hand" gowns on Monday had caused a flurry of activity for an afternoon. Yesterday a marathon session of fittings with Madame Angelique for the rest of her wardrobe had provided a welcome distraction from brooding about Tristan. The remainder of the gowns were promised for next week, although she foresaw little use for most of them as apparently she was to neither be seen nor heard in society.

Tris had called on her every evening, to share Mrs. Parker's delicious cuisine and to relate the news of his progress in securing her a position. A distinct lack of progress, actually. With all the people Tristan appeared to know, in London and all over England, she'd steeled herself for the inevitability of a swift departure from Lammas House. To her surprise, he'd had no success at all. Surely, one person, somewhere in all his acquaintance, needed a companion or governess.

After the third evening of disappointing results, Violet had decided to take the reins into her own hands. She proposed to go out herself in search of a position with one of London's less illustrious seamstresses. It was respectable work and usually plenty of it, as long as the seamstress didn't think she'd be absconding with Tris's mistress.

She'd have thought she'd plotted to steal the crown jewels.

"Absolutely not!" Tris had paced back and forth in front of the fireplace, the flickering light catching glints of gold in his brown Jacquard silk suit. "You cannot venture out of the house, Violet. It's not safe."

"Thomas or Charles and Susan can accompany me. No one would dare accost me with such an entourage." Patience with the situation at an end, she'd pointed this out while clinging to her temper.

"But someone might recognize you." He'd made it sound like she was a criminal.

"What if they do? They don't know where I've been living for the past week. You are worrying needlessly, Tristan."

"What if they saw you come out of the house? Or go back into it? Certain men know this was my mistresses' house. If there were even a hint of a suspicion you lived here under my protection—"

"I know. I'd be ruined beyond even your repair. You have mentioned it." Of course, he feared for her safety and thought her a retiring woman who couldn't take care of herself. She must disabuse him of that notion as soon as possible. For the sake of peace, and against her better judgment, however, she had agreed not to go out of the house except for the back garden, a small patch with wilted grass and a few half-hearted blooms in pots. The air at least was fresh, except for the days when the smoke and fog lay heavy on the city.

So she had poured herself into her music, reveling in the familiar thrill of the keyboard under her fingers. If only she had her harp she wouldn't mind being locked away so much. At least she did have Tris's company, although it was brief. His nightly visits were the most welcome part of her day. They dined and chatted together on so many evenings he became as comfortable to be around as an old shoe. They never ventured into such personal subjects as they had over tea last week, still she watched him when he wasn't looking. His carefree nature showed itself in full force as he laughed and teased her. Yet, she had caught him several times in unguarded moments when he stared at nothing, a frown marring his otherwise handsome features. Did he think of Miss Harper during those pensive moments? Or of her?

"You will not entertain those thoughts, my girl," she scolded herself as she swept the music from the stand and stacked it on the music chest. Any thought of Tristan other than as a friend or protector would lead to nothing but disappointment or worse. Life was seldom fair. Best for her to acknowledge that and find a way to move on, despite the ache in her heart each time she saw him.

"Penny for your thoughts."

She whirled around to face Tristan, standing in the doorway, so handsome in a rust and jade striped jacket she had to catch hold of the chest as her heart beat wildly. "You of course." She tried her best to sound flippant and flirtatious.

"Indeed." His brows rose, a mischievous twinkle in the blue eyes. "Wondering if I'd abandoned you completely because of the glorious weather?" He nodded toward the widow and the brilliant sunshine that drenched the small back garden.

"Hardly." Steadying herself, she walked nonchalantly toward him. "You've been as faithful as a puppy, visiting me every evening. I wouldn't blame you if you had more interesting things to do than have dinner with me." The afternoon shadows had scarcely begun to creep across the yard. "You're very early today, however. Does that mean you have news?" Elation warred with despair. If he'd been successful she'd soon be on her way to her employer and out of his life.

"It just so happens I do. And it was such a lovely day, quite exceptional for early December, wouldn't you say, I thought you might venture out in the carriage with me?" He grinned broadly and a dimple appeared in his left cheek. "Show off one of those devilishly pretty gowns, perhaps?"

Violet squealed and threw her arms around him. "Oh, yes, Tris. Thank you, thank you! I would love to go riding with you." She let go reluctantly, aware as always of how good he felt pressed against her. "I confess I'd been fretting because I couldn't go out. The beautiful weather just made it worse. You are an answer to a prayer." As he'd always been. She stood on tiptoe and brushed a kiss on his cheek.

Heat sizzled as her lips touched him. The shock rippled through her, rocking her back on her heels. Had he felt that?

His jaw tightened, and his eyes, so blue at first, now darkest black with desire. Her own eyes must be as dark.

She dropped her gaze and stepped back.

"Violet." His hoarse whisper rasped in her ears, tempting her to stay and appease their mutual hunger.

"Let me fetch my cloak and bonnet." Quickly, she backed away from him, then turned and fled the room, pounding up the stairs as though a fiend nipped at her heels. Dear God, she needed to leave this house, leave him before her willpower snapped and she did something disastrous they would glory in and regret.

* * * *

Tris clenched his fist, fighting the urge to run after her, seize her and give in to the passion raging within them both. He breathed in slowly, willing the storm to pass. God, the past week had been torture. Sitting across the dinner table from Violet, watching spellbound as she sipped her wine, or laughed, or teased him. He seemed to hang on her every movement, like a besotted stripling with his first lass. As soon as that became apparent, he should have stopped the visits. However, like a reckless moth compelled toward the blaze with the ultimate power to destroy it, he had returned again and again, fluttering closer and closer to her entrancing flame. Now he teetered on the verge. A touch, a kiss, hell, a smoldering look from those amber eyes might push him off the precipice into an act of unspeakable folly. One night he'd dreamed of marching into Lord Downing's study to break the betrothal and awoken in a cold sweat. Society's censure in such a case would be absolute. No honorable man would jilt an innocent woman, thus destroying her reputation. He'd end up a pariah. But he'd have Violet.

Tris headed for the brandy decanter, pleased it had been refilled. Thomas had promise as a butler if he had an eye for such details. After two healthy gulps, the excellent vintage managed to relieve some of the tension that had him tied in knots. He breathed slowly, stretching out the hand he had curled into a fist. Perfectly steady. That was a wonder. He wouldn't have wagered a sixpence on it.

"I'm ready." Violet appeared in the doorway, her black velvet cloak covering her from neck to floor. When she moved, however, the vivid blue silk of her new gown peeped out, giving an enticing glimpse of her full breasts.

Angelique was taking too much time with this order, damn it. He'd wanted Violet outfitted completely by the end of this week. Especially crucial as he'd had to abandon his first plan to find her employment. Between the holiday distractions and his reluctance to apply to any close friends or family who might know the circumstances of James Carlton's death, he'd had no luck at all turning up a post for either a governess or companion. As a result, he'd had to contemplate another way to provide for Violet. This outing served a twofold purpose—to give her a much needed respite from the looming walls of her gilded cage, and to introduce her to the alternate plan of action. One he hated to consider, yet by far the best choice for her.

"You look stunning, my dear. Heads will turn, mark my words."

"Ha. The sensible people have all returned to their comfortable estates for their Christmas revelry. There will be no one in the park to pay me a bit of mind." She secured her hat to her head with a wicked-looking pin whose jeweled end glinted with small sapphires and diamonds.

Another most inappropriate gift from him, but he couldn't help himself.

"I'll wager you nonetheless. How about…" It was on the tip of his tongue to say "a kiss.' Too dangerous by half.

"I know. A trip to the theatre," Violet broke in, her eyes sparkling.

"Done. If you win, I will take you to Drury Lane next week. If I win, however…" He paused, staring at her lips and sighed. "If I win, I demand a musical performance in which you exhibit your great talents. Just for me."

A charming blush tinted her cheeks and she smiled. "Very well, it is a wager." She leaned forward, hand outstretched as if for a handshake. At the last second she glanced at his face and abruptly withdrew it.

It was as well. Much as he desired her touch, he could only stand so much skin-to-skin contact. "Let us go, my dear. The park awaits." He offered his arm, praying the clothing between them would act as a sufficient shield.

Once seated in his phaeton, he drew a lap robe over her and gathered the ribbons. The high perch allowed them to look down on the world, a vantage point he had always secretly enjoyed. Hyde Park was a little distance from Lammas House, but they should arrive in good time to meet some of the fashionable set.

Violet sat on the edge of the seat, her neck constantly craning to catch the sights of London as they sped by. The sun glinted on the stands of her chestnut hair, turning them as gold as the autumn leaves that lingered on the ground here and there. She raised her chin and laughed as the cool air brought roses to her cheeks.

Tris swallowed hard, her beauty overwhelming him once more. Pray God others saw it as well.

"Thank you so much for this lovely treat," she said, tucking the robe more securely around her as they approached the park entrance. "I confess I've longed for just a bit of adventure this past week. This outing is a blessing."

"I'm very happy to oblige you, my dear." Tris turned the horses onto the well-used lane. In the distance, several carriages headed toward them. Perhaps his scheme would work after all. "Excellent luck." He nodded at the approaching vehicles. "I'm hoping to introduce you to some of my acquaintances this afternoon."

"You are?" She peered at him, eyebrows raised. "You've made me remain secluded at the house, forbidden to stick my nose outside the door because you feared someone would associate me with you, yet now you want to introduce me?" A frown darkened her features. "What is really going on, Tris?"

"I've come to the conclusion that the best possibility for your future would be a good marriage." He kept his eyes on the horses' heads, but heard a sharp gasp. "You yourself said you had been seeking marriage this past summer. We will merely be renewing that search. With the Christmas round of holiday parties at hand, we can reintroduce you into Society. And a good first step is to meet people in a public arena, like Hyde Park."

"Indeed." The single word dripped frost. "So you have decided I should marry. Did you not think it necessary to consult me on the matter?"

Afraid to look at her, Tris could nevertheless feel her eyes boring into him. He put on his best face and turned to her. "I am consulting you now, Violet. I have thought it through many times, but I do not see a better solution at present."

She slid well back in the seat, and her excitement vanished.

He slowed the horses. Better to have privacy for this conversation. "You know I have scoured London, written a sheaf of letters to out-of-town acquaintances, and still I have nothing to report. There appears to be a dearth of positions at the moment. These things seem to run in cycles. A month from now I'll have ten people requesting a companion. But a month from now won't do, I'm afraid."

"Your approaching nuptials, I assume." Her chest heaved as she tucked the robe up under her chin.

"Yes." What else could he say if he would be honest with her? "It may well be your best chance for a happy life, my dear." At least one of them might have a chance. He gripped the ribbons until his knuckles ached. Still he had no options left. Lord Downing had set the wedding day for early in the new year. Scarcely a month from today. Violet must be settled in her new life before his husbandly duties called him elsewhere. Before someone discovered he had been keeping her like his other mistresses.

She sat biting her lip. Then she sighed deeply and nodded. "Very well, my lord. If that is our only choice, then by all means, let us resume the hunt."

Her resignation squeezed his heart but he ignored it. It was better for them both thus.

"You realize it still will not be easy, Tris? I've no dowry, no connections, and a scandal attached to my name. What prospects do you think will magically appear? They certainly did not exist last summer."

"Leave such worries to me. Simply be your charming self and I will take care of the rest." Ah, here was a blessing indeed. Lord Donningham and his sister sat in a carriage at the end of the path. As good a start as any.

The viscount had been widowed for almost a year now, and Tris's sources told him he'd been avidly searching for a new wife at the end of last Season. The man had no vices to speak of, although he certainly wasn't good enough for Violet. Would anyone ever be?

Tris drew his carriage nigh and hailed them. "Lord Donningham, Miss Tate. I see you are enjoying this glorious afternoon. It seems to have brought many out of hiding."

"Trevor." The man nodded to him, but his attention fastened immediately on Violet, his appraising glance undisguised.

Fury seared Tris and he clenched his jaw so tight it ached. The rack would be more merciful a torture than Donningham's scrutiny.

"How splendid to see you again, Lord Trevor," Miss Tate cooed in dulcet tones, telling him she'd obviously not heard of his betrothal.

"Delighted as well, Miss Tate. Miss Carlton, may I make known to you Lord Donningham and his sister, Miss Tate."

"So pleased to meet you, Miss Tate." Violet nodded, then batted her eyes at the viscount. "My lord."

Well, she'd certainly not be a shy violet. "Miss Carlton is in town for the holidays. An old friend of the family who I am escorting about."

"Excellent, Miss Carlton," Donningham said, so eagerly he could scarcely get the words out. "You must give me a dance at the next ball you attend."

Gads, the man wasted no time a'tall. Tris fought the urge to rail at him. Such interest was what he desired for Violet. Damn it, he must let his feelings go. He'd not expected it would twist his heart this badly, though.

"It would be my pleasure, my lord." Violet flushed becomingly, her cheeks the perfect rosy shade to attract a man. She played her role extremely well.

"Do we know which entertainment we will be at next, my lord?" Gaily, she leaned toward Tris, a sickeningly sweet smile on her face.

Enjoying his discomfort, by God. "I believe the Braeton's Christmas party on the fifteenth is the next one, my dear." Then, to Miss Tate, "Miss Carlton is a particular friend of Miss Forsythe." He might as well build up Violet's reputation when he could. A connection with the red-haired heiress would be good cachet for her.

"Oh, wonderful," Miss Tate broke in, suddenly more animated. "We will be attending as well." Arching her neck, she smiled at Tris, her interest too obvious. She'd partnered Tris several times over the summer and he'd found her amiable enough, but clingy. At the last ball he'd attended he'd steered clear of her. Now of course, she'd expect him to offer for one of her dances as well.

"I would ask you for a dance, Miss Tate, but I must consult my betrothed first as to which dances she prefers me reserve for her."

Miss Tate's smile froze. "Of course, my lord. I...I didn't know you were to be married." She glanced at her brother, whose face had suddenly gone sour. "Allow me to wish you happy."

"Thank you. Miss Harper and I suit very well. Still, I will make sure we have that dance, Miss Tate."

"Miss Harper? You're engaged to Lord Downing's daughter?" Donningham's features relaxed. "Capital, Trevor. My felicitations as well." Grinning at Violet, he puffed out his chest. "I must have the first dance, Miss Carlton. I would not be able to stand looking on if you partnered another man first."

In his scarlet waistcoat and jacket, Donningham reminded Tris of a male bird with mating plumage in full display.

"Then I will make no demur, my lord. I look forward to our dance with anticipation." Violet cast her gaze down shyly.

By God, she played the game well. Had she possessed a dowry, she'd have been married long ago.

"I fear we must press on, my dear." He leaned over and patted her hand. "We must return before dark and the light goes so early this time of year." Tris inclined his head, relieved to take his leave. "Donningham, Miss Tate."

"It was such a pleasure to meet you, Miss Tate. Lord Donningham. I do look forward to seeing you again." Violet nodded to them.

Almost before they'd finished speaking, Tris had urged the team back onto the path that circled the park. The carriage had scarcely gotten out of earshot of Donningham's carriage when she turned to him.

"That went rather well, don't you think?"

"Lord Donningham certainly seemed taken with you." Refusing to look at her, Tris snapped the ribbons and the horses picked up their pace.

"He was still in mourning when I was out last summer or I daresay we'd have met already. I am surprised I didn't meet his sister, though." Violet cocked her head. "And I hardly think asking for a dance qualifies as being 'taken with me.' I will admit, however, I was rather flattered. He's very handsome."

Tris grunted. Damn Donningham.

She laughed and drew the lap robe close up over her shoulders. "Brrr. It has gotten quite chilly." A sly glance at him and she smiled. "I suppose we should go home, then. We seem to have accomplished what you wanted."

"What I wanted?" Tris almost yelped, then sighed and got himself in hand. "Yes, I believe we have. Home it is." He compelled the horses on and they completed their circuit of the park at a fast trot. At least he'd made a step toward finding a suitable marriage for Violet. Of course, watching her dance and flirt with Donningham and others would be difficult, but he'd manage. Beginning anything unpleasant was always rough on a chap. Still it was necessary.

Their return to Lammas House proved uneventful. Tris gave Thomas their cloaks as they entered.

"Allow me to repair my appearance before dinner, Tris. I'm terribly windblown." She dashed up the stairs, her feet pounding softly.

"Everything is in place?" Tris spoke quietly to the butler.

Thomas nodded. "Just as you wished, my lord."

"Excellent. You have the light supper ready?"

"Yes, my lord. Mrs. Parker is keeping it hot."

Violet reappeared and raced down the stairs, her skirts swirling around her. "High-perch phaetons are not conducive to stylish or even neat hair. What is wrong?" She stopped on the last step, her gaze riveted to his face.

"Not one thing, my dear. You are a vision of loveliness, phaeton or no. Come, I have a surprise for you. Close your eyes."

She narrowed them instead and approached him warily. "Am I going to like this surprise?"

"I believe so. It will assist you in paying your forfeit. You must admit, you did turn heads." He extended his hand to her.

"One head," she conceded, placing her hand in his.

"One was enough. Close your eyes," he said, leading her to the door of the music room. Letting her go, he wrapped his hands over her shoulders where the gown ended and her soft, white skin began. He positioned her at the threshold of the door. "Step inside, please. And no peeking." This close to her all he need do was take a breath and her sweet jasmine scent filled his head.

She giggled, nervous tension flowing through her into him as he guided her into the room, alight with candles that flickered and danced along the walls and spilled from the crystal chandelier.

"Open your eyes, Violet," he whispered, still clutching her shoulders, not wanting to let go.

Her eyes flew open, blinked, and then her gaze fell on the golden harp, placed beside the spinet. She stiffened, gasped, and raised her hand to grip his.

Then she tore across the polished wood floor to the gleaming instrument, her eyes wide. Mouth agape, she stared at it. Reverently, she lifted her hand to touch the strings, sending a soft discord through the still air.

The hunger in her eyes sent a burst of happiness through him, as if that look had been for him.

Her gaze shifted to him, the longing to run to him transparent on her face. "Oh, Tris."

The catch in her voice melted his heart. If he must torture himself, let it be at her hands.

"I don't know what to say." She caressed the golden wood and he shivered, feeling her touch on his skin.

"Be happy, Violet," he said, and gathering the pieces of his shattered heart, turned and left.

Chapter 10

The Braetons' ballroom shone almost as bright as day with the light of at least three hundred candles. Their soft glow bathed Violet in a radiance she found she had sorely missed. Never take for granted what you have today. She should have understood that last summer, the last time she had danced in this elegantly appointed room. Violet sighed, drinking in the beauty of the green and gold leaf paper that glittered on the walls. Gilt sconces at intervals along the wall reflected the candles' light as well. The cut-crystal chandeliers overhead swayed slightly, casting shadows over the dancers and seeming to keep time to the music.

"You are enjoying yourself tonight, Miss Carlton?" Lord Donningham spoke loudly to be heard over the lively music of the allemande.

Even leaning toward him slightly, Violet still had to strain to hear everything the man said. He had a thin, quiet voice. "I am, my lord, although you must ask me later in the evening. This is only the first dance." Affecting a carefree air, she laughed as she swept under his arm in the first figure of the dance. Both playing and dancing had always been a treat for her. As this evening marked her return to society, she was especially determined to enjoy herself.

"Oh, you will not need further inducements, my dear. I shall seek you out for another dance before the evening grows too old." His lordship took advantage of the moment he had to spin her around to glide his hand along her waist.

Her practiced smile in place, Violet sighed inwardly, hoping his interest ran deeper than mere flirtation. She wanted desperately to marry and leave Lammas House. The past week had proven to her just how unpleasant the pleasant house could be when she sensed she no longer belonged there.

After giving her the exquisite harp, Tristan had walked out without another word. She had neither seen nor heard from him since, save for a curt note to the butler instructing Susan and Thomas to accompany Violet to the Braeton's ball. No word of whether Tris was to attend or not. Exceedingly awkward if he did not, for she'd be unaccompanied by *ton* standards.

"I beg pardon, my lord?" Violet had caught the end of a remark from Donningham. Best not to brood over one man while trying to entrance another.

"I said we seem well-suited, Miss Carlton. Although you are charmingly petite, my limbs are long, therefore we dance well together." He smiled showing very white teeth as he ducked under their clasped hands.

A pleasant man in all respects. She'd pressed Susan for any information she had on Lord Donningham and the maid had proven herself resourceful in gathering a wealth of intelligence. John, sixth Viscount Donningham, had lost his wife and infant son to childbed fever in March of this year. From Susan's source, the couple had been fond and Donningham truly mourned his wife's death. However, because he was in his middle thirties, the practical man had realized he had no time to waste finding another helpmeet. According to Susan's source—Donningham's valet, Susan's cousin's son—the viscount was a sober gentleman, given to few vices, and a considerate master. All sterling qualities for a husband, if a trifle dull.

As they turned again, Donningham going beneath her upswept arm this time, she admired his even features, dark brown hair and eyes. His nose was straight, if a little narrow. Still, his jaw was firm and he had an air of cool composure about him that she liked very much. A man seemingly ready for any contingency. In truth, she knew him not at all, but if he asked for her hand, by God, she would bestow it before he could draw another breath.

Tristan's sudden and complete neglect of her this week had forced her to the conclusion she had come to depend on him far more than she should. They had become so comfortable together Violet quite often forgot for days at a time that he would marry soon. She must be gone from Lammas House before that happened.

"We do seem well matched, do we not?" She gave her partner a half smile and a flirtatious flutter of her lashes. "In the dance, of course, your lordship."

"Indeed, Miss Carlton." He rose to the bait like a hungry pike. "We might be well matched in other ways as well."

She cast her gaze down as they came together, then whirled in a series of rosettes. Perhaps she could begin to hope all would be well after all. No, not well. Life would not be well or pleasant or anything but miserable without Tris. Tolerable at best. Still, Donningham appeared to be a kind man. If she could give him children in exchange for respectability, then it was a bargain she could bear.

Her friend, Alethea Forsythe, twirled by in the arms of Lord Manning. Violet would speak to her tonight about the possibility of removing to the Braeton's house until she was sure of Donningham's interest. Pray God the man would take her without a dowry. She had one final piece of business with Lord Trevor. Then she could begin in earnest to plan a future without him.

* * * *

Tristan lurked in the shadow of a pillar on the edge of the Braeton's ballroom floor, resolved to pay Miss Carlton no mind this evening. He was a minimal escort, nothing more. The woman was on her own. A good plan in theory, however, his gaze seemed to have acquired a mind of its own. It riveted itself to Violet and Donningham as they chatted and refused to waver while the couples gathered for the first set.

His heart had beat faster the moment he had seen her this evening, bringing a curse to his lips. 'Sblood, why wouldn't this obsession with her abate? The night he'd given her the harp he'd been within a hair's breadth of saying "to the devil with it," scooping her into his arms, racing up the stairs, and ravishing her until both of them were sated to the point of oblivion. Reputation be damned.

Amazingly, he'd been able to walk away and, through some miracle of fiendish self-discipline, had remained away. Until tonight. Of course, he'd known he'd see her at the ball. He was her symbolic escort. Somehow, though, he'd not understood how much it would hurt to see her with Donningham, or any other man to whom she'd granted a dance.

He jumped at a light touch on his elbow.

Miss Harper stood at his side, her pale, sweet face flushed with a tinge of color at the cheeks. "I beg your pardon, my lord. Mamma said as we are betrothed, I should dance the first set with you."

Lady Downing, a severe matron in a dark, blood-red gown, nodded at him from across the floor. Had she seen his interest in Violet and sent her daughter to remind him of his duty? Intentional or not, Miss Harper's presence broke Violet's spell. "Forgive me, Miss Harper. I was remiss in my duties not to ask you sooner." He offered his arm, achingly aware of a lack of sexual tingle, no heat where her small hand rested in the crook of his arm. His gaze shot to Violet, now laughing with Donningham. Oh, but it was insufferable. He dragged his gaze away and patted Miss Harper's hand.

She accompanied him meekly to the floor.

A sweet girl indeed.

Once they stood in their places facing one another, Tris took her hand. "Do you dance often, Miss Harper?"

Glancing away from him, she shifted from foot to foot. "I do not dance as often as I would like, my lord. Unfortunately, since my sister-in-law has taken ill I have no one to partner me." She knit her brows together, which gave her a charmingly fretful look.

"How does Mrs. Harper fare?"

Dora looked away. "No worse but no better, I am sorry to say. Father has postponed our wedding because of it."

"Yes, so he informed me." Lord Downing's letter to that effect had arrived last week, doing nothing to appease Tris's dismal mood. He wanted to be married, to put the constant temptation of Violet to rest. "Please relay my wishes for her recovery."

"I will do so. I too pray for it every day." She gave a little sigh. "Before she fell ill, we used to practice dancing every day." A blush painted her cheeks. "I am quite fond of it."

Interesting admission. He'd not have guessed the shy creature would profess a fondness for dancing. "And which is your favorite dance, my dear?"

"Oh, the minuet, my lord. So beautiful and elegant."

"I believe the first set will be an allemande. Are you familiar with that as well?"

"Of course, my lord." Miss Harper pursed her lips, the first hint of displeasure he'd ever encountered in her. "I am out of the schoolroom and well versed in all the social graces, particularly the dances. I have been learning them since I was six. I hope you will be pleased." Her eyes shone with an earnestness that made him regret his baiting of her. She did seem eager to gratify him. Just like a child.

"I am sure I will, Miss Harper." He squeezed her hand and her cheeks turned rosier. Lord help him, she was no more than a child, not someone he should be marrying. The thought of taking this young creature to his bed was indecent. Tris dropped her hand and looked about for something else to focus on. His gaze landed on Violet, flirting with Donningham, which was even worse. He pulled his attention back to Miss Harper, who stared at him with innocent eyes. Damn, he needed to keep his mind on the dancing. The safest thing he could do, apparently.

The musicians struck up the tune and Tris and his partner bowed, then leaped to the side as they began the opening series of turns under their upraised arms. Damned if Miss Harper didn't acquit herself superbly, lifting her hands high enough to accommodate him going under easily.

Tris relaxed and ducked under their hands again. They came to the balance figure and he couldn't resist shooting a look at Violet just as Donningham ran his hand around her waist.

Tris stopped in the middle of the floor as his breath whooshed out. A wave of rage flushed his neck and face with heat. He gripped Miss Harper's fingers, wishing they were the viscount's neck.

"Ouch, Lord Trevor."

The room came back into focus as he blinked and shook his head. Her cry, soft but insistent, brought him back to himself, thank God. Another moment and he'd have created a scene that would have scandalized the whole company.

"I am so sorry, Miss Harper. Please forgive me a lapse in memory. I fear you know the dance much better than I after all."

The other couple broke apart and most of his tension drained away. Damn it, he shouldn't care about her any more.

"I understand, my lord. You must concentrate or the steps become a muddle." Miss Harper's smile grew wider as she drew them together for a series of rosettes.

Tris twirled obediently, their hands firmly clasped, until he became dizzy with the effort of concentrating only on the steps. How much longer before this abysmal exercise was over?

His partner laughed as the allemande ended at last, clearly relishing the dance that had been a torture for him. "Thank you, my lord. I enjoyed partnering you very much." She gave his hand a fleeting squeeze, so light he couldn't swear he'd felt it. But she looked down and smiled shyly, so it must have happened.

"Fortunate, don't you think, since shortly we will be partners for life?"

Her eyes widened until the white showed all around the China-blue irises. She backed away from him. "Y...yes, my lord." She bumped into Lord Donningham and Tris had to grab her arm to keep her from falling.

"I beg your pardon, Miss Harper," the viscount said, bowing to her but keeping his eyes on Violet who was at his side. "Good evening, Trevor. Splendid dance, splendid, don't you think? I enjoyed myself as I haven't in years." His grin split his face and he actually beamed at Violet. "As did my charming partner, or so she tells me. She declares me the most exquisite dancer, but of course, I cannot say the lady nay, or I will have a fight on my hands, I daresay. Unfortunate that we cannot dance the second set as well." A fleeting frown replaced his smile. "But that would cause quite the scandal, wouldn't it?" Amiable once more, he turned to Miss Harper, who seemed to be trying to hide behind a large potted fern. "Would you do me the honor, Miss Harper?"

"Yes, do, my dear. You deserve a better partner than I, certainly." He handed her over to Donningham, who tucked her hand into the crook of his arm, already talking a blue streak as he led her to the outer edge of the dance floor.

"Will you dance this set with me, my lord, or will you continue to ignore me?" Violet's eyes flashed amber fire. She bit her lips, then stopped and looked him in the eyes.

* * * *

Violet prayed he wouldn't simply walk away from her again. She wanted this one dance so she could tell him her plans to move from Lammas House, to marry Donningham if he asked her, to put paid to their friendship once and for all. She grabbed his hand, ignoring the sizzle that shot up her arm and made her hand burn. It hardly mattered now.

He followed her onto the dance floor and they took their places in the line of couples waiting to exhibit themselves in a minuet. Not the best chance for conversation, for it called for each couple to dance one by one with all the other guests looking on. Still, a few words might be spoken. That would suffice.

"Miss Harper looks delightful, Tris. I hope you will be very happy." Leading the first salvo would be to her advantage. He had always made her feel as though she couldn't keep up with his wit or conversation. Not this time, by God.

"She is a sweet girl. I am sorry I didn't have the chance to introduce you. Perhaps later in the evening." The stiff, formal manner he affected was off-putting but would make this conversation easier, if she could match his aloof demeanor.

"I daresay we will meet eventually as I am out in Society again."

"Next Season, I suspect. Her family is removing to their estate by the end of this week for the holidays. Her sister-in-law is in poor health." He looked away then continued. "Lord Downing has postponed the wedding as he fears his daughter-in-law is more gravely ill than first believed. We must wait in hopes of her recovery."

Violet sighed. Thank God she had made plans to leave Lammas House. She could not stay there any longer with its memories of Tris, knowing him still unmarried yet not free. "I am sorry to hear of her ill health, especially since it will delay your happiness."

"You know what delays my happiness, Violet." Spoken so low she could scarcely hear them, his words seized her heart in a strangle hold.

"You must bear it as best you can. As do I."

He shot her a look, eyes dark and dangerous. "You seem to bear Lord Donningham's company exceedingly well. Enough to accept his liberties, at least."

"I did not find them particularly offensive." How dare he criticize her? "His interest is welcome. Your plan is working well, it seems. You should be happy for me." Bitterness seeped into her voice but she didn't care. "I must marry someone, Tris. It if cannot be you, then I do not care who it is."

His scowl darkened his countenance and deepened the lines in his face. Before he could speak, however, the couple on the dance floor completed their minuet, and she and Tris had to hastily assume the opening position.

Violet tried to think only of the dance, the music, not of the eyes watching her or, God forbid, of the man who danced at her side. Somehow they managed the beginning steps without trouble, although she found it hard to concentrate. She made sure a pleasant, practiced smile graced her lips, the facade of a happy, carefree woman. That in place, she could watch Tris as he circled around her, drink in the sight of his elegant form, dressed in glittering black and gold, as he completed the intricate steps effortlessly, and not give away the agony his closeness created in her. The moment she dreaded, however, was where the minuet called for them to clasp hands. She feared she could not bear his touch without weeping.

As they spiraled in, the mincing steps bringing them closer and closer, she raised her gaze to his face. A mistake she regretted immediately.

His eyes radiated a depth of passion, a hunger she'd never seen on any man's face before.

It struck her like an arrow piercing her heart, surprising a gasp out of her. He seized her hand and leaned toward her.

Her mouth went dry as dust.

"I care too much. I plan to ask Lord Downing to release me from my promise."

Icy prickles cascaded down her back and Violet stopped, unable to move. Shock shot through her body and elated cries rang in her head. "You are mad."

Gripping her hand, he compelled her to follow him in the circle movement. "Not mad. Heartsick. I cannot live without you, Violet. My heart will break if I cannot marry you."

They spun out of the circle, unwinding the spiral they had created, drifting apart. Once away from his intoxicating presence, Violet's mind cleared and the horror of his words crystallized. Society would never forgive such a dishonorable act. No matter how loudly she screamed inside to let him carry out his plan, she knew in her soul she could not allow him to ruin himself, his honor, his reputation for her. Should he jilt Miss Harper, he'd be an outcast in their trenchant society, party to a scandal neither he nor she would ever recover from. Even if he then married Violet, their lives would be spent in seclusion, shunned by all the people they knew. She could not do that to him, to their children, or to Miss Harper. Better to trade their misery for honor than their honor for happiness.

They spiraled in again. He clasped her hand, and once more the rush of heat engulfed her. "I will not marry you, Tris." The words burned in her throat.

He stopped dead, mouth falling open.

Determinedly, she continued to turn them in a circle, the steps automatic, her mind seared into a blank.

"What?" he hissed. "Why not?"

"I won't allow you to become an outcast for my sake."

"It's as much for my sake as for yours. I love you."

The words echoed in her ears and she wanted to weep with joy, but there was none.

"I love you too. Too much to be a party to your downfall. You must marry Miss Harper. There is no other way."

He gripped her hand unmercifully. "Violet."

Wincing, she shook off his hand, continuing the minuet steps as best she could. Thank God her body remembered what to do, for her mind and heart had gone astray, the agonizing ache of regret pulsing all through her.

The dance ended with them at the far end of the ballroom. They did not take hands again. She doubted Tris could bear her touch and she certainly would not think of touching him. Her resolve hung on a thread ready to snap at the merest contact. Still, one thing remained unfinished between them. "Will you come to the house Christmas Day? We have much to discuss, I think, and I have a present of sorts for you."

His face might have been chiseled out of flint. "I hardly think that would be wise."

"Neither do I, still, I need you to come. I have a forfeit to pay if you remember."

He stared at her and she waited for him to refuse. Then he gave a terse nod and turned his back, making his way through the crowd.

Violet wanted to sink onto the floor and never arise. She'd just managed the most difficult request of her life. Welcoming a customer at Madame Vestry's paled in comparison to willingly throwing her happiness away with both hands. She could only pray now the worst was truly over.

Chapter 11

Violet sat at her toilette table on Christmas afternoon, turning a small tin horse over in her hands. Christmas had always been a time for food and revelry at her home. When she was growing up, her parents had held a weekend party each year for the children of the family at Yuletide. She remembered with fondness the sleigh rides, snowball fights, hot cider and special gingerbread, and various parlor games she had played with her brother and cousin. During these events she and Jamie and their cousin Kit had grown especially close. She still had this small tin horse she had won one year, one of the few possessions she'd managed to keep through all her recent travails. She set it back on her toilette table, a reminder of happier times, and rose to head downstairs.

This year she enjoyed the creature comforts provided by Tristan's generosity, although she sadly lacked the spirit of the season. She and Susan had ventured out to a midnight service last evening, in an effort to reclaim the special feeling of the holiday. Tris's absence these past weeks had cast a pall over everything, for she had truly missed his company. His visit this evening would hardly be a joyous one. An ending rather than the beginning suggested by the Christmas story.

After a small festive luncheon eaten, at her insistence, with Susan, Mrs. Parker, and Thomas in the kitchen, she'd retired for a nap and now made her way to the music room to practice and await her guest.

She'd done little in the way of decoration since she hadn't been in a holiday mood at all. Susan had tucked some greenery throughout the house, bringing the fresh scent of pine and bayberry into the rooms. The candles gave off a golden glow as she settled at the harpsichord first. She had progressed from the Scarlatti and ventured into Bach, now pouring her sorrow into the keyboard as she worked to once more perfect the selection before Tris's arrival. At last satisfied with the pieces, she moved to the harp.

As always, she caressed the instrument before she sat down, imagining a particular person beneath her fingertips rather than the harp. It had been bittersweet to practice on the wonderfully generous gift. She always thought of Tris when she played, great joy mingling with sadness. Today he would finally hear her play, the only time perhaps, so she sought to make it a memorable one.

One touch of the strings and the world fell away as she became absorbed in the music until the instrument became an extension of herself. Even after so many months of not rehearsing, it had come back easily, quickly consoling her for the loss of a different love. Today she practiced one song alone. Into this one she poured her heart and soul. So he would remember her.

"Violet."

Susan's voice brought her back from the trance-like state she achieved when playing her best.

"Lord Trevor is in the parlor."

Violet's stomach twisted and her hands trembled, but she rose and nodded. "Please show him in here." Hurrying from behind the harp, she took her position just inside the door to welcome him.

He rounded the corner, a splash of deep scarlet brocade, gold braid and buttons catching the light. She caught her breath at the sight of his powerful body, broad shoulders, narrow waist, strong legs—a splendid figure she drank in with a bold, greedy gaze.

"Good evening, Miss Carlton."

Icy formality it would be then. "Good evening, Lord Trevor. Merry Christmas." She indicated a chair placed before the instruments. "Please be seated."

He complied, although he did not meet her eyes until she crossed to stand directly in front of him.

"I asked you here, my lord, to pay the forfeit I owe you. I…" Much as she wanted to, she simply couldn't look into those deep sapphire eyes, see all the anger and, farther back, the hurt in them, and say everything she wanted to say. She loved him too much to doom him to a life of dishonor. That hurt and anger were her burden to bear because of her love. The only path left to her was to tell him in the only way left to her.

"I am here, Miss Carlton. I am listening."

Unable to say more, she fled to the harpsichord, her heart battered. Beginning with the Scarlatti, she poured herself into the music. At first painfully aware of his gaze on her, she managed to push through until the music overtook her and she forgot everything except for it.

The next two pieces rolled from her fingers one after the other with only a break to change the sheets of music. She'd practiced so diligently she hardly needed them. When she finished the Bach, she rose and looked at Tris for the first time since she began to play. The stunned look on his face made her want to weep. Hurt and anger had been replaced with wonder and regret.

"Violet. Oh, my dear." He came to his feet and strode toward her, taking her hands and kissing them with a fervor that made her toes tingle. "You are magnificent, my love."

My love. A wonderful Christmas present, indeed.

"Truly one of the finest performances I have heard. Why didn't you tell me you played so well? We should have been looking for a manager for you. You should be playing professional engagements."

His words, his touch, overwhelmed her, made the blood pound in her ears and her legs threaten to collapse. If only they could remain this way forever. "I never thought myself very much better than the other young ladies who exhibited. I simply wanted it to be perfect for you tonight." Joy came flooding back as the icy stranger melted into the man she adored.

He smiled, boyish once more. "I declare your forfeit paid most handsomely." He raised her hands and kissed them, his warm lips leaving prickles on her skin.

"I am so happy that debt is satisfied," she said, relishing their intimacy. This was the companionship she had sorely missed these past weeks. She forced herself to note each word, every touch, every glance, storing them up to cherish in the months and years they would be apart. "And now I have something else for you. A Christmas gift."

With a twinge of regret, she pulled her hands from his grasp and seated herself at the harp. She smiled and nodded at him, stroked the pillar of the harp, then rested the sound board on her shoulder, nestling it against her. The magic of the harp coursed through her as it always had and she plucked the strings with sure fingers, all her soul, all her love, all her passion flowing into the piece. She had nothing to give him as a remembrance of her save this, so she'd make sure it would remain with him the rest of his life.

As she played the final notes, for the first time the sense of devastating loss welled within her. She would never play for him again, never share their passion for music. She stared at the now silent strings, wanting to recall the minutes past, relive them and cherish them to the fullest, yet knowing it impossible. She blinked back tears.

A shadow fell across the harp.

She looked up into Tris's face, so full of love she burst into tears.

"Violet, love." He raised her and gathered her into his arms. "Please don't cry. That was the finest harp performance I have ever heard. I will treasure it in my heart forever."

She cried harder. Why had the Fates set themselves against her? First her brother's death, now the man she loved snatched from her and married to another. She tightened her grip on him. "It's not fair. It's simply not fair."

"No, it's not, my love," he whispered, his warm mouth in her hair. "And we make choices to try and even the odds, although rarely do they turn out in our favor. We must find a way to go on." Wrapping his arms around her, he cuddled her close against him.

"How?" she wailed.

"I don't know, love. It's a tangle, an impossible knot we cannot loosen." His gentle voice held no sliver of hope. "We must savor our remaining moments together, etch them in our hearts and memories. Which reminds me." He loosened his hold on her so he could look into her face. "I recognized the works you played on the harpsichord, but not the harp piece. What was that?"

"'Minuet for Tristan and Isolde.'" She stared into his beloved face, her heart bursting with love. "I wrote it for you."

Her gaze met his, love and desire crackling between them in a tense charge that threatened to explode them into a million pieces.

Then his lips were on hers and Violet dissolved, the music and the magic of him merging into one. She continued to cry, tears of joy now, as she molded her body to his.

He pushed his tongue through her lips, igniting even more heat between them.

She welcomed it, pulled him in greedily, demanding all of him.

With a groan he wrapped his hands around her head, cradling it, angling it so their mouths melded together perfectly.

As they were meant to be.

Determined not to let him go, she slid her arms around his neck. Somehow, she would make sure they could be together, no matter what.

With agonizing deliberation, he skimmed his hands down the length of her back, each inch he touched coming to life with a heat of its own. When he reached her buttocks, he cupped them and squeezed, pressing her against his granite-hard erection.

Dizzy, she moaned, surrendering to his will with an abandon she'd never suspected of herself. Her world had shrunk to the two of them. She'd never need anything more than this.

He scooped her into his arms, their lips still locked. When he broke the kiss it was to press her face to his chest as he strode from the room.

She rubbed against him like a cat, the scent of bergamot and citrus filling her head. The unique, comforting smell of him.

Then they were bounding up the stairs. He pushed open the door to her chamber and kicked it shut. Panting, he carried her to the bed and seized her mouth again. Bending her back onto the mattress, he kissed her long and thoroughly before leaving her lips to caress the tender flesh below.

Frantically, she arched her neck, baring the whole of it, hoping to tempt him into exploring all of her. The feel of his lips on her sensitive flesh sent chills down her arms, through her body to lodge low in her belly, an unusual ache deep inside.

The ache increased as he kissed and sucked her breasts where they spilled over her stays, then licked the deep cleft between.

"Ahhh." Her moan emerged from the back of her throat. She was on fire. A spark had started a blaze in her that would not be quenched save one way.

Tris groaned in answer and lurched to his feet. He ripped his breeches open, then pushed her into the middle of the bed.

First cool air touched her thighs, then his big, hot body pressed her into the mattress.

"This is where we began," she said, tugging at her stays until her breasts popped free.

"But so much better than then." He wrapped his lips around her nipple.

Violet surged up into him, pressing her breasts into his mouth while she ground her lower body into his hips, seeking what she craved.

Licking first one, then the other breast, he surprised her anew when he blew gently on them. They cooled immediately, gooseflesh popping out all over her. Below he stroked his fingers through the gathering moisture, pressing one finger inside.

It burned, but she forgot it instantly. When he pumped the finger in and out, caressing her without and within, her channel began to pulse. Heat poured through her. She yearned to be skin to skin with him, but disrobing would take too long. She should have heeded Madame Vestry's rules, but she hadn't expected this to happen.

"I can…do you want me to stop?" he panted, the aching need in his voice confirmed by the stiff cock he rubbed along her thigh.

Oh, how she wanted to appease that eagerness.

"No, do it now, Tris. Now." If he didn't take her this moment she feared he'd think better of it and refuse.

Without protest, he withdrew his finger and pushed himself to her opening instead. One vigorous thrust and it was done. He slid inside her, bringing some pain, but not nearly what she had feared.

Groaning his need, he gave another short thrust, and filled her completely.

The lovely fullness of him, knowing they were joined as if one, made her long to savor the moment. Each movement, however, left her with no thought for anything save the feel of him inside her.

He moved again, withdrawing and plunging forward in a rhythm like music—beautiful, exquisite music playing only for them. He increased the tempo, thrusting into her until the pulse became stronger, and without warning her body exploded, gripping him inside her.

"Oh, oh, Tris!" She clutched him to her, thrusting her hips toward him, unable to get enough.

Suddenly he cried out, thrust one more time, and slumped onto her.

As her sated body relaxed, she lay motionless, completely happy for the first time in a long while. But what should she do now?

"Christ, did I hurt you?" Tris raised his head to peer into her face.

"I don't know. But if you did, you can do it again right now." She cupped his dear face. Her racing heart slowed, returning to something like normal.

He laughed and kissed her, long and slowly. Let it never end. Finally, he lifted his head. "You were exquisite, my love. I've never felt such passion with a woman. I cannot let you go." To make good his words, he clutched her tighter. "And to think I almost did." One by one, he kissed her lips, nose, eyes. "Now you're mine. Donningham can go hang." He eased out of her and drew her against him. A sigh escaped his lips as he slid his hand over her breasts. "All we need do is rid ourselves of the rest of this clothing, my dear, and I will be happy to start your second lesson here and now."

Chapter 12

Violet awoke to the familiar tap, tap on her chamber door. "Come in," she called. Drowsy and sated, she settled her head back on Tris's chest, too tired to want even tea. Susan should come back later. Her eyes flew open and she started up in bed. "No!"

The door swung open anyway as the maid strode in.

"Good—" She stopped. Her brown eyes widened as she took in the scene before her. Scattered clothing, rumpled bedclothes, and a large man in bed beside Violet. Coolly recovering her composure, she drew a deep breath, and continued into the room. "Good morning, Violet." She set the tea on the dresser. "Would you like the curtains pulled or not?"

Violet glanced at Tris, his naked arm flung over his head, dark-haired chest blatantly on display, fast asleep. "Best leave them closed for now," she whispered. "But maybe make up the fire." Her face glowed like the hearth embers. Might as well be comfortable, then, in the chilly room. Although she and Tris had generated quite a bit of warmth throughout the night. And that magnificent body beside her radiated heat like a small sun burned within him.

"Very good, miss." Susan poured tea, handed her a cup, and set about her task as though the morning was no different from any other since her arrival.

Sipping her tea, trying to remain nonchalant about being caught in bed with a man not her husband, Violet determinedly avoided looking at her maid. Of course, Susan must be used to such a scenario. A pang of jealousy swept through her. Visions of Tris in bed with other women, something she had never really contemplated on a practical basis before, suddenly made her heart ache. She put the tea aside and slipped down under the thick covers, stretching her arm over his broad chest. The dark mat of hair rubbed against her skin in a new, intimate sensation that made her even more possessive.

"Shall I tell Mrs. Parker to hold breakfast?" Susan had finished poking up the fire and stood at the foot of the bed.

"I think that's best. I'm not sure of…" Her cheeks were an inferno, but she managed to continue, "Lord Trevor's plans this morning. I'll ring."

"Very good, miss." With a warm smile that spoke volumes, Susan nodded and left.

If her maid approved of her change in status, Violet supposed the situation couldn't be too bad.

"You handled that excellently, my love." Tris rolled up onto his side to face her. "You've bought us some more time." A flip of his hand and the covers slithered down, exposing her breasts, her nipples pebbling in the cool air.

"More time?" She stretched, arching her breasts toward him.

"To satisfy other appetites." He skimmed his finger over her flesh, making it tingle. When he reached the hard tip, his nail rasped the sensitive bud, setting a pulse leaping down below.

"Ummm. I believe I am hungry again." Suddenly impatient for him, she pulled his head to her, seizing his lips to taste him once more. They had made love three times in the night but she hungered for more. Would she ever get enough? She put her hands on his shoulders, pushed him onto his back, and rolled on top of him. Straddling him, she rubbed herself against his hard abdomen.

"I see you are." He grinned, his eyes half-closed. His cock prodded her backside, an insistent thumping that made her wet.

Grabbing his hands, she drew them over his head, then rubbed her breasts over his face. Her body ached with wanting him. Where these wanton feelings had come from she had no idea. She'd never thought much about the marriage bed until she'd been instructed by Madame Vestry. Neither had she expected the things she had learned to be so pleasurable. Perhaps they wouldn't have been, had they been done with someone other than Tris. She brushed her nipple across his lips.

He opened his mouth, trying to capture it.

She laughed and dangled it just out of reach.

Lightning fast, he snaked his tongue out, teasing the tip with tiny rapid strokes that made her whole body shudder. Taking advantage of her momentary distraction, he broke her loose hold, pulled her down, and engulfed the nipple.

Further languorous strokes hardened the little peak to a bullet point, aching in a wonderful way that drove her wild. She rubbed her cheek against his hair, moaning quietly as he sucked the tight crest.

With one hard pull on her breast, he slid his finger deep into her slippery channel.

"Ahhh, Lord, Tris." God, any part of him felt good inside her.

He withdrew and returned with two fingers. They weren't nearly as big or as long as his cock. Yet when he moved them like that her whole body trembled, tension gathering at her core. He pumped slowly, setting all her nerves on edge. Then, releasing her nipple, he slipped out of her and pushed her up to sit on him once more. "Pose for me, Violet."

Wicked man. Feeling wanton, and loving it, she sat straight, her lower lips pressed to his hot flesh. Moving slowly, she raised her arms and positioned her hands behind her head, her breasts jutting out like a ship's prow. As he'd intended perhaps. His eyes glittered like black diamonds seeming to drink in the sight of her. She'd make him drunk with wanting her, then. She draped her hair over her shoulders so the shiny brown locks fanned over her breasts, hiding most of them from his view. Turning to the right she batted her eyes at him over her shoulder. What else could she do to enflame him? She twisted back, then leaned over him, brushing her hair across his broad chest, teasing his dark brown nipples.

"Vixen," he growled, and wrapped his arms around her, crushing her against him.

"I'll show you a vixen." Her pulse raced, excitement brewing as she reached behind her and stroked the length of his cock. Smooth. Hot. Big. She closed her hand around him and pumped twice, gliding her thumb over the crown, gathering his juices. Carefully, she brought her thumb around so he could see it glistening.

His breath rasped as his body tensed. He swallowed hard.

Slowly, she licked the gleaming drops from her thumb, then poked her tongue between her lips and wiggled it at him.

"Christ." He grabbed her waist and, in one sudden movement, lifted and impaled her on his rock-hard erection.

"Ahhh." The absolute fullness of him, touching every inch inside her almost brought her to immediate completion.

He smiled up at her, hunger in his eyes.

Her heart stuttered so she could hardly breathe. "I love you, Tris."

"And I love you, Violet." He thrust his hips upward, touching the farthest reaches of her.

"Ohhh, you know just what to do, don't you?" She strained upwards, then slid slowly down him.

"To do what?" He rocked them, grinding into her with a circular motion.

"To drive me mad." God, she never wanted this to end.

He stroked through her curls, finding the little nub he'd shown her last night. "Yes, I do." With his thumb, he brushed it, circled it, faster and faster until she spun out of control.

"Tris, Tris. Oh, yes." She gasped as the tension gathered, spiking within her. "Almost there."

"Ahhh." He pounded harder, kneading the sensitive part with skillful changes of rhythm.

Until she burst, shimmering pulses throbbing within, sending her over the edge.

"Violet." Moments later he cried out, thrust again, and drenched her with his hot seed.

She collapsed on top of him, sweaty cheek meeting sweaty chest, his heart hammering in her ear. Her own thudded dully, slowing bit by bit. She didn't care if it took wing and escaped her chest. Serenity settled over her. If she never moved again, she would be satisfied.

Tris drew the covers over them, and gathered her into his arms.

His heart calmed, the strong regular beat lulling her toward sleep. As long as she and Tris were together she would be content. "I could stay like this forever."

"You say that now," he chuckled, the vibration tickling her ear. "But if it came down to you having to miss a meal, I believe you would throw me over for a nice minced pie or Mrs. Parker's Yorkshire pudding."

She giggled. "I have more willpower than that."

"But you forget, my dear, I've seen you eat."

"Wretch. How ignoble of you." Running her hand through the silky hairs on his chest, she closed them in her fingers, made patterns in the thick mat, delighting in the feel of him. "My other appetites are stronger now." A growl from her stomach set her to laughing. "I don't suppose we could have breakfast in bed?"

He laughed and slid her over to the side. "Kill two birds with one stone?"

"I am nothing if not efficient." She trailed her hand along his sleek body, reveling again at the beauty of it. "And I have no plans for the day other than to serve your pleasure, my lord."

Tris tensed, ran his hand over his face, lines emerging where an instant before there had been none. "Christ." He pulled her to him and buried his face in her neck.

"What's wrong?" A glimmer of foreboding rose in her.

He sighed and lay back, his hand flopping over to cover his eyes. "I am supposed to travel into Wiltshire to Lord Downing's estate near Devizes. I am to spend the New Year with them."

Cold dread threaded its way through Violet's veins. She slid off him and pulled the cover over her shoulder. In the joy of discovering their passion, she'd forgotten he wasn't hers to keep. Her stomach churned, all idea of hunger fled. He'd have to leave her to be with the woman who had a claim on his name, if not his heart. In this world, unfortunately, the former held more importance. She stifled a sob, even though tears had begun to flow.

"Violet." He put a hand on her shoulder.

She shrugged it off.

"Violet, love, I must go. I have to see Lord Downing so I may tell him I wish to withdraw from the betrothal."

She spun around, her heart beating wildly. "You can't do that. You'd be ruined."

"My love, I've just ruined you."

Chills crawled down her spine and she shuddered. It was true. Her circumstances had altered irrevocably last night. Any hope of a respectable marriage had vanished with her maidenhead. She didn't regret it one iota, however her future prospects, never good, now seemed bleaker than a mid-winter's night. She clenched her teeth, biting back a sob.

He gathered her into his arms, stroking her hair, his cheek pressed to her head. "Shhh, love. I promise it will be all right. I'll pay a call on my friend, the marquess. If anyone knows how to survive scandal, he does. I suppose we will not be completely beyond the pale of Society if the Marquess and Marchioness of Dalbury stand by us."

"But it would not only be us, Tris." She took his and, threading their fingers together, as if to bind him to her. "It would be our children and Miss Harper as well. Her reputation would be in shreds. Her father might even call you out." Violet bolted up in bed, her heart freezing. "No, no, no you cannot do it. I will not risk you." Tears spilled down her cheeks and she sniffed and wiped her eyes. Damn, but she seemed to cry at everything this morning.

Tris looked defeated. Obviously, he hadn't yet thought of it, but Violet could remedy the situation quickly and with very little fuss.

"I'll become your mistress, Tris. Then there won't be a scandal, nor possibility of a duel."

A storm swept across his face, a squall followed by steady thunderclouds.

"We will have each other."

He glared at her.

"It is done all the time in polite society."

"I know." His voice was stern, emotionless. "It will not, however, be done by me." Lips pursed, he narrowed his eyes until they glittered like hard jet. "I told you about my father. My feelings about that have not changed. God knows I understand perfectly now how he felt, but that does not excuse how miserable he made my mother all those years. Or his children. Believe me, we were not a happy household. I will not put you, myself, nor Miss Harper through it."

"Tris, you must see sense." Lord, if he decided to be stubborn she feared she would lose the battle. "It will be less hurtful to all concerned if you marry Miss Harper."

"You cannot know what you are saying, Violet." The sharp lines of pain around his eyes stabbed her heart. "I will never be free to be with you publicly. I will not be able to spend time with you as I have, but will have to spend time with her and her family." He came to a complete stop and his face reddened. "I will have to get heirs on her. Did you think of that?"

"Of course I did." The image of Tris holding the golden-haired Miss Harper in his arms in a bed tightened a band of iron around her chest. "I've thought of nothing else but you and her together, dining, talking, laughing, making..." She didn't want to think it, much less give voice to the idea, but it must become real to her. "Making love to her. Having children with her. Oh, yes, I have thought of all that and more. Still, I would bear the heartache of sharing you gladly if it kept you free from scandal and the threat of a duel." Tears cascaded down her cheeks and she threw herself on his chest, clutching him to her. "My brother was killed in a duel. Did you forget that? His death sent me eventually down the path that led me to you. If you were to be killed, I...." She choked and buried her face in his shoulder. "I would never recover. I went to Madame Vestry's before because I didn't want to die. If something happened to you, I wouldn't want to live."

Wrapping his arms around her consoled her somewhat and her trembling lessened. His silence lengthened so she finally dried her eyes and twisted to look at him. He stared at the canopy overhead, his jaw firm, brows knit.

The inscrutable look caused her to shiver again, but she could be firm too. Although he wouldn't want to give in and take her as his mistress, he would see the necessity of it in time. God knew she didn't want to share him with anyone, but better to share him than lose him. "Don't be sad, my love." She kissed his mouth, trying to tease a smile from his stern countenance. "It is still Christmas. We must be merry a little." When that didn't seem to work, she raised his hand and kissed it. "We certainly made merry last night." Still no response, so she continued kissing his knuckles, then turned his hand over and pressed her mouth fiercely to his palm.

That seemed to awaken him from his reverie. He caught her to him, pulling her hard to his chest, enfolding and holding her close. "No matter what, love, you must remember I love you. Above all others and to my dying breath."

"Tris." She started up out of bed, his hopeless tone sending a wave of fear through her. "You are scaring me. Please don't talk like that."

He grazed her forehead with his lips. "It will be all right. Trust me." The smile he gave her was forced, which boded ill. "Now I think you should ring for breakfast before Mrs. Parker complains we don't appreciate her." At last he produced a real grin, all gloom gone. "That would be a tragedy."

Chapter 13

Tris pushed past Grayson, the Marquess of Dalbury's butler, and strode down the hallway into his friend's office unannounced. He'd made a muddle of everything, but if anyone could help him sort it out, Duncan could.

The marquess, sitting behind his huge mahogany desk, penning some missive, jerked his head up, rose and drew his sword in one liquid movement.

Skidding to a halt, Tris pulled his own weapon from its scabbard.

"Oh, hell, it's you." Duncan's shoulders relaxed, he sheathed his sword, and sank back into his leather chair.

"S'blood, Duncan. Who the devil did you think it was?" Tris eyed him warily. He'd never seen his friend so edgy.

"That French fiend, St. Cyr. I expect him to come demanding Juliet at any moment." A dangerous scowl appeared as Duncan frowned, then picked up an engraved tumbler of what looked like very good whisky, and gulped a third of the contents.

"Christ, what happened on Christmas Eve?" Thinking it apparently hadn't been a merry holiday for any of them, Tris sauntered over to the sideboard and poured himself a drink. God, he needed more than one. "I was at the back of the ballroom, talking to Lord and Lady Bellamy, when that ruckus broke out at the entrance. By the time I'd excused myself and made it to the foyer, I could find no one who would tell me a thing."

"Servants who wouldn't talk? Perhaps it is the Second Coming." Duncan sobered. "That damned scoundrel St. Cyr brought a Runner and a warrant and forced Juliet to leave with him."

Tris snorted and whiskey went the wrong way down his throat. Coughing and sputtering, he tried to draw breath.

Duncan watched him, fear in his face. "Are you all right, Tris?" He sprang up, but Tris waved him back.

"I'm fine," he wheezed. "Why aren't you out looking for Juliet this minute?" Tris cleared his throat one last time and the spasm passed.

"My father died of such a coughing fit at the dinner table." Jaw quivering, he shifted in his seat, averting his eyes from Tris. "Morley followed them and found her an hour or so later. His military skills are top notch, I must say. Tracked her like a hound to the hunt. She's now in hiding until either the marriage is annulled, proven false, or someone kills the bastard." Duncan swallowed the rest of his drink at a gulp. "I thought it was him when you burst in." The haunted look in his eyes ceased, and he reared back in his chair, eying Tris. "What brings you here? I thought you were to go into Wiltshire to Downings's after Christmas."

Tris slumped into a worn leather chair. "I was. Now I can't."

"Can't? Why ever not?"

Suddenly preoccupied with his drink, Tris dreaded the next few minutes. *We who are about to die salute you.* "I need you to help me break the betrothal with Miss Harper."

"What?" Tension snapped back into his body as Duncan sat bolt upright. "Are you mad? You can't jilt the daughter of a peer. You can't jilt anyone and hope to escape the *ton* unscathed. But Downing's daughter? The man's related to half the kingdom and has more money than Croesus." He narrowed his eyes and drummed a finger on the desk. "Talk sense, Tris. What has happened?"

"Miss Carlton happened." God he hated to give this confession to Duncan of all people.

"What do you mean?" The voice dripped ice.

"I mean that I love her. I want to marry her and be happy for the rest of my life instead of tied to a woman I will never love."

"You'll be ruined, as will Miss Harper." Drawing himself up like some avenging god, the marquess rose. "I forbid it. I will not allow you to commit social suicide and live in exile for the rest of your life, much less help you do it." He marched over to the decanter. "You are merely infatuated with Miss Carlton. You need a good and thorough bedding is all. You'll forget all about her."

"Like the ones I had last night? And again this morning?" The memory of those encounters made him long to hold Violet's body against him again. Never to let go. "I assure you, I've forgotten nothing about her."

"What the devil does that mean?" Duncan stared at him, his hand poised with the decanter over his glass.

Tris met his stare and shrugged.

"Good Christ in heaven. You didn't…After I told you to get as far away from her as possible you took her to bed?" The decanter thumped down on the sideboard.

"I tried, tried damn hard to stay away from her." Jumping to his feet, Tris headed toward his friend. "Managed it for a week or so, although I thought about her constantly. And when she asked me to visit her on Christmas Day, I thought we would say goodbye." After seizing the bottle, Tris sloshed brandy into his glass and took a long sip. "Donningham had shown an interest, you see. So I was sure she wanted to tell me she'd be leaving soon."

"Well, at least she had the good sense to know you couldn't marry."

"Yes, but then instead of saying goodbye, she played a composition she'd written for me. And it was over. I couldn't resist her any longer. Didn't want to."

"She composed a song for you?"

"She's an accomplished musician and I had given her a harp—"

"You did what?"

Tris frowned. "She mentioned she loved playing the harp, so I bought her one. What was the harm in that?"

"I suppose you visited daily, had late suppers with her, and took her driving in the park?" Duncan's lips had twisted into a sardonic smile.

"And if I did, what of it? I did nothing improper." His friend's attitude had become irritating in the extreme.

"What you did was treat her like a mistress in all ways save one, until last night."

"I did no such thing." The nascent protest died on his lips. Save for not sharing a bed with Violet, he had indeed treated her much as he had Serena, Grace, and Fanny. "And if I did so, what was the harm?"

"Had you stayed strictly away from her, your infatuation would not have been allowed to grow." Returning to the chair behind the desk, Duncan continued his admonishments. "This predicament would never have come to pass."

"Perhaps." Tris doubted it though. "I somehow believe Miss Carlton and I would still have forged a bond. Something about her touched me from the moment I saw her."

Duncan snorted. "You met her in a brothel, Tris. I know what touched you about her."

Tris met his friend's gaze unwavering. "Yes, I'm sure you do. You met your wife in the same brothel, as I remember."

The marquess paled. "That was totally different. She'd been kidnapped and brought there."

"And you paid for her just as I did for Violet. I know—" He waved away the protest brewing in Duncan's face. "The circumstances were quite different. But the question is this. Had you been betrothed when you met Lady Dalbury, would you have been satisfied to keep her as your mistress? Or would you have fought to make her your marchioness?"

"Huh." Duncan swirled the liquid remaining in the glass, first one way then the other. "Katarina didn't want to be my wife, much less my mistress. God help the man who asked such a thing of her. But I take your point." Slowly sipping the rest of the spirits, he studied Tris. "And now you've ruined Miss Carlton, you want to marry her?"

"I've wanted to marry her from the beginning. At first for honor's sake, true, but now, not only do I love her, but it's become more urgent. After last night she could be increasing." Tris ran a hand through his hair, wanting to tear it out. That thought had occurred to him as he galloped Lucifer to Dunham House.

"Then you must pray it has not come to pass as you cannot marry the lady. Do you not remember Lord Staunton?"

"I've heard the name, and associate it with something vaguely scandalous. Why?"

"He set the *ton* tongues to wagging the year we went on the Grand Tour. That's why you don't remember him. It was all over by the time we made it home. I had to ask my father what the whispering was all about when Staunton's name came up." Shaking his head, Duncan drained his glass. "Nasty bit of business, the whole affair. Staunton was engaged to Lady Mary Cafford, but then ran off with Lady Georgina Myers. It was two months after Hardwick's Law had been put into effect, so they had to go to Coldstream Bridge in Scotland to marry. The scandal raged the whole time we were abroad. I'm mightily surprised we didn't get wind of it in Italy."

Tris laughed. "They could have shouted it from the rooftops of Venice and I'd have no recollection of it. Signora Maccari, however, I still remember very well."

Duncan chuckled and sent him a sly glance. "As you say." He sobered again. "Here in England, however, they received the cut by every person in the *ton*. My mother knew Lady Georgina's mother. She said the episode tore the family apart, for they couldn't defend the couple nor receive them either. Such ugliness upset my mother greatly. Staunton was refused admittance at White's, at Vanes, even at Charbury's."

"Impossible." That brought Tris upright, alarmed. Charbury's was the notorious gaming hell he frequented sometimes. They allowed the dregs in if they had the money to gamble.

"True, nevertheless." Duncan leaned all the way back in his chair. "The other patrons complained about his presence so loudly and threatened to riot if he wasn't removed, so they escorted him out. The last straw for Staunton, though, was his father's reaction. He disinherited him, stripped him of every means of income and publicly declared him no longer his son. The next day Staunton put a ball through his head." With a shudder, Duncan poured another drink. "And Lady Mary, although everyone held her blameless, has never married."

The story shook Tris. As he'd told the marquess, he didn't remember the scandal, but then he'd just been back from the continent, still feeling in fine fettle and spoiling for a bit of skirt after six weeks of voyage without female companionship. Society's doings had interested him not at all at the time. Now they did. Still he shrugged it off. "I already hold my title and estates, Duncan. No one can disinherit me. My sisters may well never speak to me again, but I will bear that as well as I can." He shot his friend an inquisitive look. "I suppose you and the marchioness will be forced to join the throng and stone us figuratively if not literally?"

Duncan grunted and waved a hand at him. "Short of a royal command I doubt anything would sever our friendship. And God forbid anyone tell Kat she could not honor you and your wife. Heaven help the society matrons who try to cross her." He chuckled, a glint in his eye.

The tension that ached behind Tris's eyes eased.

"So you are determined to proceed with this madness? I'm frankly surprised Miss Carlton accepted you after you told her about our part in the duel and the death of her brother."

Tris stiffened. Hell. Oh, hell and damnation. When Violet had mentioned the duel this morning he had known he must confess to her. Not telling her then had been the one cowardly act he'd ever committed.

"You did tell her, didn't you?" Duncan's eyes had narrowed, his brows furrowed in a monstrous frown.

"I thought I'd never see her again after we said goodbye yesterday. Then last night happened so quickly…" Raising his chin, Tris stared him down. "No, I didn't tell her."

"Christ, Tris." The scars on his friend's left cheek reddened. "You must tell her what happened before you break your betrothal. She may well refuse you and then where would you be?"

In hell, most likely. "I know she might," he snapped. "I'll go now." He drained his glass and set it on Duncan's desk. He looked up, hopefully. "If it all comes right, you'll go with me to Lord Downing's? I may very well have need of a second."

"Of course. There was never need to ask."

"I know." Tris grinned, though his heart sank. Facing Downing would be pleasure compared to the interview he now must undertake with Violet. Pray God he still need worry about Downing when it was over.

Chapter 14

Violet sat before the mirror of her toilette table, rapt as Susan put the finishing touches on her hair. The maid had curled her straight locks with a heated iron poker so now curly wisps of her plain brown hair framed her face. The majority of it, however, lay confined by pins under a lacy cap that exactly matched the dark pink in her deep blue and salmon print gown.

"I've never before made so much fuss over my appearance just to stay at home." Laughing, Violet turned her head this way and that. The bouncy curls swung with every twist, making her smile. "Only when I was about to attend a ball or an assembly."

"Well, miss, you'd better get used to it. Lord Trevor likes his lady well-dressed when entertaining at home. Here." Susan placed a red velvet box on the table in front of her. "His lordship sent this for you."

Violet caught her breath. Tris had sent her a gift? Heart beating frantically, she opened the box and removed a piece of paper, revealing a pair of exquisite girandole earrings. The three pendants in each earring contained brilliant sapphires that danced when she lifted them from the case. Joy washed through her at this tangible proof of his regard. Smiling broadly, she opened the note.

> *My dearest one,*
> *I am sorry I could not be there to present these to you myself. However, I wished you to have your morning gift while it was still morning. I must conduct the business of which we spoke earlier, so I will be with you later today and all through this night and every night.*
> *All my love and regard,*

Tris

Delight warred with confusion. "Do you know what a morning gift is, Susan?"

Her only answer was a shrug. "No, miss. I've not heard of such a thing." She grinned at Violet. "I suppose it means his lordship had a pleasant night." Cheeks burning, she glared at the woman. "Likely so."

"I'd say it's a good thing, Violet. They are beautiful and complete your outfit perfectly." Susan grabbed Violet's green silk-figured banyan, shaking it out as she headed toward the dressing room.

The girl might be saucy, but she must know Tris's tastes well. She'd been maid and companion to three of his mistresses, not counting Violet. That information had made her grit her teeth and clench her fists when Susan had mentioned it in passing. Still no need to deny or ignore the fact Tris had had powerful appetites before he met her. Her duty now was to fulfill those as best she could. Fortunately, Susan would prove a wealth of knowledge on how to please him.

Her nether regions tingled at the prospect. Of course, it would be hard to say who would be giving whom the most pleasure. She'd been sore when she'd bathed earlier—the hot water had stung as she washed streaks of blood from her inner thighs. Still, she eagerly waited for Tris's return and the continuation of last night's passions.

"Did Lord Trevor say when he would arrive?"

"No, miss." Susan emerged with an armful of linens. "Only the box and that note arrived. No other word."

Tris had dressed, eaten scarcely a bite of breakfast, and hurried out to his carriage to call on his friend the marquess. That was all well and good, however, nothing short of a consultation with the king himself would change her mind about Tris's offer to marry her. She couldn't live with herself if she caused irreparable harm to his honor. She could live here quietly as his mistress and share a life together. Not the perfect life perhaps, but better than her prospects had been a short time ago.

Children would be a problem, although she could begin Madame Vestry's herb tea immediately to prevent increasing. The dried flowers and seeds of Queen Anne's Lace, the Madame said, taken each morning after "entertaining," kept her girls from conceiving. Violet had a pouch full of the concoction. She'd have to find it and have Mrs. Parker brew her some. Perhaps later, once their lives were more settled, she and Tris could discuss children. If he could establish them in a home on one of his outlying estates, she'd be more than happy. Often, she'd heard, noblemen would set their mistresses up in a separate establishment just like Lammas House. Why not in the country?

"Will there be anything else, miss?" Susan had finished gathering the laundry and stood at the door.

"Could you have Mrs. Parker send up tea and some of her delicious scones? I fear I didn't eat enough breakfast." Her stomach had been in knots, worry over their situation preventing her from doing more than nibble a piece of toast.

"Very good, miss." Susan nodded and shut the door.

Violet dabbed jasmine perfume behind her ears, then slid the cool glass stopper against her neck. She trembled, thinking of Tris nuzzling her there as the sweet scent filled his head. Hastily, she dragged the stopper between her breasts. Yes, she'd love for him to bury his face there, feel his warm breath tickle the valley between. She'd press his head to her hot flesh and never let him go. Closing her eyes, she groaned, wanting him here now.

Perhaps she should instruct Susan to have their supper laid here, in the bedroom. Although she had little true experience with a man's appetites, she understood the power of food and could think of several ways she could use their repast to arouse her lover. She was finding being a mistress more to her liking than she had believed possible. Being wicked and wanton with Tristan, in ways a wife might not be willing to explore, carried a strong appeal. God knew she understood little of the expectations of either wife or mistress. Still her pulse raced when she thought of the things from Madame Vestry's instruction she could do to her willing victim.

Shortly, Susan entered with a tray and Violet pounced on the hot, sweet tea and tender scones.

"You haven't put your earrings in, miss." Susan nodded at the jewelry still lying in the open case.

"I fear I was woolgathering for far too long." Violet sipped her tea and then slipped the heavy gold earrings into her ears. Hard to believe they were truly hers. She watched herself in the mirror and touched the sparkling gems, stilling them as they swung with her movement. A plan to thank Tris very thoroughly for her morning gift began to form.

All now in readiness for his return, Violet finished the last bite of the delicious scone and headed downstairs to the music room. The moment she entered, the scene from last night played itself out before her, as though she were watching a drama on the stage. She and Tristan locked in that bone-crushing embrace. Her cheeks flamed even as her body quivered. He could not arrive too soon.

Violet shook herself, discipline returning, and sat down at the harp. She strummed the strings softly, a caress for an old lover. No, this would never do. Determined to focus on her task, she forced herself to play some scales, limbering up her fingers. The final one flowed into the opening strains of the composition she'd written for Tris. She hadn't given it a name until the hasty one last night. Before she'd merely thought of it as Tris's Air. But if he liked that one, then so be it. Plucking the familiar strings, she lost herself as always. This time, however, not in the music, but in the memory. The candlelight, the warmth of the room, the faint scent of beeswax. Tristan's gaze on her, his eyes black with desire. She reached the crescendo of the piece, pouring all her heart, her passion, her soul into the music until it engulfed her, as if in a lover's embrace.

The last of the quivering strings fell silent and she sat back, almost as sated as this morning. Movement to her right. She turned.

Tris stood in the doorway, breathtakingly splendid in a jacket of emerald green, embellished with gold braid and topaz buttons over brown leather breeches that hugged every curve of his magnificent body.

She jumped up, the harp thumping to the floor, ran to him and threw her arms around him.

He bent his head, seizing her lips, crushing her body against him so tightly her ribs ached. Without warning, he thrust his tongue into her mouth, possessing her totally. The word "mine" echoed in her head.

Catching the urgency of his passion, she strained into him, kissing him back with sweet abandon fueled by the power of the music that still coursed through her.

At last he broke the kiss and cupped her cheek with his palm. His gaze bore into her, revealing a longing she didn't understand.

After that kiss she'd expect flaming hot desire, not sadness. "What's wrong, Tris? Didn't you get to see your friend, the marquess?"

He dropped his hands from her face and turned from her.

"Did he convince you not to marry me?" What else would cause such devastation in his eyes? "Truly, it's all right, my love. I told you as long as we can be together, I don't care if we are married or not."

"Violet." He reached toward her, then jerked his hand back. "Can we sit down, please?"

"Of, course." Concern welled within, frightening her, though she schooled her face to nothing but a pleasant smile. Truly, he looked very ill. "Come, let's go into the parlor where it will be more comfortable." She took his arm as they sedately walked the few steps.

The parlor fire had burned low, but she didn't want to wait for a servant to build it up. Whatever it was, he needed to tell her now. She should have known it would take him some time to agree they could never marry. As long as she assured him of her love and that she would stay with him despite society's censure, he would find a way to accept it.

They sat on the sofa and she took his hand. It lay limp in hers and her concern rose. He had never acted this despairing before. "Please tell me what troubles you, my love. I cannot bear to see you so distressed. Did the marquess dissuade you from breaking your betrothal to Miss Harper?"

"He asked me to put it off until I had talked to you." Hard lines etched themselves into his familiar face, turning it to granite.

"About becoming your mistress?" She clasped his hand, cold as a midwinter's morn, and squeezed it. He obviously didn't believe she loved him enough to sacrifice her honor for his. For him and no other.

"No, my dear. Not that."

"Then what, my love? Why are you so distraught?"

"Because I have a tale to tell you I would give my fortune and title not to have to tell." He lifted her head, his palm cradling her face. "Let me look at you, Violet, as you are at this moment." He gazed intently into her eyes, the sadness in his even deeper.

Dread seized her heart and squeezed it with icy fingers.

"Please believe I love you. That will not change until the land falls into the boiling sea at Judgment Day."

"Tell me." The croak emerged from a mouth gone bone dry with fear.

He kissed her hand, then released it and stood up. "When we met at the House of Pleasure, I told you I knew your brother."

"Yes, you said you had a slight acquaintance with him. You never told me how you met." The abrupt change of subject confused her. Why bring up Jamie now?

"I did know him briefly, just before he died." Tris paced to the sideboard and poured a full tumbler of brandy.

"How did you know him?" Jamie had never spoken of a Lord Trevor to her recollection. He certainly hadn't traveled in the same circles as Tris.

"In the spring of 1760, Duncan, my friend the marquess, was obliged to fight several duels defending the honor of his sister, Lady Juliet. Her fiancé had broken off their engagement because rumors had surfaced regarding insanity in the Ferrers family. You remember the scandal regarding the Earl Ferrers?"

Violet nodded. When the earl had killed his steward, the *ton* had been shocked. He'd actually been hanged for the crime, creating an even bigger sensation. "They are part of that family?"

"Through marriage only, but of course, people will spread wild stories. One of the men who slandered Lady Juliet was Christopher Davies."

"Kit?" Her cousin. A chill swept through her. The marquess, Tristan's friend, had fought Kit? "When did you say this was?" A hothead all his life, Kit had fought several duels.

"May of 1760."

"Oh, God." On May 25, 1760 Kit had been killed in a duel. She leaped to her feet. "Your friend killed my cousin and my brother?" Blood throbbed in her ears. Tris had known. He'd been there and had seen it. And he hadn't told her.

"No." Tris shook his head. "Duncan fought your cousin and, yes, killed him in a fair fight." He set his glass on the table and looked her in the face. "I killed your brother."

Chapter 15

Roaring deafened her. She couldn't comprehend what he had said. He hadn't said what she thought he'd said. He hadn't. She was mistaken. Black spots crowded out the sight of Tristan's face, white as parchment, shouting something.

Violet sat up and gasped.

"There you are, miss." Susan stood up, a vial of smelling salts in her hand. "She'll be all right now, my lord." She left and closed the door.

Violet lay on the pink parlor sofa, her feet atop a pile of pillows.

"Are you all right, Violet?" Tris sat down beside her. "You swooned."

Had she? "Oh, God." She did remember. "Get away! Get away from me!" With a shriek, she sprang off the sofa and ran behind it. "You killed him. You killed Jamie." She burst into tears, the rage and pain of betrayal licking through her veins. How could he have done such a thing?

"I had no choice, Violet. Don't you know what happened?" He took a slow step toward her.

"Stop. Don't come near me." Oh, but she wanted to die. The sharp sorrow of Jamie's death reared itself from the shallow grave she'd fought to keep it in all these months. She'd had to move past the agony of grief in order to survive. That hurt, however, paled in comparison to the raw agony of Tris's betrayal. "How could you?"

"I had to, Violet. You told me you knew what happened." Misery stared out of his eyes. "Duncan had just pierced your cousin below the heart. As he lay dying, your brother knelt beside him, comforting him for the few minutes he had left." Pacing between the sofa and the sideboard, he opened and closed his fists. "I was standing next to Duncan when from the corner of my eye I saw your brother leap to his feet, draw his sword, and run toward Duncan." Sudden anger flashed in Tris's face. "Duncan had his back to them. I had only seconds to act. I pushed Duncan out of the way. I drew my sword as your brother lunged and he ran onto my blade."

Despicable man. She glared at Tris and backed up. Oh, she'd known Jamie's actions were dishonorable. That was why she'd been shunned by almost all the *ton*. But he hadn't deserved to die. Tears tumbled down her face.

"It's all your fault." She managed to stop the tears long enough to throw that at him. "If you hadn't killed Jamie I wouldn't have ended up at Madame Vestry's to be bought by you." Betrayed. Betrayed by the man who had killed her brother and stolen her heart. "Why? Why didn't you tell me that night? You knew and you didn't tell me you had killed him."

"Because I wanted to help you and I feared you wouldn't take my help if you knew." Slowly, he shifted from one foot to another.

"Of course I wouldn't have gone with you if I'd known." He must be mad himself. She squeezed her temples, praying the doors of Bedlam would open and swallow her, making this a lunatic's dream.

"Violet." He eased toward her another step.

"Stop!" She skittered back from the sofa. "Don't come near me." Blast the luck, he stood between her and the doorway.

"I won't." Tris raised his hands, palms out, and backed away. "I won't come near you. I'm sorry I've hurt you. More sorry than you can know. Because I still love you."

"Oh, you wretch!" She grabbed a vase of dried flowers and hurled it at him. He ducked and it crashed into the wall.

"Don't you ever say such a thing to me again. Don't speak to me at all!" Seizing a China figurine, she heaved that at his head.

When he ducked it, she sprinted out the door, up the stairs and into her room. She slammed the door and turned the key. Chest heaving, she leaned against it, sobbing, unable to breathe.

Someone pounded up the stairs.

"Violet. Please just talk to me." Tristan's muffled voice sent a spike of pain through her head.

"Go away. I never want to see you or hear from you or speak to you again." Her throat hurt from all the screeching. Gripped with a sudden madness, she turned the key in the lock, jerked the door open, and came face to face with Tristan.

"Violet." Wide-eyed, he just stared.

"Ever again!" She slammed the door and locked it.

Chapter 16

Tristan leaned his head against the door to Violet's chamber, resisting the urge to bang on the smooth wood. He'd prayed against all odds she would understand at least a little. Her brother's death had been mostly accidental. The man had lunged at the exact time Tris had drawn his sword. He hadn't aimed to kill James Carlton. Of course, his sister wouldn't see it that way at all. Only a fool would hope so, especially given Violet's circumstances. His blade had dealt the mortal blow. Not something lightly forgiven. Perhaps never.

Her sobbing squeezed his heart. He laid his hand flat against the door, as if he could touch her through it. In his heart, he feared it would be the last time he did. Turning away, he dragged himself down the stairs.

Susan stood at the bottom, hands on hips. "You should have told her, my lord. The very first night she came here."

How could he be angry at her impudence, when she was completely right? "You should go to her, Susan. She has need of a friend now." He passed the disapproving servant, collected his cloak and hat, and let himself out. The afternoon had turned dark and a light snow blew around him as he mounted Lucifer.

The ride to his townhouse seemed interminable.

No matter how hard he tried to distract himself, his thoughts always circled back to the devastated look on Violet's face when he spoke those damnable words. God, the image was seared on the inside of his eyelids. The silence of the deserted streets only emphasized the sound of her voice in his head, telling him she never wanted to see him again. Well, he would make sure she got her wish.

Relief washed through him as he trotted Lucifer into the mews behind his house in Mayfair. Here at least he could mourn her loss in solitude.

"I am home to no one, Marks." He drew off his cloak and handed it to his butler. "If you value your position you will allow no one to cross this threshold." Tris paused, an impossible hope raising its head. "The sole exception would be a young lady or a maid. The name would be Miss Carlton." If her anger cooled and by some miracle she forgave him, he damned sure wouldn't want to turn her away.

"Very good, my lord." The tall, thin servant whisked his outer things away without even a questioning glance.

Tris hauled himself up the stairs to his room, cold despite the roaring fire. He might never feel warmth in his life again. When Saunders, his valet, approached, he waved the man away. For once clothes and appearance meant nothing. He paced the room, shedding jacket and waistcoat and untucking his shirt as he went. The garments fell unheeded to the floor, leaving him in shirt, breeches, and boots. At the writing desk he paused to grab the decanter and a glass. Flopping into the chair before the fire, he poured the expensive cognac into the tumbler until it slopped over the rim. He raised the dripping glass, contemplating the swirling liquid. If only he could drown in it. Then, with a practiced hand, he poured the fiery spirit down his throat, gulping it until he drained the glass. The only way he would endure this long afternoon and eternal night would be through oblivion.

* * * *

Violet allowed Susan to undress her, although she refused a bath. It might have soothed her and she didn't want soothing. She wanted to hold on to her anger, revel in her pain. She wanted to feed the outrage each time she recalled the man she had thought she loved had killed her brother and ruined her. Oh, yes. She wanted no possibility of calming enough to consider Tristan's...Lord Trevor's explanation. He had killed her brother, forced her to destitution and a life of prostitution, and debauched her into the bargain. There was no other way to view it.

"Shall I brush your hair, miss?" Susan bustled around the room, setting everything to rights.

Except her. Never again would she be right.

Violet shook her head, tears flowing. So many things lost. Her brother, her reputation, the life she might have had with Tris that could never be.

"It will do you good, miss. You've had a shock. Let me get you some hot tea with a drop of brandy in it and then brush your hair." Susan turned down the bed and fluffed the pillows.

Fresh sheets on the bed. Bless Susan for a thoughtful and efficient maid. Violet wanted no reminders of the night past. She needed none. Every moment had been scorched into her memory.

"Thank you, Susan. I would like that." The brandy might dull her enough to let her sleep. If not, the decanter on the sideboard had been replenished, so she could doctor her own tea.

The maid finished the bed and left Violet sitting on it to brood and weep, as she'd been doing ever since Tristan's departure. She must put the scoundrel out of her mind, look to her future instead, with Lord Donningham perhaps. He was an honorable man, one who could provide her with a safe and secure life.

Oh, Lord. No, she couldn't do that. Violet twisted back and forth on the bed. She couldn't pursue Lord Donningham or any other decent man. The one thing of value she'd had—her virtue—was gone, swept away in that night of passion by a man who couldn't marry her. A man she would rather die than marry now.

Sinking down beneath the covers, she couldn't stop the tears streaming down her face. No friends, no money, and now no virtue to recommend her. On the marriage mart she'd be less tempting than a used suit of clothing. What was she to do? She couldn't stay at Lammas House one minute longer than it took to make a plan and pack her things. Packing would take no time as she intended to leave with only the same clothes she'd arrived in. She refused to take anything Tristan...Lord Trevor had given her. She'd not give him the satisfaction of providing anything for the family of his victim.

Then where was she to go?

The door opened and she peeked out from the cover.

"Here you go, miss." Susan entered with a tray in her hands.

Violet poked her head all the way out. Pray God Susan had been generous with the brandy. "Thank you." Sniffling, Violet dragged the sleeve of her nightgown across her eyes and wiggled into a sitting position.

"I brought some of Mrs. Parker's scones, hot out of the oven. You need to eat something, miss." Susan settled the tray on her lap and tucked a napkin over her gown.

"I suppose you heard our whole conversation?"

"Rather hard not to hear in a house with thin walls." Concentrating on the tray, Susan straightened the dishes slightly. "Have you decided what to do, miss?"

"Not exactly." Violet shook her head and took a sip. Sweet and strong. The brandy trailed a comfortable burn all the way down her throat. Bless

Susan. She would miss her terribly. "I haven't worked out a plan, but I won't remain here."

"That's as I thought, miss. So I was wondering if you'd consider leaving London? Go away somewhere they don't know you."

Hope flared, then died. "The *ton* would know me wherever I went." She gripped the cup. There was nowhere to run to. "Brighton, Bath." She gulped the tea. The more she thought of her bleak outlook, the more she needed the brandy.

"Not if you went somewhere the *ton* doesn't go. Like Shotesham St. Mary. That's the village I came from, though I've not been back in years." Susan eased down onto the bed. "It's in Norfolk, but I've saved a bit. I could take you there, introduce you as a cousin or a friend. No one would think anything of it." She cut her eyes at Violet and hurried on. "There are prosperous farmers in the area who'd marry someone who looked like you, miss, and not think twice. They'd want a woman to take care of their house and bear their children. And believe me, they'd pay no mind as to whether you were a virgin or not, although we could say you were a widow lady. That would take care of that. Someone as lovely and talented as you, they'd be lined up to court you. You could have your pick of the men."

Violet sipped the tea, the brandy not making quite the difference she'd hoped. Somehow the image of her in a cozy house, surrounded by children and a man who wasn't Tristan still seemed intolerable. Nonsense to be sure because she hated Tristan. She willed the memory of his face away.

"You think about it, miss. Unless you can find a way to forgive Lord Trevor, Shotesham is likely your best chance." Susan rose and straightened the covers.

"Forgive Lord Trevor?" Violet jerked upright, upsetting the tray.

The maid dove for it and barely caught it before it spilled over the bed. "Yes, miss, begging your pardon. I did hear his lordship's explanation and it seemed to me it was more accident he killed your brother."

"You don't understand." Tears coursed down her cheeks. "I loved my brother. He and our cousin were closer to me than anyone, even my grandmother." Her jaw ached where she clenched it. "When Jamie died, I lost everything. I can never forgive Lord Trevor."

"Suit yourself, miss." Susan sniffed. "But it's my opinion your brother wouldn't have died if he'd behaved as he should." With a piercing look, she flounced out of the room.

Violet grabbed the teacup and drained it. Not enough brandy by far. She gazed longingly at the decanter on the desk. If she could summon the energy, she'd fill the cup brimful and down it. The less she remembered about Lord Trevor the better. Still, she needed her wits about her. She needed to come up with a plan.

Susan's scheme tempted her. It promised security and anonymity. Why not grasp both and be done with it? What did the man matter? She'd never feel about any man the way she had felt heart and soul for Tristan. Lord Trevor. She must remember him as Lord Trevor, by God, nothing but the lying scoundrel she hated.

With a clatter, Violet set the cup on the tray, then pushed it away and curled up on her side, tears starting from her eyes again. If she hated him, then why did her heart hurt so badly? It wasn't right to feel this ache along with the anger. She should feel one or the other. In Shotesham St. Mary she would likely never have to see him again. Probably the best thing for her. Still, her heart thudded painfully in her chest. Leaving London sent another pang through her.

It wasn't as if she was without friends in Town. If she paid a call on Miss Forsythe in the morning, she could beg for assistance. She might be refused, but she didn't think so. Sinking down into the covers once more, she closed her eyes, her mind made up. Tonight would be her last one in Lammas House, with its torturous memories and reminders of the man she could not forget.

* * * *

Hammering on his chamber door roused Tris from the brandy-induced stupor he'd fallen into sometime during the night. Marks had replenished the decanter twice. It rested on its side on the floor, empty. He winced and ran his hand through his hair. His mouth tasted foul as an un-mucked stable.

The pounding increased.

"Stop that infernal noise!" He plastered his hands over his ears. His is own voice tore a swath through his head until he feared it might explode. The drumming on the door ceased abruptly. The thumping inside his skull, however, worsened.

Gingerly, he peeled himself from the chair where he'd been sprawled for hours, and crossed to the door. By God, this had better be good or Marks would be sacked with no notice and no reference. He pulled the door open, about to lay into his butler.

Susan stood at the threshold, her brown cloak covering her figure completely and accentuating the pallor of her face.

"What are you doing here?" He blinked, still befuddled from the spirits and now confused by the presence of Serena's maid. No, Violet's maid. Violet.

He grabbed her by the shoulders and hauled her into the room.

She squeaked and pulled out of his grasp.

"Violet? Where is she? What's wrong?"

"That's just it, my lord. I don't know." Frowning deeply, Susan shifted backward, twisting her cloak.

A bad omen. He'd never seen her so flustered. "You don't know what's wrong or where she is?"

"We both know what's wrong, my lord." She glared at him.

He shrugged off her censure. "Then where is she?"

"I don't know!" Her wail pierced both his head and his heart. "When I went to her chamber late this morning, Miss Carlton wasn't in bed. I checked the house, but she was nowhere to be found. She'd said nothing about going out. She never leaves the house, you know."

Tris nodded. Violet had only been out a time or two and always with him or Thomas as escort. "Did she take Thomas with her?"

Susan gazed at the floor and wrung her hands. "Thomas is still there. The only things missing are her old satchel and the purple gown she was wearing when she arrived at Lammas House."

God, this was all his fault. Obviously, she intended to show him she needed nothing of his. "I suppose she didn't take the carriage either?"

"No, my lord. Nothing. But I did have a bit of luck. I asked around, different servants who were out and about this morning, if they'd seen her. I'd no idea what time she'd left. Andrew, Mrs. Lyman's coachman from next door, had been up early with a colicky horse. He said he took a breather around dawn and went out to have a pipe in the mews. He saw Miss Carlton."

"He knew her?" Insane to feel jealous at a time like this, and of a coachman, no less, but his rational mind had flown.

"No, my lord. He described her—brown hair, deep purple dress, black cloak—and said she came out of our mews gate, looking furtive-like over her shoulder. She headed on foot down the mews and then turned right at the end."

"Toward St. James Square." Tris rubbed the heel of his hand against his eyes, praying to God his brains didn't leak out. "Who might she know in that direction?" He lowered his hand and stared dully at the maid, hoping she had an answer, but the woman shrugged.

"Miss Carlton's had no callers and paid no calls in the time she's been with me. If she has friends or family, she never told me of them."

Tris tried to focus, though his thoughts jumbled as they spun around his head. Out of the fog, her voice, clear and strong came back to him. *I finally had the great good luck to make the acquaintance of a Miss Forsythe, who had just arrived from Ireland.* That was it. He nodded at Susan, his heart finally lightening. "I think I know where she's gone." Pray God he was right. So many things could happen to a woman alone in London. "I'll take care of this, Susan. Thank you for coming to me."

She gave him one exasperated look, and left.

"Saunders!"

The valet materialized immediately from his dressing room. He'd likely been lurking there all morning in hopes of a summons. The rotund little man took as much pride in Tristan's appearance as he did himself.

"Yes, my lord?"

"You must make me as presentable as possible in fifteen minutes."

"Very good, my lord." Saunders sprinted to the dressing room. Loud thumping sounds ensued.

Tristan grabbed his head, praying it didn't explode. He dreaded showing himself in public in this disgraceful fashion. Rarely did he indulge in spirits to this excess, but his guilt last night had driven him to this sorry state. And he deserved every pain-filled moment.

* * * *

"Lord Trevor." The shrill tone of the butler made Tris cringe as he entered the large reception room at the Braeton's townhouse.

"How lovely to see you again, Lord Trevor." Lady Braeton, beautifully attired in a sky-blue gown that somehow muted her flaming red hair, purred and patted the seat on the sofa next to her.

"Haven't seen you this season down in Kent, Trevor," Lord Braeton said, raising a tumbler half filled with pale liquor. He arched his brows in invitation.

Tris could almost taste the smooth spirits. Through his wife's family in Ireland, Braeton always procured the best Irish whiskey to be had in England. Just a couple of mouthfuls would take the edge off this infernal pounding in his head. But he needed to hang onto the few wits he had that still worked. He slowly shook his head at Braeton, and sat down.

The earl shrugged and took another sip. "Damned shame you missed the hunt in October. Some really good riders turned up, including young Manning. Have you met?"

"Yes. He's the Marquess of Dalbury's brother-in-law. He's got quite the reputation as a good judge of horseflesh." Hoping it wouldn't make his internal matters worse, Tris accepted a cup of tea from Lady Braeton. "Thank you. Two lumps of sugar and a splash of milk, please."

"And such a pleasant young man," Cocking her head, her ladyship chimed in. "My cousin, Miss Forsythe, is quite an admirer of his." Her blue eyes bore into him. "Have you met her, Lord Trevor?"

"Yes, my lady. At your ball in April. Such a beautiful and spirited young woman." Had the woman forgotten she'd insisted he dance the opening set with her? Still, her question gave him the opening he'd hoped for. "Is she receiving visitors today?"

The countess shook her head, clucking her tongue. "No, I fear my cousin has been indisposed for quite a while now. She has not been able to receive anyone for several weeks. Ever since our Christmas ball."

Damn. "I wondered because Miss Carlton mentioned she intended to call on Miss Forsythe."

Lady Braeton sighed and sipped her tea. "No, I'm sorry to say we have not seen Miss Carlton since the ball. Alethea took such a fancy to her last summer. I encouraged it as my poor cousin had made so few friends since her arrival in London. I do wish she had called. I'm sure Alethea would have made an exception for her. Perhaps Miss Carlton's presence would have raised my cousin's spirits."

Damn. If Violet wasn't here, where the devil was she?

He remained with the Braeton's another agonizing quarter of an hour, although he wanted to flee and continue his search. But search where? He'd thought of every place she might have gone and discarded them all as impossible due to her lack of funds.

When he took his leave of the Braetons, he headed back to Lammas House. Perhaps the woman had come to her senses and returned. If so, he'd shake her until her teeth rattled. If she had not made herself known by tomorrow morning, he'd contact Duncan. His wife had a relation employed by Bow Street. Perhaps the man could locate her.

Susan met him at the door, her eyes hopeful until she realized he was alone, and slumped.

"Any word?" he asked, already knowing the answer.

"Nothing. I've sent a message to my family in Shotesham St. Mary to see if by chance she'd gone there."

Tris frowned and pushed forward into the house. "Why would she visit your family?"

"We had talked of the possibility of her moving there, posing as a widow so she could get a well-to-do husband with no expectations of her virtue." Candle in hand, Susan pursed her lips and led the way into the parlor. She lit the lamps and faced Tris. "She could have stayed here in London, my lord, and married Lord Donningham. But she said she couldn't deceive a decent man like him and she'd rather die than tell him she was no longer a virgin." She glared at him, her breast heaving. "If you needed to lie with a woman that bad, begging your pardon, my lord, you should have gone back to the House of Pleasure. It's not like you've never been there before. You should have left Miss Carlton alone." She turned on her heel and stamped up the stairs.

Impertinent wench. Tris trudged to the sideboard looking for a drink. Still he couldn't summon true anger at Susan. She was as worried as he about Violet. She was also right. He poured a short shot of brandy and tossed it back. If only he'd kept as tight a rein on his cock as he had that night at Madame Vestry's.

He stopped mid-toss, his breath stilled in his chest. The brandy hit his throat and Tris choked. "Good Christ, no." He slammed the glass down, wheezing and coughing as he grabbed his cloak and ran for the door. Fear flooded his mind and heart. Now he knew where she had gone, damn her. Dear God, if he was right please let him be in time.

Chapter 17

Violet stood once more—cold, tired, and hungry but determined—on Madame Vestry's doorstep in the thin afternoon sunlight. Willie opened the door and his eyes widened. With a leer, he silently led her into the Madame's office.

Pen poised over an open ledger, Madame Vestry raised her head and met her gaze evenly. "You have returned Miss Carlton? Or is it now Cassandra?"

Violet squared her shoulders. The long walk from Lammas House, made even longer by the circuitous route she'd taken, just in case Susan or, God forbid, Lord Trevor had tried to follow her, had given her time to make peace with her decision to return to Madame Vestry. "Cassandra."

"Your other option did not work out, I suppose?"

"No." She'd returned to the House of Pleasure where a ruined woman belonged. Ruined by her own folly in letting the guard down around her heart and allowing herself to be swept away by Lord Trevor's charm and attentions. "I discovered I had no other options after all."

Of course, she could have left for Susan's village; no one would have been the wiser. Or begged Alethea to take her in and pursued a marriage with Lord Donningham or some other man of the *ton*. She could even have tried again to gain employment with a mantua maker.

"That is truly a pity." Madame Vestry's big brown eyes flickered with compassion for an instant before hardening once more. "I don't suppose we are still able to sell your virtue?"

A curt shake of her head told the tale. She'd refused to be party to deceit, to foisting herself off on an unsuspecting suitor. It would only be a matter of time until her shame was known throughout the *ton*. She might as well get on with the life she was fated to live as Cassandra. The life she deserved. Tris had ruined her in more ways than one.

"A shame. You'd have fetched a pretty price once more." With a shrug, the Madame turned over another page in her ledger and wrote the name Cassandra at its top. "The green room tonight at eight o'clock."

* * * *

"What pleasure my I give you this evening, my lord?" The question came back all too quickly as Violet sat once again in the green room at the House of Pleasure. She adjusted her skirt for the hundredth time, her gaze locked on the door.

The latch rattled.

She jerked up straight in the velvet chair. Her heartbeat pounded in her ears. It would be all right. This was the life she was fit for now. She would see it through.

The door opened and she rose. "What pleasure may I give you—" The words cut off in her throat.

Fashionably dressed in brown and buff, the gentleman stepped smiling into the room. Then his eyes widened and his jaw dropped. "Miss Carlton?"

* * * *

Tris pushed through the throng of merry gentlemen, laughing and drinking in the public rooms of the House of Pleasure. He had no idea where Violet might be, but one person would certainly know.

"Trevor. Over here." An acquaintance from White's waved him over, but Tris shook his head and continued wading through the packed room, with even greater urgency. A terrible constriction in his chest persuaded him he would be too late.

"Lord Trevor. Didn't think I'd see you here so close to your wedding. Getting in one last bit of skirt before you don the shackle, what?" The man put a hand on Tris's shoulder.

He threw it off and shoved the startled patron out of his way. God in heaven, where was the doorway? Fighting his way through another tangle of guests, he turned a corner, out of the raucous fog and into a dim corridor. He hurried forward to the Madame's office where he pounded on the door then hit the latch.

The door swung inward revealing Madame Vestry seated behind her enormous black lacquer desk. Tonight she had dressed in an expensive blue silk gown, cut daringly low. Ready for business.

"Where is she?" Tris strode up to the desk, his sword banging against the shiny wood. He wasn't above using intimidation if the woman proved reluctant to give him what he wanted.

"Where is who, Lord Trevor?" A slight smile on her too red lips, the Madame rose. "You were not scheduled for an appointment this evening, my lord, however, for such a good customer I can always make—"

"Damn you to hell." He leaned over the shiny desk until his nose hovered a mere inch from her dark, brooding eyes. "Where is Miss Carlton?"

Madame Vestry shrugged. "There is no one of that name here." Seating herself once more, she picked up her pen. "As I was saying before the interruption, I believe I can accommodate you despite the lack of a prior arrangement." She consulted the ledger before her, turned a page. "Daphne is new and available now. Perhaps not to your exact taste—"

"To hell with Daphne, to hell with you, and to hell with this accursed place." If she didn't tell him he would go mad. "Where is Violet Carlton?" He clenched his fists, blood roaring in his ears. By God, he'd not be responsible if he throttled the bitch. Every second counted if he were to stop Violet.

Mirth danced in Vestry's dark eyes for a fleeting moment. "Violet Carlton is a gently born woman who has never worked in this house. A sultry temptress named Cassandra, however, has returned."

"'Sblood, I'll wring your neck" Tris raised his hands, and his gaze fell on the ledger. He seized it with fingers that shook. "Where is she?"

"The green room." Vestry smiled and ice slid down his spine. "With a gentleman, of course."

Tris tossed the book at the smiling face and bounded out of the room. She'd cost him precious minutes. If he was too late to save Violet, he'd kill Vestry with his own hands. He pelted down the familiar corridor, his cloak billowing behind him like an ominous black sail.

Before the door, suddenly terrified of what he might find behind it, he froze. Pressing his ear to the gray-streaked panel, he strained to hear something, anything.

Silence.

His breath rasped in his own ears. Had he come too late? Were they even now in bed, the man already spent?

A chair scraped the wooden floor.

Tris hit the latch with enough force to snap the handle off in his hand. He gazed at it, amazed, then with an anguished cry, raised his booted foot and kicked the door. It crashed inward, rebounding off the wall and jolting his shoulder as he strode into the room.

Violet, eyes so wide they looked like tiny red-gold dots in a sea of white, rose from her chair by the fireplace clutching her chest, still covered by the fabric of her bedraggled purple dress, thank God.

"Violet, are you all right?" He strode into the room, hands outstretched.

A blur of movement to his right and the tip of a rapier pricked his chest.

"What the devil?" Tris danced backward, sweeping his cloak aside and drawing his own weapon to meet the unknown threat.

"You may retire, my lord." His tall, solidly built opponent stood directly in front of Violet, shielding her from sight. "You have no business with this woman." The man raised his sword into the high *en garde* of the second position. "I'll thank you to leave us." His face remained in shadow, however his rich voice had a familiar ring.

"The devil I will." Tris countered by lowering his arm into the fourth position, tearing at the strings of his cloak and tossing it aside. He squinted in the poor firelight, still trying to make out the identity of the stranger. "The lady is under my protection."

"I am not!" Violet's voice rang out. "He has nothing to do with me anymore." The denial cut like a dagger to Tris's heart.

"I am afraid the lady is correct, my lord." The shadowy figure rotated his hand, the blade twisting inches from Tris's face. "It's Lord Trevor, is it not?"

"Who the deuce are you?"

"I beg your pardon." The man lowered his weapon. "Lord Manning at your service."

"Manning? Good God." Breathing a sigh of relief, Tris sheathed his sword.

The Earl of Manning took a step into the light, revealing the dark hair and chiseled features of Duncan's brother-in-law. Thank goodness the scandal would go no further. "What are you doing here?"

The young man's face darkened. Was he actually blushing?

Heat rose in Tristan's as well. Damn it, he had nothing to be ashamed of.

"Hrmph." Manning cleared his throat and glanced at Violet who had come from behind him, glaring at Tris. "No need to go into reasons for my presence tonight. Suffice it to say I have rescued a damsel in distress."

The sight of her in that rumpled purple dress—the one she'd been wearing when he met her—almost undid him. He wanted nothing so much as to enfold her in his arms, feel her heart beat against his chest, and never let go. His own heart thundered like a sudden storm that drenched his body in cold sweat even as his mouth dried to dust. Damn it, what could he do? He blew out an explosive breath. Stop staring at her for a start.

Violet raised her chin and met his gaze. Her piercing eyes and stubborn jaw made his stomach clench.

"Thank you for your rescue, Manning. I hope we can keep this whole unfortunate episode private." By God, when he got her home he'd shake the woman like a terrier with a rat. How dare she run off to this place?

"My desire as well, Trevor." Manning picked up his cloak and draped it around Violet's shoulders. "I would not want it to get about the *ton* that my wife had been seen in a brothel."

"Your what?" Tris jerked his attention back to the handsome lord. Had the man gone mad? "What the devil are you talking about?"

"Lord Manning asked for my hand in marriage. I had just accepted his proposal when you burst in and interrupted us." Violet straightened, a triumphant smile settling like a mantle over her face. "Will you wish me happy, Lord Trevor?"

Tris nodded, the ice in his belly freezing the rest of him. She'd accepted another man. Numbness spread from his middle outward, like rays of a dead sun. Dead or not, he must show nothing. "Of course, Miss Carlton. My heartfelt felicitations."

Her gaze searched his face without finding what she sought. Her smile slackened to a pitiful drooping of the lips.

Manning's frown darkened his face. He tugged on the sleeves of his golden brown jacket. "You cannot imagine my shock and dismay when I discovered Miss Carlton here. I immediately thought of Kat's ordeal."

The earl's sister had been kidnapped and sold in the House of Pleasure not quite a year ago.

"Naturally, I assumed the same circumstances applied to Miss Carlton but she explained her unfortunate situation." He shook his head, his jaw firming, as he stared at Violet. "Of course, as a gentleman I could do nothing less than offer her the protection of my name." His gaze swung toward Tris, skewering him with an accusatory glare.

Tris ground his teeth, aching to clarify his relationship with Violet to the earl. But it was done. He'd lost her. Years of training to withhold any outward display of emotion rose automatically to mind. He summoned an inscrutable mask and donned it without thought. "Miss Carlton has been most fortunate to encounter you, my lord. You will wed immediately, I assume?"

Certainly for the best if they did. Remove any sort of temptation to renege on the betrothal. Manning was a good sort, according to Duncan. He could be sure the man would treat Violet well enough. How she'd cope with keeping regular company with the marquess who'd had a hand in her brother's death was anyone's guess. Had she even stopped to consider that? At least she wouldn't have to see him every day.

"We were about to leave when you came in, Trevor." Lord Manning stared pointedly at the broken door behind Tris. He sighed and shrugged. "Although I'm deucedly at a loss for where to lodge Miss Carlton this evening. Tomorrow I can hire a maid and set her up at a reputable inn until

I can procure a special license. But tonight…I suppose I could take her to Dalbury's, although he's still in an uproar over Juliet."

Violet started, then backed away from the earl, wringing her hands. The dim light cast mottled shadows on her strained, pale face.

"That would not be wise, I think." Perhaps the last place she should go, save one. Still, under the circumstances, he'd have to offer it.

"Do not worry, my dear." Manning took Violet's hand. "Good Lord, your fingers are like ice." He set to chaffing it vigorously. "Something will come to mind."

Tris dug his nails into his palms until the ache became intolerable. "If I may suggest it, Manning, allow Miss Carlton to return to Lammas House for the night. Or until you marry. She has a maid and a full staff there to attend her."

The earl left off rubbing her hands, now rosy with his attentions, and frowned. "Lammas House?"

"Where I stayed when I was under Lord Trevor's protection, my lord." Violet's lips trembled, but she stared at the earl calmly.

Manning shrugged. "Will that arrangement be acceptable, Miss Carlton?"

With a searing look at Tris, she opened her mouth.

Steeling himself for a resounding "No," he wondered what the hell they were to do with her then, but she closed her mouth and nodded, not meeting either his or Manning's eyes.

Manning relaxed, a boyish smile lighting his face. He'd been worried as well it seemed. "Good. Much obliged, Trevor." He nodded and motioned for Violet to go to the door. "I'll send the boy for my carriage. What's the direction?"

"It's in Soho, not far, off of…"

Resting his hand on the small of Violet's back, Manning ushered her out the door.

"I'll lead you there." He'd thought he'd gotten himself in hand, but the intimate gesture from Manning had jerked the response from him as though he'd been stabbed with a hot poker.

They passed Madame Vestry's office on the way out, but the room was dark; the woman had wisely made herself scarce. Just as well. He might have kept his promise to throttle her if he'd found her there.

Chapter 18

The damp cold soaked into Tris's bones although he kept Lucifer to a quick trot all the way to Lammas House. The ride seemed interminable and not just because of the chill weather. He could scarcely wait to be alone with Violet. He'd pounce upon her so hard her ears would fall off. Why in God's name had she gone back to The House of Pleasure? To insult him? Obviously. She'd done that when she'd left everything he'd given her. That should have been enough to wound him to the quick. So why hadn't she gone to her friend? Round and round the arguments raced, with answers unlikely to present themselves.

At last they drew up before the small, comfortable, lapped board front of Lammas House. Tris rode around to the mews, handing Lucifer over to a groom with strict instructions for the horse's care. Unnecessary, of course. The groom had been here for years. The knots in his stomach, however, told him he needed time to steel himself for the coming confrontation.

When he finally entered the parlor, Violet perched next to Manning, who had seated himself—or been seated—on the sofa.

In Tristan's accustomed place.

Fiendish woman. Determined to show him he'd been replaced. Well, he could play that game as well.

Tris shrugged off his cloak and strode to the sideboard. A drink, always welcome, was especially appreciated tonight. He poured a hefty libation and held the tumbler out to Manning who stared into the glowing hearth. "You'll take one against the cold, I trust?"

The earl leaped to his feet and joined him at the sideboard. "Thank you, yes. As you say, it's a bitter night." He seized the glass and bolted a large mouthful.

The man seemed skittish, although anyone might be unnerved having gone to a brothel for an evening of sport and come away with a wife.

"Good vintage." Manning nodded and took another sip. "Will you stay here tonight with Miss Carlton?"

"He most certainly will not." All but forgotten on the sofa, Violet now marched toward them, a glint in her eye like an avenging fury. "I have always stayed here with only the servants. I see no reason to change that plan now."

Tris fought the urge to remind her that had been true of all save one night. Then his shoulders slumped and he poured himself a full glass. What would such a declaration accomplish? He should be pleased Violet would be well taken care of. Still he could muster very little pleasure from the situation. "Miss Carlton is correct, Manning. She will be perfectly safe here for as long as she needs to stay. You have my word on it."

One scathing look at him, then Violet took her seat again.

"Much obliged." Contemplating the contents of his glass, the earl swirled the liquid slowly around, knitting his brows into a frown as he sat once more on the sofa.

Of course, the man must be puzzled over his relationship to Violet. God knew what she had told him, although the current look on his face suggested she'd mentioned some aspect of it. Still, Manning had accepted her, virgin or not. It was none of Tris's concern any more. He had to convince himself of that.

An awkward silence settled over them, Tris glancing from one figure on the sofa to the other. They sat like opponents over a game of chess, neither one wanting to make a move. Tension wound him up, each tick of the clock on the mantle accusing him of folly in letting her go. As if he could have stopped her from accepting Manning.

"Miss Carlton! Thank goodness you're all right." Susan sailed into the room, making everyone jump. She swooped down on her mistress like a hawk grabbing a mouse. "Where have you been?"

Manning sprang to his feet, wide-eyed as an owl.

Eyes narrowed, Susan appraised first the earl then Tris. After a long moment, she sniffed and returned her attention to her charge. "You had me in three kinds of fits and Lord Trevor worried to death." She continued tsk-tsking as she took Violet by the arm. "You come right along with me, miss. Look done in, you do."

Tris smiled as Violet opened her mouth, perhaps to protest, though she had no chance.

"I'll brook no argument, miss." Susan urged Violet toward the door with a none-too-gentle hand. "You need a bath and some hot broth, a hot brick at your feet to help you sleep and we'll pray this madness didn't cause you any mischief."

Violet shrugged sheepishly as Susan propelled her out the door. "You see I am taken captive. Good night, Lord Manning," she called from the staircase.

"Captive my eye," the maid grumbled as she headed up the stairs behind her mistress. "You'll be lucky not to catch your death. Mark my words."

Some of the tension eased from Tris's neck. Susan had her charge well under control. "You see Miss Carlton is in very capable hands. Rest assured no harm will come to her here."

"Indeed." The young man smiled, the first time he had done so all evening. "Will this woman accompany Miss Carlton to our home when we marry?"

The words stabbed Tris like an unexpected knife in the dark. He sobered immediately, his mask firmly back in place. He shrugged and tipped another good tot of the brandy into his glass. "That is for Susan to decide. I've employed her for several years now…" Damn. How much could he say and reveal nothing?

"Yes, for your mistresses." Manning tossed back the contents of his tumbler. "Of whom Miss Carlton is your most recent."

God, this would be awkward. "Not exactly. Is that what she told you?"

"She told me enough."

The dark countenance of Manning's face—brows taut, nose flared, mouth set with a downward turn—made Tris wish he had not given his sword to Thomas when he entered the house. Lord Manning had a legitimate grievance with him as the debaucher of his bride-to-be.

"I would have married her myself when I found her at the House of Pleasure a month ago. But I had just affianced myself to Lord Downing's daughter. I couldn't go back on my word." Fool. "And there is the matter of her brother."

"Yes, she told me that as well."

"She's been quite the chatterbox this evening, hasn't she?" Tris stared evenly at the earl, then downed his drink. "The situation has been intolerable from the start. I am sorely grieved by my own shortcomings in regards to my actions toward Miss Carlson, whom I hold blameless. Your brother-in-law told me to get as far away from her as possible and I paid him no heed." Despite his strong desire for another drink, Tris set his glass down. Getting drunk again would do no good either. "She is a delightful woman, intelligent, talented. I am sure she will make you the perfect wife." The words wanted to stick in his throat but he forced them out.

"Not when she's in love with another man."

Tris hefted the decanter, the liquor making a high-pitched *glug glug* as he topped his tumbler off. So much for not getting drunk. "I'm afraid you are mistaken, Manning. She abhors me. I killed her brother for Christ's sake."

"Yes, and she'd like to hate you for it, I'm sure." Grim-faced, Manning set his glass down and picked up his hat. "Much to her distress, however, she doesn't. She told me in great detail how you'd found her at the House of Pleasure and taken her away. Rescued her, she said. The look in her eyes when she said that did not bespeak hatred."

Tris's heart thudded against his chest. If only that were true. And yet…

"As I cannot marry her, it still doesn't matter whether or not she would have me." Slowly, he curled his hands into fists. "She has agreed to be your wife. That should be the end of it."

"Somehow I doubt it will be." Manning donned his black tricorne, elegantly appointed with gold trim. "I could never have left her in that place any more than you could. I did the only thing I could do, as you say, and offered to marry her." With precise motions, he adjusted the hat to a jaunty angle. "I had to insist upon it, in fact. The woman was deucedly unwilling. And although she told me a great deal about her life here, what she didn't tell me is why she left it and returned to the House of Pleasure." The earl's cold stare unnerved Tris. "Can you perhaps shed some light on her motive?"

More weary than ever before, Tris slumped into the Chippendale chair. "I have no idea, although I suppose I can conjecture. When I told her I had killed her brother, I suspect she felt so betrayed she wanted to punish me in turn. I don't know how she knew what a blow her returning to that place would be to me, but it was a master plan. To think I drove her back to that life…well, suffice it to say when I realized where she had gone, having my heart cut out with a dull dessert spoon would have been a treat in comparison."

"You will make sure she does not attempt to return a second time, won't you?" Manning's voice blew through Tris like a cold wind.

"I will leave strict instructions for her to be watched. She won't be able to use a chamber pot without someone knowing she's done it." Thought of Violet stealing away to Madame Vestry's in order to punish him made him sick inside. He'd gotten lucky this time. Another time he might not.

"I doubt she will take such confinement well. She's a spirited woman. Even our short acquaintance has shown me that. You'd best make sure your servants understand Miss Carlton's mettle if they don't already." Manning headed for the door then swung back around. "I will hasten the wedding to the best of my ability. By the end of the week, say?"

"Thank you. I believe I can manage that long." Too long for his taste. He wanted to see Violet as little as possible if he were to keep the pain of her leaving to a manageable level. If it were done, then were best done quickly.

"I'll send round a note tomorrow, informing Miss Carlton and you about arrangements for the special license."

"If you have any trouble I'm sure your brother-in-law can help. He's gotten one before." His friend's wedding had been a quick affair under strange circumstances.

"Yes, I remember clearly." Manning pursed his lips, but said only, "'Til tomorrow then." With a curt nod, he left.

Tris sat in the deserted parlor, the events of the past two days playing themselves over and over in his mind. How had it gone wrong so badly so quickly? He'd like to believe Violet still loved him, although he could scarce give credence to the earl's statements. The man had known her for only a few hours. Certainly not long enough to be able to ascertain her deepest emotions. Even if true, their situation was hopeless. He and Violet would marry other people and live comfortable if empty lives. Few men or women could claim true happiness in marriage. Why should they be any different?

After leaving strict instructions with Thomas to have Violet watched, he reluctantly prepared to venture out into the chilly January air. He regretted the need for departure, however, he'd rather face the raw air than Manning's sword. In any case, the softest bed he'd get in Lammas House tonight would be the sofa, so unlike all the other nights he'd stayed here. After calling Thomas to have his horse fetched, he donned cape and gloves, and finished off his brandy against the bitter night.

The ride home—past women who made their living walking the streets, past homeless figures huddled near a blazing fire in an alleyway—was mercifully short. Each person he passed could have been Violet had he not found her. His stomach sickened at the thought. He'd not be able to relax until she and Manning were safely married. He kept Lucifer to a fast trot and arrived at this door in Mayfair in mercifully quick order.

Tris strode into the foyer of his townhouse, shedding cape and gloves into the waiting hands of Marks. Hurrying up the polished stairs, into his suite of rooms, he called for Saunders.

His valet emerged from the dressing room. "My lord?"

Thankful for a well-run household, Tris dropped onto the bed and Saunders bent to remove his boots. "Call Marks, please."

"Very good, my lord." The efficient Saunders made short work of the boots, rang for the butler, then began to remove Tris's coat and waistcoat with practiced ease.

"Yes, my lord?" Marks entered just as Saunders unbuttoned the last silver button.

"Inform me of the day's goings on, please. In trying to solve the problems of others I have sadly been remiss with my own affairs."

"Very good, my lord." Standing ramrod straight, the butler began the recitation of household matters. "Nothing of much consequence happened downstairs. Mrs. McGregor had a falling out with the butcher over a brace of fresh hens. She's now declaring she'll give her custom to Hodges instead. There were two notes delivered earlier, one from Lady Gorham and one from Sir John Propst. Three letters arrived in the late post."

"And they are from…?"

"Lord Rothbury, Sir Anthony Deal, and Lady Knolls, my lord."

Two notes were likely thank-yous for some advice he had given Propst and for a birthday bouquet sent to his aunt. The letters from the gentlemen should be related to business on his estates. The one from his sister was an invitation to dinner before she left London for her home near the Scottish border. She'd told him of it last week at her Christmas party.

"All of those are on your desk." Marks drew forth a folded piece of heavy paper, with a large black wax seal. "This one came by hand, not an hour ago, my lord. I thought you would want to see it first thing." The butler held it out to him.

Tris sighed and took the letter. From Lord Downing. The writing and the black seal were unmistakable. His heart stuttered. Had the viscount found out about Violet? He stared at the creamy paper, dreading opening it. "That will be all tonight, Marks."

The butler bowed and made a hasty retreat.

Tris rubbed the rough paper between his fingers, a strange foreboding surging through him. He shrugged it off and broke the seal. The man had likely sent to remind him to come down to Wiltshire. He had planned to leave tomorrow, which might still be possible. Violet was now taken care of so there was no reason for him to remain in London. A pang of regret seared through his heart but there was nothing else to do but accept the new situation and move forward. He ripped open the letter and winced at the three brief lines.

Yes, duty called. Little as he'd like to do so, he should make every effort to leave tomorrow. A vision of Dora, sweet in virginal white, arose as though the letter had conjured her to rebuke him for his thoughts of infidelity.

He strode to the sideboard and splashed his favorite brandy into a glass until it slopped over the rim. The sooner he could put Violet Carlton out of his mind the better off he would be. If only his heart would believe that.

Chapter 19

Sunshine streamed in through the dining room windows, brightening the pale green walls and infusing the room with a false sense of warmth. Violet sat at the table, her breakfast nearly untouched. She sipped the cooling tea and pinched off miniscule bites of the toast Mrs. Parker had set before her. Even that little bit of bread stuck in her throat. A huge yawn almost dislocated her jaw. She'd passed a fretful night alternating between wakefulness and sleep plagued by menacing dreams in which shadowy figures lunged toward her from the dark corners of the green room at the House of Pleasure. Her eyelids fluttered and drooped. Nothing would please her more than to return to her bed, crawl beneath the covers, and sleep—aided this time by a large slug of brandy.

First thing this morning, however, Lord Manning had sent a note around requesting permission to call upon her with urgent news. The earl seemed frightfully young and energetic. Violet sighed and turned her teacup this way and that. Most likely this visit had something to do with the special license. She straightened in her chair. Perhaps the wedding must be postponed. That would suit her just fine.

She did not want to marry Lord Manning.

Violet crumpled her napkin, tossed it on the plate, and rose. She'd wait for his lordship in the parlor. She chose to sit in the Queen Anne chair rather than the sofa. Less chance of having to sit near the earl. She gripped the chair arms then shook herself. This would not do if she was going to marry the man.

If. Why did she not want to marry him? From her friend Miss Forsythe she'd learned in addition to his title he possessed reasonable wealth and a number of estates. He was always kind, even gallant as evidenced last night. And handsomely made, with broad shoulders, slim hips, and a chiseled face that would make a nun swoon. A dream come true, in fact. Just not her dream anymore. Because he wasn't Tristan.

The truth hurt abominably but it was truth nonetheless. She still loved Tris. The moment he broke into the room last evening she'd known. Her heart had beat like a racehorse thundering down a track. Her whole body had quivered as with an ague. Her gaze had lingered on his face, his dark eyes, although she'd tried to force herself to look away.

God knew she'd tried to rekindle her outrage at his actions. He'd killed Jamie and hidden it from her. She should hate him for the rest of her life. That she could not pained her almost as much. Better to have stayed and plied her trade at the House of Pleasure. There she'd have had no complications of the heart or honor to distract her, only focus on the cold business at hand.

She dropped her head into her hands. She'd need to think the same way about her marriage to the earl, at least in the beginning. Do her wifely duties as one would with a stranger or customer. Eventually she'd get used to him. They might find they suited after a fashion. Tears slid down her face. Had things been different she could have had so much more. Damn. She had to put Tris out of her mind, out of her heart.

Thomas appeared in the doorway. "Lord Trevor, Miss Carlton."

Hastily, she wiped at her eyes and sat up straight in her chair. He'd not see her teary-eyed and think himself the cause.

Tristan swept in, his big body filling the room as he always did, filling her vision with him alone. The wretch had worn the blue velvet suit he'd worn the night they met. A message for her? He'd pulled his dark hair back in a queue, accentuating his taut jaw. Had something not gone to his liking this morning? His eyes blazed like sapphire flames.

"Miss Carlton." He gave an almost imperceptible dip of his head.

His formality cut her to the bone. With an effort, she managed her own curt nod.

"Lord Manning sent me a message to meet him here at eleven." Glancing out the window, he removed his gloves, finger by finger.

Meet with him? Why on earth would he want to meet with her and Tris together?

He continued staring out the window.

Damn him for his reserve. He might have been speaking to one of the men at his club. Well, two could play that game. She sat, lips pursed, hands folded carefully in her lap. Patience was one virtue she still had intact, thank goodness.

"I trust you are well?" He spit the words out grudgingly.

Violet bit her cheek to keep from smiling. A small victory, yet hers. "Very well, Lord Trevor. And you, after your late night? No ill effects, I hope?"

"None whatsoever." Voice neutral, face a blank mask.

His impersonal nature saddened her. She had enjoyed their warm friendship so much. No matter what he had done, he had helped her and tried to make it right. Although she might not have forgiven him yet, the wheels had been turning ever since that dreadful confession. Last night in bed, as she tossed and turned and punched her pillow, she'd brooded on his explanation. Enough to understand a little bit better at least.

"Do you know why Lord Manning needs to meet with us both?" If he needed Tris's presence it could scarcely be about the wedding. She slumped in the chair. The nuptials were likely galloping apace.

"I've no idea, Miss Carlton. I thought you might be able to shed some light on the subject." He stared down his nose at her, then sauntered to the sideboard. "I hope he makes haste, for I must leave immediately for Wiltshire."

Violet drew a deep breath, stung by his reference to Lord Downing's estate. He was leaving to go pay court to his betrothed. Wretched woman. No, she shouldn't blame the girl. It was her own folly to have fallen in love with a married man. She would need to work long and hard to quell her feelings for Tris. For now, best to focus on Lord Manning's visit.

Both summonses were a puzzle. What reason could Lord Manning have for wanting to speak to them together? Perhaps he couldn't get the special license immediately and they would need to wait for the banns to be read. She would need to continue at Lammas House under Tris's protection. A plausible and very agreeable excuse for this assemblage. Tris would have nominative control over her while she resided here. Perhaps she'd even see him once in a while when he came to check on things. On her. Her heart thumped noisily in her chest.

Of course, Lord Manning would likely have her and Susan retire to a respectable inn until the reading of the banns could be completed. Nothing could be simpler. So again, why summon Tris?

He raised the decanter, let it hover a moment over the glass, then set it back down on the sideboard. "I am sure there is no impediment to procuring the special license. Manning may simply wish to gift you with a wardrobe more suitable to your coming station."

Violet's cheeks burned and she jerked her head downward, staring at her lap. He masked his anger at her leaving with a reproof for leaving behind the clothes he'd bought her. Well, she had been angry too. Angry enough to want to keep nothing from him whatsoever. "I doubt that is the case, although perhaps he wishes for me to have a special gown made for the wedding." She shrugged. "But then why summon you here?"

"Why indeed?" He grasped the neck of the decanter, squeezing somewhat harder than absolutely necessary. His knuckles showed white as bones.

She would have dearly loved a drink at this moment. Sparring with him in this manner kept her on edge, to be sure, however, she'd appreciate a moment to just relax in his presence. "Let me ring for tea." Violet pulled the bell mechanically, needing to do something. She couldn't simply sit here in the parlor with its genteel furnishings and do nothing but ring the bell. Nor could she continue to look at her lap.

"Yes, Miss Carlton?" Susan appeared, fixing Tris with a gimlet eye that took no quarter.

"Bring tea please, Susan. My special blend." A wink at the maid as she prayed the girl understood to add a healthy dollop of brandy to the beverage.

"Right away, miss." Raised eyebrows, but no other indication Susan had understood the signal.

Violet turned back to Tristan, who hovered just behind her. "Please be seated, Lord Trevor. You make me nervous hanging about so."

"Far be it from me to discommode a lady." He smirked, but came around the end of the sofa, drink in hand, and sat in the Queen Anne companion chair. His face, set in harsh lines, had laid grooves about his mouth. So forbidding he scarcely seemed her Tris at all.

Because he was not her Tris and never had been. Asking him to sit had been a mistake. They had nothing to say to one another save for the one subject that kept them silent. If she brought it out in the open, would it break this hideous stalemate between them? Like ripping a bandage off a wound to make it bleed—and begin to heal.

Gathering her courage, she faced him again although she could not bring herself to look directly into his eyes. "Tris."

He tensed, his hand frozen with the glass before his mouth. His dark gaze shot straight to her face. "Yes?"

"I am sorry—"

"Lord Manning, miss," Thomas announced the earl.

Violet jumped as the servant made a hasty retreat.

Manning strode into the room and headed directly for the fireplace. "Bitter cold out this morning." With a shiver, he held his hands out to the well-laid blaze. "The wind chilled me to the bone just coming from the carriage." He looked up from the flames and stopped, his gaze flitting from her face to Tris's.

Violet turned her head sharply, afraid her face would reveal more than she cared to tell the earl.

"So what brings you here, Manning?" Tris rose and sauntered toward the younger man. "And more particularly, why was I summoned?" He sipped his brandy, although his gaze narrowed keenly on the earl. "I am leaving town as soon as this business is concluded."

Rubbing his hands, Manning nodded toward the sideboard. "May I?"

"Of course." Tris swept his hand outward, in a broad circle that took in the whole room before coming to rest at Violet. "What is mine is yours."

"Hardly." Manning chuckled. "Still, many thanks. This should warm me up nicely." He poured a tumbler half full and took a gulp. A shudder ran through him as the fiery liquid hit. Then his shoulders relaxed.

"Good morning, my lord." Uncomfortably aware of Tris's gaze on her, Violet rose and nodded to the earl. "I received your note, but couldn't help wondering if you'd encountered a difficulty with the wedding plans." She strove to keep eagerness out of her voice, though it was devilishly hard to do.

Manning stared at her for a moment, then swirled the remaining brandy in the glass. "You are very perceptive, Miss Carlton. That is indeed the reason for my visit. I have discovered an impediment to our plans."

"Impediment?" The word raised a hope in Violet's heart.

"Impediment?" Tris set his glass down with a dull thud. "You have found a blood connection between your family and Miss Carlton's?"

"No. At least, I have not heard of such." Gazing at the tumbler in his hand, Manning rubbed his thumb across the cut-crystal stars. "Rather I have found when I asked Miss Carlton to marry me I was unaware I was not free to do so." He up-ended the glass, gulping the brandy until he'd drained it.

"Not free?" Tris's brows lowered almost to his nose. "What the devil do you mean, Manning?"

"I mean that for reasons I discovered only last night, I must withdraw my offer of marriage to Miss Carlton." Quietly, he placed his glass precisely in the center of the white linen runner covering the sideboard.

Violet clutched her chest, her heartbeat thundering in her ears. Salvation.

"I have obligations that prohibit me from marrying Miss Carlton." The earl drew himself up, squaring off with Tris. "This is the reason I summoned you here, Trevor. You have been acting as Miss Carlton's protector and as such it is your right, should you wish, to challenge me for this insult."

Chapter 20

"No!" Violet's heart leaped like a wild thing. "There will be no such challenge offered on my behalf." Dear God, from salvation to damnation in the blink of an eye.

"The devil there won't." Tristan's eyes flashed indigo blue and narrowed as he turned that piercing gaze on Lord Manning. "You wish to withdraw from the betrothal with Miss Carlton? Then name your seconds, my lord."

"I forbid it, Tris."

"I will not brook this insult, Violet." The blood had drained from Tris's face.

"I'll not have either of you killed in a stupid duel." If she had to bash him over the head with a brick, she would not allow him to jeopardize his life in such a manner.

"He offered to marry you and you accepted that offer." Tris paced briskly toward the window and back. "You have a legitimate and legal claim on him. He cannot make a proposal one day and renege on it the next. It's simply not done."

"But is has been done. By me." Manning's raised voice overpowered them both. "Despite any other feelings I may have, I cannot marry Miss Carlton."

"Then you will meet me, Lord Manning." Tris squeezed his hands into fists. "I will have satisfaction for this smirch on her honor."

"Tris, there is no dishonor in this." Violet pressed her hands to her cheeks. Would the stubborn man get himself killed just to prove a point to her? "Can you tell us why you want to break the engagement, my lord?"

With a heavy sigh, Manning ran a hand over his face. Dark smudges beneath his eyes gave him a haunted look. He appeared to have slept even worse than she had.

"I am not at liberty to divulge that information, Miss Carlton. Suffice it to say the situation is dire enough I must take this deplorable action as the lesser of two evils. Would to God I did not have to make such a choice, but it cannot be helped."

"And what of the injury to Miss Carlton's reputation?" Tris stalked over to her, towering above her like an oak shielding an acorn.

Manning shrugged. "At the moment there is none."

"Of course there is." Tris's voice boomed in her ear. "You are jilting her. The whole *ton* will know. She will never be able to marry."

"They won't know unless you tell them."

"Here you are, miss." The conversation stopped as Susan bustled in with the tea tray. "I've made it just the way you like. Nice and strong." She cut her eyes toward Violet with a subtle nod of her head and a raising of the eyebrows.

Bless Susan.

Tension thrummed through Tris so strongly she could feel the vibrations. She needed to dismiss the maid quickly or he might combust right before their eyes.

"Thank you, Susan. That will be all." Violet raised her chin. The girl would expect all the details as soon as the guests left and she would absolutely have them.

She gave a hurried curtsey and left.

No sooner had she closed the door than Tris erupted. "No one knows about the betrothal?"

The earl shook his head. "Who would know? I've told no one. Have you?"

"No."

"And if I release you from your obligation, there will be no stain on either of us." Violet took Manning's hand, startling him and drawing his attention away from the still bristling Tristan. "Much as I am grateful for your gallant offer, my lord, I believe it would be a mistake to press the issue if you have a responsibility elsewhere." The relief in his eyes confirmed this was the right decision. He was an honorable man who would not have made nor retracted the offer capriciously. Something unexpected had forced him to this decision. She would let him go and be grateful. "I wish you nothing but well."

"Violet, do you know what you're doing?" Tris suddenly loomed over her.

He wanted to intimidate her, which made her angry. Still, she hastily dropped the earl's hand. Best not antagonize him when she suspected she would get her way in this.

Grasping her arm, he drew her behind the sofa. "Your circumstances have not changed," he whispered fiercely. "Unless you have employment of which I am unaware, or another offer of marriage." He peered into her face, his bright eyes blistering her soul.

"No, I have neither of those things," she said, willing him to understand. "However, I know I cannot in good conscience hold Lord Manning if he has a prior claim on his name. Especially, as I suspect, if the reputation of another lady lies in the balance. Perhaps she will fare even worse than I if he doesn't come to her rescue." She squeezed his arm and murmured, "Please, I truly do not wish to marry the earl."

A long moment of silence before he laid his hand over hers then nodded and in a normal voice said, "Then against my better judgment, I will agree to break the betrothal."

Violet smiled until he pulled her chin up to meet his gaze, a stern cast to his face.

"On certain conditions, Miss Carlton, which I believe Lord Manning will insist upon as well." He glanced to the earl.

"Name them, Lord Trevor." Manning strode over to stand beside her.

"First and foremost, you will give your solemn oath you will never, under any circumstances, return to The House of Pleasure or any other such establishment." The intensity of his glare made her drop her gaze and step back for fear his anger would scorch her.

Lord Manning's countenance was almost as stern.

A chill oozed down her spine. Both men were quite angry at her, with just cause she must admit. With a sigh, she clasped her hands and addressed both men. "I know it was folly to return to Madame Vestry's." Heat rushed into her cheeks, still she continued. "I should not have let my anger at Lord Trevor lead me to such a rash and dangerous action. For this I do apologize to you both."

The easing of Lord Manning's features seemed to indicate he accepted her contrition.

Tris's face, however, remained unmoved, as though Michelangelo himself had carved the visage.

"I give you my solemn oath," she began in a small voice, "on pain of hellfire and eternal damnation I will never seek out employment, succor, or sanctuary in The House of Pleasure or any other such establishment." The sound of a door closing echoed in her mind. Of course, she never wanted to darken Madame Vestry's door again. But the question remained what was to become of her?

After staring at her a moment longer, as if searching her soul for confirmation of her words, Tris nodded.

She gasped in air, unaware she'd been holding her breath. "You said 'certain conditions' my lord. Are there any others?"

"Only that you promise to consult me before making any decisions about accepting either a position or marriage." Turning from her, Tris raised his glass toward Manning. "Another one, my lord? I assume you will be hastening off into the cold to attend your next damsel in distress?"

"Hmm." Manning grunted as he headed to the sideboard where he armed himself with a fresh glass. "I do have my affairs to put in order directly, still I wish to assure Miss Carlton I will do everything within my power to assist her in securing a respectable and permanent position."

Tris poured a healthy amount into both their glasses. "That should keep you from freezing during your travels."

"Indeed." Eying the glass, the earl shrugged and took a sip. "You are preparing against the cold as well? I recall you said you were leaving town?"

"Yes, for Lord Downing's estate in Wiltshire. I'm expected there day after tomorrow." The shadows of the shrubbery were lengthening along the garden wall. Where had the day gone? "I'd hoped to leave today, but I fear it's simply too late. If I leave early tomorrow morning, I'll be there in time for dinner. Excellent roads to Devizes."

"You should have good weather as well." Manning drained his glass. "I am off. Do not fear, Miss Carlton." He turned to Violet with a smile. "I shall not let my other duties make me neglect your cause."

"I would never believe that, my lord." She followed him to the door. "I cannot thank you enough, Lord Manning, for coming to my rescue last night. I will make the most of this chance to start again."

"I am sure you will, Miss Carlton." With a deferential touch, he raised her hand and brushed his lips over her knuckles.

A warmth lingered there momentarily then was gone.

"Should you need anything further, especially while Lord Trevor is from town, please send to me at once." The earl made a deep bow and strode out of the room.

"When…" Violet turned toward Tris and stopped, unable to move or speak.

Tristan leaned against the mantelpiece, his forehead pressed against his arm, staring intently into the fire. His hair, clubbed back in a neat queue earlier, now swung free.

"What…what happened to you?" She waved her hand toward him, moonstruck at the sheer beauty of him in the flickering firelight. His eyes glittered, staring out of the chiseled planes of his face where a faint stubble was beginning to show. The blue jacket molded to his shoulders and arms, proclaiming their rugged strength. But his hair, burnished chestnut in the light, hung loose, scattered wildly over his shoulders, as it had been Christmas night. The only other time she'd seen it so. She stared, unable to remember how to breathe.

"This?" He brushed the hair back over his shoulder. "The band that bound it back broke. My valet will have another. Why?"

"It just surprised me, is all." Violet made herself sit and pour more tea. It was cold but she didn't care. The brandy steadied her nerves and warmed her nicely. "So you will be gone for a week or more?"

"Most likely more. Lord Downing will want to discuss the Yorkshire property he's settling on his daughter. There will be a series of entertainments when the betrothal is officially announced. I may not return to town until the end of the month."

"Oh." Keeping her eyes carefully on her tea cup, Violet now wished for brandy alone. She was back to where she had been at the beginning of this wretched affair, without the hope of a happy ending for her. "Is there anything you wish for me to do in your absence? I suppose I will be at home the entire time, but if you can think of something, I will be happy to attempt it." Time would hang heavy on her hands with only her music and perhaps some embroidery to keep her occupied. "I cannot attend social functions without an escort, of course, but I wondered if you would allow me to call on Miss Forsythe? Or Miss Tate. I could perhaps renew my acquaintance with Lord Donningham."

Tris cocked his head and frowned deeply. "Susan told me you had relinquished all hopes of Donningham."

"I may have to reconsider that stand." She stared down at her lap rather than meet his eyes. "I must have somewhere to go, Tris. I cannot stay here forever. And I need to find a life I can live without you. If Lord Donningham will take me as I am, then I will accept him." It seemed the most direct route to a decent existence. Donningham appeared a kind man. At least, he would have no ties to the marquess and that horrible memory. "I could do worse." Much worse.

"Yes, I suppose you could." He shook his head back, setting his hair to swinging.

Her stomach clenched and she braced against the ache in her heart.

"If you'd prefer him, I can still challenge Manning. Make him fulfill his promise to you."

"No." She leaped to her feet and grasped his hand. Flames licked through her veins. "There has been enough bloodshed. Let us forget and try to forgive."

Gazing softly into her eyes, he raised her hand to touch his lips. "Does that mean you can now find it in your heart to forgive me, my dearest one?"

Her body trembled and she tried to draw away, but he clasped her hands to his chest, heat blistering her as though she stood in an inferno.

"I scarcely dare to hope you can forgive me, Violet, still I must ask again. I swear to you, if I could return your brother to you and forfeit my life instead, I would do it this instant."

"No!" She wrenched her hand free and pressed it against his lips. "Do not say such a thing, ever. I would not have my brother back at the expense of your life." Giving in at last, she leaned against his stalwart frame, soaking in his warmth and the spicy bergamot scent inextricably linked in her mind to Tris. "I have come to understand he was in the wrong. I would have you both, if God could change what is past, but as he cannot, I will be content with the man he chose to let live." Looking up into the softly shining pools of blue, she cupped his cheek. "It would be a poorer world for me were you not in it, Tristan."

He folded his arms around her and clasped her to his chest. The regular thud, thud of his heartbeat the sweetest sound imaginable. "You may visit whom you will, Violet. I only pray you find the place in someone's heart that is not mine to give you."

Heart breaking, she wrenched herself away. He was right. She must do what must be done. Unable to bear the thought while in his presence, she grasped her skirts and ran for the stairs, tears pouring down her cheeks despite her attempts to stem them. Some things simply could not be stopped.

Chapter 21

"Damnation." Tris peered at the sky as the light snow of the early morning gave way to thick, wet flakes. He'd left at first light and planned to arrive at Harper's Grange no later than 6 or 7 o'clock. The weather, however, had not cooperated. He rapped on the trap.

"Yes, my lord?" Hunched against the cold, Stokes squinted through the thickly falling snow.

"How much longer to the Grange?"

"I'd say about another six or seven hours." He glanced around at the swirling snowflakes. "Maybe more if this gets worse."

Tris sighed. His raw mood had deteriorated with the long journey and little but his thoughts of Violet to keep him company. He'd done nothing all morning but think of her. At least if he'd made it to Lord Downing's he would have had companions to distract him from brooding. Dismal to think of spending the night on the road with no company, but there was nothing for it. "What's the nearest inn we can make?"

Flipping his collar up to avoid the blustering wind, the coachman shivered and said, "Woolhampton's the closest, my lord. 'Bout an hour, I expect. The Angel would be my choice."

"Right, then. We'll stop there for the night."

"Very good, my lord." Stokes' relieved face vanished as the trap dropped into place, leaving the carriage colder than before.

To keep his sanity, Tris elected to spend the evening in the common room, drinking the inn's best ale and being regaled with stories from the innkeeper about the local squire whose stallion kept trying to kill its master. He'd been thoroughly entertained until the group broke up to wend their ways home through the still blowing snow.

As soon as Tris closed the door of his chamber, however, the image of Violet, warm, sweet, beckoning him to bed filled his mind. "God, help me." Rubbing his hand over his face, he attempted to dispel the vision, to no avail. She would haunt him the rest of his life and he had no one but himself to blame.

A hesitant knock on the chamber door brought him a thankful respite. Even if it were only Saunders with some question about tomorrow's outfit or warm water to wash with, it would save him from more thoughts of her.

A ready smile on his face, he opened the door on Meg, the serving girl from downstairs, a porcelain ewer in her hands. What the devil...?

"Beg pardon, my lord, but I was told to bring up your washin' water by Mr. Saunders." She ran her gaze down the length of his body and a smile touched her lips. "I'll just put it behind the screen for you." Before he could protest, she strode past him and disappeared behind the folding screen in the corner.

A minute passed, but the girl didn't return. Letting his head droop, Tris groaned aloud. Damn Saunders. In the past Tris hadn't minded the valet scaring him up a bit of entertainment for the night, and he'd certainly not be able to relieve his needs once he arrived in Harper's Grange. Possibly not until the wedding sometime this spring. "Meg?"

The girl stepped from behind the screen. She'd removed her fichu and plumped her breasts so they almost spilled over her white and gray striped bodice. "Yes, m'lord?"

Tris swallowed hard. To his dismay, his cock had perked up at the sight of the girl's pale, rounded mounds. "You can go now." A surge from below made him wince.

Meg's brow puckered. "I thought...I thought I might help you, my lord." She faced him and jerked her bodice open. Round and dark, her nipples peeked over her shift and stays.

Temptation to give in overwhelmed him. The girl was willing and his stiffening flesh ached for a warm nest. But not this one. "Not this evening, I think."

Her face flushed red and she flew behind the screen.

He gazed about, searching for a decanter. He'd need a drink, no, several drinks as soon as the woman left.

Meg strode out, her clothing askew, but covering the essential parts, and made a silent beeline for the door, her face still the color of a ripe persimmon.

"Wait."

She skidded to a halt in front of him, her eyes narrowed.

Tris opened his valise and grabbed a coin from the pouch of traveling money. He laid it on the table. "Thank you for fetching the water, Meg."

She glanced from him to the coin, a gold sovereign. In one liquid movement, she scooped the coin up, curtsied, and sped out the door.

"Oh, Christ." Tris spied the decanter at last and helped himself to a healthy glass full. Agonies raged in his groin. At least he could take care of that later if need be. The more burning question was what if he couldn't put Violet out of his mind? And worse, what would he to do if he couldn't bring himself to take Dora to his bed?

* * * *

Next morning dawned cold and crisp, the sun glinting off the new fallen snow. With only forty miles left to Devizes he certainly should arrive in time for tea. The night before, as he'd tossed and turned thinking of Violet, he'd decided his time in the carriage might be best spent by concocting a plan of courtship for Dora. If he could find some shared interest, some mutual pastime, perhaps his affection for her would grow enough so he would want to attend to his husbandly duties. There was time. They would not be wed for almost three months, although on second thought he should urge Downing to move the date up. Once married, he would have to cease his obsession with Violet Carlton for there would be no way to break the marriage bond.

The carriage started and Tris settled down to listing outings, activities, and topics of conversation with which to draw out his bride-to-be. If the girl would be his wife, he'd best try to find a way for them to scrape along amiably.

Five hours later Tris gladly relinquished his list, with its measly four items, as the carriage swept up the long driveway to the massive stone building—half Tudor manor, half medieval fortress that was Harper's Grange. The original structure, the castle that formed the rear portion of the house, had been standing since the Conquest. The Tudor section had been added after a fire had destroyed the Great Hall two centuries before. That he was marrying into one of the oldest English families hadn't impressed Tris until now.

The doors opened as he walked toward them.

"Lord Trevor?" The ancient butler, eighty years old if he was a day, ushered him into a long foyer hung with medieval battleaxes. "Welcome, my lord. The family has been expecting you." The stooped, little man neatly peeled the heavy cloak from Tris's shoulders as he stared at the full suits of armor lining the corridor leading toward the main portion of the house.

"Lord Downing is quite the collector of antiquities." Tris gestured to the walls as he removed his gloves and hat and handed them to the butler.

"Not so much a collection as family history, my lord," the man replied, carefully handing the outerwear to another servant, then headed down the corridor at a sedate, almost snail-like pace. "These are all family heirlooms passed down from the earliest Viscount Downing who came over with William the Conqueror as a squire to Sir Jacques de Main." They continued into the Great Hall, also decorated with all manner of weaponry. Swords, daggers, maces, helmets, sets of chainmail hung as if a reminder—or a warning—of the martial ancestry of the house.

Tris shivered. The room was chilly even without the hostile decorations.

"Lord Downing gave instructions for you to be brought to his study immediately." The wizened servant crossed the Hall and continued down another corridor, his heels tapping on the slate-paved floor. When they reached a dark oak door, bound with black metal strips, he halted. "I will see your things and your man settled." He bowed and opened the door.

Although less war-like, Downing's study nonetheless presented a severe decor. Walls papered a pale gray should have lightened the room considerably, had not the deep maroon carpet and the dark polished wood molding cast a somber pall over it. The gloom seeped into Tris's bones, weighing him down as soon as he entered.

"We expected you yesterday, Trevor." Lord Downing looked up from a letter he was writing, a frown on his deeply lined face.

"Snow held me up." Tris bristled, then plopped down in the chair opposite the man. He damn well didn't have to account for his time to his future father-in-law. "I lodged at The Angel in Woolhampton.

"Holman runs a decent establishment." Downing gave Tris a nod, whether to commend his choice or the publican remained unclear, then he returned to his document. The scratching of the pen warred with the loud, steady ticking of the longcase clock to his right.

If the man wasn't going to tell him why he'd been summoned before he could even wash and change, he could at least offer him a drink. Tris eyed the massive sideboard, where several decanters displayed tempting libations and licked his lips.

"Solmes thinks he can outlast me." Lord Downing placed his pen in the inkpot, shook pounce onto the sheet, gently swirled the letter then poured the sand back into the pounce pot. He raised the paper toward Tris. "I've had a bill in my pocket for well-nigh four years, just because Solmes wanted it passed. I suspect it will come up for a vote only if I die before him." He folded the piece of foolscap and held a stick of black sealing wax in the candle's flame.

The hiss as the fat drops of wax sizzled into the flame reminded Tris of the sound of searing flesh and he shivered again. God, he needed a drink.

"Now, Trevor," Lord Downing said as he dripped the molten wax onto the letter and plunged his signet ring into the puddle. "We have several matters to settle regarding your marriage to Dora." A narrow face and pinched nose made the viscount resemble a hawk. He turned furtive eyes that missed nothing on Tris. "There is an adequate property only a mile away from the Grange. I've made inquiries of old Leinster and he will be willing to sell it at a fair price."

"Indeed? Has it just come up for sale?" Did Downing need guidance on buying the estate? Had he been brought here to give business advice?

"It's not for sale." The pale, watery blue eyes gazed at him with thinly veiled contempt. "Leinster hasn't parted with an inch of land in twenty years. But I have sufficient inducement that assures me he'll sell it to you."

"Sell it to me?" Tris bolted upright in his chair. "I've no notion of buying an estate out here." His gut tightened. He sensed a trap closing around him.

"I doubt Dora will wish to leave her home or the society she's grown up in. I trust you will be willing to accommodate her wishes." The keen gaze sliced into Tristan's heart.

"Of course I will consult her, but it is fairly customary for a man's wife to leave her home and cleave to her husband, is it not?" He was not about to be coerced into burying himself in the country because his wife's father wanted him under his thumb.

"She can cleave to you just as well down here as elsewhere. However," Downing scratched his chin, "if you prefer not to purchase an estate quite yet, we can make arrangements to lodge you here at the Grange. Simon and his wife have been happy here for the past eight years."

Eight years. Tris's stomach lurched. Christ, but he needed that drink now. He'd be damned if he'd give up his freedom and live with this tyrant. "I believe that won't be necessary, my lord. I shall inquire of Dora at dinner as to her wishes in the matter." He shot to his feet, eager to quit his lordship in record time. "If you will excuse me, my lord, I will refresh myself before the dinner gong." He bowed and made himself saunter out the door. Damned if he'd run like a scared rabbit, but he'd never seen this side of Downing before. And he didn't like it one bit. What the hell had he gotten himself into?

* * * *

"Smithfield is overrated, if you ask my opinion."

After enduring Simon Harper's ongoing conversation during dinner, his opinion would be the last thing Tris would ask for. "I'll go to Barnet in April and come back with a horse that will stop everyone in their tracks."

Dinner had been family only, which didn't help to raise the pall Lord Downing's revelation had laid over Tris. Harper trying to monopolize his conversation had been abominably tedious.

Worse, he'd not been able to speak with Dora, even though she was his dinner partner. Every attempt to engage her had been thwarted by Simon. He'd been painfully aware of her presence, however. She'd worn an elegant rose-colored gown that accentuated the pink cheeks in her otherwise pale face. The ensemble, with her hair swept up on top of her head in a masterful coiffure, made her look older than eighteen, more womanly, which was encouraging. Still, she kept her head bent through most of the meal, avoiding his eyes. He'd managed a few remarks to her, all answered with a mumbled "Yes, my lord."

Frustration made him stab at the food on his plate, spearing hunks of potato and venison viciously, like a caveman on a hunt. He was willing to try to make their match work, but she had to make some effort on her part.

"Simon," Lord Downing fixed his son with a stern eye, "I received a bill today from Tanner's for a new post-chaise. I do not recall giving an order for such a conveyance. Pray, shed some light on this for me."

Harper's face went white then red. He turned to his father and Tris seized the reprieve to engage to Dora.

"Have you ridden in a post-chaise before?"

She tucked her golden head and whispered, "No, my lord. Only the family carriage."

Tris had to duck his head toward hers to catch the answer. He waited for her to elaborate, but nothing else seemed forthcoming. This would never do. She must talk about something or he'd never learn anything about her. If he could get a rise out of her there was a chance she'd forget her shyness for two minutes. "Perhaps your brother will take you out now that he's apparently ordered one." He indicated the end of the table where Downing and Harper were arguing bitterly over the carriage, Harper banging his hand on the table, raising his voice to be heard over his father's stentorian tones.

"I very much doubt it, my lord." Dora shook her head, her attention on the roll she was shredding onto her plate.

"Tris."

Startled, she raised wide blue eyes to him. "I beg pardon, my—"

"We agreed I would be Tris when we were *en famille.*" He grinned and her shoulders relaxed. Good.

"Very well then, Tris." She smiled at him and he caught his breath. The gentle curve of her lips lit her face in the loveliest way. Her cheeks pinked and her eyes crinkled in a charming fashion.

"You should smile more often, my dear. You are quite lovely when you do." Her face suffused with a deep red and she hastily grabbed her water glass.

"Why do you doubt he will take you riding?"

The light in her eyes extinguished as if snuffed by a cold wind. "Simon hates me." She set the glass down on the table with a dull thud.

Surprised by the anger in her voice, Tris leaned back in his chair. Dora had just become much more interesting.

"He has never done one nice thing for me my entire life, save marrying Judith." The liquid blue eyes turned to him again. "She has been my best friend since she came here. I'm sure if Simon had known we'd like each other so much he'd have married someone else." Abruptly, she returned her gaze to her plate. "I am so worried for her. She's been in poor health for so long. I don't know what I will do if...if..."

"Don't fret yourself, my dear." Tris covered her small white hand with his and gave it a pat. "The doctor has been tending to her, hasn't he?"

"Yes, but he cannot say what is wrong with her."

"Then we must pray very hard she recovers quickly enough to attend our wedding." He squeezed her hand and was rewarded with a fleeting smile.

"Yes, my...Tris."

With a laugh he picked up his wineglass. He was apparently marrying a neglected younger child. Not the heir, not possessed of a forthcoming nature, she'd likely been overlooked all her life. So a little attention might go far toward forging a bond between them. "I happen to have a post-chaise in my carriage house in London. When you're next in town I'll take you out. The world goes by very fast in a post-chase. They are rather sporty."

"Oh, I would like that so much." Though her smile was not as bright as before, still it transformed her face into beauty. "I love carriage rides almost as much as riding horseback."

"Do you enjoy riding, Dora?" He'd not have guessed that any more than her fondness for dancing. Apparently, he understood her as little as her family.

"I do. I have my own mare, Gretchen. I try to ride every day in good weather, but am forbidden to go out unless the ground is bare and dry."

"Why don't we ride out tomorrow after breakfast if it's still clear?" An excellent way to get his little bride-to-be alone, out from under the watchful eye of her family. "You can show me the estate and perhaps the village."

"Father won't allow me to go out with snow on the ground." She shook her head sadly, trying to smile. Her hands twisted the napkin in her lap.

"He thinks I cannot handle a horse if the ground is sloppy, even though I've ridden all my life."

"Leave the permissions to me." Tris shot a look down the table at her father, now talking amicably with his son. "As your betrothed I will demand you accompany me on pain of forfeiture of his best boots."

Dora sputtered with laughter.

She deserved a husband who could draw out her good nature and love her. He seemed to be the former, but could only hope, eventually, to be the latter as well. Several times during dinner his thoughts had wandered back to Violet. What was she doing? What was she practicing? Was she dancing with Donningham or some other fortunate suitor? He feared such images would never leave him.

Shaking off the melancholy that threatened to drape itself around him, Tris turned to his hostess. "Are you fond of riding, Lady Downing?"

"No, indeed, Lord Trevor. Give me a carriage every time, I say." She nodded so fiercely one of the combs securing her coiffure flew onto the table.

A footman leaped forward and retrieved it.

"Oh, how sad." Feigning a dour countenance, Tris sent his future mother-in-law a woeful glance. "I was going to ask you to join Dora and me on our ride tomorrow morning. I thought it would be a nice adventure to explore the countryside and get to know one another before the wedding."

"But the snow, Lord Trevor." The viscountess's eyes seemed to pop at him, like the frogs he used to gig as a boy.

Tris bit the inside of his mouth to stifle a laugh. "I assure you, my lady, I will take excellent care of your daughter."

With pursed lips, which only enhanced the froggy look of her, Lady Downing straightened her shoulders, laid her napkin next to her plate and rose. "Come, Dora. We will retire to have tea and leave the gentlemen to their brandy."

Dora rose obediently, but sent a merry smile at Tris before following her mother from the room.

Tris shook his head as Lord Downing poured a stingy dollop of brandy into a glass and handed it to him.

"Dora seems rather taken with you, Trevor." His lordship sipped his own libation before returning to his seat at the head of the table. "I don't think I've seen her so animated since…well, ever."

"Not that you pay her much mind, Father." Harper, who had downed his splash of spirits, rose and headed for the decanter. "Let me warn you, Trevor. She's a pathetic little mouse. Father should have told you what you were in for before he accepted your offer for her."

Surly pup. Tris gripped the fluted tumbler then tossed it off. He hadn't believed Dora when she'd said her brother hated her, although he might have been mistaken to do so. Never would he have dreamed of dishonoring one of his sisters so, and certainly not in his father's hearing. This Captain Hackum needed to be given his oatmeal. "Of course, I made her acquaintance before I offered for her, Harper. She suits me as she is, if it's any of your business."

"Oh, not my business at all." Throwing his head back with a laugh, Harper plopped himself down. "I've just always found her to be a mopus. But if that's to your taste, then have at her. Keep her out of my way and I won't give a damn."

"That will hardly be a problem, I think." Tris eyed the wretch, malice in his heart. "After our wedding trip we'll likely remove to London for the Season. I'll take my seat next session but as soon as that's through we'll head to Yorkshire. A visit to the property at Bromley, and then we'll settle in. You will likely not see your sister for some time." Never again if he could help it.

"Have you given no thought, then, to old Leinster's property?" Lord Downing's voice cut the air crisply. His chair screeched on the stone floor as he pushed it back.

"I have not consulted Dora yet, but I suspect she will be glad to spread her wings a bit and see other parts of England save London and Devizes." Tris forced himself to speak lightly. No need for a fight. After all, she'd be his wife. He could command her to go wherever he wished. But it would be a cold day in hell when he lived under Downing's roof. "As Lady Trevor she will be much in demand in Society. I will insist she take full advantage of her new position." And stay the hell out of her family's clutches.

Knuckles white, Lord Downing slammed his glass down so hard the candelabra in the center of the table jumped. "You had best remember your position, Trevor. Dora's a fragile girl who will not thrive far away from her home."

"In that I do hope to prove you wrong, my lord." Tris grinned into the red face. He grabbed the decanter and tipped the cognac in until it filled half the glass. "By the way, Dora and I will be riding around the estate tomorrow. A little tour to familiarize myself with the countryside. I'll be able to discuss the issue of our residence with her then."

Downing's face went purple. His eyes protruded almost from their sockets and one large vein in his neck bulged. Sputtering incomprehensibly, he stalked out of the dining room, the loud clicking of his heels echoing down the corridor.

"Whew." Harper whistled as he rose and snagged the brandy. "You've no fear of baiting the bear, have you, Trevor?"

"I won't be held hostage by a tyrant no matter if I have married his daughter." Tris gulped the remaining brandy, relishing the burn. He held his glass out. The evening would likely require more than one glass for him to survive.

"Well, you'll make my life a damn sight easier. The pater will be so set on dealing with you he won't come after me so often." Harper poured a generous amount into Tris's tumbler before filling his glass almost to the brim. "I wouldn't take up for Dora too much. She's always been a thorn in Father's side. Too shy, too awkward, not nearly as pretty as my other sisters."

Careful to keep his temper in check, Tris leaned back, sipping slowly. "You don't like your sister much, do you, Harper?" he drawled, aching to chalk the man one in the face.

"She's been my ruin since she was born."

"Come again?"

"My grandmother's money was meant to come to me. The old lady doted on me, even over my sisters. I would have inherited her estates in York and Brighton and a considerable fortune as well." He took a swallow, dribbling the spirits down his chin, then grimaced and wiped his mouth with this sleeve. "Until the day the little darling was born. The moment my mother named her for the old lady she had no use for anyone else."

"You've got the title and all your father's property coming to you. Why would you need more?" Greedy Turk.

Harper rolled his eyes. "One does need money in the meantime to go on with. I wouldn't have to be called on the carpet every time I spend a farthing. With that inheritance I could have bought a post-chaise for each day of the week." He leered at Tris. "Or I could set up residence in the best punch house in London. There are several girls I wouldn't mind patronizing on a regular basis."

Tris sputtered, mid-sip. Christ, did the man go to Vestry's? Could he know about Violet? He shot a glance at Harper, but he was busy emptying the decanter into his glass. Tris hadn't ever seen him at the House of Pleasure, but that meant nothing. Hopefully he patronized Madame Bontemp's establishment instead. She catered to more wanton tastes if rumor was correct. Best not make much of the comment. "You'll survive without Dora's inheritance, Harper. And you might have a thought for your wife's recovery rather than patronizing brothels."

"Huh. Wait until you've bedded Dora and then give me that advice." Harper's lip curled in an ugly sneer. "I wager you'll be in London and in bed with a cat inside a month of your marriage."

"I'd take that wager, but I won't dishonor my wife with even the contemplation of it." Enough was enough. Tris set his glass down and rose. "Good evening, sir." He strode from the room, shaking with rage at the slight to Dora and with a greater fear that Harper might prove right.

Chapter 22

Crisp air crackled in Tris's nose as he sat atop Rufus, Downing's roan gelding, surveying the five inches of fresh snow that sparkled over the front lawn of Harper's Grange next morning. A bracing morning for a ride. He hoped Dora lived up to her estimation of herself as a horsewoman. If not he'd feel like Jack Adams having gone on about how she'd be fine to ride out in the snow. Downing had grumbled, but finally acquiesced.

A slow *crunch, crunch* of hooves on the fresh snow carpet drew his attention to the corner of the manor. Dora rounded the side of the house on a gray mare who pranced and arched her neck, ears flicked forward.

She smiled and patted the gray's withers. "There, there Gretchen. We'll be away in no time." Seeing Tris, she nodded to him. "Good morning, my lord."

"It is always a good morning when I'm met with such a charming sight." His gaze swept her form from top to toe, taking in the trim figure in pale blue wool riding habit, trimmed in dashing gold braid. A fashionable small black tricorn, also trimmed in gold and cocked at a jaunty angle, perched on her golden hair. Her cheeks, already pink from the cold, grew even redder. She ducked her head and adjusted her grip on the reins.

"You are too kind, my lord." She surveyed him in turn, leaned toward him, her lips slightly parted, then hesitated and sat back in the saddle.

"Shall we view the estate first, then the village?" Tris hurried to fill the silence left by her unspoken comment. "We won't want to stay overlong out in the cold."

A shy smile and enthusiastic nod and he nudged his horse toward hers. They set out down the drive at a sedate walk. The countryside spread out around them, covered with a blanket of snow, reminded Tris of a particular sugary cake the family cook used to make. The clean expanse looked so pure he almost hated to mar it with their hoof prints.

"If you truly want to see the estate, we shall have to leave the road, my lord." Dora's voice sounded unusually loud in the cold air.

"By all means." Was she actually taking the lead?

"This way." With a practiced hand, Dora turned the mare to the left and struck out across the untouched lawn, urging her horse to a trot.

Tris gave her her head and followed, amazed at the change in his bride-to-be. Here with him she seemed more confident, more at ease.

They headed toward a stand of tall oaks on the perimeter of the parkland, passing a large pond, frozen solid. Particles of snow skittered across it in the brisk wind. Dora pulled her horse to a stop, waiting for him to catch up. "The pond is stocked in summer with all manner of fish—carp and pike mostly, I believe. Do you enjoy fishing, my lord?"

He had to chuckle. "Although I will eat it, I confess I have never attempted to actually catch one. Do you enjoy it, then?"

Shaking her head, she frowned at the frozen water. "I have never been allowed. At one time my father spoke of building a folly at one end." Dora waved toward the near bank. "I would have liked that. Perhaps I might have been permitted to sit there and watch the fishing." After she stared at the expanse of ice a moment longer, her brows puckered into a frown, then pulled her mount to the right. "Come, Gretchen." A gentle tap of her heel started the mare for the woods, once more at a trot.

Tris hung back, enjoying the sight of his bride-to-be handling the high-spirited animal with ease. There was more to Miss Dora Harper than met the eye. He urged Rufus into a trot to catch her up.

Reaching the line of trees, she halted, waiting for him, not impatient. Simply waiting. As though she'd been schooled to wait on other people's whims without complaint.

"This stand of oaks marks the boundary of the Grange on the north side of the property. The estate is some five hundred acres, so I doubt we can see it all today." She smiled and tapped Gretchen's flank, heading them into the trees. "I've always thought this a pretty wood. So leafy and green in spring and summer. And a blaze of color in autumn." Her eyes sparkled and she motioned to the trees before her. "Even in winter they are beautiful. Black lace on white."

"I agree," Tris said, pulling alongside her. "Very pretty indeed."

Startled, she jerked her head toward him, her body tensing as for a blow.

Why was she so skittish? Reassuringly, he smiled and patted her hand. "I am only sorry I shall take you away from it."

Dora gazed down at his hand on hers. "I will not mind much, I think."

"No? Your father seemed to think you would prefer to continue to live at home after we marry. Either at the Grange or on a neighboring estate."

She stiffened, her lips thinning until they resembled a pink slash across her face. "He is mistaken, my lord."

"Tris, please, Dora." He gave her hand a little shake, then drew his away. Still, he needed to be quite sure. "You are certain you would not prefer to stay here? Your father has even made enquiries about an estate close by."

"You may be assured, I will be most happy to remove to your estate, Tris." A fleeting curl of her lips passed for a smile. "It is in Yorkshire I believe my father said."

"My principle estate is, yes. I live in London most of the year, where I have a townhouse in Mayfair. After the wedding, I thought we might journey to Italy for some months."

"To Italy?" Her voice rose almost to a squeak.

"It is a lovely country and I would like very much to show it to you. When we return we'll journey to Yorkshire." He took her gloved hand between both of his and placed a warm kiss on it. "Perhaps you will find it as lovely as this estate."

A slow, satisfied smile spread across her face and she grasped his hand. "That sounds wonderful, Tris."

Her horse stamped. Almost reluctantly, she let go Tris's hand and clucked to Gretchen, patting the animal's neck. "I cannot wait to see Yorkshire. Is the estate large?"

"Almost two thousand acres."

"Goodness." Gathering her reins, she stared off into the distance. "The temperature is dropping. Let us head to the village."

"Should we perhaps return to the house?" He had an idea what her answer would be, still he'd ask.

"Oh, I believe we can pay a short visit," she spoke quickly, slipping her reins through her fingers over and over. "If we're in luck, Mrs. Pierce will have some warm bannocks in her shop. They are quite the best I've ever had."

"I cannot wait to taste one." Tris motioned for her to take the lead. "Would you like to hear more about my estate? You will be mistress there soon."

Her blue eyes matched the sky. "I'd like that very much."

Once they cleared the woods, Tris pulled the roan up beside her and they started at a brisk walk. "The estate is called Marshall Manor, on the border of Cumbria. A lovely prospect in summer, but the Dales are fierce in winter." He eyed her and nodded. "I think you'll love it."

* * * *

Finishing Mrs. Pierce's warm bannocks, which were every bit as good as Dora claimed, Tris marveled at all the people who seemed to know of their visit to the village. Before he'd taken a bite out of the delicious bread, slathered with fresh butter, half the populace seemed to have entered the baker's shop. They admired Mrs. Pierce's new grandson, swaddled and in his mother's arms, spoke to the head crofter, Mr. Craddock and two of his six daughters. Young Jimmy Vyne arrived to purchase bannocks and stayed to talk about the spring crops while Tris's toes froze in his boots.

He finally urged Dora outdoors, and toward her mount, when she spied a black and white dog, bounding over the drifts.

"Jasper!" she called, backing away from her horse and kneeling to embrace the shaggy shepherd. "Where have you come from?" She peered around, then glanced at Tris, brows puckered. "He belongs to old Mr. Blake, but I don't see him anywhere. I hope nothing is wrong." Fending off Jasper's enthusiastic advances, Dora continued searching for sight of his master.

"Does Mr. Blake live in the village?" Tris asked, grabbing the reins of both horses. He, too, scanned the fields and roadway for sight of the dog's master.

"No, he lives at one of the outlying farms." She rose, her brows set in a deep V. "I hope he's not ill. Jasper's usually right at his side."

"Shall we ride out to his farm to check on him?" Tris took measure of the sun's position. Much as he commended Dora's concern about her tenants, the shadows of afternoon lay deep on the snow. He wouldn't want to be caught far from the manor house after dark. "We may just have time before tea."

"Yes, thank you." Cheeks pink with the cold, she flashed him another brilliant smile that went straight to his heart. "It would put my mind at ease." She loosed Jasper and Tris cupped his hands for her to mount.

The small foot, encased in shiny black leather, made him smile unaccountably. She would be a gracious and caring viscountess for his estates. Guilt assailed him for taking her away from the people she obviously loved and who loved her, still he'd be damned if he settled here. He had his own people to think of. Dora settled into place and Tris grabbed his horse, preparing to mount, when a loud call of "Halloo, Jasper," rent the air.

"Mr. Blake?" Dora twisted in the saddle.

Yipping, Jasper raced toward an ancient board wagon pulled by a small pony just rounding the corner of the baker's shop. The elderly little man at the reins could be no one but Mr. Blake. His worn brown coat, threadbare in places, barely seemed to cover his diminutive frame. His face lit up at the site of Dora. "Miss Harper it is. I've not seen your lovely face these two months. A Merry Christmas to you."

"And to you, Mr. Blake. I was surprised to see Jasper and not you." At once, Dora slid nimbly out of her saddle to the ground. "I never see one without the other."

"Aye, well, Jasper's a sight faster 'an me these days." He ruffled the fur on the excited dog's ruff. "He's always loved boundin' through the snow."

They continued speaking, but Tris heard nothing.

Christmas. Christ, had it only been three days since he'd seen Violet? It seemed a year at least. The fleeting contentment he'd enjoyed with Dora vanished like a snowflake in the sun. Much as he was coming to admire his future wife, his heart twisted at the thought of the woman he'd left in London. The woman he might never see again but would never forget. His love, his soul.

"My lord?"

Dora's raised voice finally penetrated his reverie. Focusing on her once again, he found her staring at him oddly.

Mr. Blake glanced from her to him with raised eyebrow.

Damn. He refused to let his lack of self-control hurt his future wife. She deserved better than that. Better than him. "My pardon, Miss Harper, Mr. Blake. I was woolgathering, I fear. Are you ready to go, my dear?"

Giving him a wary look, she nodded slowly.

He tossed her up onto Gretchen again, and swiftly mounted Rufus.

Mr. Blake eased himself down out of the seat and slowly tethered his pony. He called to Jasper, who bounded to his side, wide doggy smile and wagging tail declaring his happiness. Blake raised a hand in farewell, then picked his way carefully into Mrs. Pierce's establishment.

"Shall we head home for tea?" Tris gathered his reins then turned to Dora.

The wide smile and animated face had gone, leaving in its place the thin-lipped woman of the morning. She wanted to return to Harper's Grange about as much as she wanted to shoot Jasper. Well, she wouldn't have to live there much longer. He would take her away from her awful family as soon as he possibly could. If he couldn't love her, he could at least do that for her.

By the time they arrived at the front of the manor, the light had faded from the western sky, leaving it deep lavender tinged with a pink edge where the sky kissed the earth. Tris hoped Lord Downing hadn't sent out a search party for them. The closer they had gotten to the house, the more Dora had withdrawn from his attempts at conversation. A scolding from her father might finish the job, leaving her sullen and silent for the rest of the night. They dismounted at the portico and he grasped her hand to tuck it in his arm. The chill that emanated from her body made him shiver.

"My dear, you are frozen." He chaffed her hand, willing the stiff fingers inside her gloves to warm. "Come, we must get you inside and before the fire."

"Oh, no, my lord. I will go directly to my room. Larkin will see to me." She clutched his arm.

"You don't think you should see your parents first? We are so late they may be quite worried." Staving off possible protest, he rapped on the door and when it opened, strode in before the butler could swing it wide. "Where are the family currently, Eccles?"

"In the large drawing room, my lord." Eccles shut the door and indicated the stairs to the first floor.

Tris flowed forward, bringing a now shivering Dora along with him. They'd shed their outerwear in the foyer and the house was quite cool. He hoped they had a good fire going. They both needed to thaw out. He squeezed Dora's hand. "It will be fine. I insist on taking all the blame on myself." He searched her pale face, noting feverish pink splotches. "I only pray you have not taken a chill. I could never forgive myself if I have been an agent to harm you in any way."

She smiled at that, though it paled in comparison to her earlier brilliance.

He steered her into the drawing room they had occupied last night, braced for the explosion. Tension in the room pricked the hairs on the back of his neck immediately. There seemed to be half a dozen people present, although in truth there were only three.

Lord Downing, Lady Downing, and Simon Harper clustered around the sideboard. The men held full glasses of port; Lady Downing looked longingly at the decanter while sipping her tea.

"That's the second one in three months, Simon." Lord Downing's florid face deepened as his eyes bulged. "I'll not stand for this kind of behavior anymore."

"Dora, where have you been?" Setting her cup down, Lady Downing rushed to her daughter. "We were quite worried." She cut her gaze toward her husband.

"We stayed overlong in the village, Mama," Dora said, making a beeline for the fireplace.

"That is no excuse for putting the household in an uproar." Her father glared at her, then emptied his glass. "What were you doing in the village?"

"She was showing me all about the estate, my lord," Tris answered smoothly in her stead, following her to the fire. This was one damsel he'd be able to rescue. "I must take the blame for our late appearance. I'm afraid we tarried eating Mrs. Pierce's excellent bannocks. We were also chatting with many of your tenants and cottagers." He eyed Downing, gauging the depth of the man's ire. It might be his own perception, but the man seemed more on edge than their tardiness allowed for. Certainly they knew he'd been with Dora and would let nothing happen to her. "No harm done. We are back safely in time for dinner."

Downing shot another angry look at Harper who flushed and took a long pull at his glass as well.

"Is anything else amiss?" Certainly, something more than their tardiness was afoot.

"Just a little domestic upset," Lady Downing answered, wringing her hands. "Miss Giles, the governess, has left, without word or reason. She didn't even stay long enough to receive the wages coming to her."

"Huh. Knew she wouldn't get a farthing from me." Downing poured another hefty libation, sloshing the tawny liquid into the glass with an unsteady hand. Spots of mottled pink smudged his cheeks. "That's why she stole away."

"I am sorry to hear that." Dora ventured to put a word in. "She was always nice to me when I went to the nursery and seemed genuinely fond of Anna. I wonder what upset her." She rubbed her hands then held them out to the fire. "Did she receive bad news, perhaps?"

"We have no idea, my dear," Lady Downing replied, tsk, tsking across the room to the teapot where she poured tea into the waiting cups. "We knew nothing until Mrs. Lane came in to tell us not half an hour ago that Miss Giles had demanded a carriage to take her to Devizes, where she could catch the mail coach back to London. Tea, Lord Trevor?"

"Yes, thank you, my lady." Leaving the fire reluctantly, Tris accepted a cup.

"Clark is going to get the sack for that too." Downing clenched his fists. "He should have asked permission before stirring a step. We might have found out the reason behind Miss Giles' treachery."

"Surely not treachery, my lord." Raising an eyebrow, Tris settled himself on the sofa and sipped the hot tea gratefully. He was chilled to the bone and not only by the weather outside. "Miss Giles must have had a good reason for her precipitous flight."

"I daresay she finally got fed up with Anna's little tricks," Harper spoke up, staring into his drink. "She can be a little terror when she wants to be."

"Simon." His mother shook her head, her mouth drawn. "Dora, stop standing there and come get your tea."

"Simon, how can you say such things?" Dora stared at her brother, a scowl marring her face. She took the proffered cup, but didn't drink. "Anna is a perfectly sweet child. I have cause to know." A glance at Tris and some of the tension left her face. "Miss Jones' departure in November put me in charge of her for two weeks. We had a lovely time together."

"Well, then, how do you explain Giles' flight today?" Simon rounded on her. "You don't know anything about it, Dora. You shouldn't speak when you have no idea what you're talking about."

"Perhaps one of the servants upset her. Here, Dora, come sit by me." Lady Downing patted the sofa beside her. "I will inquire of the housekeeper, Mrs. Lane."

"Whatever the reason, we are left once again without a governess." Pacing like a tiger, Simon stalked back to the sideboard. "Children and servants can be a terrible nuisance, Trevor. Be sure you have both well in control."

"I'll be sure to take that into consideration, Harper." Tris eyed him askance. His brother-in-law seemed strung tight as a bow over the departure of a governess.

"Dora, you will have to take over as governess to Anna until other arrangements can be made." Lady Downing nodded as she sipped. "She seemed to respond well to you last time."

"That is fine, Mama. You know I don't mind. I like children very much." She smiled shyly, her gaze on Tris.

"Because you are a child yourself, Dora." Her father snorted into his drink.

"I beg to disagree, Lord Downing." Tris sent a warm smile back to his betrothed. "I'm glad the future mother of my children will enjoy caring for them. Dora is a kind and gentle woman who has very maternal instincts." In truth, Dora had shown today she could be both womanly and compassionate, hardly the child he'd mistaken her for in November. Perhaps her impending marriage had changed her. He smothered a laugh. Or he'd simply misjudged her.

"I hope you find her so when the time comes." Lord Downing snorted, completely oblivious to the presence of his daughter. "In any event, Trevor, what about this relation of yours. Will she do?"

"What relation?" When had he lost the thread of the conversation? "And do for what?"

"You told me some time ago a relative of yours was in need of a position as companion or governess." Scowling, Downing peered at him. "So is the woman engaged elsewhere or not? We need a governess for Anna at once."

If he hadn't already swallowed his mouthful of tea he'd have choked. He coughed, sputtered and sucked in a breath. The man wanted Violet.

Damn. His heart beat like a drum as he strove to answer nonchalantly. "I believe you are referring to Miss Carlton, a very distant relation, who is nevertheless dear to me." Surreptitiously, he cut his eyes toward Dora, but she was deep in conversation with her mother.

"I don't care about her name, Trevor. Can she come immediately is the question?"

He'd rarely been in a situation so fraught with peril. The position was exactly what Violet had been looking for, what she needed to be able to survive. Yet how could he bring her here, see her every day, at least until he married, and not acknowledge her? Still, if she were a governess he'd likely have little chance to see her. Knowing she was under the same roof would likely drive him to madness, but if that was the price he had to pay to provide a position for her, then he'd manage it somehow.

Oh, but it was folly. How could he withstand being always near her and never with her? Even worse, could he keep his feelings for Violet hidden from Dora? Could he risk it to give Violet her chance? Damned if he did and damned if he didn't.

"Why yes, Lord Downing. Miss Carlton is available, or she was when I left London." He forced himself to speak calmly. "Shall I write to her extending the offer?"

"Yes, thank God." Downing's voice boomed and echoed in the chamber.

Tris nodded and, with a stricken glance at Dora, hurried to the door. He sprinted to his room, cursing Downing, Dora, Violet, and himself.

God help them all.

Chapter 23

Violet sat in the music room, staring at the curt note she clutched, her head spinning as she tried to stop her hands from shaking. She'd recognized Tris's handwriting and broken the seal with a pop that shot it into the air. Hungry for news of him after nearly a week, she'd almost torn the paper unfolding it. The summons to Harper's Grange, however, had left her troubled and wary.

The offer of a position as governess to Lord Downing's granddaughter was as manna from heaven. The Lord had obviously answered her daily prayers for a respectable position. She smoothed out the cream-colored paper again, running her fingers over the masculine script, afraid to feel elated. Did she truly want to take this position? There were pitfalls whatever choice she made.

Spending the better part of four days sitting idly, reading, or practicing on piano or harp had convinced her she must find some employment to keep her occupied. Mrs. Parker had offered to teach her some of her best baking secrets, so yesterday she'd made a valiant attempt at an apple tart. After one bite of the misshapen, blackened thing, she dumped it in the trash bin. "I wouldn't even feed it to the pigs—if we had any," she'd confided to Susan.

There must be something she could do to be useful and earn her living. Perhaps she should take up her needle again. She might find employment with one of the other mantua makers. And now here the ideal position had presented itself, and she hesitated.

She'd never taken care of children before, true, but surely she could teach one little girl all the things she'd been taught. The letter didn't mention why the post had come open, but she doubted the child herself was the issue. If so, she could certainly manage a six-year-old.

No, the true reason she hesitated was Tris. If she became governess at Lord Downing's estate, she'd most likely have to see Tris again on a regular basis and in the company of his betrothed. At least until their wedding. Could she bear being in such proximity to him without exposing her feelings to him or anyone there?

A shattering pain struck her heart. To see him, knowing him beyond her reach, would cause agonies enough. To see the woman who would be his wife smile at him, look adoringly at him, take his arm by right, and show her possession of him might be more than she could bear. Her body ached, every muscle tensed against the pain. No, she would send to Tris tomorrow telling him to thank Lord Downing, but she must refuse his kind offer.

"Susan," she called. The maid hovered incessantly these days, never out of earshot. As though she expected her mistress to vanish, like a magician's assistant. Of course, she had good reason to do so.

Sure enough, before the echo of her name faded, Susan appeared. "Yes, miss?"

"Fetch my pen and ink, please."

Once the girl had gone, Violet sat to the harpsichord, fidgeting with the keys. She worried her bottom lip, pulling it until it bled. Trish would be furious with her. They'd been waiting for just such a respectable position for so long. It offered the chance to go on with her life with honor. Did she have the right to refuse it?

"Here it is, miss." Susan laid pen, inkpot, and paper on the top of the spinet, the creamy sheet a stark contrast to the shining dark wood.

Violet nodded and flexed her fingers. She'd been practicing all morning. Her fingers should be limber by now, yet they acted stiff as pikes. "Thank you, Susan," she said, giving a wave of dismissal. She would write this letter alone.

"Shall I pack your belongings, Miss Carlton?"

Violet jerked her head up, the pen tumbling from her fingers. "How did you know I'm to leave, Susan?" Had her maid been snooping in her mail?

"Lord Trevor sent a note instructing me to pack your clothes and accompany you to Devizes, miss." Susan peered oddly at her. "Has he told you differently?"

"No, I...I'd simply no idea he'd written you as well." Then he assumed she'd take the position, expected her to take it. A wave of sadness washed over her. This truly was the end of his relations with her. She must take it with as good a grace as she could muster and move on.

Straightening in her chair, her back now like a ramrod, she grabbed the pen and dipped it in the ink so furiously drops flew willy-nilly across the spinet. "Here." She scribbled a dozen words, blew across the paper, folded it and handed it to Susan. "Have Thomas post this immediately. Tell him to make sure it is on the next mail coach to Wiltshire." She thrust it into the maid's hands as if it burned her.

Through narrowed eyes, Susan shifted her attention from her mistress to the letter.

"As soon as Thomas is off, come to my chamber. We have much to do if I am to leave tomorrow." The catch in her voice hurt abominably.

"Very good, miss." The girl stared at her dry-eyed, but her lips trembled. A nod and she hurried from the room.

Violet rose from the bench, an air of unreality descending on her. She would leave tomorrow, never to return. Her hand rested on the polished wood of the spinet and she rubbed over the smooth, shiny surface lovingly. She would miss it so much. She cursed herself for being a terrible coward. Rather than bend to his will she should have been able to stand firm and sever the ties between them. If such a thing were even possible.

* * * *

The raging fire in the formal drawing room at Harper's Grange had done its job too well. Violet stood before Lord and Lady Downing, beads of perspiration trickling between her breasts. Her hands, however, anchored in the folds of her sapphire blue gown to keep them from trembling, were icy.

"Miss Carlton? You are Lord Trevor's cousin, I believe he said?" Lord Downing's bushy gray eyebrows rose slightly.

"A distant relationship, my lord. Although he has been kind enough to assist me in my search for a position." Violet smiled then thought better of it for fear his lordship might think her frivolous. His stern visage certainly held no such sign. "The death of my grandmother left me quite alone."

Lady Downing, however, a fluttering bird-like woman in dove gray who perched on the edge of the sofa, gave her a wavering smile. "Lord Trevor is such a thoughtful young man."

"Let us be to the point, Miss Carlton." Lord Downing broke in, giving his wife a withering look. "Have you prior experience with children? I would not wish to place my only grandchild in the hands of an unqualified governess."

His lordship's narrow nose and thin lips sent a shiver of foreboding cascading down Violet's back. Still, she must forget everything except securing this position. Planting her feet firmly, she met Lord Downing's eyes. "This will be the first such position for which I have applied, my lord. Until earlier this year I was companion to my grandmother, Lady Crenshaw."

"Edwina Crenshaw?" Lady Downing broke in excitedly. "I hadn't heard she had died."

"No, my lady. Her first name was Aurelia. She was the widow of Sir Robert Crenshaw, of Headley Hall in Essex." Fervently, Violet prayed her ladyship was not acquainted with her grandmother. If she could keep them from finding out about the scandal with her brother, she'd have a much better chance of securing this position. They hadn't seemed to recognize her name, which boded well for keeping that secret.

"Oh." Lady Downing looked disappointed, but shook her head. "No, I am afraid we were not acquainted."

Violet released a grateful breath. "She became increasingly reclusive after my grandfather's death almost twenty years ago. I cared for her until her death in March. After a suitable period of mourning, I contacted Lord Trevor for assistance."

Lady Downing tapped her lips with her forefinger. "Did I not see you at the Braeton's Christmas ball?"

"Yes, my lady, you may indeed have." Violet's stomach twisted, but she forced herself to maintain a pleasant demeanor. "I had made the acquaintance of Miss Forsythe earlier in the season. She asked her cousin, Lady Braeton, to invite me." Dreading where the conversation seemed to be heading, she cast her gaze to the floor.

"Trying to secure a title, Miss Carlton?" His black eyes staring her down, Lord Downing leaned back on the sofa, his lips twisted in a smirk.

"I had hoped to marry, yes, my lord. As is every woman's duty." Heart in her throat, Violet struggled to remain calm. "A titled gentleman was not a requirement. Unfortunately, I have not been so fortunate as to secure the affections of a respectable man. Therefore, when Lord Trevor told me of your current difficulty, I thought it could be another way for me to lead a useful life." If they would not have her, God knew what she would do. Perhaps take Susan up on the offer of an introduction in her village. Glancing from the harsh lines of Lord Downing's visage to the nervous fluttering of Lady Downing, she began to hope for rejection.

"Have you ever had charge of children before, Miss Carlton? Younger brothers or sisters, perhaps?" Head cocked, Lady Downing leaned forward, a gleam in her eyes.

"I am sorry, my lady, but no. I was the youngest in my family." Violet bit her lip, thinking furiously. "I did have charge of the children of our church one year." That much was true, although the sum total had been two little girls. Still, she had been in charge of them at the age of ten.

"You managed them with no incident?" Her ladyship's beady eyes flitted toward her husband, then back to Violet.

"Yes, my lady. We got on well, no trouble whatsoever." Apparently, the tide of opinion was turning with Lady Downing. "I thought at the time I would enjoy having children of my own one day."

Her ladyship gave a curt nod of her head and rose. "Then I believe this interview is at an end, Miss Carlton."

"What?" Lord Downing jumped to his feet. "What do you mean, my dear?"

"I think Miss Carlton will do excellently as governess to Anna." His lady gestured toward the door. "If you will come with me, Miss Carlton, I will introduce you to your charge."

"Harriet, you are too…too… hasty," Lord Downing sputtered, scowling at Violet.

"Nonsense." With a dismissive wave of her hand toward her husband, the lady continued toward the door.

"She has almost no experience. She won't be able to handle the child." Lord Downing trailed behind them, his face reddening to the color of brick.

"I see no reason why she couldn't try." Lady Downing shot him a look that made Violet hastily revise her opinion of the viscountess. The woman had a lot more steel in her than her looks gave on.

Violet expected further argument from his lordship, but Lady Downing silenced him by leading her out of the room, leaving her husband behind, fuming silently. She could hear the heavy breathing diminish as she followed her ladyship down the corridor to a different part of the house.

"The nursery is in the east wing," Lady Downing said over her shoulder. "You will have a classroom for Anna's lessons. Her bedchamber is next to it with your chamber beyond. Did you bring your belongings?"

"Yes, my lady. They are in the carriage, but my…companion can see to their removal if you think I will suit." As she strode after the viscountess, Violet managed to take in the quiet cream-colored walls, the gold carpets, and the rich tones of the artwork hung at intervals along the corridor. Most were landscapes that brought the beauty of the outdoors into the house.

"These paintings are wonderful, Lady Downing." She paused to examine one depicting a riot of trees in bold autumn golds and reds. "Such excellent brush strokes. One thinks one is gazing out a window." Violet had taken drawing lessons when she was younger, but music had been where her talents lay and she had turned her attention to her instruments. Still, she could recognize superior talent when she saw it. "Are these your work, my lady?" Each painting was signed with the initials DIH only.

"No, no, Miss Carlton." Lady Downing's voice held a touch of pride, despite her denial. "These are the works of my daughter, Dora. She has always excelled in water colors."

Violet's heart lurched so badly her face twisted against the sudden pain. She tried to mask it by stopping to peer at another picture. Lord, she needed to sit down before her legs gave way. Nonsense. She gritted her teeth and locked her knees. If she was going to live in the same house as Tris's fiancée, she had better get used to hearing her name. Steel herself for the inevitable meeting. She had just missed an introduction to Miss Harper at the Braeton's Christmas ball. That would have been even more awkward, now she was employed by the girl's family. Decidedly awkward in any case. Perhaps tucked away here in the east wing she would not see either Miss Harper or Tris very much. A blessing and a curse. At least she could hope to settle in and get her bearings before stirring up a hornet's nest in her heart.

After a moment to compose herself, she continued down the corridor with Lady Downing. They arrived at the nursery door.

"Sweetheart?" Lady Downing called. "Grandmamma is here with a nice new lady for you to play with. Won't that be ever so much fun?" She pushed the latch and the door swung open into a cozy room, the soft pink walls glowing in the bright afternoon sun. A small girl, dressed in a gown a shade or two lighter than the walls, had been sitting by the fireplace, a doll in her lap. She looked up, her round, cherubic face bursting into a wide smile. Fine porcelain skin, red cheeks, and golden curls made the child look like a doll herself.

"Grandmamma!" She ran to Lady Downing and threw her arms around her. "Come listen to the story Aunt Dora is telling me. All about a knight who rescues a fair maiden from a terrible castle and the two ogres who are holding her captive."

Violet stopped dead, her face draining of blood so quickly she clutched the doorframe to keep from fainting. Her gaze skipped from Anna, tugging Lady Downing toward the fireplace, to the figure sitting in the other armchair. Another blond head, this one belonging to an older girl with a sweet face and worried eyes. Violet's chest tightened and she forced herself to breathe.

Miss Harper's gaze fell on her and her shoulders relaxed. She smiled and nodded, then turned her attention back to her mother and niece.

Violet's heart gave a terrible thump, then resumed its normal beating. Her breathing too seemed easier, thank goodness. Perhaps she would get through the next minutes without disgracing herself.

"Anna, Dora, come meet Miss Violet Carlton. She will be your new governess, Anna. Make your curtsey, my love." Lady Downing beamed as the child bobbed a short curtsey, her skirts held out awkwardly at her sides.

"How do you do, Miss Carlton?" Anna spoke carefully, looking at her with frankly inquisitive eyes.

This was the unruly child who had driven off two governesses?

"I am quite well, thank you, Anna. How are you today?" Aware of the eyes on her, Violet forced herself to focus on her charge only.

"Oh, Aunt Dora and I have been having such fun," she said, her sweet high voice hinting at giggles. She smiled in delight at her aunt. "We've been telling stories and singing songs." Her brows puckered. "Will we still be able to do that, Miss Carlton?"

Immediately, Violet crouched down before the thin child and smiled at her. "I believe we can manage stories and songs as well as other lessons. Do you know your numbers?"

"Of course I do. I can count all the way up to twenty." The shiny blond head nodded fiercely.

"I see. That's very good. But can you count it in French?" She studied the grave face and watched it fall.

"No." Shaking her head, Anna sighed. "I don't know how to do that at all."

"Well," Violet said, holding out her hand. "I can teach you. There's a counting game I know where you tell stories about the numbers in French. Would you like to play it with me?"

The cherub's smile returned. "Oh, yes, please." She grabbed Violet's hand and pulled her toward the fire. "I love to play games."

They sat together, the heat of the flames finally bringing some feeling back into Violet's frozen fingers. "Very well. First, let me hear your numbers in English."

As Anna began, Violet glanced up to catch Lady Downing's eye, trying to gauge her acceptance. The room, however, was empty save for her and her student, although the memory of the beautiful blond Miss Harper lingered, like a ghost in the air, unseen but felt like a cold hand on her heart.

Chapter 24

"Mind your sleeve, Anna. Don't get it in the jam." Violet pushed back the endangered garment and poured herself another cup of tea. Her third day as Anna's governess found her rather proud of how well they had been getting along. And how easily she seemed to fit the role.

The first day the little girl had been shy and withdrawn, surprising Violet because of the easy way Anna had accepted her the day before. Violet made sure to keep a pleasant but firm tone as they went through their lessons, ending with the story of The Little Glass Slipper. The next day at tea, Anna offered Violet some of her cake, which Violet took and praised her for her good manners. Today Anna bubbled with chatter, asking Violet all kinds of questions, and showing off her skills in reading and sums.

Violet sipped her tea and shook her head, staring at the six-year-old in total bewilderment. How could anyone think this precious child incorrigible? A sweeter girl she'd never seen.

A maid entered to clear away the tea things. Violet sighed contentedly until she glanced up to find Miss Harper in the doorway. Her throat closed as if a hand had seized it. She leaped to her feet, banging her knee on the low table so hard it made the dishes dance.

"Miss Harper. What a pleasant surprise." Lord, but she'd been dreading this encounter. Jealousy and guilt hammered her heart by turns. She'd slept with this woman's betrothed. Was in love with him as well. How could she speak a word and not let on?

"Aunt Dora." Anna ran to her, flinging her arms around her.

Pray God Miss Harper never found out her feelings. Such treachery could scarcely be forgiven. Therefore, she must play her part as well as any actress in a Covent Garden theatre. She straightened her dress and gazed expectantly at the younger woman.

"Oh, I am sorry." Miss Harper nodded at her skirt, presumably where her knee still smarted, while held in Anna's death grip.

"It's nothing, really." Violet's gaze darted around the room, making sure all was tidy. It wouldn't do for her to appear disorderly. "Anna, you must greet people properly and not attack them as if you were a savage from darkest Africa."

"Have you come to play with us, Aunt Dora?" Reluctantly, Anna let go of her aunt's waist. "We've had a lovely morning tea party with all my dolls." She pouted her lips. "But you've come too late for tea."

"I see that, poppet." A soft gleam in her eyes, Miss Harper took the small chin in her hand. "I'll have tea with you one day very soon, if Miss Carlton is agreeable." She shot Violet a questioning look.

"Yes, of course." Violet nodded, her head spinning. Her stomach twisted even as she smiled. She suspected entertaining Miss Harper would be akin to swallowing glass, but Anna's peaked face lit up in joy at the suggestion. If Miss Harper wanted to eat jam and bread with them, she'd brave it out somehow.

"Hello, darling. How is my pet?" Simon Harper's voice, coming unexpectedly, startled Violet so badly she staggered toward the fireplace.

"Simon." Miss Harper seemed as happy to see him as Violet. "Whatever are you doing here?"

"Can't a man look in on his only daughter from time to time without being a nine-days wonder?" He swung Anna up into his arms, making her squeal with laughter. "Miss Carlton won't mind, I'm sure." His gaze trailed over Violet's face, a flicker of interest that extinguished itself immediately.

"Of course not, Mr. Harper." Violet noted the delight on Anna's face. "You must come visit Anna whenever you can spare a moment. You seem to have made her very happy today."

Arms around her father's neck, Anna giggled and laid her head on his shoulder. "You can come have tea with Miss Carlton and Aunt Dora and Countess Hepplewhite and Princess Beatrice. And me."

"Who are Countess Hepplewhite and Princess Beatrice, poppet?" Mr. Harper grinned at his daughter. He seemed very devoted to the child.

"My dolls, of course, Papa." The little girl snuggled against him. "They would love for you to come to tea tomorrow. Ever so much they would."

Violet struggled to keep from smiling at Mr. Harper's look of alarm. She'd have company in the nursery tomorrow. She'd lay a wager on it.

"Well, we shall see, my love." He kissed the pale face and set her down. "I don't expect it would be much trouble, would it, Miss Carlton?"

"None whatsoever, Mr. Harper. Shall we expect you as well, Miss Harper?"

"I don't…" Miss Harper glanced from Anna to her brother, her gaze finally coming to rest on Violet. "Yes, I believe I will come as well."

"Hmph." Mr. Harper narrowed his eyes at his sister and strode from the room.

"Oh, goody." Anna clapped her hands. "We will have a party." Her round face and blue eyes peeking out from beneath her white mob cap made her look more like a cherub than ever.

"I suppose it shall be, lovey." Miss Harper took Anna's hand, drawing her toward the warmth of the fire. Her gaze met Violet's and she shrugged. "Quite a party indeed."

* * * *

"Shall I give you more tea, Lady Hepplewhite?" With exaggerated motions, Anna pretended to pour into her doll's cup.

Tea with Anna and her guests had proved a pleasant surprise for Violet.

"Oh, no more for me, my dear," Anna answered in a squeaky voice.

Miss Harper smiled, delighted with her niece. She held out her cup. "I, however, will take some more from Miss Carlton's teapot, if you please."

"Certainly." Violet lifted the pot and poured with a steadier hand than she expected. About halfway through the party, she'd finally stopped trembling at Miss Harper's presence. The girl obviously had no idea of her liaison with Tris. Of course, he would never have divulged such a thing to his bride-to-be. Even so, her cheeks kept heating at the slightest provocation. She bent her head over the teapot to hide them. "Would you like more as well, Mr. Harper?"

"No, I fear I must leave you now." He touched Anna's golden curls and sighed. "There's some business Grandpapa has asked me to do, poppet."

Anna's mouth turned downward like a waterspout. Her brows lowered in a dark frown. "But you promised."

"Yes, and I have kept that promise, lovey. I have taken Miss Carlton's excellent tea with you, and Aunt Dora, and Princess Hepplewhite." He glanced at Violet, his gaze lingering on her a beat too long. "Thank you, Miss Carlton."

"Her name is *Countess* Hepplewhite." The girl poked her bottom lip out, two tears rolling down her face.

"I beg your pardon, Countess," Mr. Harpers said, rising to bow to the doll propped up beside Anna.

"No, Papa. Don't go." Anna jumped to her feet and threw her arms around her father's legs. "I don't want you to go."

"Thank you, my love." He lifted his daughter in his arms, hugging her to him. His gaze met Violet's. "Then I certainly must come again, shan't I?" Anna nodded and burrowed her wet face into his shoulder.

"Good. I shall look forward to it." Kissing the top of the golden head, he set her on the floor. "I will return another day and stay longer for more tea." He bowed to his sister. "Dora."

The sneering tone caught Violet off guard. She stared at him, unsettled by the thinly veiled contempt in his voice.

"Miss Carlton, good day." Mr. Harper stalked out of the room without a backward glance.

"Papa." Anna's forlorn face brought Violet out of her trance.

"Come, my dear. Let's have a story and then a nap. If you're good and go straight to sleep, we will go out into the garden and make a snowman when you awake." She held her hand out to the woebegone little girl, who looked as if she would burst into tears anew, but instead she gulped and took her hand. With a nod to Miss Harper, Violet led her charge into the bedroom.

"When will Papa come back?" Anna asked as she crawled onto her small bed, festooned with frothy pink and white drapery.

"I'm sure it will be soon, my dear." Violet kept her tone soft as she pulled the embroidered coverlet up over the child. "We shall have to think of something very special to serve him when next he comes. Do you know what he particularly likes for tea?"

"Treacle tart." A huge yawn interrupted Anna's words.

"Your favorite is treacle tart, I believe," Violet said with a smile.

Anna smiled back, her heavy eyelids drooping.

"I'll find out from cook what he likes and make sure we have it the next time he comes to tea with us."

The girl nodded, winking now in an effort to stay awake. "Miss Carlton." She reached for Violet's hand, clasping her thin fingers around it. "Stay here."

"I will, lovey. Go to sleep. I'm right here." Gently, Violet squeezed the small hand.

Anna squeezed back, then her hand fell limply onto the coverlet.

Violet smoothed the tiny brow as the child's breathing became slow and regular. "Poor darling."

She'd been told Anna's mother had been ill for months. The little girl had been kept away from her for fear she would catch the mysterious illness that had kept Judith Harper unable to leave her bed. No wonder poor Anna clung to her father so.

Violet waited until she was deeply asleep, then rose and headed for the nursery. She'd found naptime the perfect opportunity to read. Lady Downing allowed her to take books from the library and she'd found a lovely volume by Samuel Richardson called *Pamela*. The antics of the maid as she fended off her employer had proven most entertaining during the past week. A chapter or two a day and the story was flying by. She wished she could still practice her music, but beggars could not be choosers. With a little hum of satisfaction, she picked up her shawl and the volume and headed for the nursery.

"Miss Carlton."

Violet stopped, shocked to see Miss Harper still seated on the sofa sipping tea. "Miss Harper. I beg your pardon. I didn't realize you were still here." Why on earth *was* she still here? "Shall I call for more tea?"

"No, thank you." The younger woman stared into the fireplace, as if avoiding Violet.

A cold dread crept up Violet's spine. Miss Harper had stayed to have her say—to finally confront her about Tristan. Heart hammering, she returned to the chair in which she'd sat during the tea party. She straightened her skirts and squared her shoulders. There was no defense for her actions, but she couldn't be ashamed of her love for Tris either. She raised her chin and gazed at Miss Harper, relieved to have the matter brought out in the open at last.

"I'd hoped to speak to you earlier, Miss Carlton, but the time has never seemed quite right since you arrived." Miss Harper fingered the edge of her black and green figured gown.

"Yes?" Violet steeled herself for the accusation.

"You and Lord Trevor have been friends for some time he has told me. You are, in fact, related?" The blue eyes across from her were neither hard nor narrowed. Rather than acting the wronged woman, Miss Harper seemed almost shy.

"The connection is remote," Violet answered carefully. "But we have been acquainted for some time." Certainly, God would forgive the lie. The lesser of her sins to be sure.

"He spoke very highly of you to my father. Praised your character and skills with children. From what I've seen of you and Anna I can tell he has spoken nothing but truth." The girl smiled and leaned forward.

"Thank you, Miss Harper." For some reason, she didn't sound angry at all. More confused than ever, Violet clasped her hands together to keep them from quivering.

"So I was wondering if you might help me." Suddenly fidgety, Miss Harper tucked her head until her chin almost rested on her chest and squeezed her hands together tightly.

"Help you?" What help could this young woman possibly need from her?

"Yes, you see..." The girl twisted restlessly in her seat, looking ready to bolt from the room. "I suppose you know I am to marry Lord Trevor this spring?"

"Yes." The word came out clipped as a wave of pain crashed over Violet, closing her throat. The innocuous question cut like a knife in her chest.

"I have only met Lord Trevor a few times." Chaotic color spread from Miss Harper's neck upward to her forehead, turning her face the hue of a summer rose. "He seems very kind, but aloof. So I was wondering..." She clutched her skirts as though they were a lifeline. "I wondered if you could tell me something of him, of his character, his background. I want..." Another longer pause. "I want him to like me." The hollows around her eyes seemed to deepen and a trick of the light cast her face in dark shadow. "If I knew more about him, perhaps, his likes and dislikes, I could please him better after we are wed."

Violet stared at Miss Harper, the room wavering until she could see nothing but the woman's pinched face. A roaring in her ears, a lightness in her head told her she was about to swoon and she fought to take deep breaths, remain conscious even as her heart ripped in two. If she could crawl off somewhere and die she'd consider it a blessing. Anything rather than this wrenching pain that wracked her body and soul. Still she stared at the pink-tinged face, unable to move or speak.

"I would not presume to ask so personal a favor, Miss Carlton, on such slight acquaintance, but I have no one else to turn to." Miss Harper sighed, smoothing out her skirts where her fingers had crushed the pretty fabric. "As I said, Lord Trevor has been very kind, but is often very remote." She gave a high, nervous little laugh. "I'm not sure, but I suspect all men may be so. My father and brother certainly are, although they have never truly liked me." Her head came up and she met Violet's gaze beseechingly. "I didn't want Lord Trevor to be like them."

Violet stared back at Miss Harper, properly chastened. She'd known the love and respect of her brother, father, mother, grandmother. The remembrance of that love would always be with her, no matter her circumstances. She couldn't fathom what it would be like not to have a brother to tease her, to play games with, to dry her tears. Jamie had done all that and more. Her father had doted on them both while he lived. Only happy memories of her childhood remained.

Miss Harper appeared to be a kind person who seemed genuinely fond of Anna and her sister-in-law. Why would her father and brother treat her so callously?

"Please don't think me impertinent, Miss Carlton." Abruptly, Miss Harper rose, wringing her hands. "I know we are barely acquainted and I would not ask such a favor except…" Her mouth trembled and tears glistened in her eyes. "Marriage is forever. I had hoped it might be a happy one, if I knew how to please my husband."

Again the sinking feeling hit Violet, like an iron chain tied around her heart dragging her down into the depths of the earth. What the girl asked was impossible. How could she even speak about Tris without dissolving into tears? Misery wrapped its cold arms around her.

Miss Harper turned to go.

What would Tris want her to do? By his own admission, he felt nothing for Miss Harper, yet he was prepared to go ahead with the marriage to avoid hurting her. He would not break his vow, would not repeat his father's mistake and take Violet as his mistress. If one of them had any chance at happiness, for love of him should she not abet it?

"Miss Harper."

The girl stopped at the threshold and peered warily over her shoulder.

"I believe I can help you." Violet gritted her teeth but managed a smile and indicated the chair opposite her. "Won't you please take a seat?"

The young woman's face lit up, her eyes wide and eager. She flashed a trembling smile at Violet and hurried back to the fire. "Oh, thank you, Miss Carlton."

Violet waved her hand toward the teapot. "Shall I send for more tea?"

"Oh, yes, please."

Violet stepped to the door and hailed a footman. "Please fetch more tea for Miss Harper."

The man nodded and left.

Gathering her courage, Violet reseated herself and looked straight at Miss Harper. She could do this for Tris. "What can I tell you about Lord Trevor?"

"Oh, please call me Dora," the girl replied, leaning forward to grasp Violet's hands with fingers like ice.

"Thank you, Dora. And you must call me Violet." Perhaps it would be easier if they were less formal.

"Such a pretty name."

Breathing deeply, she forced a smile. She could do this. "What would you like to know?"

"Oh, I have no idea, really." Dora gave a shrill little laugh. "Everything you can think of. How does he take his tea? What foods does he like? Does he prefer town life or country?" She ran on excitedly, her face animated for the first time in Violet's memory. "There are a thousand things I want to know. He dances so well. What music does he like?"

Violet closed her eyes and the music room at Lammas House appeared, bathed in candlelight. "The harp, I would say, is his favorite instrument. Do you play?" With a shake of her head she opened her eyes. It wouldn't do to be carried away by her memories.

"Only the pianoforte. Does he like that as well?" Dora asked eagerly.

"He does. I have played both instruments for him and he seems to enjoy both." Violet fought the memory of Christmas Day, even as the remembered smell of beeswax candles filled her head.

"But he prefers the harp?" Dora cocked her head, her face falling. "I can see it in your eyes. I do wish I could play, but we only have the one instrument. Mama thought it the best one for ladies to learn. I see she was wrong in my case."

So tempting to just sympathize and continue the conversation. But that would not further the plan for Tristan's happiness. "If your parents approve, I will send for my harp. I could teach you and later Anna." The tight band that encircled her chest eased a trifle.

"You would do that for me?" The astonishment on Dora's face, the unshed tears, spoke candidly of the kindnesses she'd been denied.

"I would indeed." Violet swallowed hard and smiled at her new friend. "Everyone deserves happiness."

Chapter 25

"Relax your hand. Let the fingers fold themselves naturally against the palm, Dora." Holding up her right hand, Violet demonstrated how the fingers curled inward. "You don't want them stiff and pointed like a lion's claw."

"Ugh. Why can I not do this simplest of things?" Dora clenched her fist, then threw her hands in the air, fingers pointed outward. "Roar."

Violet couldn't help but laugh. Dora's lessons had only begun two days before, but the girl seemed to think she must play perfectly from the beginning. An excellent trait, perfection, but better if a bit more forgiving. "You are a credible lion, but I think you'll be a better harpist before long."

"I shall never play as well as you." Fretfully, Dora pushed the instrument upright then slumped against the chair.

"You will if I have anything to do with it." Violet ran her hand softly down the strings, making them whisper a discordant tune. "You are at the beginning of your studies. With time and practice you will play beautifully."

"But I have little time, Violet." Dora sat up, rubbing her arms as if suddenly chilled. "The wedding will be in two short months. Then I will be gone. No more lessons." She sighed, almost a sob.

"Of course you will have more lessons. Once you are…married, I am sure Lord Trevor will insist you keep up your studies." Almost no hesitation now when speaking of Dora's marriage. The pain had dulled recently, as a wound does after the initial shock to the severed flesh gives way to a muted ache. Coming to know Dora had been a two-edged sword. The constant reminder of Tris's impending marriage was pure agony, but as she came to know Dora's sweet nature, she took perverse comfort in thinking she would hand Tris a wife he could come to love and be happy with in time. If she could not have him herself, then who better than Dora?

"Come, let me show you how to perform a glissando." Violet sat in the chair next to her pupil and pulled the harp over onto her shoulder.

"What is that?"

"A glorious sounding movement that is actually very simple." Strumming again, this time she played down the strings using her left thumb. "You go upward with your right hand and downward with your left. Watch." She repeated the sweeping movements twice, watching Dora's rapt face turn into concentration as her brows dipped almost to her nose. "Here. Now you try."

"But I—"

Violet didn't bother arguing. Instead, she shoved the pillar of the harp over to Dora's shoulder. "Now curve your hand as I showed you."

Dora obediently curled her fingers inward.

"Good. Now place your forefinger bent on the lower 'C' string. Keep your thumb up."

Biting her lip in concentration, the girl followed the instructions step-by-step.

"Pull that finger back against every string."

Gingerly, Dora placed her finger on the center of the string and pulled back as instructed, one string at a time. Her pace was too slow and she wobbled once, but completed the movement at last.

"Excellent, Dora."

"I did it!" A wide grin broke out across her face.

"And well." Her pleasure in her achievement made Violet's heart ache. The poor thing seemed to have had little praise in her life. "Now let's do it again, a little faster this time. Imagine you are pulling a bow back as if you were playing at archery."

"Oh, yes. I see." Brows furrowed as she concentrated, Dora set her finger on the middle "C" string once more and pulled back smoothly and rapidly. The notes rang out loud and sweet in the small parlor they were using as a music room.

"Excellent. Now strum down with the other hand."

Dora shot her a wild look but took a deep breath and did as she was told. The resulting notes were soft but sweet.

"Curve your thumb a bit to cup the sound and make it louder. First, up with the right hand."

The harp sang the scale beautifully.

"And down with the left."

The descending notes rang louder.

"Continue up and back."

The joy of accomplishment in Dora's face made Violet's heart swell. Her pupil was a delight to teach.

Dora continued for several more sweeps of the strings, each pass stronger, more sure.

"It's like I'm actually playing, Violet." Her smile stretched across her entire face.

"You are indeed playing, my dear." Tris's voice cut through the glorious notes.

The sound stopped Violet's breath dead.

Dora gasped and jumped up.

The harp crashed to the floor, rocking on its base until Violet grabbed it to prevent it toppling over.

"My lord, I...I." Dora's cheeks bloomed a bright pink.

"Good morning, Lord Trevor." Violet had caught her breath and forced her head to clear, for the sight of him after so much time made her giddy. Dressed in a bronze brocade coat, brown breeches, and a deep maroon checked waistcoat all trimmed in gold braid, he cut a magnificent figure in the doorway.

"Good morning, Miss Carlton. I thought you had been engaged to teach Lord Downing's granddaughter, not his daughter." Mischievously, he looked from her to Dora, who had now turned white as the sheets of music scattered on the floor.

"I am a woman of many talents, my lord." She bent, intent on retrieving the papers.

"I am fully aware of that, Miss Carlton."

His arch tone made her jerk her head up. The hot gaze he turned on her made her bones turn to water.

He stooped and snared the last page. When he rose, they stood face to face. He handed her the music, brushing his finger along hers.

A bolt of heat shot straight to her core, like an arrow to its mark. "Thank you, my lord." In need of support, she stepped back and laid her hand on Dora's shoulder. The chill of the girl's skin, even through her gown, jerked Violet out of her trance. "Are you all right, Dora? You're cold as ice."

"Yes, I am fine," she whispered. "I was just startled by your appearance, Lord Trevor."

"We had hoped to surprise you, my lord," Violet continued, still unsure if Dora was about to faint or not. "I am teaching your future bride to play the harp."

"You are? That is indeed a surprise. And very thoughtful of you." He turned a softened gaze on Dora. "The harp is my favorite instrument."

"I know." Dora glanced from Violet to Tris. "Violet told me."

"Then I am most pleased and flattered you have undertaken the instrument, my dear. I will look forward eagerly to hearing you play again." His gaze lingered on her pale face, a wistfulness appearing in his eyes. "I am therefore most sorry I must interrupt your lesson, but I am sent to fetch you. Your mother awaits you in her sitting room. Your aunt, the Duchess of Ostroda, has arrived."

"Aunt Mimi is here? All the way from Prussia? That is a surprise." Some of the color had returned to Dora's face. She stood lost in thought, then dipped a curtsey. "If you will excuse me, my lord. I must go greet her."

"Of course. I shall see you at dinner." Tris grasped her hand, lifted and kissed it. "Until then."

With one last piercing look at Tris, she left, the *tap tap* of her shoes in the corridor escalating as they faded.

Tris swung around to face Violet, the love shining in his face heartbreaking.

Unable to bear it, she clutched the sheets of music and fled to the small wooden cabinet where they were stored. She took her time, rearranging the pages until all were facing up. The movements were mechanical; she listened with all her might to him—the rustle of his coat against his body, the soft puff of his breath in the still air behind her. She bent and thrust the sheets inside, all the while seeing his face before her.

It had been weeks since she'd seen him, the morning he'd met with her and Lord Manning. Not weeks but a lifetime. Her heart filled with sadness. Soon she would see him much more seldom, and eventually not at all. Still, she could not make herself turn and look at him. She stood slowly, straightening her spine inch by inch, all the while willing him to leave because she didn't know how long she could restrain herself.

"Violet."

Her back prickled with gooseflesh. He stood so close she could feel his warm breath on her nape. So close that if she turned around she would be in his arms. She wanted that. Wanted it more than she wanted air to breathe. Yet he was not hers to have.

He slid his hands over her shoulders, the big, warm, strong hands she remembered so very well. Hands that had explored her body and given her the utmost pleasure. Tugging gently, he turned her toward him.

Dreading each inch that brought her to face him, she closed her eyes. She couldn't bear seeing his desire for her again. The scent of his cologne, spicy bergamot steeped in citrus, filled her head. She breathed him in, like coming home.

He cradled her head, guiding it until he found her lips, then plunging his tongue home.

An exquisite hunger swept through her body, as though she'd been starving and suddenly been given a feast. She slid her arms around his neck, pressing her eager body along his, seeking to touch every inch she could. The world stopped and they stood frozen in this one blessed moment in time.

He came to his senses first, pulling away, though he still cupped her face. "Oh, Violet. I do love you. I have missed you so much, my love."

Tears started from her eyes. Her throat threatened to close completely as her heart beat painfully in her breast. She stepped back, staring into the beautiful sapphire eyes and shook her head, flinging drops to and fro. "We shouldn't have done that."

"I don't give a fiddler's damn about what we should and should not do." He crushed her to his chest. "I cannot do this, Violet. I cannot marry Dora and condemn us to a life of misery."

She struggled to push away from him, though she was loath to do so. Her body sought his warmth like steel to a magnet. He was her true North. "You would condemn her too then?" She wiped at her streaming eyes with the back of her hand, then groped in her pocket for a handkerchief. "You cannot abandon her, Tris. She needs you. Needs to leave this house before it kills her spirit."

"I know her circumstances. Believe me, I know." He grabbed her shoulders and gave her comforting squeeze. "Her father is a right bastard to her. Her brother too. I've seen the way they treat her. It is an impossible situation." He dropped his hands and stared into her eyes with an intensity that scared her. "But I cannot rescue you both, Violet. She's managed to cope with her family's disdain thus far. Certainly Downing will arrange another marriage for her." He leaned his forehead against hers. "I cannot lose you, Violet. I cannot."

"Tris." It cost every ounce of her resolve to step back from him. "You must marry her, not only for honor, but for her sake." She clutched the handkerchief, already damp with tears. "And for my sake you must never see me again."

"Violet!"

"No, my dear." She swallowed hard, but met his eyes unflinchingly. "My dearest love, if you love me, you must swear you will not seek me out again. To do so will rekindle this unbearable pain that even now rips at my breast."

"My love." He ran his hand around the back of his neck where the tendons had popped up in thick, rigid lines. With a groan he stepped toward her, arms outstretched.

She threw her hands up to fend him off. "Tris, no. Do not touch me. I swear to you my heart will break if you do." A lie, of course. Her heart already lay in a thousand throbbing pieces, so painful she could scarcely draw breath. But what else could she do to preserve his honor and Dora's salvation?

"I cannot—"

"You must, my dear. For me." Violet choked on the words, but forced herself to continue. "Promise me you will marry her and be kind. She deserves that, Tris. She will make you a good and loving wife, one who only wants to please you if you give her the chance. For my sake, my love, give her that chance." Completely overcome, Violet turned and fled the room. Tears streamed down her cheeks once more as she ran toward the safety of the nursery, toward a life of service. To a life without Tris.

* * * *

Tristan stood in the cold receiving room furious and forlorn by turns, which infuriated him even more. How could she refuse him when he was willing to sacrifice everything for her? They deserved to be together. Why could she not see beyond the scandal and come away with him now? His hand itched to throttle someone—Violet, Downing, his father, himself. The latter more so than anyone else. God, what a muddle he'd made of his life.

A glance showed the room held no comforting decanter. If this affair lasted much longer he'd become a tosspot and probably happier so. With an effort, he unclenched his fists and dropped his shoulders, although the ache of tension lingered in his body.

For the past two weeks he'd consciously avoided any contact with Violet, though he'd been peculiarly aware of her presence in the house. Several times he'd enter a room and feel her essence, as though the ghost of her lingered on the currents in the air. Temptation had gnawed at him, urging him to seek her out, see her beautiful face, hear her lovely voice if only for a fleeting moment. He'd quelled every impulse until today, when the unexpected arrival of the duchess had thrown the household into a panic.

Lady Downing had set the maids to freshening the second-best guest room, then nervously requested him to move to that chamber, allowing the duchess to occupy the best chamber. He'd graciously acquiesced, smiling at the woman's shattered poise. When Lady Downing rang the bell for a footman to find Dora and none was forthcoming, Tris had volunteered to go.

That had been a grave mistake.

As he had approached the upstairs sitting room, where he'd been directed, he'd been amazed to hear two voices raised in laughter. His heart had given a fierce jolt that shook his chest. He'd recognize Violet's laughter anywhere. Amazed anew at the beautiful strains of harp music, punctuated by the murmur of voices, he'd eased into the doorway and stood transfixed. His bride-to-be and the mistress of his heart laughed together as Violet strummed the strings in demonstration. The picture they presented made his heart ache.

Dora, blue eyes shining, trim figure shown off to perfection in a fashionable pink gown *d'Anglais*, was absorbed in her fingering. Unselfconscious, she exuded a grace and *joie de vive* he'd never seen in her before. No man could resist her like this, unless he looked beyond her to her companion.

Violet sat easily in her chair, natural poise and charm in every line of her. The green *saque* gown, one of Madame Angelique's creations, subtly emphasized her full breasts and neat waist. Her hair glinted in the lamplight, strands straggling as they always did from beneath her pinner. Eyes sparkling and laughter bubbling from her lips—lips he'd give anything to kiss once more—she could be the goddess of love incarnate.

The vision disintegrated into the chilly room where he stood staring at the harp, all illusion of warmth dispelled. He strode to the harp, touched the strings reverently, hoping for a trace of her presence on them. The strings whispered the discordant notes he'd raised, but no more. Violet had gone from this place, gone from him, and by her word, gone forever.

Much as he hated to do so, he must honor her wishes and cease his pursuit of her. How many times had he vowed that very thing, yet here he stood, once again guilty of trying to persuade her to run away with him. Would this madness in his blood ever cease? He feared it unlikely. She had bound him to her with ties sunk bone-deep in his heart. That would never change. His manner, however, must.

Resting his hand on the shaft of the harp, he lifted his head. "I vow, from this day forward, I will not see nor speak to Violet, though she be my own true love. I will abide by her decree and take Dora as my wife to honor and cherish above all others. I swear it on my life."

He hoped the oath would give him peace and a renewed sense of purpose. It did not. Indeed, nothing save an icy desolation swept through him so he stood empty as the harp strings awaiting Violet's hand to bring them to life once more. At least they had the hope of such. He had none.

With a muttered curse, he quit the haunted chamber in search of an empty room with a full decanter. He could deal with the pain as long as the brandy held out.

Chapter 26

Violet smoothed the covers over the angelic sleeping child and turned down the lamp on the mantle. The late afternoons were so dim she left a light on for Anna who feared the dark. One more fond look and Violet left the girl to her nap.

She stretched as she made her way to the schoolroom where she had begun eating her lunch. Anna tended to dawdle whenever they ate together, prattling on and on about her dolls, her dogs, anything and everything she could think of to avoid the inevitable naptime.

Smiling, she laid her napkin in her lap. She and Jamie had resisted naptime and bedtime, going so far once as to set a book on fire to create an alarm and thus postpone the dreaded nap. They hadn't been model children by any means, but they'd never managed to run off a governess either. Miss Baker had remained with them until Jamie had gone to school, at which point she'd left and Miss Connors had taken over Violet's education.

Her own predecessors' behavior at Harper's Grange still puzzled her. Anna could not be a sweeter child. What could she have done to drive away not one but two governesses in the span of three months? Had her mother's illness affected her in some way Violet had yet to discover? She sipped her tea, letting the deliciously sweet brew sooth her.

She needed soothing after yesterday's encounter with Tris. Every time she closed her eyes his face appeared, as though it had been etched on the inside of her eyelids. Her hands trembled so the cup chattered in the saucer and she set it down.

Think about something else.

She pushed away her uneaten lunch—the pork pie would choke her if she attempted it—and rose. Perhaps another chapter or two of *Pamela* would take her mind off her misery. If it truly loved company, then she could find it in Mr. Richardson's plucky heroine. She turned toward the end of Volume One. When last she'd stopped, Pamela had tried to escape the clutches of Mr. B, her employer, but had been frightened by a pair of bulls, who actually turned out to be cows, and had returned to Mr. B's house. What would the maid do now? Violet bent her head and dove into the perils of Pamela.

The creak of the door opening jolted her from the novel just as Pamela discovered the person in bed with her was not Nan the maid, but Mr. B himself. Violet started up, wheeling toward the nursery door, but it remained ajar. No small figure there.

Her attention swerved to the door to the East Wing corridor to find Simon Harper standing at the doorway, grinning at her discomposure. He lounged against the frame, his suit of uncut burgundy velvet the height of fashion, although the dark color with his dark hair and pale face gave him an almost sinister air.

"Mr. Harper, you gave me a fright." Violet closed her book and set it neatly on the table. "I am sorry, but Anna is asleep. I know how disappointed she'll be to have missed your visit." She straightened the dishes and cutlery, wishing Mr. Harper had come a bit later. Then he could have seen Anna and she would have had time to clear the lunch things.

"Ah, yes, a pity that." Mr. Harper strolled over to one of the chairs before the fire and sat, looking expectantly at her. "How is Anna getting on?"

Dear Lord, he must want to discuss his daughter's progress, although she had little to report really. They'd only been together for a few weeks. Of course, her report would be quite a good diversion, if only Mr. Harper scrutiny wasn't quite so keen. "For such a short time, she has gotten along very well. She is progressing well in both reading and writing so we have started her on French lessons as well." Violet's quick smile as she praised her pupil dimmed.

Mr. Harper was not attending her report. He lounged far back in his chair, hands laced over his stomach, a smug smile on his lips. Every so often he chuckled. How rude of the man. Why had he sought her out to tell him about Anna if he didn't want to listen to the report?

"Did I say something amusing, Mr. Harper?" She forgot to keep the acid out of her tone. If she didn't come up with a suitable manner for dealing with her employers and their son, she'd likely end up out of a position. She wanted to keep this job, needed to keep it if she wanted to live. Her difficulty in finding a post before this one had shown her the precarious nature of her foothold here. One slip, one disrespectful word and they would sack her and put her out on the streets again. As she dared not return to Madame Vestry for fear of the wrath of Tris and Lord Manning, she could very easily starve in a matter of weeks. She must curb her tongue. "I beg your pardon. I did not mean to be impertinent, but I did wonder what you were laughing at."

Mr. Harper, all warm eyes and merry mouth, fell silent, the chuckling replaced by a salacious leer. "Why at you, Miss Carlton."

"At me?" Unaccountably the hairs on the nape of her neck bristled.

"Yes." He stood, towering over her, a giant in the small nursery.

Wary, Violet inched her way to the far side of the table. "I had no idea I was so amusing."

"Let us say the situation is amusing rather than your lovely self." The leer on his face deepened.

Violet glanced about, searching for some sort of makeshift weapon. The man was speaking and acting exceedingly strange. Better safe than sorry. "I don't understand."

"Oh, I am sure you do." Quick as a lightning strike he shot his hand out, snaring her arm and wrenching her across the table.

"Mr. Harper!" Off-balance, Violet fell hard, scattering the dishes.

In a flash the man was behind her. He grabbed her hair and pulled her up, arching her against him until her back bowed. "Wouldn't you call it most amusing that my father hired a whore to teach my daughter how to be a lady?" He wrapped his arm around her neck.

She gasped for breath, hoping a scream would bring someone in time to save her.

Harper clasped his hand over her mouth. "I'd think twice before raising an alarm, my girl. You wouldn't want Anna to wake up while I'm taking my pleasure with you, now would you?"

Violet whimpered, terror making her arms and legs numb. He meant to rape her here, not ten feet from where his daughter slumbered, and there was nothing she could do to stop him. She sobbed against his hand. "Why? Why would you do this?" Though indistinct, he seemed to understand her question.

"Let us say your talents are being wasted in the nursery." He chuckled and jerked her head back. "Except for today." Keeping one hand over her mouth, her neck bent cruelly back against his shoulder, he grasped her skirts and hauled them upward.

Cool air on her bare backside jolted Violet into action. "Hup. Hup!" She squirmed and kicked at him even as she dug her nails into the hand muffling her cries. Why couldn't a footman appear? Or the maid? Or even Dora? Better discovered than violated so brutally by this fiend.

She continued to struggle, hope of rescue waning with each passing second.

He slapped her buttocks and pushed her legs apart with his knee.

Violet opened her mouth impossibly wide and bit down on the side of his hand. Blood spurted into her mouth.

Harper yelped, releasing her so suddenly she sprawled across the table, sending the lunch things crashing to the floor.

Before he could recover, she kicked out, connecting with his leg and propelling her the rest of the way across the table. She slithered onto the floor then popped up on her feet, gasping for breath as her heart pounded. The coppery taste of blood filled her mouth. She spit it out and swiped the back of her hand across her lips.

Harper shook his hand, ruby drops flying along the tabletop. "You'll pay for that, bitch. See if you don't."

"You've gone stark staring mad." Violet couldn't stop shaking. She kept a wary eye on her attacker, but couldn't help glancing at the doorway. Too far to make a dash and Harper stood closer to it than she did.

"Don't you believe it." He sucked the wound, his dark stare promising dire retribution.

"Why else would you attack me?" She rubbed her neck and her hand came away bloody. Her blood or his? He sported a large square-cut ruby on his index finger.

"Because you'll warm my bed and say nothing about it unless you want me to reveal your secret." He pulled out a handkerchief and wound it around his hand.

"I have no idea what you're talking about." Violet stiffened and locked her knees before they buckled. He knew. Knew about her night with Tris, although how he could have found out boggled her mind. Suddenly dizzy, she swayed then fought the urge to collapse. He'd be on her like a jackal on a fresh kill if she didn't stay alert. "I have no secrets."

"Hah."

She cringed. He knew. But how? Tris would never have told him.

"Seeing is believing, although I admit I didn't place you at first."

"What are you talking about, Mr. Harper? I've never met you before. You've obviously mistaken me for someone else." She eyed the door again. Anna would be in no danger from him. She had to get out of here, find Tris, and leave.

"We didn't meet, true. But I never forget a face. Especially not a looker like you." He licked his lips, sending a sudden chill down her back.

"But if we didn't meet—"

"I saw you. With Trevor. At the House of Pleasure."

All the spirit ran out of her, leaving a great hollow shell in which her racing heart echoed. But they'd seen no one there save Madame Vestry. She saw again the small dim office, the darkened foyer where...Damn. Tris had spoken to three masqueraders. She recalled Zeus and the scantily clad shepherd with the jeweled ring that had caught the candlelight.

"So you see, Miss Carlton, I hold you in thrall. If you so much as breathe a word of our encounter here I will make it known you were Trevor's mistress, a common strumpet from a brothel. My father will be livid when he finds his future son-in-law has brought his lady-bird with him in the guise of a governess. He might even break the betrothal." Harper sneered as he stalked around the table toward her.

Dear God, what must she do? Every instinct cried flee the brute and beg someone, Tris, Dora, even Lady Downing to save her from him. Her pulse beat a staccato rhythm in her ears and she tensed for flight as he closed on her, shaking his wounded hand.

If she sought help, however, Harper would expose her. Her reputation would be in ruins, never again able to pass for a decent woman. No one would ever receive her again—not even Tris's considerable influence could mend that.

The vile fiend reached her, but she stood still. Submit and she might retain her position here and the pretense of respectability. Defy him and she could cost Tris his marriage to Dora and find herself fit only for Madame Vestry.

Violet raised her gaze to the smirking face as he grabbed her arms and pulled her to him. Steeling herself, she yielded to him when he crushed his lips against hers, bruising her mouth and cutting her lip on his teeth. The coppery taste of blood filled her mouth once more.

He fisted one hand in her hair then thrust his tongue into her so far she almost gagged. His other hand fumbled at her bodice until finally he shoved it under the fabric and pulled her breast free. With brutal fingers he pinched her nipple, pulling and rolling it until tears started from her eyes.

She braced against the pain, but refused to cry out.

Harper dug her other breast out, squeezing that nipple so sharply she couldn't stifle a moan. He chuckled. "I knew you'd like this. All sluts do." He lowered his head and latched onto her left nipple, sucking on it hard while he squeezed the other one unmercifully.

Violet bit her lip to keep from crying out. The ache in her breasts soared, yet she must stand it and silently. Tears trickled down her cheeks.

Suddenly the pressure of his mouth decreased as he set his teeth against her tender nipple.

She gasped and clenched her jaw, dread of worse pain to come hurtling through her. In desperation, she grabbed his shoulders, digging her fingers into his wool coat as her breasts swelled against his harsh treatment.

"Miss Carlton! Miss Carlton!" Cries from Anna's room pierced Violet's numbed mind, snapping her back to sanity.

Harper raised his head, turning toward the sudden noise, freeing her breast.

With a great shove, she pushed him away, gasping in a breath that dispelled the cobwebby feeling of powerlessness. Stumbling back, she automatically pushed her breasts back into her bodice. Avoiding Harper's red, leering face, she raced into the nursery to Anna's bedside.

"There, there, now." Calming her own fears, Violet eased onto the bed where the little girl sat up, shaking in terror. "Was it a bad dream? You're awake now, lovey." A fervent glance at the open door, but the fiend did not appear.

"Oh, Miss Carlton." Anna threw her arms around her governess, her slight body trembling as she nodded.

"Well, you are safe now, my dear." Trembling, Violet pulled the distraught child to her, taking as much as giving comfort. "What was the matter in your dream?"

"I was being chased by a big dog." A stranglehold on her, Anna buried her head in Violet's bosom.

"A very big dog?"

A nod, though she still hid her face.

"As big as Sadie?"

The child sat up, her petite brows fixed in a comical frown. "Sadie is a Yorkshire terrier. She is not big enough to frighten a flea."

"Well, then, was it as big as Johnny?"

"Much bigger than him." Anna leaned back on the pillows. "Of course, Johnny is a basset hound and old. He wouldn't scare anyone."

"Well, then, it must be as big as Duke." Sensing an unwelcome presence outside the door, Violet rose.

"Oh, yes, indeed. It was just as big as Duke."

The family Great Dane was taller than Anna, but as good natured as any animal Violet had ever met. "But Duke wouldn't hurt you, would he?"

"No, of course not. I love Duke."

"And he loves you. He wouldn't try to frighten you, do you think?"

"No, Duke wouldn't do that."

"And he wouldn't let another dog frighten you, would he, my dear?"

"Duke would protect you, poppet, no matter what." Mr. Harper rounded the doorframe and stood looking as though he'd come from church, not a hair out of place, pious expression on his face. "Just like Papa would."

"Papa, papa!" Anna jumped out of the bed and ran to her father. She launched herself into his arms.

He caught her to him, hugging her with all his might. Over Anna's head he caught Violet's attention and nodded slowly.

She stood and backed toward the servant's entrance to the nursery behind her. She tried to forget the slimy feeling of his skin on hers, his mouth on her.

He held her gaze and mouthed the word, "Tonight."

Violet's knees turned to water. She'd escaped this afternoon by the grace of God. Tonight she could not hope to be so lucky. With a strangled cry she fled the nursery, grateful to have this short respite from this loathsome man's attentions. Certainly it would not be long enough.

Chapter 27

Violet fled downstairs to the kitchen under the guise of needing assistance with the broken dishes in the nursery. She could think of no better excuse in her shocked and battered state. Her breasts still ached with his abuse and she trembled in fear, which was hard to hide. She kept checking her bodice to assure her appearance didn't breathe a word of what had transpired upstairs. Each time she did so, however, she could feel Mr. Harper's hot mouth on her and the trembling increased.

Mrs. Rose eyed her oddly, but nodded to a footman. "James, go fetch the tea service from the nursery." She bustled about the kitchen, checking a batch of bread in the oven, supervising two young scullery maids who were paring vegetables, and another footman who sat polishing the silver. "Did you need more tea sent up, Miss Carlton?" She dipped a spoon into a bubbling pot on the stove and tasted it.

"Yes, please, Mrs. Rose. I'd best get back to Anna." Violet wanted to dawdle in the warm kitchen that recalled the comfort and safety of home, but there was Anna to think of. Perhaps if she hurried and got the girl ready for a walk while the footman was there, they could leave with him and avoid being alone with Mr. Harper. That might help with this afternoon, but what about tonight? "Mrs. Rose, I wonder if I might take my dinner in the servant's hall this evening? I can put Anna to bed and come straight down."

Again, a piercing look from the cook, though she shrugged and nodded. "Makes no never mind to me, Miss Carlton, if the governess wants to eat here. Less work for us in the long run." She took her rolling pin and banged it into the lump of dough on her counter. "Suit yourself. Best be on time, though, or you'll do without dinner."

Breathing a sigh of relief, Violet crept back upstairs. Outside the nursery door, she listened intently for movement inside. The soft swish of a broom on the hardwood floor told her the footman was still about. She squared her shoulders and marched into the sitting room.

All seemed quiet. James had cleared the broken dishes and discarded food onto a large tray and had swept up the mess on the floor. "There you go, Miss Carlton," he said, hefting the tray in one hand. He deftly tucked the broom under his arm and grabbed the dustpan.

"Did you see Mr. Harper and Anna?" She kept her voice low in case the man was in Anna's bedroom.

"Yes, miss. He dressed her and they left only a few minutes ago." James headed for the door.

"Did Mr. Harper happen to say where they were going?" She prayed it was not to his mother to demand she be dismissed.

"I believe they were going to walk about the garden, miss. Miss Anna seemed excited about the snow, though it's almost gone. If you'll pardon me, miss." The footman left, taking his blanket of security with him.

Violet crept to the sitting room window and peeped out between the dark green-damasked drapes. This window gave onto the larger of the house's two gardens.

The failing light revealed Anna squealing in delight as her father chased her around the cold, empty fountain. Suddenly he seized the child and lifted her high in the air, twirling her around while she screamed with laughter. He caught sight of Violet and stopped, a grin spreading over his ruddy face.

Her heart surged, as if clutched by a phantom hand. What must she do? She might be able to thwart his advances for a day or two if she was very careful, but eventually he would corner her. Now more than ever she wished for Susan who would shadow her every move and keep the hellhound at bay. The reality of the situation was stark, however. She had two choices: leave or accept Mr. Harper's advances. If she left, she had nowhere to go. Tris had closed Lammas House and dismissed the servants. While she might apply to Lord Manning for aid, she would hate to involve him further in her wretched affairs. She could not consult Tris without telling him why she wanted to leave, after which he would kill Mr. Harper and be hanged himself. Just like the Earl Ferrers.

Which left her precisely two options: Madame Vestry's establishment or mistress to Simon Harper. Both odious choices but she'd had no say in creating them. At least if she remained at Harper's Grange she need only service Mr. Harper rather than a horde of different men each night. Cold comfort perhaps, yet a relevant point. Better the devil she knew.

Violet backed away from the window, her mind whirling with the magnitude of her decision. She'd avoid Mr. Harper as best she could for as long as she could. See how difficult it would be to keep out of his clutches without rousing the suspicions of the household and go on from there.

The unsettled nature of the next few days would grind her nerves to a fine point but it could not be helped. Violet prayed she could find a way to avoid the man although she held out little hope of it. She might as well attempt to escape the notice of the Almighty. With that cheerful thought, she headed into her bedroom to repair her appearance for a dinner she'd likely not touch. Still, her presence in the servant's hall would keep her safer than dining alone in her room.

After sending a footman to collect Anna when she returned to the house, Violet read to the girl, gave her dinner and put her to bed with remarkably little fuss from the child. She yawned throughout her meal and fell asleep almost instantly, apparently worn out from her playtime with her father. It seemed the man was good for something at least.

Still on edge, Violet jumped at each creak of a floorboard, expecting Mr. Harper to appear and ravish her on the spot. She didn't really believe he would force himself upon her in front of his daughter. He used that threat as another tactic to buy her compliance with her own debauchery. Still, she would put nothing past the odious man in the end. Best spend most of the evening with the other servants.

Luck shone a glimmer on her and she walked to dinner in the company of Madge, an upstairs maid who had been sent to fetch a shawl for the duchess. Once in the servant's hall, Violet relaxed a measure, enough to enjoy the excellent chicken that was Mrs. Rose's specialty. She spoke little unless asked a question, keeping an ear on the conversations surrounding the Downing's doings. Lady Downing had repaired to the drawing room with the ladies when Violet and the others had sat down to eat.

"Have the gentlemen joined the ladies, Mr. Eccles?" she asked nonchalantly when the butler returned from a summons upstairs.

"Yes, Miss Carlton. They've just now gone in. I'll take another slice of currant cake, Mrs. Rose, if you don't mind." The older man sat wearily at the head of the table.

"Right away, Mr. Eccles." Mrs. Rose brought the whole cake to the table and cut a slice for him. "Another for you, Miss Carlton?"

"No, thank you, Mrs. Rose. The first was delicious, but I'm quite full enough after your delightful chicken." Violet could be enthusiastic, for the cook knew her business well. "I believe I will say good night now. I need to check on Anna. Thank you for allowing me to dine with you."

She wished she could do so each day for the servants here were a friendly if somewhat reserved crew. She'd like to get to know them, but that was frowned upon as beneath her position. "Good night."

Violet smiled and nodded to each person, then quietly slipped from the hall. A swift trip back to the nursery and she could lock herself in her bedroom for the night. She hurried down the main corridor, first past Lord Downing's study, then the library. The creak of the library door shot a jolt of fear down her spine. The hairs on her arms stood straight up and she bent her head and put on a burst of speed.

Too late.

Simon Harper stepped out of the library and snagged her hand as she raced by. He hauled her into the dim room and closed the door quietly behind her. The rasp of the key in the lock sent chills down her back.

"Thought you'd be sly didn't you, Violet?" He pulled her against him. His hot breath in her ear made her clench her teeth. "I like a little spirit in my girls." Seizing her head, he dragged it up to his. "But only a little. You'd do well to remember that." With more force than last time, he mashed his lips against hers, trying to push his tongue into her mouth.

She clamped her lips together, determined to fight, and backed away, only to find her way blocked by a library table.

He stabbed at her mouth with his tongue, advancing inward only to be stopped by her clenched teeth. He clamped his hand into her hair and jerked it, almost tearing it from the roots.

Violet cried out, her eyes tearing at the sudden pain.

With a triumphal cry he thrust his thick tongue into her mouth, almost choking her.

She pummeled his chest, then gave a great push, sending him reeling backward into a chair. She wretched, coughing to dispel the sickening sensation of his tongue in her throat.

"Don't worry, my dear. You'll get used to that in no time. I've a fondness for ladies' mouths as you'll find out." His dark eyes brightened, as a gleam of candlelight revealed his excitement.

Violet's stomach lurched, almost gagging her anew. Madame Vestry had told her all the places men liked to have women put their mouths on them. She staggered backward, bent on flight.

He grabbed her arm, then grasped her face in a cruel grip. "You'll come to like it eventually." He scrutinized her face, then let go and let his gaze wander down to her breasts. "Yes, these beauties must be let out to play." Grasping the top of her bodice, he ripped the garment open.

"No!" Violet started back, trying to grab the pieces of her gown and cover her exposed stays. Tears of rage streamed down her cheeks. To hell with safety. She had to get away before he threw her onto the library table and debauched her right here. She opened her mouth to scream.

He spun her around, his brutal hand clamped over her mouth, his arm round her neck. "None of that." He chuckled in her ear. "Struggle and I'll call Father to witness your depraved nature, though I'd rather this be our little secret. Stuck down here in the country with an ailing wife, well, a man has needs as I'm sure you know." He slid his hand into her corset and hauled her breasts out one at a time. "There. They look so pretty when they're free, don't they?" He nodded toward the Venetian curio cabinet whose mirrored back reflected a dim image of his hands on her naked body.

Violet sobbed, terrified and humiliated as he slid busy fingers over her nipples.

He pinched one suddenly, bringing fresh tears to her eyes. "I might have had you at Madame Vestry's had I seen you first. Damn Trevor for taking you away before I got a taste." He ran his tongue up the back of her neck. "Of course, I'll have more than a taste now." He gave her nipple a vicious twist.

Violet screamed in agony.

The library door burst open.

The wrath of God blazing from his eyes, Tris strode in.

Harper pushed Violet toward him and made a mad dash for the door.

Violet staggered, but stayed on her feet, relief washing through her.

Tris grabbed Harper by his throat, lifted him off his feet, and threw him into the towering glass curio cabinet. Shattered glass cascaded over him. Several small volumes, a china figurine, and a jet-black stone statue of a cat fell onto Harper, lying sprawled on the floor. A large quartz rock teetered on the edge of a broken shelf then toppled onto his head. He yelped, then grasped his head and moaned.

Disregarding the broken glass, Tris seized the man by his jacket, hauled him up and drove his fist into his stomach.

Harper doubled over, retching.

Shaking as though she'd emerged from an ice-cold pond, Violet tried desperately to repair her appearance. She pushed her breasts back inside her stays and clutched the ends of her torn bodice, trying to cover herself. Her hands shook so hard, however, the material kept slipping through her fingers. What could she do? Nothing save cross her arms over her chest, and huddle in the corner of a leather chair.

Before Harper could straighten, Tris slammed his fist into his face.

He flew backward into the tattered remains of the curio cabinet and lay still.

Tris started toward him again, and Violet gasped, certain he meant to murder the wretch. He stopped and whirled around, seemed to see her for the first time.

"Violet." In two strides, he reached her, dragged her out of the chair. He clutched her to him. "My God, are you hurt?"

Tears rolled down her cheeks. She hung her head, weeping with shame and joy and relief. It was over.

"Violet, my love. Please. Tell me what did he do?"

The horror in his voice brought her head up, her gaze riveted to his as he took in her disheveled hair, torn dress, tear-stained face. She clasped her arms across her ripped bodice, and her breasts ached at the slight pressure. God knew she looked like a strumpet and worse. "He tried to make me his mistress."

Tris's blue eyes darkened, his nostrils flared and his jaw tightened so hard it creaked. Death looked out of his face as he stalked over to the still form. He stood over him, chest heaving, hands opening and clenching. "Had I a sword or a pistol this piece of filth would never rise from this spot. He's nothing more than a rabid dog that wants killing."

"What in hell is going on here?" The imperious tones of Lord Downing sounded from the doorway.

Violet froze.

His lordship stood half over the threshold, his eyes popping out of their sockets. Standing behind him, Lady Downing, the Duchess of Ostroda, and Dora, all wide-eyed and white faced, stared silently at the carnage.

Chapter 28

The women's shocked faces, carrying almost the exact scandalized expression, made Violet want to giggle hysterically.

In an instant, Tris appeared beside her, doffed his coat, and wrapped it around her. He stood in front of her, shielding her from their prying eyes.

Gratefully, she sank into the warmth of his steel-gray velvet jacket, even more comforted because it enveloped her in the fragrance of bergamot, citrus, and him. An overwhelming sense of safety settled over her and her tears renewed, although now they were tears of joy.

Lord Downing stumped into the library. "What have you done to Harper? Eccles!" he bellowed. "Eccles."

The butler appeared at a sedate trot, but skidded to a stop at the bloodbath before him. Simon Harper lay bleeding from a dozen tiny cuts.

"Fetch the surgeon at once." Downing gazed around, helpless. "Harriet, for the love of God, do something. Harper may be dying."

"I sincerely doubt that." Flexing and shaking his hand, Tris twisted his mouth in disgust as he viewed the moaning man. "Only the good die young, so they say. By that reckoning, your son will live to see one hundred."

"How dare you." Lady Downing knelt beside her son, patting his hands and face. "Eccles, fetch my reticule. It has smelling salts."

"Oh, I have some here." Dora darted forward to offer the vial. She stared first at Tris, then at Violet. Then more decidedly at Violet's dishabille.

Heat touching her cheeks at her friend's scrutiny, Violet pulled the coat more securely across her chest. Oh, why must Dora see her like this? Bad enough to be disgraced in front of her employers, but for her friend to be part and parcel of her ruin was another stinging blow.

Lady Downing applied the smelling salts to Harper's nose.

From the floor he sputtered, gasped, and sat up. He pushed his mother away, knocking the vial from her hand, and it spun across the room. "What in damnation is that? Get it away from me before I choke to death."

"Simon. Thank God you're alive." When Lady Downing tried to grasp him around the neck, however, she was soundly rebuffed, and promptly burst into tears.

The duchess, who seemed made of sterner stuff, helped her sister to her feet. "Come along, Harriet. Let's get you a good strong cup of tea."

"I demand to know what is going on." Lord Downing planted himself in the doorway. With his cravat askew, his jacket pulled open, and his wig cocked at an impossible angle, he could have been mistaken for an inmate escaped from Bedlam.

"A gross deception, Father." Easing himself up off the floor, Mr. Harper winced when his hand crunched on a piece of glass. He sidled over to a long sofa and sank onto it.

"A deception? What do you mean?" Wide-eyed, Lord Downing glanced from Tristan to his son to his wife.

"I mean Trevor here has perpetrated a fraud upon us."

Everyone in the room turned, staring at Tris who continued to stand nonchalantly, arms folded across his chest, glowering at Harper.

"What fraud, boy?" Downing knit his brows, his gaze shuttling back and forth between his son and his future son-in-law. With each subtle movement, his wig slid lower.

"Miss Carlton has been brought here and foisted upon us under false pretenses by Lord Trevor." Harper thrust his finger toward her.

Violet shrank back into the coat, her stomach sickening. Now the whole sordid story would come out in a room full of people. In front of Dora, who she'd come to like very much. If the floor could swallow her whole she would count it a blessing.

"What are you talking about, Harper. Spit it out." Downing drummed his fingers on the back of a chair.

"Miss Carlton is his mistress." With a triumphant toss of his head, Harper threw the words at them.

Gasps from the ladies near the doorway sent Violet shrinking further behind Tris.

"Is this true, Trevor?" Downing's voice deepened, he leaned toward Tris, and his wig finally slid down his back and plopped onto the floor.

"No, it is not true." Tris spoke calmly and Violet started at the lie. He put a hand on her shoulder, urging her to stay silent.

"The devil it is." Harper sprang out of the chair, then turned pale and slowly lowered himself back into the seat. "I saw you leaving the House of Pleasure with her in November."

A wailing moan arose and Lady Downing sank to the floor in a swoon. The duchess shook her head and motioned to Dora. "Fetch the smelling salts again, my dear." She knelt beside her sister, fanning her with Lord Downing's wig, which she had snatched from its resting place at the viscount's feet.

Searching for the vial, Dora scrambled under the library table. When she stood again, she handed the bottle to her aunt, without taking her attention off Tris and Violet. She stared at the two of them, completely ignoring her mother's plight.

"What do you have to say about this, Trevor?" Downing's complexion neared a frightening shade of puce. "How dare you bring your light-skirt from a brothel to take care of my granddaughter? Under the same roof as my daughter, your soon-to-be wife?"

The look of contempt Tris fixed on Harper was so severe the younger man slid back in his seat. "Miss Carlton is not, nor has ever been my mistress. I'll swear an oath to that on a stack of Bibles as tall as you, Harper."

Violet trembled.

"But I saw you leaving with her the night of the Zeus' Desire masquerade at Madame Vestry's." Petulant to the point of irritation, Harper's voice rose shrilly. "If she's not your lady-bird, then she's certainly a trollop. Not one to bring into a decent household to teach my innocent child."

"Or mine." Lord Downing pointed to Dora. "The good Lord knows what salacious things she'd been teaching Dora."

"Just to play the harp, Father," Dora spoke up eagerly, with a quick nod to Violet. "She taught me the fingering for a glissando."

"Fingering a glissando!" Shrieking from the chaise, Lady Downing bolted up from her sister's arms, ignoring the duchess's attempts to wipe her face with a handkerchief. "Oh, I shall never live down the shame." Eyes rolling back in her head, she flopped into her sister's arms once more.

"It's a way to strum," Dora added helpfully, peering at her prostrate mother, then at her father. "The strings, you know. That's all."

"Of course it is, Dora." With a sigh, Her Grace pushed Lady Downing into a sitting position. "Do get up, Harriet. Your swoons are just as bothersome now as they were when you were a girl. Melchior, take her." She waved a hand at Lord Downing. "She's your burden, not mine."

Swearing under his breath, Downing bustled forward, grabbed his wife beneath the arms and heaved her up. "So what do you have to say for yourself, Trevor?" After a tussle, the viscount managed to get his wife on her feet long enough for the duchess to move to the chair. He lowered his wife down again and wiped his brow. "Eccles, fetch the brandy." Tenderly, he patted his wife's cheek. "Do you deny what my son says? Will you declare him a liar before us all?"

Tris stared malevolently at Harper, who sat picking shards of glass from his clothing and hair. "No, I may accuse him of being depraved, but not of lying in this instance. He may indeed have seen me leaving—" Hesitating, he rested his gaze on Dora's rapt face a little longer than necessary. "An establishment of interest to certain men, young and old alike." He glared at Downing, who grunted and looked away. "I do remember speaking to a friend that night in November. I had not made Harper's acquaintance at the time, and if he was disguised for the masquerade I would not have recognized him in any case. If you say you were the shepherd I will not gainsay you." Tris's lips quirked in a smile. "Why you, a married man, would be entering such a house I will leave for you to explain."

The bright red tinge of Harper's cheeks rivaled a ripe pomegranate. "Why I was there is none of your business. Why were you there?"

Again Tris searched the duchess's and Dora's faces and shifted. "This is hardly a conversation to be had in front of ladies. If the duchess, Dora, and Lady Downing would retire—"

"Well, I for one want to hear the end of the story." The duchess's gray eyes snapped with excitement.

"And I as well." The determined set of Dora's jaw belied her soft tone. "He is my betrothed, after all."

Moaning anew, Lady Downing, burrowed her face into the chaise.

Tris shrugged. "Very well." He looked straight at Dora. "I had gone there to deflower a virgin."

Lady Downing's shriek rent the air.

The duchess's eyes widened.

Dora paled until the only color left were two pink spots on her cheeks.

Scandalized, Violet hung her head, stifling a sob. Why would Tris shame her this way?

"By God, Trevor." Lord Downing took a step toward him. "You cannot speak this way before my wife."

"My pardon to Lady Downing, although I believe she has swooned again."

The duchess glared at the figure lying supine on the daybed and sniffed. "Proceed young man."

Tris's lips trembled, with repressed laughter Violet would wager, the wretch. This was no laughing matter.

"My wedding day was approaching. I wanted to be able to control my baser urges when I lay with my wife for the first time." Turning to Dora, he softened his gaze. "I didn't want to hurt you or frighten you, my dear."

Face as white as the plastered walls, Dora clenched her jaw and studied the gold and purple feathers on the duchess's hat.

"So instead you terrorized this young woman." Downing stabbed a finger at Violet.

The words hit like a blow. Cringing, trying to disappear within herself, she sobbed aloud. If only she could sell her soul this moment to be anywhere else in the world, she would do it gladly.

"No, I did not."

That brought her head up with a jerk. Peering up at Tris, she recoiled at the stern set of his jaw, the demonic gaze he threw at Lord Downing.

"What do you mean?" Downing's frown almost touched his nose. "You don't think you terrorized her? She's trembling there this very moment."

Ducking behind Tris, she tried to make herself as small as possible.

"But not from fear of me." He turned to her, stroked her cheek.

Soft as a kiss, his touch steadied her.

"When I found Miss Carlton in the House of Pleasure, I immediately noticed her reluctance. Her fear. So I asked her why she was there." His gaze lingered on her face, his eyes pools of love. "She told me she had been kidnapped."

Astounded by the lie, Violet sucked in a breath. What tale was Tris concocting now?

"The devil you say." Lord Downing staggered back.

"My word." Raising her quizzing glass, the duchess peered at Violet anew.

Dora stared at her, white-faced and speechless.

"Don't believe a word of it." Harper stepped forward, still rubbing his jaw. "She was a whore who spun him a story, nothing more. Madame Vestry probably told her what to say, in order to make more money."

"Indeed, she was not, Mr. Harper." Tris's eyes glittered and his fist tightened. "I will have a word to speak with you directly, never fear." Slowly he returned his attention to Lord Downing. "This sort of unfortunate occurrence has happed there before. If you doubt my word, I suggest you call upon the Marquess of Dalbury and ask him."

The elder man sputtered and backed away, a hand outstretched. "Dalbury, you say? Dalbury has experienced such a thing before?"

"Ask him."

"Oh, no, no. That will not be necessary. I take your word on that, Trevor. No need to bring Dalbury into this at all." Sweat popped out on Lord Downing's lined brow.

Puzzled, Violet glanced from one man to the other. Tris's satisfied smirk startled her.

"Yes, I expect you wanted no further dealings with the marquess." Tris stared pointedly at Harper, who refused to meet his eyes.

The tenor of the room had changed. Never had two men looked so uncomfortable as Harper and Downing. She hoped she could tease the tale out of Tris at some later time. For now, it was enough to draw his coat closer around her. Unless she missed her guess, the drama in the room had not yet seen its climax.

"Since that night in November, I have been assisting Miss Carlton in finding respectable employment. Her family is dead and she has no friends, the reason, I suspect, she was the target of the kidnapping in the first place." He drew Violet from behind him to his side.

She was loath to move out of the shelter of his tall frame, into the pool of light that exposed her to the curious stares. Like the bugs Jamie used to stick a pin through, anchoring them to a board so he could watch them squirm. The family seemed to have abandoned good manners, for they stared unabashedly at her, even Lady Downing who had regained her senses once more.

"So you can imagine my outrage that, having at last secured Miss Carlton a position in what I believed a decent household, Lord Downing, I find her being attacked by your son." He clutched her to his side, shielding her from their gaze.

The room erupted into furious cries, screams, moans and shouts.

Violet drew closer to Tris, in an attempt to cover her ears against the deafening uproar.

Poor Dora sank down on the sofa, whiter than milk. She twisted her hands in her lap, staring first at Violet, then Tris, and finally her brother. The unmasked hatred in her face sent a shiver through Violet.

All Violet could see of the duchess was her eyes, like two huge saucers with gray centers. She glared at her nephew, who stood sputtering, opening and closing his mouth like a huge carp.

Her sister moaned and slumped back onto the chaise, her head lolling over the side of the lounge, while Lord Downing stared stonily at Tris.

"That's a damned lie." Harper finally found his voice and leaped toward Tris.

"That is the second time in ten minutes you've impugned my honor, Harper." Tris grabbed the man by his ruffled cravat that had come undone. He twisted it until Harper's face went red. "One would be enough for me to call you out. However," Tris let go the necktie, shoving the man into his father, "I will take greater pleasure in demanding satisfaction of you for the assault and slanders you have heaped upon Miss Carlton. Name your seconds, sir."

No, no, no. The words screamed inside Violet's head. Her heart beat at a frantic pace, as though trying to hammer its way out of her chest. "No, Tris…Lord Trevor, I cannot allow—"

He turned sharply, his finger raised and she gulped back the words.

"I will defend your honor, Miss Carlton, if it is the last thing I do on this earth."

She bit back a moan at the import of his words.

"I cannot believe you would do this, Trevor." Lord Downing straightened, gathering his dignity. "Such an accusation is cause for Harper to challenge you."

"He is welcome to do so if he survives my challenge." Calmly, Tris pulled down the sleeves of his rumpled shirt, as though he had not a care in the world. "Although such behavior on his part goes far in explaining why you have lost two governesses in the span of three months. The child is obviously not the cause." With that pronouncement, Tris slid his arm around Violet's shoulders, drawing her close once more.

Harper had attempted to straighten his clothing, though it remained bedraggled and blood stained. The tendons on either side of his neck stood out like thick ropes. "I'll meet you, Trevor. Glad to do it. Swords. Tomorrow. There's a nice clearing in the woods about a mile from the house at the pond. The ground may be a bit soggy, but it should serve to mix your blood with the mud." He sneered. "Lord Stanley of Witsop and Mr. John Cox will stand as my seconds. I'll write them now."

Tris shook his head. "We must postpone the date to allow my seconds to arrive from London. I will write them directly I remove to the inn at Devizes." He chuckled and Violet shivered at the icy sound. "Although the Earl of Manning and his brother-in-law, the Marquess of Dalbury will not be pleased at such a summons, I am certain they will be here as soon as the post roads allow."

Florid face paling considerably, Lord Downing sucked in a breath and sat down hard, narrowly missing his wife's outstretched body.

"Lord Dalbury will attend your seconds as soon as he arrives." Tris glanced down at Violet, warming her with his gaze. "I will lodge Miss

Carlton at the inn as well. She will be well enough tonight. I can get one of the servants to serve as her companion for now. I'll instruct Dalbury to bring her maid." He returned his searing gaze to Harper. "Three days, sir." Then to Downing, "Your servant, my lord." Pressing his hand into the small of Violet's back, an intimate touch that thrilled her despite the disastrous swirl of events that had just transpired, Tris urged her toward the door.

"Lord Trevor." The quiet voice reverberated like a bell in the silence.

Everyone turned toward Dora, standing behind the sofa, chin raised, lips firm.

Violet's heart went out to the girl she had been able to call friend so briefly.

Tris stopped and faced her. "Yes, Miss Harper?"

Twisting her hands until her fingers were white, Dora finally managed to speak. "Under the circumstances, as you have challenged my brother, I regret to tell you I must release you from your promise of marriage. I cannot, in good conscience, marry a man who would cause my brother harm." Her eyes flashed like hard gems at Tris. "I think we will not meet again, my lord." With one agonized look at Violet, she picked up her skirts and fled.

"Dora! Come back this instant!" Downing roared at the figure in white disappearing out the doorway.

"Oh, let her go." Harper gingerly pulled another sliver of glass from the leg of his breeches. "Trevor would never marry her now he's got his whore back with him. And you shouldn't—"

Tris's right fist connected with Harper's nose, producing a spectacular crunch.

The man flew backwards again, into a tall stand holding a bust of Caesar. The bust shattered into a thousand pieces of plaster, raining down on the still, bloody figure on the floor.

"Three days." Tris gathered Violet to him and strode from the room.

Chapter 29

"Go upstairs quickly, change and gather your things, love." Tris murmured as he walked her to the staircase.

His arm a comforting and welcome weight about her waist, Violet sighed, reluctant to lose contact with him. "But—"

"No. Nothing you can say will induce me to leave you in this house one minute more. I shall wait here for you." He brushed a kiss over her lips and her heart sang with joy. "I love you."

A burden she'd not known she carried fell from her shoulders. He did love her. She floated up the steps, her head whirling. Her fortunes had shifted like the March wind blowing a stray feather to and fro. Pray God it now headed her on a true course for happiness.

She opened the door to the nursery, heading for her room when a rhythmic creaking of the floorboards in the next room stopped her where she stood. Had Anna awakened and gone looking for her? She changed course and peeped into the girl's bedroom.

The golden head slumbered peacefully, beautiful in its innocent repose. The maid assigned to watch her until Violet returned from dinner rose, putting aside the bit of mending she'd occupied herself with.

With a finger raised to her lips for silence, Violet beckoned the girl. "Bess, you must stay the night with Miss Anna. I am to leave Harper's Grange and she cannot be alone. Go fetch your night things. I shall wait until you return."

Wide-eyed, Bess stared at her as though she were spouting Latin, then nodded and sped from the room.

Squaring her shoulders, Violet returned to the nursery sitting room. She'd discover who the trespasser was and dismiss them as well. At least it couldn't be Mr. Harper, so she would deal with whoever it was swiftly.

The door to her chamber stood ajar, the constant creaking continuing within. Boldly, she pushed it open.

Dora stood at the end of her bed, folding one of Violet's gowns, the trunk at her feet half-filled with clothing.

"What are you doing here?" Violet's voice wavered. She was surprised she could speak at all. The last person she had expected to see was Dora.

"I'm helping you pack." The young woman's stare pierced Violet to her core.

"You needn't bother, Miss Harper." She hated addressing her friend that way, but best not rely on the familiarity of a friendship most likely blasted to Hades.

Dora cringed then laid the gown gently in the trunk. "I'd think you'd want to shake the dust of this house from your feet without delay." Abruptly, she straightened, wringing her hands. "My brother behaved abominably toward you."

A glimmer of hope raised its head. "He did. You must believe me when I tell you I gave him no encouragement for his attentions whatsoever."

"Oh, I believe you." Dora picked up a pair of stockings from the bed and began to roll them. "I also believe Lord Trevor is in love with you."

Violet bowed her head but could not deny it. "Yes, and I am in love with him." The weight of that admission rolled off her shoulders like the globe of Atlas, and she'd swear on her grandmother's grave she'd not take up that guilt again. She sniffed, determined not to cry, and raised her head. "How did you know?"

"The way he looked at you the other day when he interrupted our lesson." Her clear blue eyes took on a faraway look. "He looked as though he had lost a great treasure and suddenly found it again. The light in his eyes…" Dora sighed. "I know he will never look at me that way."

Violet's heart went out to her, but she suspected it was the truth.

"I am glad my brother provided a way for me to release Lord Trevor from his promise. He saved me the trouble of inventing a reason." After grabbing a chemise from the chest on chest, Dora laid it on the bed and straightened every line until the garment lay in a perfect square. "I was leaning toward accusing Lord Trevor of the theft of a particularly dear parure my grandmother left me. I had shown it to him just last week. It might not have held water as far as an excuse, but I could have worked it up into an issue of trust that would have sufficed." A smile broadened into a grin. "I'd even figured out a way to slip the items into his room."

She gave a little laugh then sobered. "Still, I am glad in the end I needn't besmirch his name and reputation with such an accusation."

"But why would you have done it at all?" How could anyone let Tris go willingly.

"I want my husband to look at me the way Lord Trevor looks at you, Violet." Tears started from Dora's eyes. "I believe I deserve at least that much happiness in life."

"Of course you do." Violet sped to her and threw her arms around her, clinging to her, comforting her as best she could. Her friend had done a brave and generous deed. Certainly such a sacrifice would merit reward. "You will find a man who is good and kind and whose face lights up like a summer morning just because you enter a room."

"Do you think so, truly?" Dora wiped her tears away with the back of her hand.

"With all my heart." Violet hugged her again. Someone as good and selfless must find the perfect man. She herself could do nothing, save pray each night to the Almighty and trust such prayers would be answered. "You must stop crying, my dear, or you will have me caterwauling as well. And I must be gone quickly, before your brother awakens and tries to stop me." A teardrop fell onto her bare shoulder where Tris's coat had fallen away.

"Hunh. From what I saw down stairs, Lord Trevor won't let him touch a hair on your head." Dora stepped back, eyeing Violet as she clutched the coat to her bosom. "Here." She thrust a gown at Violet. "You must change. It would be most scandalous to be seen leaving the house in such a state." Waving her hand at Violet's forlorn apparel, she leaned forward and whispered, "My aunt would be most thrilled."

"Thank you." Violet managed a smile and took the garment into her dressing room, grateful her new stays laced up the front. She could dress herself without Dora's help. A few minutes later she emerged in a tailored gray traveling suit of wool, and a hat of deep wine red perched on the back of her head.

Dora let the lid of the trunk fall with a solid thunk. "I believe those are all your things. If I or the maids find anything after you go, I'll make sure it finds its way to you."

She grasped her friend's hands. "Dora, I cannot thank you enough. You have my oath I will entreat Lord Trevor to spare your brother if it is humanly possible. I do not know what skill he has with the sword, however—"

"I hope he kills the cur."

An icy finger skittered down her spine and Violet jerked back, appalled at the vehemence and malice in Dora's voice. "Surely, you do not mean that?"

"Only with every ounce of feeling I possess." Dora stiffened, but waved the death of her brother away as a matter of little consequence. "You are not the only one he has assaulted. As Lord Trevor surmised earlier, Simon has attacked both Miss Martin and Miss Giles. I'll wager my horse on it." She met her eyes with a piercing gaze and Violet trembled, a sudden premonition sweeping through her. "Simon is the reason Judith is still abed."

"What?" All the air rushed from Violet's lungs. From the family's earlier comments, she'd thought Mrs. Harper ill with some incurable disease.

"They had an argument in November, while we were in London." She continued to twist her hands until her fingers looked knotted. "I happened to be in the corridor outside their apartments. I had come to ask Judith to ride with me. I heard voices raised. Judith was upset because Simon had gone to that...that pleasure house." Her cheeks flushed bright pink. The poor girl would have little innocence left by the end of the day.

Violet grasped her hand and gave a comforting squeeze.

"I heard a sharp slap and a thud. Then Simon called out for help." Dora wiped tears away from her face once more. "He gave out she had tripped and hit her head on the marble hearth. But he hit her, Violet, knocked her down and when she fell, her head struck the ornate andiron. Her right temple was bruised for a week. She's lain in the bed ever since. She doesn't know anyone, doesn't speak. She barely takes any nourishment. She used to be so pretty, so vivacious. I always wanted to be like her." The stare Dora turned on Violet made her blood freeze. "I pray Lord Trevor kills the monster who did that to Judith."

If Violet had one regret in leaving this house, it was abandoning Dora. No one seemed to care about her. She clasped her hands. "That must rest in God's hands. I will pray for a miracle for your sister-in-law that she will recover." The words seemed pitifully inadequate, but she could do nothing else.

"Best pray too I find a husband who will take me away from here." Dora's grim-set mouth and sad eyes smote Violet anew.

"I will with all my heart." She squeezed Dora's hand one last time. "Much as I hate to leave you, I fear I must go. Lord Trevor is below—"

"Yes, yes. Please. You must go." Dora broke from her and bent, hiding her face while fastening the trunk. "I believe that is everything."

"Yes." After peering about the room for any forgotten item, Violet at last looked toward the doorway. "Will you say my goodbyes to Anna? I don't wish to wake her, but neither do I want her to think ill of me for leaving without saying goodbye."

"Of course. I will tell her your true love took you away, like in the fairy tales." Dora smiled bitterly. "I think she will enjoy thinking such things can happen in real life." She embraced Violet fiercely. "I know I do. I wish you and Lord Trevor every happiness."

Tears started from Violet's eyes. She gave one last squeeze and stepped away. "Goodbye, my friend."

"Goodbye." Dora swallowed hard.

Heading for the door to call a footman, she halted at the threshold. "My harp. What must I do—"

"I will take good care of it until I can send it to you in London," Dora said, coming to push her out the door. "Go. Your true love awaits."

Laughing, Violet raced down the staircase. True to his word, Tris stood exactly where she'd left him in the foyer, pacing the polished floor.

He looked up at her and the scowl on his face turned into a wide grin.

All the horror and strife of the day were whisked away as the love shining in his eyes melted her heart. She faltered on the stairs, the enormity of her change in circumstances overwhelming her. Then she pounded down them, straight into Tris's arms.

"Did you pack everything in the house?" he grumbled, stepping back after an embrace that left her giddy. She handed him his coat.

"I had to say goodbye to Dora."

"Indeed." He paused in the act of slipping his arms into his jacket. With a shake of his head, he settled the garment over his broad shoulders. "I'd have expected her to give you a wide berth and the rough side of her tongue, if she has one."

"You might be surprised, my lord." Violet chuckled.

His eyebrows shot up, however, instead of pursuing the subject, he snapped his fingers at a passing footman. "Fetch Miss Carlton's trunk from the nursery. Take it to my carriage out front."

"Right away, my lord." The servant hurried up the stairs.

"Your cloak, my lord." Eccles appeared with both Tris's and Violet's outer garments.

"Thank you." Tris shrugged into his and gently settled Violet's new blue wool cape around her shoulders.

The bustle of activity swirled around her, but time seemed to have slowed. She could focus on nothing but the fact she was leaving with Tris, who was not marrying Dora.

He took her by the elbow and escorted her into the carriage, then supervised the loading of her trunk and his before settling himself in the seat beside her. With a rap on the trap, Tris sank back on the soft leather seat. A jerk as the coachman started the horses and Harper's Grange faded behind her.

"You look frozen, love." Grasping her hands, Tris raised them, and blew on her frigid fingers.

In her haste she'd forgotten her gloves. She'd never believed gloves could keep the hands so warm, but her fingers were like ice, just coming from the house to the carriage. Now, however, his hot breath on her skin sent warmth pulsing all through her.

"Oh, Tris." Heart too full for anything else, her head spun as he began kissing her fingers one by one, firing off sparks that hurtled straight to her core. To have his mouth on her body again was to gain heaven. Fire erupted at the apex of her thighs. Though a moment ago she'd been cold head to toe, she would swear her body had turned a scalding red from the attentions of his lips.

He grinned wickedly, assuring her the rising temperature wasn't imagination.

Her face was doubtless cherry red, and the warmth radiated throughout her body, arms, and legs. She'd be tearing off her cape soon, trying to cool down.

"There, that's better, isn't it?"

"A thousand times better." She could drown in the blue pools of his eyes. "I haven't thanked you properly for rescuing me."

"Believe me, love, it was completely my pleasure." He engulfed her hand in both of his, sending her pulse leaping. "Had Harper not given me an excuse to punch him, I'd have invented one. The man's a bully and a bounder. Not fit for the society of decent women."

"He struck his wife, according to Dora." She loosed her hand and sat back. The soaring heat in her blood subsided. "She hit her head and has been insensible ever since. Such a shame, too. She'd been Dora's only friend in the house."

"Damn." He rubbed his jaw. "Forgive me. Downing gave it to me she was recovering from a wasting fever. I suppose he must defend his blighter of a son. Or cover up the more sordid details." His face sobered. "At least I may put an end to his tyranny day after tomorrow."

"You will fight to the death?" All of the recent warmth leeched from her, leaving her frozen on the seat.

"I will confer with Duncan when he arrives, hopefully late tomorrow."

The name of the marquess who killed her cousin always brought a taste of metal to her mouth. She understood with her head the man had to defend his sister's good name, and God only knew what had prompted Kit to insult her in the first place. But her heart had not yet forgiven Lord

Dalbury. Tris's forgiveness was altogether different. How could she hate her own leg or eye or heart? He was bone of her bone, and now she could lose him once more in this duel. Might as well put a ball through her head or a sword through her breast.

"I sent to him as soon as I left Downing's library, while you were upstairs changing. My valet, Saunders, should make good time this evening. There is a full moon so I expect him to make Reading at the least. If he's up and on the road by first light he will reach Dunham House by tomorrow afternoon. Duncan and Manning can leave first thing on Tuesday morning."

"They won't want to leave immediately tomorrow?" With such urgency as the situation warranted, she'd expected them to travel through the night as well.

"Ah, well, I have given Duncan a commission he must needs wait to perform." Tris's face lay in somber lines.

A prickle of fear inched down her back. Had he sent to make a will? Her stomach churned and her gorge rose. She seized his hands and drew him close, staring into his eyes not an inch from hers. "Promise me you will not fight to the death, Tris. Will honor not be served just as well without your life hanging in the balance?"

"Fear not, my love." He cupped her cheek, the warm skin of his naked hand like a benediction to her soul. "I will make sure my life is long enough to satisfy us both."

"You cannot claim immortality, my dear, and that alone would satisfy my hunger for you." Violet pressed his hand tighter against her cheek, then placed a deep kiss on his palm.

He groaned, a deep, haunted sound, and grabbed her head with both hands, bringing their mouths together.

The kiss seared her, shooting flames of lust to her toes.

He made a slight adjustment to the angle of their heads and their lips melded, soft skin to soft skin, in perfect harmony.

A growl started deep in her throat. They had been too long apart. Denied their love too long. She opened her lips and thrust her tongue into his mouth. He tasted like sweet wine and brandy, an intoxicating mix. She pressed closer, wanting to feel all of him.

He sighed, and drew her into his lap. Their tongues tangled in a glorious duel of their own, the only conflict she might be willing to lose.

Her body steamed, as though the sun had pierced the dark night and shone only upon her, bringing its warmth, making her pulse with need. She never wanted to let him go.

The carriage slowed.

Tris gently disengaged them.

"No. No, Tris." Her hunger had scarcely begun to flame, much less be appeased by such a brief caress. She pressed against him, seeking his mouth again.

He chuckled and slid her back into her seat. "I fear we must abate our ardor for the moment, my love."

The trap opened and the coachman peered down at them. "The Black Horse Inn, my lord."

Chapter 30

Tris forced himself to calm. His major worry since leaving Harper's Grange was Violet's reputation. If a simple lie would suffice, he could proclaim them man and wife. Unfortunately, he was somewhat known in the area, so gossip would bubble up. He could say she was his sister and since they'd be in different rooms, it might serve. However, if she was known in the area as governess to Lord Downing's granddaughter, there would be hell to pay in the rumor mill. Of course, honesty was likely the best policy, but even that was never a sure thing. Guess he'd have to take this one on the fly.

He scarcely waited for the carriage to stop before jumping to the muddy ground and handing Violet down the step. Grasping her waist, hardly bigger than his hands' span, he whirled her off the step onto the less muddy cobbles of the doorway.

Just touching her, even through layers of clothing and cloak, set his cock to aching. She had ever afflicted him thus. It had been so long since they had been together, just themselves in an embrace that stretched forever. His blood raced hotly through his veins, igniting a fire within him he never wanted to quench save in her sweet self.

"What are you going to tell them?" Violet whispered when he lifted her.

"Allow me to handle it all, my dear." Firmly, he put the distraction of her presence aside. He must concentrate on securing two rooms with no harm to her reputation. Given her lack of a maid, this could be a challenge. He strode to the bar in the Black Horse's taproom and raised his voice. "Innkeeper?"

A moment later a familiar thin, older woman appeared from somewhere in the shadowy recesses of the inn, a mug in one hand, a towel in the other.

"May I help you, my lord?" Her eyebrows rose. "Lord Trevor. An honor, milord." She gazed first at Violet, then back to him, a sly smile on her lips. "How may I help you?"

Tris could see the wheels turning in her greedy little mind. How much she could charge for her silence and how much she could sell the information for. He'd squash that directly. Summoning all his charm, he smiled at her. "How kind of you to remember me. I require two rooms and a parlor, if you please, for myself and my ward, Miss Carlton." He spoke with deliberation. "I will also require the services of one of your maids for the night."

The wild look the woman shot him made him bite back a laugh. Oh, yes, she'd be telling tales the moment he headed to his room.

"I'm sure I don't know what you mean, my lord. The Black Horse is a respectable inn." She managed to sound outraged, although the excitement showed plainly in her wide eyes and raised brows. She tapped the bar with her towel.

"My ward has lost her maid due to an injury." A stretching of the truth, but still a plausible lie. "She will require the services of one of your maids to fill the breech until other arrangements can be made. Do you have such a girl you can spare for the evening?"

"Oh, ah, well." The woman cut her eyes from him to Violet once more, clearly puzzled. "I s'pose I could spare Betsy for the night. 'Specially as how we're not full up." She shrugged and handed him a key. "I'll send her out to show you to your rooms. Dinner's past, but I've got some keeping hot in the kitchen if you're hungry. Roast chicken with a ragout of vegetables, potatoes en croute, and there's still some apple tart."

Food was the last thing on his mind, but Violet might need something to fortify her. One glance at her told him she was nearing the end of her strength. She'd stood this entire time, speechless, almost in a trance, a vacant look on her usually animated face.

"That sounds delicious, doesn't it, my dear? And apple tart is your favorite, isn't it?"

Violet nodded vigorously, a frozen smile and glassy eyes heightening his concern.

"We will be down directly we refresh ourselves and change." Thank goodness the taproom held only a handful of men sipping ale and talking quietly.

"You don't want to dine in your parlor? Privately?" The woman cocked her head. Her beady eyes flicked from him to Violet.

Tris would love nothing better. What he truly wanted to feast on was not chicken and vegetables. But for the sake of Violet's reputation, the game must be played out down here. "I believe we would enjoy a little company this evening, wouldn't you agree, Miss Carlton?" He affected a careless demeanor, all the while willing her to agree.

"I…" She cleared her throat. "I think I would like that, my lord."

Sighing in relief, he beamed at Violet. "Then it's settled, Mrs.…"

"Cheeley, my lord. Mrs. Elmira Cheeley. My husband's the innkeeper, but he's been called away to his grandda's funeral and left me to run things." Mrs. Cheeley bobbed her head, a new respect in her eyes.

"My condolences to your husband. If you would be so kind as to fetch Betsy and some warm water for washing, we can be back down by the time you've set our places." Tris allowed himself to relax a trifle as the woman headed into the kitchen, calling for Betsy in a shrill voice. He returned his attention to Violet, who stared at him, wry amusement on her drawn face.

"Your ward?"

"The best I could think of when the woman recognized me."

"How?"

"Downing and I stopped here once for a drink on our way from London. I thought it had been the Black Swan, which is why I told Stokes to make for the Black Horse. I was unfortunately mistaken. I'd rather not be known, but I believe it will be all right." He helped her off with her cloak, breathing in the soft jasmine scent of her hair. Soothing and exciting in the same instant.

"What will be all right? And why are you engaging a maid for me?" Her eyes flashed a deeper amber, almost golden in the uneven light. She must be recovering her faculties. "I don't need a maid, especially when I want to be with you tonight."

"And I with you, my love." He ran his hand down her arm and shuddered as the need to enfold her almost overtook him. "If we wish to preserve our reputations, however, we must wait a little longer and play out this blasted charade."

"But I don't want—"

"It's only until Duncan arrives, which with any luck will be tomorrow evening." Thought of the commission he'd charged his friend with shot a jolt of desire through his body. God, it would be agony to control himself tonight.

"What difference will the marquess's presence make?" She'd set her mouth in a peevish pout.

"He's bringing a special license." Grinning broadly, Tris couldn't hold back the news any longer.

"A special license for what? Dueling?" Her golden eyes flashed beneath threatening brows.

Tris bit back a laugh. God, but she was beautiful when she was angry. And arousing. His cock was stiff as a maypole. He must remember to enrage her more often. "No, my love. A special license to allow me to marry you."

* * * *

The room spun. Violet staggered back, so shocked she groped for something to hold her up. He wanted to marry her?

Tris grabbed her arm and drew her to him. "Be careful, love. We've come too far for you to fall and do yourself a mischief."

She stared at the beloved face, mind churning, unable to utter a sound.

"You cannot truly be shocked, Violet." He gave her a small smile and squeezed her hand. "I've told you for months if I were free I would marry you."

"But…" That single word was all she could summon. If she could only think what to say.

"Did you think me a liar?" Quick as a wink, he pounced on her inability to speak.

"No, but—"

He rubbed his knuckles across her hand. "Then all it requires is your answer, love."

Her heart beat strangely, first pounding in her chest as if trying to hammer its way to freedom, then constricting so hard it hurt. She opened her mouth, not knowing if anything would come out.

A short woman, dressed in a dark green striped skirt and modest rust-colored bodice rounded the corner from the kitchen. "I'll take ye up to yer rooms now. This way m'lord, m'lady." With a disinterested air, Betsy grabbed a taper and led the way to the stairs at the end of the bar.

"I'm not 'my lady,' Betsy." Violet hastened to put the matter straight. She couldn't allow herself to think the girl might soon be correct in her address. "Miss Carlton will do."

"As you will, mistress." They had reached the first floor landing. "Here you go. Your bed chamber is this first one, on the right." She indicated a dark, stout door. "M'lord, ye're in this one, across the hall." Shouldering her way past Tris, she marched into the dim room on the left.

Light glowed suddenly and the maid reappeared.

"I've laid the fire and lit your candles, m'lord." Betsy headed back to Violet's chamber. "Just here, mistress." She opened the door and hurried inside.

Following her into a good-sized room, Violet gazed about at the ample furnishings: a high wooden poster bed, a trundle beneath, a nightstand, and a screened corner.

The maid lit the candle beside the bed. "The parlor's yon, through that door." She picked the candlestick up and stabbed it toward another stout door, just past the bed. "Mrs. Cheeley tells me ye've lost yer maid, mistress, and have need of one for the night?"

Violet nodded, her mind a jumble.

"I've never been maid to anyone afore, but I'll help ye with yer farthin'gales and fol-de-rols as best I can."

"Thank you, Betsy." Tris broke in, God bless him. "If you would fetch us both some warm water to wash with, then you can come back and help Miss Carlton change."

"Very good, m'lord." With a brief bob of a curtsey, the maid vanished out the door.

Alone with Tris once more, Violet found herself trembling in anticipation. Dare she dream he would continue their conversation from the taproom?

In answer to the unspoken question, he dropped to one knee and clasped her hands.

Blood roared in her ears. Her hands went from dry and hot to icy, as though all heat had fled her body. A metallic taste flooded her mouth.

His eyes were deep sapphire, a private ocean crashing over her, sweeping her out to sea.

"Violet, I love you." The quiet conviction in his voice would have melted her heart had it not already belonged to him.

Tears trickled down her cheeks, but she let them flow rather than release his grip and lose the power of his touch on her skin.

"I own I have betrayed you, have caused irreparable damage to your family. Yet, I would beg your forgiveness once more. Violet, please show me mercy beyond grace, beyond forgiveness, beyond my hope of heaven, by agreeing to become my wife." His beloved face shone with love, his mouth parted in a smile both fearful and expectant.

Gallant fool.

"Oh, Tris." She struggled to speak louder than the whispery words he had to cock his head to hear. "Yes. Yes, I will marry you, my love."

He jumped to his feet, wrapped his arms around her, and kissed her madly before she could draw another breath. His lips crushed hers and her happy tears drenched them both.

"You are caught now," he said, pausing to whisper in her ear. "You cannot take it back. I won't let you."

"Nor I you, my darling." She threw her arms around his neck, happiness throbbing in every inch of her being. "You will have to kill me to get rid of me."

"If I may slay you with pleasure, then you may indeed have fear for your life." Expertly, he settled her between his legs. "For I mean to give you every pleasure invented by man, and a few by women."

"I will die a happy woman, then." She rained kisses over his face, his neck, enjoying anew the very taste of him. Never had she believed such a thing would come to pass. How could she wait these two long days? When she'd had no expectation of his love and happiness time had proceeded at a normal pace. Now that she possessed those things, a snail's pace would be fast in comparison to the crawl of time.

"I prefer you to live a happy woman, Violet, so I may live a happy man." He kissed her hand, an eagerness about him he'd never shown before. "You've made me so very happy, love."

"And we can marry as soon as your friend arrives?" She could scarcely believe it still.

"Yes." Pressed this close, the citrusy smell of him filled her head. "First thing tomorrow we'll discover the local church and seek out the vicar. I shall entreat him to marry us as soon as the special license arrives. We will have no time to waste." He ran his hands lightly over her back, the movement soothing and arousing all at once.

"Ummm." She settled herself against him, trying to touch every inch. "You will find no argument from me, my lord." The sooner they could be man and wife, the sooner they could lay the past to rest. "But why such haste, my love? We could marry in London once this business of the duel is over. Then your friends could be present to wish you happy."

Stepping back, he left her bereft of his warm comfort and took her hands once more. "I would have us married and you my viscountess before the duel." He twined their fingers together, smiling at them, though not at her. "In case things go badly wrong, I would have you provided for. Duncan will make certain you will never want for anything."

"Tris." She pulled her hands away, cold dread filling the spaces where moments before there had been only joy and warmth. "You mustn't say such things. Jamie…" As her brother's face rose before her, she winced. Their situation had been much different, and he had been most confident of returning. Still, he'd had the forethought to give her the advice that had led her in the end to Madame Vestry.

Tris ran a hand through his hair. It came loose from its tie, giving him a wild, forbidding look. "I must make sure you are safe." He stared at her with an intensity that sent her back a step. "I believe myself the better swordsman, though even the best have met their match to their dismay." With an effort, he relaxed his face and forced a smile. "I'd be even happier to know I'd left you with my child in your belly, but I trust you would have told me by now if you even suspected you were increasing." His smile turned rueful, so he looked like nothing so much as a small boy about to be scolded. "I confess I have prayed you'd come to me with such news, for with that circumstance alone I would have cried off the marriage with Dora despite yours or Duncan's protests."

She sighed and hung her head. "No, my lord, I have had my courses since we were together at Christmas." That circumstance had occurred to her as well, and knowing what Tris's reaction would likely be, she'd resolved to simply disappear. If she'd sold all her things, she could have lived quietly in Susan's village until the child was born. Thankfully, she'd been spared that decision when her courses had appeared a week later. "But let us not speak of such things now." She forced a smile to her lips. "We are to be married, which means we should make merry this evening."

"Indeed we must." Tris's brooding countenance lightened. "Let me retire to my chamber. Betsy will return any moment to dress you. Wear something blue for me, love. You are a vision in blue gowns." His gaze roved eagerly over her figure and her cheeks burned.

"I will do so, my lord, and happily so, if you in turn will wear a certain blue velvet suit if you have it with you." Despite their history, or perhaps because of it, the thought of him in that garment always lit her with desire.

With a grin, he pulled her to him once more, cradling her against him. "Your wish shall be my command."

* * * *

The candle in her bedchamber had burned low as Violet tossed and turned in the big four-poster. A comfortable bed, a well-banked, and a room toasty warm should have sent her to sleep immediately. Instead, she sat up, punched her pillow, and lay down again, no more or less comfortable.

She wanted Tris in her bed.

After they'd finished the late supper in the taproom, Betsy had helped her undress, wash, and dress for bed. Violet had attempted to send the girl away, back to the kitchen or her room. Anywhere but here where she would know if Violet stole across the corridor to her "guardian's" chamber for a night of passion.

Betsy now slumbered peacefully on the trundle bed beneath her, snoring loudly enough to drown out a full orchestra.

Another reason she couldn't fall asleep.

Violet peered over the edge of the bed at the maid's swaddled figure, the edge of her mob cap fluttering with every breath and rattling of noise. How deeply did the girl sleep was the question.

With the stealth of a starving tiger, she eased back the covers and slithered to the end of the bed. Inch by agonizing inch she slid off the mattress until her toes touched the icy floor. Peeking around the bedpost, she held her breath.

Betsy slumbered on.

Still refusing to breathe, Violet crept to the door, her gaze fixed on the figure lying in the trundle. She'd insisted on the candle remaining lit in a strange bedroom and now she was doubly glad of it. When she reached the door she exhaled at last. So far so good. A quick turn of the key and she was ready. Grasping the handle oh so gently, she closed her eyes and pressed down, praying the latch wouldn't click so loud, nor the door creak. She was so focused on easing the door open, when it swung wide easily she stumbled backward in surprise, trod on a discarded shoe and almost cried out.

Violet clamped her hands over her mouth, staring in horror as Betsy sat up in the bed.

The girl blinked unseeing eyes, grunted, and turned over to face the big bed. She settled down in the covers once more and the rattling snores began afresh.

Clutching her chest, Violet was certain she'd have a seizure of some sort. Her heart gave a huge thump, then subsided to a normal beat. The dim corridor remained quiet as well. Perhaps the Fates would stand on her side tonight. She stepped over the threshold and closed the door as carefully as she could, then sped across to the door on the left.

Should she knock or simply open the door? Of course, he'd probably locked it. She raised her hand to knock. What if he didn't want her in his bed tonight? She lowered her hand. He hadn't intimated it either while they ate or afterward when they kissed goodnight. Surely, he would have at least hinted at it if he desired to spend the night with her.

The door behind her remained closed, a faint buzzing through the wood the only sign of life. Her resolve firmed. They were to be married tomorrow or the next day. He wanted her. The memory of the touch of his skin on hers, the thought of his heavy body pressing her into the mattress as he claimed her as his once more drove her to scratch at the door.

"Tris?" She could scarcely hear the whisper herself. To hell with doubt. She plunged the handle down and the door swung inward. She scurried in and shut the door quietly, mindful of being caught in the corridor.

The room was cloaked in darkness. Not even a crack of light showed through the break in the curtains, although the dim glow of the fireplace became apparent as her eyesight adjusted. She peered into the shadows where she believed the bed might be.

The click of a pistol being cocked reverberated in the cool air.

Chapter 31

Violet stopped dead and clamped her hand over her mouth. She had entered the wrong room and was about to be shot for her mistake. Should she dive for the door? Drop to the floor? The room's inhabitant would likely aim high. Or should she call out and announce herself? She could explain she'd gotten into the wrong room—which was nothing but the truth. The man—she assumed the occupant was a man—might fire first, without letting her identify herself.

"I'd suggest exiting the room now, whoever you are, unless you wish a ball in your buttocks," a man spoke in an even voice from the inky blackness to her right.

"Tris?" Violet swayed, almost swooning at the familiar sound of her beloved.

"Violet!"

A light flared, illuminating Tris propped up in bed, clothed but for his boots and jacket. "What the devil…what are you…" His eyes seemed huge and dark in the dim light of the single candle. The scowl on his face, however, was plain enough. He scrambled from the bed, tucking the pistol into his waistband. Two strides and he stood before her. "I could have shot you."

"I'm rather glad you did not, my love." Giddy with relief, she laid her head on his shoulder. "There are so many more peasant things I can think of for you to do to me."

His chest heaved and he clutched her to him. "What on earth are you doing in my chamber?" Stepping back, he peered at her, all the lines in his face hard as stone. "I paid for a maid to keep your reputation spotless until we can marry."

"My reputation hasn't been spotless since I met you." She tried to suppress a giggle at his frown and failed. "And I am here because I cannot wait one more day to be with you, my love." She ran her hand down his firm jaw, the scratch of his night beard thrilling to her fingertips.

"Violet. Love." Shaking his head, he gathered her back to his chest. "I could wish for nothing more either, than to have you in my bed." He sighed and a tremor ran through him. "However, should anyone find you in here…"

Determined to have her way, she laid her hand over his lips. "Let them. I do not care what they will say, if anyone is even interested. Simon Harper may put out lies about me, but we shall be married tomorrow, God willing. And I doubt anyone will want to besmirch the reputation of Viscountess Trevor, especially after you trounce Mr. Harper." She turned his head until all he could see was her face. "Please let me stay. Love me, Tris. Please love me."

"Darling. Oh, my love." He kissed her lips until her breath ran out. "I have dreamed of this moment ever since I left you." His arms around her in a fierce grip, he seemed to never want to let her go. "We shall love one another tonight, and damn the consequences." Kisses rained down upon her as he caressed her eyes, her cheeks, her neck.

Chills raced down her spine. Her toes tingled and her body flashed hot and cold by turns. Nothing had ever felt as wonderful as his lips on her. "Oh God, what are you doing to me, Tris?"

"It's what I want to do to you, my love, that matters most." He growled, the vibration tickling her neck.

"Hmmm." She rubbed her breasts against his shirt, the snowy linen sheer enough she could see the interest in his puckered nipples, hard as bullets. Dropping her head to his chest, she licked one of the tiny points through his shirt. The feel of his flesh on her tongue, even through the material, made her core ache with need.

With a groan, Tris squeezed her arms. "We need to remove your clothes. Now."

At last. "What you will, my lord." She backed toward the bed, inching her nightgown over first one, then the other shoulder. Her training at Madame Vestry's would be put to good use tonight. She twitched her shoulders and the garment slid down her arms until it barely covered her nipples, creating the illusion it would fall at any moment.

Tris's gaze, fixed squarely on her breasts, certainly avowed he believed it so.

In truth, she held the cloth in place by squeezing her arms tight to her sides so she controlled the moment of revelation. The hot, dark eyes of her betrothed told her time was nigh. She breathed deeply, expanding her chest fully, and let the gown drop.

With a hiss, he sucked in air and tore at his cravat, even as his eyes feasted on her naked body. A flurry of white cascaded to the floor at her feet as he ripped off his clothing and pounced, bearing her onto the mattress. His hungry mouth devoured hers as his hands caressed and kneaded her breasts.

She arched into his hands, his long awaited touch so welcome she almost dissolved into pleasure the moment he claimed her. Lord, but he made her want to be wanton.

"Violet. Oh, God." His hot breath tickled her ear. "I'm sorry, love. I cannot wait." He urged his knees between her thighs.

"I don't want you to." God knew she'd been wanting him long enough.

With his groan sounding blissfully in her ear, he surged forward, filling all of her.

"Ahh." The fullness of him was almost too exquisite to bear. She slid her arms around him, urging him to thrust harder, deeper. Let him sear her to the bone so she could dissolve into a puddle of sated desire.

He quickened his pace, grunting, straining faster and faster until she cried out, the sudden blinding pleasure taking her unawares.

Wave after wave washed through her. As from a distance she heard Tris cry her name, then he sagged onto her, his warm weight better than any blanket ever made.

They lay panting, her frantic breaths in counterpoint to his. She could lie entwined like this forever, but a twitch of her hips sent him rolling off her. No, he couldn't go so soon. A frantic grab and she rolled with him, coming to lie with her head upon his chest. His heart hammered in her ear, slowly quieting to a steady thump, thump. Oh, but she couldn't wait to make it race again.

"Ahhh," Tris groaned, flinging one arm over his head. "I'm ruined. I'll never be good for anything again."

Pretending to pout, she poked her lip out at him. "And here I thought we might try that once or twice more before the night was through. However, if you don't feel capable…"

He growled, flipping her easily underneath him once more, pinning her arms to the mattress. "Not capable?" He dragged his tongue down her neck to her breast. "I'll make you incapable of walking down the aisle at you own wedding, vixen."

What a delicious thought. She giggled.

"You think I jest?" A wolf-like smile on his lips, teeth gleaming, his hair shaggy around his face made him look deliciously dangerous. Slowly, he drew first one, then the other hand up over her head, making her breasts thrust impudently into the cool air. He lowered his lips to the right one, clasped them around her nipple, and sucked.

An explosion of heat rocked her, streaking down to her core where it became a slickness that made her moan. "Oh, do that some more," she breathed, pushing herself against his mouth. God, she was ready for him even now.

In response he flicked his tongue rapidly back and forth against the sensitive nub.

"Tris! Oh, please—"

A floorboard outside the door creaked.

Tris bounded up off her and stood before the door before she had raised her head. Dear Lord, he was fast. "What is it?" she whispered.

He shook his head, then pressed his ear once more to the oak panel, and grasped the latch. A minute later he relaxed his watchful pose, then hefted the room's one armchair and placed it against the door, under the latch.

"What on earth are you doing?" Raised up on her elbows, Violet frowned at him.

"What I should have done before we were consumed with desire." He shook his head. "I was a fool. Anyone could have burst in on us."

"Why didn't you simply lock the door?"

"The latch is broken and the landlord hasn't had it fixed yet." Tris bent and fished in the heap of his clothing on the floor. When he straightened, the pistol gleamed in his hand. "That's why I was sitting up in bed with this, waiting to see if anyone would show up."

"Other than me?" She smiled, although she kept her gaze on the gun.

"Yes, other than you, sweetheart. You were actually a surprise." He chuckled.

"Then who were you expecting?" Surely not another woman. Cold now he no longer warmed her, she snaked the covers over her naked body.

"Simon Harper." Tris padded to the fireplace, probed the embers into a blaze, and tossed on another log. His stern profile, lit by the flickering flames, as much as his words made her heart thud painfully in her chest.

"Goodness." That was probably the last name she expected to hear. "Why would Mr. Harper follow us here? Your duel is set. What reason would he have for seeking you out?" She sat up, pulling the covers over her shoulders. Even the newly blazing wood couldn't drive out the cold that touched her heart.

"Because he's a coward who would rather kill me in cold blood in a surprise attack than face me honorably in a fight he will likely lose." Another chuckle, deeper this time, more dangerous. He climbed into bed, laid the pistol carefully on the table, and slid down next to her, instantly allaying her fears. Once he'd tucked the covers around her and settled her head again on his shoulder, he asked, "Did you wonder at Downing's horror at the mention of the Marquess of Dalbury?"

"I scarcely realized I was standing in the library after that attack and the whirl of events. But I remember thinking it odd he seemed frightened of the marquess." She ran her fingers through the mat of dark hair on his chest, soothed by the touch of him, by the warmth of the crackling fire. Nothing could come between them now.

"Well, Lord Downing would give much to never set eyes on Duncan again. Simon Harper was one of the first men to dishonor Duncan's sister Juliet with his slanderous lies."

"He what?" She shot up, hovering over Tris. "And your friend let him live?" If the marquess hadn't killed Harper, then why had he killed Kit for the same offense? And led to Jamie's death. The old wound bled afresh. Why of all people had Tris been the one to defend his friend and inadvertently kill Jamie?

"Shhh." As if he knew her thoughts, Tris wrapped his arms around her and drew her to him. "Had Duncan been allowed to meet Harper, his wife would likely have been a widow long before he injured her. Downing came to Dunham House, Harper at his heels like a whipped puppy. He wanted the duel, was mad to pit himself against the marquess. Downing, however, had found out about Duncan's reputation with a blade and pleaded with him to spare his heir. Harper had to make a public apology to Duncan and retract his statement about Lady Juliet." Tris stroked her arm, soothing her prickly mood. When his strokes moved to her breast, tension of another kind began to build.

"Ummm."

He slid down beneath the covers until only his head poked out. "Let us see if I can do better." Beginning at the tip of her breast, he kissed the tender flesh, then pulled the nipple into his mouth, laving it with his tongue.

"Ahhh." Her body flushed, exquisite heat rising all over her.

He stroked the other breast, tweaking the nipple in counterpoint to the ravages his mouth was making on the other.

How had she believed she could ever live without him? He knew her body better than she did, certainly how best to pleasure it.

"Ohhh." She couldn't keep silent as she caught fire. Her hips twitched, seeking his other heat.

Swiftly, he lifted himself over her, settling between her thighs, and the ache there became excruciating.

"I need to feel you inside me, Tris." She kneaded his back, ready to beg him to fill her again.

"Soon, love." He kissed her lips, then vanished beneath the covers. His kisses continued to roam along her body, over breasts, stomach, the tender flesh above her mound. Heat seared her cheeks and she moaned as he searched through her thicket, his tongue like a hound nosing out game. When he brushed a sensitive spot, she shrieked and shot bolt upright as tongues of fire filled her core.

Tris slid his hand up her body, soothing her, urging her back upon the mattress.

Bit by bit she relaxed back onto the bed, moaning and writhing as he continued to stroke her intimate flesh. Madame Vestry had told her of such a spot, but never had she given it any thought. Until Tris had shown her on Christmas Day. Now, each time he ventured there with his mouth, she thought the pleasure it gave would overwhelm her. Could someone die from such attentions?

He slid a finger into her wet channel, all the while swirling his tongue around the little bead of passion. Oh, what a fire he stoked, stroking in and out, deliberately triggering the coiling sensation in her belly toward that wonderful release. When he slid a second finger in, her toes curled and she clutched the mattress as wave after wave of her shudders shook the bed.

Tris rose above her and in one liquid move filled her again with his long, hard, burning member. He thrust smooth and strong, until he claimed her completely.

Her body, still twitching from its previous release, now surged anew, gripping him time and again with an intensity that took her breath away. She stared into the blue eyes above her as intent on her face as she was on them, and abandoned herself to the bliss that consumed her.

"Violet. Oh, God." His face contorted, mouth open, head flung back as he erupted within her. He collapsed onto her, sweet heaviness pressing her into the mattress. His breath rasped in her ear, and then he rolled off her and lay panting. "You've truly killed me this time."

Drowsy now, she managed a chuckle. "And you have done for me, my love."

"Then I'll see you in heaven."

"I'm already there."

* * * *

Furious knocking brought Violet out of a sweet dream of Tristan and her playing on a grassy hill with nine children, all of them theirs. She wiped her hand over her eyes, yawned, and sat up in bed.

"Who's there?" A shadowy silhouette of Tris stood at the door, swiftly tying the belt of his gray silk banyan. Early rays of sun creeping through the window glinted off the pistol in his hand.

"Oh, m'lord!" Betsy's terrified wail penetrated the door easily. "She's gone. Miss Carlton's been spirited away in the night. I swear I scarce shut my eyes, m'lord, and when I looked again she was nowhere t' be found."

"Damn," Tris swore under his breath.

Violet bit her lip to keep from laughing. It truly wasn't funny. She didn't need the maid spreading tales about her and Tris, even though they might be married today. Married. The word echoed in her mind. She drew her legs up and clasped her arms around them, pure joy radiating throughout her. The cold air penetrated her dazed mind and she snagged the cover, drawing it up around her shoulders.

Tris frowned at her. "What must I say?" he whispered to her, uncocking the pistol and laying it in the chair that still barricaded the door. Without waiting for an answer, he called through the door, "Are her things missing?"

"No, my lord. All is just as she left it when she went t' sleep."

"Help, please," he hissed.

Stifling a laugh once more, Violet mouthed a word. "Privy?"

"Have you checked the privy, Betsy? She may have gone down there."

"Oh, no, m'lord. I came straight to ye. I'll run right down and see. I hope to goodness that's where she is." Her footfalls hurried away.

Tris moved the chair, cocked his head toward the door, waited a beat, then cracked it open. "She's gone." He shut the door and leaned on it, exhaling. "Quick, before she returns."

Laughing softly, Violet threw back the covers, wincing as the cold air pricked up gooseflesh all over her body. Every hair must be standing on end. "Where's my gown?" She slid out of bed and padded toward him.

He retrieved it from the floor and dropped it over her head. The regret in his eyes as it covered her body warmed her better than the fabric. He pulled her close, his kiss urgent and lingering.

"Tris, I must go." She broke the kiss, little as she wished to.

He sighed and nodded, chaffing her arms as though loathe to lose touch with her.

"Shall I order breakfast laid in the parlor?" They could be together, just not in bed.

"Please." He cupped her cheek and she gloried in his warmth. "I'll dress and be there directly."

She nodded, then flung her arms around him, pulling his head down for one last kiss.

At last he broke them apart, pushing her away and breathing hard. "Go now before I throw you back in that bed."

A floorboard creaked in the corridor.

"Damn. Go!" He wrenched the door open and Violet sped out of the room, no thought for who might be about. Fortunately, at this early an hour, few stirred.

She crossed to her room in two swift strides. What a morning. Before she entered she turned back to Tris's door. What a night. Humming, she continued into her room, stripped off her gown and darted behind the screen to wash. By this evening she wouldn't have to sneak into Tris's room, thank God.

The door opened.

"Oh, miss. Wherever can ye be?" The maid's soft plaintive cry hung in the air.

"I'm here, Betsy," she called, trying to put the right amount of nonchalance into her voice.

"Oh, Miss Carlton!" Betsy popped her head around the screen.

Startled, Violet attempted to unsuccessfully cover her nakedness with her hands.

The girl had dressed in haste, her cap askew, apron hanging to the side of her skirt. "Wherever have ye been, miss? I been searching for ye all morning long."

"I went down to the privy earlier. You were still asleep. Then I came back up here, just now, but you had gone." Violet grasped the pitcher. "Can you fetch me some warm water? The cold is brisker than I thought."

"Of course, miss." Betsy seized the pitcher and disappeared.

"And please order breakfast laid in the parlor for me and Lord Trevor. I'll step across and invite him as soon as I'm dressed."

"Very good, miss."

The door closed and Violet slumped. She simply wasn't cut out for a life of intrigue.

Chapter 32

Tris sat savoring his coffee after a very enjoyable breakfast. Not that he could say exactly what he had eaten; it could have been shoe leather for all he cared. His full attention had been taken up with staring at the beautiful woman across the table from him, the wonder that she would soon be his wife stealing all awareness of the food placed before him. Which brought them to the next matter. "If you are quite done, my dear, we have an errand to attend to."

Violet beamed at him over her teacup. Her eyes were rimmed with dark circles, testament to the lack of sleep they'd gotten. Still, the glow in those amber orbs sent a bolt of desire straight to his groin. They'd get precious little sleep for a long time to come after the wedding. "Where are we going, Tris?" She set her cup in the saucer and clasped his hand. "I'd hoped we might…rest a while after breakfast." The rush of pink to her cheeks belied that resting was on her mind.

"Perhaps we may 'rest' this afternoon, love," he said with a rueful smile. "This morning I propose we seek out the parish vicar and arrange to be married as soon as Duncan arrives with the special license."

The broad smile that burst forth made her face glow, as if happiness itself shone there. "Then I will get my cloak while you order the carriage around, my lord. We must make 'haste to the wedding.'" She leaned closer and whispered, "I would not waste a precious moment in making our marriage come to pass."

"Neither would I, sweetheart." He dropped his napkin on his plate and rose. "I will get my cloak and meet you downstairs." The closeness of her drove him wild. Every time he looked at her, his desire to possess her sweet body must show clearly on his face. The sooner they married, the sooner he could stop feeling guilty about their illicit liaison.

He spent the short ride into Devizes mooning over Violet, who sat beside him chatting animatedly about their return to London, and dreading the upcoming interview with the vicar. The niggling fear the man would refuse to marry them, special license or not, ate at him like a cankerworm. She must become his wife before that blasted duel. He would not risk leaving her destitute once more should Harper somehow manage to best him and take his life.

"You look rather grave, my love." She grasped his hand and drew it onto her lap, the warmth of her stealing into him. "Does the thought of returning to London distress you?"

"There could be no greater joy for me than to enter a London ballroom with you on my arm, my sweet." There was nothing he looked forward to more than presenting her to London Society as his viscountess. Pray God he would be able to do so. Still, he wouldn't alarm her with morbid speculations. He raised their clasped hands and kissed hers, tingling with the anticipation of further delights when they returned to the inn. "No, I merely wish these preliminaries done and over so we may celebrate the beginning of our life together."

"Ummm. I like the sound of that." Violet raised their hands and returned the kiss. When he thought she was letting go his hand, she instead stripped the glove from it, made as if to kiss it again then licked the flesh on the back of his knuckles.

"Good God, Violet." His cock stiffened as if by magic. "Where did you learn to do that?"

"Need you ask, my lord?" The mischievous twinkle in her eyes gave away the answer.

"I suppose not, although I will insist on exploring more of your erotic knowledge later…in our chamber."

She kissed his hand again, a quick peck that did nothing to dispel the discomfort in his breeches. "I shall await that encounter with great anticipation."

An urge to turn the carriage around and head back immediately seized him. His blood had heated to a feverish boil the instant she touched him. Where else might she employ that tongue? Damn. He scooted an inch or two away from her enticement. Not since Bathsheba tempted King David had a man faced worse torture. They must present themselves before the vicar if they intended to be married. Pray God the interview was short.

Fortune shone on them in the person of Mr. Ezekiel Curry, the vicar of St. Mary's. Once the little man understood what they wished, he agreed to hold the wedding in the event the special license was properly presented with witnesses. After this agreement had been reached, in a mercifully short time, Tris and Violet were left to inspect the stained glass windows behind the altar.

Unfortunate he and Violet could not be married with all the pomp and circumstance of a proper wedding at St. George's in London. Dressed in a spectacular gown, with a bevy of attendants also in their finery, she would have been the talk of the town. An equally impressive wedding breakfast with all their friends and family—quite half the *ton* would be in attendance. He'd wager a good horse on it. Did she mind having to settle for him, Duncan, and Manning? If only they need not make haste. He would make it up to her somehow.

They left the church arm in arm. The sun showed brilliantly, though the bitter wind had picked up. Tris put his arm around her to help shield her from the chill. He started toward the carriage, glad to be heading back to the toasty inn.

"Tris!"

"Duncan!" Tris had jerked his head up, instinctively drawing Violet behind him, though he recognized the voice almost immediately. He leaped forward and clasped the man standing in front of a strange carriage about the neck. "By all that is holy, how do you come here so soon?"

* * * *

Violet's heart lurched, startled by the unexpected appearance, then beat furiously as Tris eagerly greeted the man who had killed her cousin. She dropped her gaze to the slate-gray pebbles and dead grass at her feet. Although she'd heard much of the Marquess of Dalbury, she had not seen him before. In the end, curiosity outweighed animosity. She raised her head just enough that she could assess him without a direct gaze.

An inch or two shorter than Tris, and with a slighter build, the marquess's imposing demeanor still proclaimed his air of command. Authority emanated from his casual stance as he leaned back, surveying her and Tris with one penetrating look. Even the offhand way his cloak draped over his shoulders gave him the appearance of someone whose word was obeyed without question. He clasped Tris's shoulder, pleasure in their meeting drawn in every line of his smiling face. Like one would greet a brother.

She'd never pressed Tris for details about his friendship with the marquess, but from what she'd gleaned, she'd thought theirs a mere friendship. The devotion evident in Dalbury's face, however, had her revising that opinion. The connection between them seemed close as a blood relation. Without a doubt the man would be a part of their lives and she couldn't imagine having to endure his presence in their home, perhaps on a regular basis. If she were to judge from Tris's reaction right now—his face animated, his stance close to the marquess, his conversation which hadn't stopped in five minutes—she'd have to learn to mask her feelings for the marquess.

"Violet…Miss Carlton." Tris took her arm, pulling her forward to stand before the marquess and his companion.

Her legs trembled. Hopefully they'd blame it on the cold. She was about to meet the father of her misfortunes, like it or not.

"Miss Carlton, may I present Lord Dalbury?"

"My lord." She cast her gaze down and curtsied to avoid meeting his eyes.

"Duncan, I think you have not met my betrothed, Miss Carlton?"

"No, we have not met, although I believe we have a connection through tragic circumstances."

Violet jerked her head up at the gentle, respectful tone. Somehow she'd expected surliness or mockery from the despicable man. Instead, his rich brown eyes held compassion, his demeanor a gravity bordering on regret.

"Allow me to extend my belated condolences on the deaths of your brother, your cousin, and your grandmother. Tristan has told me of the misfortunes my encounter with Mr. Davies and Mr. Carlton have cost you. I wish, for your sake, the outcome of that meeting had been much different."

Uncertain how to respond, she drew into herself, murmuring, "Thank you, my lord." She could hardly rail at him in front of Tris, and of course, the circumstances were not completely his fault. No one had forced Kit to insult his family.

Brows swooping down into a scowl, Lord Dalbury's face darkened. "I have since discovered the author of those unfortunate events was one Thomas Redmond, who used your cousin most cruelly to strike at me. I can tell you, although he has not been brought to the justice he deserves, he has suffered a loss." The marquess shot a look at Tris, who turned away smiling. "Still, if there is any service I may do you, Miss Carlton, you have but to name it. I am yours to command."

On the tip of her tongue to tell him to jump in the ice-caked River Avon, she took a breath instead and settled. It would do no good to disparage a man so obviously Tris's friend. Best then to make him help her in the only way that counted. "Thank you, my lord. My one request is that you keep Lord Trevor safe during this hideous duel tomorrow. I would have him come back to me whole and well."

He bowed, an elegant gesture full of charm and grace. "I will do everything within my power to return him to you unscathed."

Violet nodded her thanks and breathed easier. Lord Dalbury would protect Tris with his life, she was sure of it.

So taken up with the shock of meeting the marquess, she'd paid no attention to the stranger he'd brought with him. Blond hair, a shade or two darker than Dalbury's, of the same height, though perhaps a bit bigger boned. Not as well dressed as the marquess, yet a gentleman certainly.

The careful way in which he scrutinized her, however, made the hairs on the back of her neck rise.

Why on earth was he here?

"Where is Lord Manning?" she whispered to Tris.

"Good question," he murmured in return. "Has some tragedy befallen Lord Manning, Duncan?" He gave a short nod toward the blond stranger. "And I don't believe I've met this gentleman."

"Manning has been unavoidably detained in London on business I am not at liberty to disclose." The marquess's eye twitched, though his face otherwise remained unmoved.

She shuddered to think what could have been so dire it prevented his lordship from coming to her defense.

"But allow me to present Mr. Reginald Matthews, Miss Carlton. And Lord Trevor. Mr. Matthews is a relation of my wife's and a man of great discretion."

The stranger bowed, a subtle air of command in him.

"Tris, a word if you please." Lord Dalbury pulled him aside, leaving her to entertain Mr. Matthews.

She curtsied, curious at his keen gaze that seemed to take in her every aspect. "You are kind to have taken on this arduous journey with no notice, Mr. Matthews. I must thank you for assisting Lord Trevor in the odious duel."

The man smiled, immediately transforming his rather severe countenance into a handsome, jovial one. "I seem to be constantly embroiled in duels on account of the marquess despite my profession."

"Your profession?" Was the man a lawyer?

"I'm a Bow Street Runner, Miss Carlton. And dueling is illegal under the law. By rights, I am bound to stop them whenever I am able." His almost merry attitude all but belied his statement.

"And are you come to stop this duel?" Hope leaped in her chest. If this man could prevent the duel, Tris would be safe.

"Well, Lord Dalbury made me swear an oath not to interfere, especially as I have been pressed into service as a second in the duel. I assure you, it would not appear favorably to my superiors, in light of the fact I am being considered for the position of magistrate. And Dalbury assures me they will be informed if I lift a hand to prevent the altercation other than my duty to attempt a reconciliation." A comic roll of his eyes and he chuckled ruefully. "I'm enjoying the irony. I don't suppose Lord Trevor wishes to reconcile?" he called to Lord Dalbury.

"I'd as soon shoot Duncan here," Tris interrupted smoothly, coming to stand by her side. "Or you, my love." He nodded to Matthews. "You can tell Simon Harper, short of someone presenting his head on a pike to me, I'll meet him at first light tomorrow as promised."

"Duly noted, my lord." Mr. Matthews bowed and retreated to the carriage.

"Duncan has carried out all my commissions with his usual dependable thoroughness and speed. The fool actually set out this morning at five o'clock—after terrorizing the Archbishop of Canterbury—and drove all through the day, arriving at the Black Horse only to find us gone." Tris chuckled. "He tracked us here on Mrs. Cheeley's advice, to deliver this." With an exaggerated flourish, he drew a piece of parchment from his jacket. "A special license. We can be married whenever we wish."

"Not the easiest document to obtain in the dead of night. Saunders staggered into my house at three o'clock." The marquess cocked his head. "You must raise the man's wages a sovereign or two, Tris. He rode straight through, stopping only to change horses and down a pint of ale along the way. Made it in eight hours, which I didn't believe possible. Must be a record of some sort. In any case, I am fortunate my Aunt Phoebe is godmother to His Grace, the Archbishop. The man didn't hesitate to see me even at that ungodly hour. At least he hadn't gone to bed yet. I suppose he'd rather deal with me than have my aunt knocking on his door to find out why he didn't accommodate me."

"Shall we go in this minute, my love, and be married before another hour passes?" Tris took her hands, staring at her with so much love tears started from her eyes.

"Oh, yes, Tris." Heart beating a tattoo, Violet squeezed his hands and they turned toward the church once more.

"Oh, no you don't miss."

Violet whirled around.

Leaning on a black hawthorn cane, her left ankle in bandages, Susan stood in front of the marquess's carriage. "You will not go to your wedding in a brown wool gown suitable for travel and nothing else."

"Susan!" Violet rushed forward, throwing her arms around her friend. "How wonderful to see you. But how do you come here?" Reluctantly, she released Susan and stood back, taking the woman in with a hungry gaze. The bandaged foot peeped out from beneath her striped skirts.

"His lordship," she nodded toward the marquess, who was again deep in conversation with Tris, "knocked on my door just before five o'clock—I've no idea how he found me—and told me of your circumstances. Of course, I had to come."

"But your foot—"

Susan waved the objection away. "I stupidly tripped coming down a narrow flight of stairs at my lodgings. My landlady helped me bandage it and called the surgeon. He says it is not broken, but I'm to rest it for at least a month."

"And here you are traipsing across the countryside clear to Wiltshire. Come into the church and sit down." Violet took her arm, but Susan winced and stood her ground.

"I've been sitting for nigh on ten hours, miss. I could do with a stretch." The penetrating way she looked Violet over, head to heels, made her suddenly feel like a small child being inspected before going to Sunday service. "I see my work is cut out for me. I've brought your blue silk with the darker stripe. Do you remember it?"

Completely awed by her maid's efficient, no-nonsense manner, Violet nodded.

"Then let us return to the inn and I will turn you out for your wedding as though we were in London and this St. George's." Gingerly, Susan eased her weight from her injured ankle and leaned more heavily on her stick. "Lord Trevor, you, Lord Dalbury, Mr. Matthews, and Saunders take Lord Dalbury's carriage. I'll take yours and accompany Miss Carlton back to the inn and get her ready. If you wish to stay, we will return within the hour."

"What do you say, Duncan?" Tris looked eagerly toward his friend "Shall we head for The Swan, grab a pint, and discuss this duel tomorrow?"

"I'd rather confront Mr. Harper now, if possible," Mr. Matthews said, moving toward the marquess's carriage. "How far to his residence?"

"Harper's Grange is only about two and a half miles farther on. You could make it there and back in an hour or so." Tris grinned at them all. "I suspect the meeting will be of short duration."

"I believe, as I have time now before the wedding, I will do just that." With a bow, Matthews opened the carriage door, then turned back. "Your terms, all joking aside?"

All humor left Tris's face and he grunted. "The terms stand as they did the last time he was challenged to a duel. He apologizes to Miss Carlton privately and upon pain of exposure never speaks to her or of her ever again. Otherwise, I shall meet him in the morning."

A cold chill sent a shiver through Violet, like a goose stepping on her grave. This duel suddenly seemed very real and menacing.

"Come, miss. I shall have the satisfaction of seeing you turned out a treat before you wed his lordship." Smiling, Susan put an arm around her shoulders and drew her toward Tris's carriage.

At the reassuring touch, Violet found her fluttering stomach calming. Stokes handed them into the carriage then leaped onto the seat and started the swift trip to The Black Horse.

Once there, Susan's fussing over her clothes and hair proved more soothing to her than she would have imagined. If she closed her eyes, she could almost believe they were back at Lammas House, preparing for dinner with Tris. After tonight, she would always prepare for dinner with him, for he would be hers alone.

Her husband.

She could scarcely take it in. A strange feeling of unreality assailed her, as though she stood outside herself, watching as Susan twisted her hair, pinning it into an elegant coil. It was actually her, however. Her wedding day.

"You're going to need to hire a real lady's maid, Miss," Susan said, sliding another pin into the back of her coiffure.

"I have a lady's maid, Susan." The woman looking back from the mirror seemed scared and unsure, eyes wide, brows drooping, hands clasped tightly in her lap. "You."

"Me!" So startled she almost dropped the pin she clutched, Susan stared back at Violet in the mirror, her hand still poised over the already exquisite arrangement. "I can't be maid to you once you marry Lord Trevor. I was maid to every one of his mistresses for the past seven years."

"Including me." Violet smiled grimly at her reflection. "Nothing has changed, save I will be true mistress of his house. I see no reason why you cannot continue."

"But it wouldn't be proper, Miss Carlton." Susan stepped back, hands on hips, glaring.

Fortunately, Violet had seen that look before. She twisted in her chair until she faced the woman she would not do without. "To the devil with propriety. I've never been a titled lady before, yet in an hour I will be Lady Trevor. You may have been a maid to women who were not accepted in polite society, but that counts for nothing. You have done nothing of which to be ashamed. I know you will be splendid as my lady's maid, and I dare anyone to try and dissuade me from that, including you."

"But miss—"

"Either you accept my proposal or I will take down my hair, remove this gown and put on the gray one you hate so much and be married in that with a thick braid down my back." Head held high to feign an assurance she didn't quite feel, Violet rose and faced Susan. She wouldn't lose her friend or her best chance at presenting herself flawlessly before society.

"That's what you call blackmail, miss." Susan's pouting lips sang a song of victory to Violet.

"Shall I change then?" Mischievously, Violet let her hand drop to the bodice of the blue changeable silk, shot through with darker stripes of blue and now embellished with crystals over bodice and sleeves. Cut low at the breast, it was a truly elegant garment that could be used for any formal occasion. Violet grasped the stomacher, tugging it from its pouch at the front.

"No, miss!" Darting forward, Susan stayed her hand. "I'll stay. I'll stay with you until you get a proper maid."

"Not good enough." Violet jerked the stiffened fabric upward, almost dislodging it.

"Stop! You'll ruin it." She clenched her hands and swore under her breath. "All right. I will remain as your lady's maid until you no longer require my services."

Violet threw her arms around her friend, hugging her fiercely. "Now, come, let me be married."

By the time she and Susan stood beside Tristan and the marquess at the entrance to St. Anne's, the shadows were lengthening on the churchyard grass. Where had the day gone?

"What are we waiting for?"

"Matthews has not returned." The marquess cocked his head. "Although I believe that is about to be remedied." He nodded toward his carriage as it rounded the corner and swept up to the door. Matthews jumped out, then extended his hand to someone in the interior.

Violet drew closer to Tris. Who on earth—

"Dora!" Two steps and she hugged her friend, unable to fully take in her presence. "But…how?" Further speech failed her.

"I saw the carriage drive up and had to take my chance." Dora's blue eyes sparkled. "It has been horrible since yesterday. Father has cursed both me and Simon morning and night. Mother took to her bed with smelling salts and my aunt has enjoyed the whole spectacle." Dora grasped Violet's hands, squeezing them so tight she winced. "Father confined me to my room, but I stole down and listened to Simon berate Mr. Matthews when he asked for the names and direction for his seconds. Simon said he could perform the formalities tomorrow in the woods, as there was no way he'd miss the pleasure of running Lord Trevor through." With a laugh, Dora rolled her eyes. "Simon is worse than a fool."

"He sounds it," Susan mumbled.

Dora cut her gaze at the young woman, then shrugged. "He is one, make no mistake. It will be his downfall, rather sooner than later I believe." Clutching Violet's hands, she beamed at her friend. "Anyway, when Mr. Matthews left the library, I accosted him and asked after you. He told me the situation and I insisted on accompanying him here to see you married."

"Alone?" Violet raised an eyebrow at that revelation. Matthews certainly looked harmless, but society dictated Dora must be chaperoned.

"Larkin is with me." Dora nodded toward the carriage where the almost invisible, painfully shy maid crouched in the seat. "Your coachman will return us and perhaps with no one the wiser." She smiled brilliantly and urged Violet toward the church. "Come, let us all see you married."

Chapter 33

"The gentlemen have gone ahead, but if you will allow me, ladies." Mr. Matthews opened the door and Violet, Dora, and Susan passed inside.

"Thank you, Mr. Matthews," Violet said.

He followed them, remarking, "At least five degrees cooler in here without the sunlight."

The smallest of the churches in the town of Devizes, St. Mary's had seemed the more discreet choice of location for the wedding. Violet and Tris had discussed it at length and decided they wanted as few people as possible to know of their marriage, certainly not Lord and Lady Downing. After the duel they could return to London and announce it in grand style. Dora's presence in the wedding party with Susan, therefore, was an unexpected boon.

Violet blinked, her eyes adjusting quickly to the church's dim interior. The gray stone walls reflected what light still filtered through the stained-glass windows on either side of the nave. They depicted scenes from the life of Christ with St. Mary a prominent figure in each. Violet spied Tris with the marquess and the vicar standing in front of the altar. Tris smiled so broadly, his eyes so full of love, she trembled, scarcely able to continue down the aisle. The longest walk of her life, perhaps, but what a glorious prize awaited her at the journey's end.

"Here, my lady. Let me take your cloak." Susan drew the dark wool cape off her, revealing her pale blue satin brocade gown, pearl trim and glittering crystal embroidery on the bodice, neck, and cuffs catching the light of the candles.

Tris's eyes grew enormous, an appreciatory gleam in them. He shook his head, frowning. "Where did you get that gown? I recall one similar—"

"She left this one behind at Lammas House, your lordship," Susan volunteered. "I occupied my time with it on the journey here. I suspected she didn't have a gown grand enough for her wedding day and made sure to provide for it." She smoothed the fabric over Violet's waist and twitched the fit at the shoulders. "My wedding gift to you both."

"Thank you once more, Susan," Violet said, blinking back tears. She would be bubbling like a fountain soon if she didn't keep control. "But I am not 'my lady' yet."

"Wait ten minutes and you will be, my lady." Smile broadening, Susan glanced at Tris. "You had best take care of her or you answer to me, my lord."

"You have my oath on it, Susan. I vow to love and protect her until my dying breath." His words sent a trickle of fear down Violet's back, but she shook it off and took Tris's hand. A wave of joy washed over her. She'd think of this only, of them being joined together forever. Happiness poured through her, and fear faded.

Tris's gaze gentled as he drew her to stand beside him. He stared at her, brows arched, lips parted as though about to speak, his love on his face for all to see. As he continued to stare at her, the vicar began the service.

"Dearly beloved…"

Violet wanted to listen, to remember each word, every detail of this perfect moment. Instead, she heard nothing save the blood pulsing in her ears, her voice rasping as she gasped for breath, the low scraping of his thumb as he stroked the back of her hand. Not the memory of her wedding she'd planned. Still, it would be enough. She would remember these things for the rest of her life.

"Bless, O Lord, this ring to be a sign of the vows by which this man and this woman have bound themselves to each other through Jesus Christ our Lord. Amen." The vicar looked expectantly at Tris.

"Oh, d—" Tris clamped his lips shut and clutched her hand. "Can we do it without the ring, Mr. Curry?" he implored the vicar.

"Here, my lord." Dora darted forward, pulling a ring from her pocket. "I never got the chance to return it to you." Smiling, she dropped the gold and sapphire Trevor betrothal ring onto Tris's palm.

Speechless, Tris nodded, cleared his throat, and slid the ancestral ring onto her finger. "Violet, I give you this ring as a symbol of my vow…"

Time stood still as Violet stared at him, love for him pouring through her so fiercely tears of joy spilled down her cheeks. She belonged to Tris now. Forever.

"Amen." The vicar intoned the final word and closed his prayer book with a snap.

Before the echo could fade, Tris grasped her face and drew her to him. "I love you and you are mine, Lady Trevor." Then he crushed his lips against her with a force that stole her breath. Not a kiss of passion, but of possession, of two souls melding.

She never wanted it to end.

At last, he broke from her, grinning ear-to-ear.

Applause shook the empty church, thunderous despite the intimate congregation. The vicar produced the register and first Dora, then the marquess signed as witnesses. Violet and Tris signed as well before she found herself in the arms of first Susan, then Dora, tears of joy still spilling down her face. "Thank you. Thank you all so much." She turned from one dear friend to the other. "I cannot believe it is true. Like a fairy story."

"And you will live happily ever after," Dora pronounced, squeezing her hand. "I wish you all the joy and happiness you deserve, Violet. But I must say goodbye. If I am missed, it will be yet another row." She sighed. "I promise to pray very hard tomorrow morning for Lord Trevor." A slow shake of her head. "And perhaps a small prayer he doesn't actually kill Simon, deserve it though he might." Throwing her arms around Violet, she hugged her close. "Goodbye, Lady Trevor. I truly hope we meet again."

Violet nodded and let her go. "On the happiest of occasions, your wedding day. Farewell, my friend."

Dora turned to Tris, her face calm, though small worry lines showed around her eyes. "My lord, may I borrow your carriage to return to the Grange?"

"I think you need more protection than a mere coachman—no offense to Stokes, of course." With a deep bow, the Marquess of Dalbury presented himself before Dora. "Allow me and Mr. Matthews to accompany you and your maid home, with the chaperonage of Miss Douglas as well." He gestured to Susan, then winked at Dora. "If need be, I'll have a word with your father."

Tris snorted. "He'll die of an apoplexy if you show up, Duncan. But then he'd see you tomorrow morning in any case." He grabbed Violet's cloak from the pew and draped it securely around her shoulders. "I wish you good luck with your endeavor. Meanwhile, I shall accompany my wife—" he lingered over the word, then squeezed her shoulders "—back to The Black Horse and prepare a celebration for us all." Solicitously, he drew her arm through his. It fit perfectly, as though made for the crook of his elbow.

They strode down the church aisle and out into the stunning pinks and purples of the winter's sunset. What a beautiful world.

Violet clutched his arm as he handed her into the carriage and climbed in beside her, not letting go of his hand for a second.

He kissed their linked hands and rapped on the carriage roof. "To the inn, Stokes."

The intense blue of his eyes seemed magnified somehow. She would enjoy diving into those luscious pools and never returning.

"My lady and I are ready for a celebration."

* * * *

Tris moved the candle close to the edge of the nightstand so it threw his beloved's features into sharp relief. She lay on her stomach beside him, her face toward him, her luxurious hair in disarray over her shoulders and back. Never would he tire of the sight.

They'd made love twice since retiring from the celebration in the taproom, but seeing her beauty, knowing he'd be the only man ever to see her thus, made his cock rise like Lazarus. He could watch her like this for hours, if only he had some self-restraint.

Brushing her hair from her shoulder, he ran his hand over her warm skin, satiny smooth and creamy. He couldn't keep his hands off her. Might as well tell a horse not to graze in a field full of sweet clover. All the while they'd had their health toasted downstairs, he'd held her hand, patted her thigh, kissed her, but couldn't get enough, never enough. Biding his time until they could steal away up here.

"Mmm." She stretched and relaxed with a little sigh. She opened one amber eye. "You need to sleep, my love. I would have your wits about you in the morning."

"I will. I promise." He slid his hand across her back, curving his fingers around her breast where it met the mattress. "I need to touch you is all."

A sleepy smile and she rolled onto her back, her breasts rising like twin mountains with small, brown peaks. "I am here for your pleasure, my lord. Do with me what you will."

"God, I love you." His heart strained in his chest, emotion threatening to spill over into his voice. For once, he didn't care. "I love everything about you. Not only your body, but your wit, your talent, your stubbornness that wouldn't let you stop, no matter what." He explored her nipple with his fingertips, its curve, the pebbly texture. His attentions made them tighten further, like a flower closed against the night's cold.

Rather than watch his hand, she met his eyes, the unfaltering golden gaze making him groan with need.

Even her look made him want her more than the air he breathed. He rubbed the tip of the nipple, scraping his fingernail lightly across the flat top.

She closed her eyes and moaned, her brows furrowing as she stretched and arched toward him.

Slowly, he slid his hand down her warm flesh, spreading his fingers wide across her flat stomach, eliciting a wiggle and a laugh when he hit a ticklish spot.

Her face changed moment by moment, her brow now lifted, now furrowed in concentration, her lips curved up in a smile or open in a silent moan.

When he reached the curls over her mound, she drew a sharp breath and licked her lips. His shaft stiffened, bending back until it touched his stomach. Not yet. Not for a long time yet. Determined, he used his forefinger to circle her nub.

"Ahh." She arched and panted.

Her sounds drove him mad with wanting to sink himself into her. Still, the beauty of her face as pleasure built inside her intrigued him. He'd seen her at different times during the throes of passion, but never at the ultimate moment. Always he'd wait for her to reach the penultimate moment, then close his eyes and lose himself in her as passion took them. While almost heart-stopping, his actions had robbed him of the pleasure of seeing her face at the moment of completion. He'd promised himself he would see that beauty tonight.

"Oh, Tris." Gasping, she writhed on the bed, raising her hips to meet his finger, still stroking her round and round. "Lower. Inside me."

"Your wish, my love." His heart hammered and his cock strained as he slid his digit inside her warm, wet channel.

"Ahh." Her moan began as a guttural sound, then rose to high pitched squeaks. Her face flushed, a lovely pink staining her cheeks and forehead, where fine beads of sweat glistened. She tried to reach his very ready member, but he stayed her hand, all the while stroking in and out. "Now, Tris. Put yourself inside me now."

"I want to watch you, love, as the passion takes you." He kissed the damp forehead and added a second finger. "Then I will join with you."

"Ahh. Ahh." She closed her eyes, her ragged breath timed with his thrusts. The slow, sure rhythm pushed her toward the edge, each stroke met with an increasingly louder moan.

He sped up his thrusts, intent on the flushed face.

Fisting her hands in the sheets, she opened her blazing eyes, and shrieked, "Oh, God," as her body clutched at his fingers. "Tris, oh, Tris," she cried as her face took on a glow, a radiance of beauty he'd never glimpsed before.

Scarcely missing a beat, he climbed on top of her and thrust home. She gripped him now and he closed his eyes, her face still before him, gave two thrusts and spent himself deep inside her. The memory of her face at that moment in time would remain with him always.

She continued to moan as her body clasped him and he remained inside her until she stopped, both of them completely spent, now eternally knit together as one.

Chapter 34

Warm lips pressed against hers. Violet reached the edges of consciousness and cracked an eyelid to see Tris bending over her, tucking the rumpled covers more securely around her.

"Shh. Go back to sleep, love. I will return shortly." A fleeting kiss and he was gone.

She sank back into the warm bed, drifting off as tantalizing images of Tris during the night lulled her back toward sleep. Where was he going so early? Not the privy. Although the room had but faint lights of the dark before dawn, she'd seen he'd been fully dressed. Was he going to meet the marquess for an appointment this morning? He would return soon he said. That was good. She missed his comforting weight beside her in the bed. Turning over, Violet rubbed the pillow next to her, the indentation where his head had lain a shadowy crater. Why did he need to go before first light? Nothing happened this early in the morning except—

"Susan!" Violet screeched and bounded up in the bed. "The duel. That stupid duel." She flung the covers back and leaped out of bed. Where were her stays?

"My lady, what's wrong?" Slowly, Susan limped into the bedchamber, a pitcher of water in her hand.

"The duel. He went without me." Cursing under her breath, Violet grabbed the first dress to hand out of her trunk, her brown traveling gown and jerked it over her head. "Quickly. He will not do this without me there."

Susan settled the gown over her and swiftly laced the back.

A rumble of wheels sent Violet stumbling to the window. The marquess's carriage pulled out of the inn yard, gathering speed.

"Tris!" She beat her hand on the window. "Tris! Wait. Wait for me." Head spinning, she reeled back into the room, grabbed the stomacher and jammed it into the bodice. "Go tell them to bring Tris's carriage."

Eyes wide and frightened, Susan nodded and hitched out of the room, calling for a pot boy.

Violet pulled on her half boots and tied the laces with fingers that shook. Why would he leave her behind? Had he a premonition? Did he see his own death and wish to spare her seeing him die? Stupid fool. Did he think life would matter a tinker's damn if he was not here with her? That she would wait calmly at the inn while he was fighting for his life? If he survived Simon Harper's blade he might well fall by her hand for his idiocy.

"Susan," she called as she passed the maid's door, running down the steep staircase at a frenzied pace.

"Here, my lady." Susan waited at the bottom of the steps, Violet's cloak in her hands. "They're bringing the carriage around now." She pulled the garment around Violet's shoulders.

Scarcely waiting for the maid to settle the cloak, she sped out into the cold inn yard, Susan following after her. The sun had at last peeked over the roof of the stables, bathing everything in a delicate pink light.

The carriage rolled up in front of them. "Stokes, do you know where Lord Trevor was to fight this morning?" Violet fixed the elderly man with a glare designed to make him quake in his boots.

"Y-yes, miss. That is, my lady. Tate, the coachman to the marquess, asked me last night if I knew where this pond was he'd be going to this morning. I did, and I told him." Stokes's face seemed to wither, his mouth quivering. "Will you try to stop him, my lady?" The hope in his pale blue eyes tugged at her heart.

"No." As swiftly as she could, she helped Susan into the carriage. "I understand Lord Trevor must fight the duel, but by God, I will be there to see him do it." She clambered in after Susan, slammed the door, and the vehicle lurched into motion.

The journey back to Harper's Grange had the same air of unreality as her earlier flight from it. Violet clenched her hands in her lap and stared out the window, seeing nothing of the countryside flashing by her in the brightening light. What must she do when she arrived? If the duel was over she would quietly have a fit and cry on Tris's shoulder. She doubted that would be the case. She'd been too quick behind him. Most likely they would have just begun.

Her stomach roiled and she bit back her gorge. Never again would she allow Tris to put her through such a thing. Her heart hammered as they passed through the gates that gave entry to the estate. The world spun and she grabbed the leather strap above her head.

"Are you all right, my lady?" Alarmed, Susan put out a hand to steady her.

"No, I fear I am not, Susan. Nor will I be until this ghastly ordeal is past." Violet tried to smile at the maid, but couldn't hold back the sob that broke forth instead.

"All we can do is pray, my lady." Susan patted her hand. "I think we are here." She nodded to the large pond that had come into sight when they topped a small rise. Two other carriages had pulled up next to the shore and two sets of combatants were milling around.

Violet spied Tris immediately and her tension eased a bit. "Thank God." She rapped on the roof and Stokes opened the trap. "Take us down there, Stokes."

"Wait, my lady." Susan grasped her arm and Violet held a hand up to stay the coachman. "Did you ever think Lord Trevor may have left you at the inn for a reason? You don't want to go down there and distract him when he needs all his wits about him."

Violet sighed and leaned back against the leather seat. "I know, but I had to come. I would have gone mad with not knowing until they came back."

"Tell Stokes to get us close enough to see what's happening, but don't get out until it's done." Susan squeezed her hand. "I cannot stand for very long in any case."

This business would be the end of her. "Very well. Stokes, close enough to see, but not close enough to intrude."

"Very good, my lady." The trap snapped shut and they crept forward.

The duelists had taken their positions by the time the carriage halted, some yards from the area of combat. The two men saluted and Violet grabbed Susan's hand, clutching it so hard her own fingers ached.

Tris raised his sword, the steel flashing in the full sunlight that lit the scene with too much clarity. He had doffed his coat and cravat, despite the cold, so the breeze fluttered his unfettered shirt. Attired informally, in buckskin breeches and stocking feet, splashed with mud, he nevertheless stood alert, like a coiled snake waiting to strike.

Simon Harper, similarly attired, lifted his sword over his head, a sickening smirk on his face. He said something and Tris smiled and replied, his gaze never wavering from his opponent. Both men seemed poised, waiting for the other to make the first move.

Suddenly Tris exploded forward, his blade ringing as it slashed back and forth, seeking the target. Harper, however, met each blow easily, both rapiers singing as they exchanged stroke for stroke. Graceful as dancers, the duelists slithered back and forth on the muddy ground. Pray God Tris did not slip.

Harper took the offensive, pushing Tris back toward the edge of the pond. The evil joy on Harper's face brought her to her feet. "I've got to go out there."

"No, my lady." Susan's hand stayed her.

She thumped into her seat and lowered her face into her hands. Much more of this would kill her.

"My lady." The edge in Susan's voice brought Violet's head up.

Tris had ceased his retreat. He stood tall and with a mighty crash, knocked Harper's sword upward, throwing the man backward, off balance. Tris grinned, pure pleasure in his face, as he swung his blade down across Harper's thigh. Blood welled up immediately, staining the white breeches.

Clutching his leg, Harper yelled, and fell to the ground.

Still grinning, Tris saluted him, then offered a hand to his opponent.

Harper batted it away and shouted a name. Two men ran to his side. They dropped to their knees and seemed to be assessing the wound.

Tris turned away, heading toward the carriage where Mr. Matthews and the marquess stood, identical smiles on their faces.

Relief washed through Violet like a tidal wave. She cried and hugged Susan. "He's alive. Oh, thank God."

"I prayed the whole time, my lady." Susan extracted her handkerchief and wiped her eyes.

"I must go to him." Violet opened the door and slid to the ground. "Come, Susan." She helped the maid to the ground, eager to set off toward Tris, who was talking to Matthews and Lord Dalbury. She slowed her gait, however, to match Susan's hobbling pace. "Be careful of the mud."

"Don't wait for me." Susan laughed, picking her way through the muck with her cane.

As Violet turned back to her, she caught movement out of the corner of her eye.

Mr. Harper's seconds had staunched the bleeding and were tying a bandage around his bloody leg. They lifted him until he could stand, leaning heavily on the young man on his left.

A flash of metal and a pistol appeared in Simon Harper's right hand. His grim lips pulled taut as he leveled his arm and pointed his weapon at Tris's back.

Time, so long her enemy, slowed to a crawl. Without thought, in one smooth movement, she plucked Susan's cane from her hand and tore across the slippery grass. With a sweeping upstroke, she knocked the pistol skyward as he fired, startling the crows roosting in a nearby tree. Their raucous cries echoed the sound of the harmless shot.

Black rage contorted Simon Harper's face. He swung toward her, reaching for her neck.

Violet let the swing of the hawthorn cane carry her arms upward. As of their own accord, in a parody of the sword fight, she reversed over Simon's head and swung the club with deadly accuracy at his temple.

Harper dropped to the ground, unmoving.

Time came back in a rush.

Tris appeared from nowhere, grabbed her up in his arms, squeezing so tight she couldn't breathe. "Violet. Oh, God, are you hurt?" Carefully, he set her down and peered at her, his face almost as angry as Harper's had been.

"I'm f-f-fine." She laughed, wiping at the tears that trickled down her cheeks. Shaking so hard she almost put a finger in her eye, she leaned against him before her legs gave way.

"What were you doing here? I didn't want you to have to witness this." His hair had come loose and he brushed it out of his face. "Although as it turns out I've very grateful you did." He glanced at Harper's still unmoving form and shook his head. "Where on earth did you learn to parry like that?"

"Parry?" Laughter bubbled up, a release she savored. "I'm sure I don't know what that means. I just reacted naturally, I suppose." She clutched his arm. "I wasn't about to lose you to that ill-begotten worm."

"She's a natural-born fighter, Tris." From nowhere the marquess appeared before them. "Here, Lady Trevor, you'll need this about now." He handed her a small flask, the sharp, sweet smell of brandy wafting from the open mouth.

Gratefully, Violet grasped it and took a quick sip. The liquid fire burned its way into her belly, soothing her clenched muscles.

"I must introduce you to my wife, Lady Dalbury. She will be anxious to make your acquaintance when I tell her she has a kindred spirit in you. She will be quite put out with me that she missed your exploits today." Lord Dalbury grinned ruefully. "I'll wager as soon as her confinement is over, she will take it upon herself to train you properly in fencing."

"I would be most honored to meet the marchioness, my lord." Perhaps they could take nothing more strenuous than tea together. She'd had enough excitement today to last a lifetime.

"Tris, we'll meet you back at the inn and make preparations for the journey home. Will we leave after breakfast?" His friend fell silent, his gaze fixed on something behind Violet.

Simon Harper's friends had managed to carry him from where he had fallen to the carriage. They loaded him, groaning insensibly, into the carriage and with a piercing glare at Tris, left.

"I think we'll leave tomorrow, if you don't mind, Duncan." Tris clutched Violet to him, his lips brushing her hair.

"If you are all quite finished, can someone help me up?" Susan's voice boomed from the muddy patch of ground on which she sat. "I swear I'll be glad to rub the mud of this town off my shoes."

With a chuckle, Matthews rushed to assist her, scooping her up into his arms and conveying her to Tris's carriage.

Tris lifted Violet into his arms as well. "Shall we return to The Black Horse, my love, and continue where we left off early this morning? A newly married couple is allowed at least a day to rest and relax from all the excitement." His eyes promised excitement of a completely different sort.

"That is a custom I believe we should uphold, my lord." She slid her arms around his neck and snuggled deeper against him. "To the very letter, if you please. We have had our share of excitement and more." With her eyes, she promised him so many things then thrilled at his slight gasp.

"As the mistress of my heart commands, so shall I obey." He kissed her, lingering just long enough to make her desire more.

Mistress of his heart, her true title, for now and forever.

THE END

Turn the page for a special excerpt of Jenna Jaxon's

To Woo A Wicked Window

Chapter 1

London May 1810

Moonlight streamed into the mews, brightening the night and making Lady Charlotte Fownhope draw back into the shadows of the stable. She strained to hear sounds from her father, the Earl of Grafton's, townhouse, but only the clink of bridles came to her ears as Edward, her groom, led her chestnut mare and his horse into the light.

"You should have taught me to saddle her. Then I could have helped you." She came forward to take the reins.

"I'll always be here to do that for you, my lady." He smiled, his white teeth a flash in the swarthy handsome face, then leaned down to kiss her.

His warm lips caressed her, calmed her even as the comforting scent of horses and leather that hung about him enveloped her. This was where she belonged, in Edward's arms. Not with Lord Ramsay, her father's choice for a husband.

A horse snorted and Charlotte jumped back. "We must be off. Dinner will last only so long. With luck no one will look in on me on me but my cousin Jane, so we will have until the morning before they know I am gone."

Edward nodded and cupped his hands to give her a leg up.

Once in the saddle, she gathered the reins and waited for him to mount, her stomach tightening with excitement. "You know the way?"

"Yes, we take the Great North Road as far as York, then over to Manchester and up to Gretna Green." He slid into the saddle. "We'll be on horseback the first two days. They won't expect that. They'll be looking for a carriage." He reached over and grasped her hands. "You'll be all right on horseback for so long?"

She nodded, prompted to sit up straighter. If she had to spend a week in the saddle to be with Edward, she would do it. "Let's go."

They walked the horses out of the light, into the darkness of the underpass, keeping quiet until they were at the end of the row of stables. Charlotte resisted the urge to look over her shoulder to see if they had been pursued. They had been careful. They would succeed. She drew her black cloak around her shoulders against the now-chill wind.

At a nod from Edward, she tapped her horse and Sophie started into a quick trot. The *clop, clop* of the hooves on the cobbled streets soothed her. After months of planning, they were on their way at last.

* * * *

Several hours later, Charlotte and Edward slowed for another toll gate. They had passed through four already and after the first, Charlotte had turned the bag of coins over to him to take care of the fees. A twinge in her hip, an ache in her thigh muscle told her that her body had begun to feel the strain of constant motion in the saddle. When they finally stopped for the night, she doubted she would want to climb back on Sophie tomorrow.

Slowed to a walk, her mare nickered, and from somewhere behind the toll gate another one answered. Charlotte patted her withers and glanced at Edward.

"Toll keeper!" he called, rending the silent night. After a moment he called again, still with no result.

"He must be dead asleep." The wind had risen, causing Charlotte to tug her cloak closer.

"Dead drunk's more like." Edward dismounted, strode to the toll house door, and knocked.

The door jerked open. A huge hand grasped his shoulder, dragging him inside.

"Edward!" Charlotte dropped the reins peeled her aching leg from around the horn of the sidesaddle and slid to the ground. She must get to Edward. As her boots hit the dirt, two men appeared from nowhere.

"Ha, got ya!" They grabbed her arms, their rough fingers digging painfully into her flesh.

Terror shot through her veins, stopping her breath in her throat. Still, she managed to pull back and forth, trying to break free. No use. Their big hands clamped down on her like a vise as they hustled her toward the tool booth.

"Edward! Help! Someone, help." Charlotte shrieked as they dragged her toward the building. Dear Lord, they must be highwaymen. She had heard sickening stories about the dangerous criminals who roamed the roads, preying on unlucky travelers. Her stomach twisted.

At the threshold they loosened their grip to get her through the door. Charlotte swung around and raked her fingernails down one man's face.

He bellowed and pushed her away, into the house.

She wheeled toward the other man, bent on a similar attack but stopped, shocked at the tableau before her.

The flickering light of the hearth revealed a large man holding Edward's head down on a crude plank table, a pistol pressed against his temple. The toll keeper in his nightshirt and cap, eyes wide, face pale stood in front of the fire staring at the scene. To the left of the table stood her father.

All the strength ran out of Charlotte's legs and she began to sink toward the floor.

The man she had wounded grabbed her arm and hauled her up. "No you don't. That's all, your lordship. Just the two of 'em."

Leaning on his silver-knobbed walking stick, her father fixed his dark eyes on her, his mouth a black line between thin lips.

Charlotte's heart thudded painfully in her chest. The light flickered, dimming to a dull gray as she began to slump again. Oblivion would certainly be preferable to what her father surely had in store for her.

Cold water hit her face and chest forcing her back into consciousness.

"You will be awake to see this, Charlotte." Her father thrust a stoneware mug at the toll keeper, who clutched it to his chest as if it were a shield. Then her father nodded to the man with the pistol.

"No! You cannot kill him." Charlotte wrenched her arms out of the man's grasp and lunged for the gun.

The side of the pistol slammed into her face, knocking her to the floor. He cocked the piece and returned it to Edward's head.

"Thrush here had the audacity to try to take what is *mine*." Her father's voice shook, his fury rising with each curt word.

Through her wavering vision, her father's face appeared impassive in the uncertain light, his voice now emotionless as he peered down at her. "If you assisted him in this, then his blood is on your hands much more so than mine."

"If you kill him, you will have to kill me as well." Narrowing her eyes at him, Charlotte carefully picked herself up off the floor, hatred of him so intense it must be oozing through her skin. "I will tell everyone exactly what you have done to Edward. As a peer you may be above the law, but you are not above the censure of the *ton*. I will make sure that they have every detail of his death and our elopement until the scandal-broth scalds you to death. If you want scandal, Father, I will choke you with it."

He chuckled, adjusting his grip on his walking stick. "Sometimes I wish you were my heir, Charlotte. You have a better mind than Caldwell, and much more of me in you." He sighed and rubbed the knob of his cane. "Pity you've begun to rave like a lunatic. I doubt you will like Bedlam, my dear. I would dislike having to put you there but if you tell such grievous lies, what else am I to do?"

A wave of horror washed over her. Tales of the appalling conditions of the infamous hospital had sickened her. Her arms broke out in goose flesh. Bitter bile crawled up the back of her throat. Tears trickling down her cheeks, she looked at Edward, who hadn't moved the whole time.

He mouthed silently, "I love you."

Staring at him, she raised her voice until it rang in the rafters. "I love you, Edward."

"Sickening pap." Her father pursed his lips as though a bad taste filled his mouth. "I *should* kill you, too." He nodded to the man with the pistol. "Cates."

"Toll keeper!"

The shout from outside froze everyone.

Dear God, a savior. Charlotte opened her mouth, only to have the dirty hand of her captor slam over it before she could shout.

"Attend to your business, toll keeper." Her father's words were clipped as he stared down the little man. "Leave me to mine and you will be rewarded."

Eyes wide, the toll keeper nodded, and headed for the door with shaky steps.

Charlotte elbowed her captor, wrenching her body this way and that, trying to break free. She bit down on the hand that muzzled her and stomped in an effort to mash his foot.

The howl the blackguard sent up was music to her ears. He jerked his hand away swearing.

"Help! Oh God, help me. Someone!" She screamed so loudly something in her throat tore.

"Charlotte!" Her father slammed his cane down on the table, an inch from Edward's face, making her jump back. "Andrews, for God's sake, stifle her."

Andrews grabbed her again, putting his arm around her neck. She almost gagged at the sour smell of his coat.

The door burst open and a tall man holding a large pistol strode in, the toll keeper scuttling behind him.

Cates whipped his gun around, training it on the stranger.

The man, who seemed to tower over everyone in the room, obliged him by leveling his weapon on Andrew. Glancing from one figure to another, his gaze finally rested on Charlotte. "What the devil is going on here?"

His deep, commanding voice sent a thrill of hope through her.

"None of your affair, sir." Her father once again leaned on his cane, his mouth pinched. "You may pay your toll and be on your way. This is a private matter."

The stranger, bundled against the cold in a blue pea coat and black felt hat with the brim pulled down shading his eyes, shook his head. "I think not." He nodded toward Charlotte. "I heard the lady scream. I'll hear what she has to say."

Andrews tightened his hold and Charlotte's vision started to gray again. A loud *thwack* sounded near her ear and the arm smothering her loosened and fell. She coughed then drew a deep, clean breath. Her father's henchman lay at her feet. The stranger now stood next to her, his gun now pointing at Cates. Hope stole through her breast once more.

"Tell me what's going on, miss."

"I apprehended this horse thief," her father spoke up before she say a word, "and was about to administer justice when you came along. As I said, it is a private affair."

"That's not true." Charlotte turned to their rescuer, her heart thundering. She must convince him to help them or Edward would die. "My betrothed and I were eloping. My father found out and waylaid us here. They are going to kill Edward." Her heart lurched at the sound of the words spoken aloud. She searched the man's face, praying with every fiber of her soul that he believed her. That whoever he was, he was a match for her father and his men. "Please, I beg of you, you must stop them."

"He was stealing my horses, taking my daughter as a hostage for ransom." Her father cut his eyes toward Cates.

Charlotte tensed. What would the wretched man try next?

"The lady seems rather enamored of her kidnapper, which I find odd, if what you say is true." The stranger gestured to Edward. "What do you have to say, sir?"

Edward tried to rise, but Cates slammed the butt of the pistol into the back of his head. He fell forward onto the table.

"No!" Charlotte shrieked, her stomach twisting anew. She darted toward the still figure.

Her father grabbed her arm and jerked her behind the table next to him. His fingers dug into flesh, biting even through her clothing.

The stranger swung his pistol around, pointing it at her father's face. "Since you didn't want me to hear his reply, I'll assume it would have confirmed the lady's tale."

"And if it did, you have no authority to aid and abet their illegal flight to Scotland," her father countered. "My daughter has not reached her majority, therefore I am fully within my rights to keep her from making such a misalliance."

"Quite correct, sir. If she *is* your daughter, she does fall under your dominion. This man, however, does not. And you certainly have no authority to kill him."

"That was never my intention."

"Oh, yes it was." Charlotte tried to pull away from her father, but his strong grip on her upper arm pinned her next to him.

"I think I will take the lady's word over yours, all the same." The stranger smiled and a chill ran down Charlotte's spine. "Get him on his feet." He gestured with the gun to Edward.

Cates glanced at her father, who nodded. The henchman grabbed Edward by the back of his coat and hauled him up.

Groaning and groggy, but able to stand, Edward stared at her, the anguish in his eyes matching the ache that tore at her heart.

The stranger clasped him about the waist and they backed toward the door.

"Make sure you do not take any of my horses." Her father finally released his grip on her aching arm. Shaking it loose, she ran toward the door shouting, "Take the chestnut mare. She's mine."

Cates blocked her way, but moments later the muffled sound of hoof beats told her they were away, Edward safe at last. Her shoulders slumped and the tears began to flow once more, relief at his escape warring with the hollow ache of her heart. She would never see him again. If she could die right now, she would count herself blessed.

"Wake up Andrews and bring my carriage around." Her father barked out the order to Cates. Glaring at the toll keeper who was now cowering in the corner, he tossed a gold sovereign on the table. "For your trouble and your silence." At last he turned his attention to Charlotte, his lips twisted in a snarl. "You will fill an ocean with those tears before I'm through with you."

He grabbed her arm again and pushed her out the door into the chill air and pale moonlight that would be the rest of her life. Oh, yes. Death would have been a blessing.

* * * *

"My lady, wake up." The insistent voice of her maid scarcely penetrated the fog of exhausted sleep Charlotte had fallen into early this morning. She grunted and turned over. If she never woke up she'd be perfectly happy.

"My lady." Sara shook her shoulder. "Your father wants you downstairs immediately."

Oh, God. Charlotte groaned and burrowed deeper under the covers. The reckoning she'd known was coming had arrived. Too heart sore to be afraid, she crawled out from beneath the covers. Best to get this over with, take her punishment as she always had at her father's hands, so she could come back here to mourn Edward's loss in private.

She peered at herself in the mirror and wished she had not. Her face was badly bruised where Cates had hit her. Anna would be hard pressed to cover the purple marks on her cheek even with cosmetics. And her arm throbbed from her father's brutal grip. Still, her heart ached more than her body. She wanted to be happy that Edward had escaped, but she couldn't ignore the empty pit in her heart.

An hour later, she entered her father's study, fighting not to wince as she straightened her shoulders and raised her chin. Unless she met the man with strength, he would trample her and never look back. She stood before the huge, worn mahogany desk, exactly as she had every time she'd displeased him in her eighteen years.

He continued writing, not even looking up to acknowledge her presence. Another of his ploys.

Remaining still, she stared at his hand as he made the small, neat letters. The trick was not to say a word. Allow him to make the first move.

At last he signed his name with a flourish, set the pen down and capped the ink. Then he raised his head and looked at her. And smiled.

Charlotte's stomach sank. The smile meant triumph. It meant whatever the punishment he had set for her, he had gotten his way with it. She firmed her lips. She'd not give him the satisfaction of seeing her fear.

"Well, your little indiscretion of last night has cost me the Ramsay alliance." He leaned back, his hands clasped.

"It has?" She couldn't keep the surprise out of her voice. The settlements for her marriage to Lord Ramsay had already been signed. So how had the betrothal been broken?

"Ramsay caught wind of your little escapade. I'm not sure how, but I'll find out which servant talked. They will never set foot in a decent household again." He tapped his forefingers together. "Nevertheless, he knows that my daughter tried to elope with her groom and now refuses to have you."

Well, good for Lord Ramsay. She had nothing against the man except she didn't know him, and certainly didn't love him.

"I could have forced the issue, but he has agreed to be discrete about the reason he now finds you objectionable. I have broken the betrothal on your behalf." His intense stare made Charlotte's skin crawl. There would be worse news to come.

"Thank you, Father." Not that this situation pleased her much more than marrying Ramsay. Of course, now he'd have to send her down into the country to wait for him to choose the next most advantageous match for her. A plan with merit, for being out of his presence was a boon. Even had she found a man this Season at least palatable to her, her father would never allow her to marry him, unless the alliance served his purposes.

"But do not despair, Charlotte. You shall have your wedding, and on schedule." His eyes twinkled and her stomach sank even further. "I have called in a favor from an old friend. He has agreed to marry you and take you off my hands."

"An old friend, Father?" Dread built slowly in her chest. This must be her punishment.

"Sir Archibald Cavendish. You remember him, I daresay. He's been my guest often enough at the hunting lodge in Kent."

Her breath stopped. No. That was not possible. Marriage with... "Sir Archibald? But...but he's your age." And balding and as big around as he was tall. The last time she'd seen him, two years ago at the lodge, he'd been so drunk he stank of whiskey and the strong clove scent he wore in his cologne made her sneeze. Now she'd be expected to marry the man? She had to clutch the back of the chair in front of her.

"Two years younger, but that's of no consequence." The jubilant tenor in his voice told her was enjoying her horror. "Sir Archibald is just the man to keep you in line."

"I won't do it. You cannot make me marry that nasty old man." She had spoken with her cousin Jane when she'd been betrothed to Ramsay and been informed that the English law required her to consent to her marriage. Well, she would never willingly agree to this alliance. Being a spinster or anything else was better than being that man's wife.

"Oh, I think you will, daughter." He leaned toward her, menace etched in every line on his face. "Because it is Sir Archibald or the lunatics at Bedlam. Any woman who would disgrace herself by running off with a servant would easily be deemed mad by the authorities. I have sent inquiries to one of the physicians on the board, telling him of your irrational behavior and asking if they would admit you if you do not see reason."

"You would really do such a thing to me?" He would. She had no doubt.

"It is your choice, Charlotte. I will not have scandal in my house. Had you behaved according to your station and married Ramsay, we could have avoided these less appealing options." He sat back again, cold, emotionless. Triumphant.

He had her trapped. She could not choose the asylum if she expected to live. Edward had not wanted that for her, even at the cost of his own life. She swallowed hard and prepared herself for the inevitable. It would have to be the odious Sir Archibald. Perhaps she could persuade the man to leave her in the country while he gallivanted around and thus spend as little time with him as possible. At least there was that hope.

With a heavy sigh, Charlotte nodded. "Then I accept Sir Archibald's suit. You can inform me of the wedding details when you have arranged them." She clenched her hands and spun on her heel, determined to leave the study without seeing her father's gloating face. Before her tears rained down again, as she knew they would, the ocean her father had predicted just beginning.

Chapter 2

London, June 18, 1816

Lady Charlotte Cavendish squeezed into the upstairs retiring room at Almack's, shaking in her new yellow slippers, half in excitement, half in terror. The parlor was already crowded with gaily-dressed women eager to show their patriotism for the Waterloo veterans. She, on the other hand, attended for an entirely different reason—a reason that gave her joy for the first time in six long years.

Charlotte glanced around, unnerved by the crush of people. She was unused to such crowds after five years of marriage and a year of mourning. Surely she could find a bit of unclaimed wall where she could wait for her cousin, Jane, Lady John Tarkington, and contemplate the freedom she'd celebrate tonight. Not the normal return to society by a grieving widow. Then again, she had never grieved one day for the odious Sir Archibald. Considering she was still a virgin, she could hardly be called a normal widow at all.

She danced out of the way as two portly matrons hurtled past her.

"And then she said Lord Fairfax dragged her into the library..." The ladies moved off, heads still together, oblivious of the others around them.

Charlotte ran her hands over her skirts, checking for tears. She had never seen so many people here before. Had half of London turned up? Spying an open spot, she hurried toward it, tread on the hem of her gown and stumbled against the cream colored rear wall.

Drat. She turned her back to the wall and inspected the edging of the garment. The modiste had apparently cut it a little too long despite her exacting measurements. Why hadn't she noticed this at home? The lace wasn't torn, however. She and sighed in relief, relaxing just a little. There was no reason to be nervous about rejoining society, yet she was on pins and needles. She must compose herself and wait right here for Jane so her clothing would not get further mussed.

She glanced down, smiling in satisfaction at her gown, which the seamstress had delivered yesterday. The fresh confection, cut daringly low in both front and back, in the most delectable shade of deep primrose yellow, boldly announced her eagerness to engage in life anew.

Time now to re-emerge, like a bright butterfly from a twelve-month cocoon, to stretch her wings. Charlotte fidgeted, shifting from one foot to the other, full of pent up energy after years spent suffering through an empty marriage to a man she had never loved. *I'd have better spent the past twelve months grieving the loss of Edward. Or perhaps I should have mourned my step-son Hal. He set me free.*

Harold Cavendish, her husband's second son, had died at Waterloo. When the news had reached Sir Archibald, he'd suffered an attack of apoplexy and died. His elder son, Edgar, now Sir Edgar, held the title to the baronetcy. What a pity the fates of the sons had not been reversed. Charlotte had always gotten along well with Hal. Edgar was another matter entirely.

Near the entranceway the press of women seemed to thin a bit. She strained to see through the throng that still surrounded her. Drat it. Had the dancing begun before her cousin arrived? She didn't want to miss a moment of tonight. Cocking her head, she strained to hear through the low din of voices. Snatches of discordant notes drifted in from the ballroom as the orchestra tuned up.

Oh, why hadn't Jane arrived? Charlotte eyed the doorway, willing her cousin to appear. As the first social function Charlotte had attended since her mourning ended, this fete represented her bid for freedom and she did not intend to miss a moment of the ball.

Thanks to her father's treachery, not since her ill-fated flight to Gretna Green had she experienced one moment of love or tenderness with a man. Her aging husband had made it quite clear on their wedding night that he would not demand his marital rights. He'd never given her a reason for his disinterest, although she had her own suspicions. During the next five years, however, he'd been as good as his word, never so much as putting a foot over the threshold of her bedchamber. A circumstance for which she gave thanks to God nightly—Sir Archibald had been short, pot-bellied, with a breath like an old chamber pot. Charlotte had often wondered who she despised more, her husband or her father.

What she wouldn't give just once to know the long-denied pleasure of a man's attentions. She imagined herself on the dance floor, held in the arms of a dashing gentleman who would sweep her around the room as if they trod on air. He would smile for her alone and perhaps hold her a bit more tightly than was proper. She would laugh and flirt with him, without a care in the world beyond who her next partner would be. Oh, yes, she had dreamed of this night for years.

Her blood beat a quick rhythm in her veins. The parlor air had grown quite stifling. Alarmed, Charlotte pulled out her fan and plied it vigorously. She simply could not faint here! Not before setting a foot on the dance floor.

Had she known Jane would be this tardy, she would have accompanied her to Lady Darlington's crush. Instead, Charlotte had preferred to have more time to dress, to perfect her first impression after so long an absence. If Jane didn't arrive soon, however, she might give in to desperation. Might even be tempted to go into the ballroom alone. A dreadful way to call attention to herself but she'd been waiting all her life for this moment.

As if summoned by Charlotte's frantic need, her cousin rounded the corner into the receiving room. Panic receded. Charlotte breathed deeply and waved to her. Ever since they were children, Jane's presence had had a calming effect on her. Though truly sorry for the loss of her cousin's husband, she had been grateful when Jane had moved into the London townhouse with her and provided her with advice on widowhood.

"Oh, Jane!" Charlotte hugged her slight frame. "I thought you would never arrive."

"I told you to come with me, Charlotte. Then you wouldn't be in such a state." Jane straightened the topaz and gold necklace around Charlotte's neck. "You seem ready to fly to pieces."

"Oh, I am." Charlotte laughed, so giddy now the flickering candlelight spun. "I'm so tired of waiting."

"Well, you likely will still have your share of that once we enter." Jane nodded toward the ballroom. "We will probably have a devilish time attracting any attention at all from the gentlemen." She frowned and flipped open her fan. "That is a major concern, my dear. The Season is all but over."

Charlotte nodded. Now that they could accept any invitation they liked, the invitations had ceased to arrive.

"Our mourning ended at such an unfortunate time of year." Jane started toward the doorway. "What few events remain will not likely be well attended by gentlemen seeking to marry. The most eligible have either been brought up to scratch already, or have managed to escape and think themselves safe for another year." She stopped and nodded to an acquaintance. "Despite the numbers drawn to the fete tonight, I fear we will find dancing partners scarce." Jane sounded miffed, but Charlotte smothered a smile at her words. She doubted her cousin would sit out a single set unless she chose to. Jane had always had a way with men.

"Then by all means, let us hurry to make our presence known." Charlotte bit her lips. Prickles of excitement coursed down her glove-encased arms. The moment she had waited for had arrived. Once again she would enter the giddy world of the *ton*. Shoulders straight, a pleasant smile carefully gracing her lips, Charlotte swept toward the glittering ballroom, ready for life to begin again.

* * * *

"Demmed slim pickings this late in the Season, eh, Wrotham?"

Blandly surveying the crowded ballroom, Nash, twelfth Earl of Wrotham, had to agree with his friend, George Abernathy.

"Well, none of them showed great promise, even when out in full force in April. Too young and too silly if you ask me." A shame too, as Nash had determined he would do his duty and marry this year. He'd come into his title unexpectedly, only eighteen months before, and at thirty had no time to waste putting an heir in his nursery. Life was a chancy thing.

"You may be right at that." George surveyed the room, his usual look of boredom unchanged.

"I suppose we must wait and hope for a better crop during the Little Season." Nash sighed as several young ladies, dressed in all manner of frothy pastel gowns, congregated not ten feet from where he stood. He smiled pleasantly to acknowledge them, all of whom he'd stood up with before, but none of whom had drawn his interest for more than a dance or two. "I do hope at least one or two here tonight can dance tolerably. Such a shame Miss Benson is now betrothed."

Abernathy cocked his head and produced a quizzing glass, through which he seemed to study Nash. "You cherished hopes in that direction?"

"Not a bit." Nash chuckled. "The chit is as flighty as they come, but she moved like a sprite. I've not had a partner such as her in ten years." He shook his head. Not that he had indulged in dancing much at all in that time. "Fortunately, the ability to dance well is not my highest criteria for a wife."

"Now there we can agree." Abernathy settled himself to gazing about the room, likely looking for a suitable candidate for the opening reel. "Fortune is the primary consideration when seeking out a wife. Fortune and good breeding."

Nash shook his head. "A consideration perhaps, but not the highest one. I'm much more interested in a pleasant woman, a good companion. A lady who will not insist on dabbling about in my business affairs, although she must be an outstanding hostess." He looked expectantly at two young ladies entering, then he recognized them as Miss Olivia Sanderling and Lady Catherine Dole. Neither one old enough for his taste. "She should also enjoy living in the country and sharing quiet pursuits. I seek a woman I will *want* to sit across the breakfast table from, which means she can't be some miss right out of the schoolroom, fortune or not."

"Humpf." Abernathy swung around toward the ballroom entrance where some sort of commotion had erupted.

Had the press of people entering become too great, creating a stoppage? The organizers should have foreseen that with this particular Ball and Fete. Everyone must want to attend this evening.

Nash peered at the little knot of people now filing through the doorway, his attention immediately drawn to a lady in yellow who chatted animatedly with another woman. The bright hue of her gown riveted his gaze on the elegant figure, an arresting, almost fierce expression on her face, as if determined to enjoy the evening no matter what.

"I say, Abernathy, do you know that lady there in yellow, just come into the room?" Nash had never seen her at any other *ton* event. Of course, this was his first full year on the Town and he certainly had not met everyone. One of the disadvantages of inheriting his title with no warning had been his lack of preparation for the duties expected of him. Including attending all these blasted functions and remembering names and faces.

I would have remembered her.

George once again raised his quizzer. "Well, well. Lady John Tarkington. She was widowed last year. I suppose this means her mourning is finished." He smiled and licked his lips. "Lady John is quite the figure of a woman, wouldn't you say?"

"Is she the one in yellow?" Nash couldn't take his eyes off her.

"In blue. With blond hair."

Nash shot his friend a sideways glance. "Bit older than your usual conquest, isn't she?"

George let the quizzing glass drop and straightened his jacket. "Yes, but ever so much more fun. She led Tarkington a merry chase before and after their marriage so I'm told. Always a breath away from scandal was Lady Jane Munro before she married. And now she's apparently back on the market." He started across the dance floor. "Come, let me present you so I can ask her for the first dance. Perhaps she will introduce you to her companion."

"But who is the lady in yellow?" Nash followed, frowning. He hated when things went on the fly. Fifteen years in the Royal Navy had taught him that lack of organization usually led to disaster.

Abernathy shook his head. "No idea. Didn't get a good look at her." He nodded toward the two women, talking and laughing together with several ladies they had joined. "But Lady John obviously does."

Nash trailed behind, weaving his way across the floor where the first set was making up. If fortune shone on him, an introduction would be forthcoming in time to ask the lady in yellow for the honor of the first dance. If not, he'd ask for the second set and admire her during the first.

They arrived at the little knot of ladies, and George's acquaintance turned toward them.

"Mr. Abernathy. How wonderful to see you again." The woman's eyes lit with pleasure and perhaps a touch of amusement. She turned her penetrating gaze on Nash and he swallowed hard, unnerved by her bold assessment of him.

Managing a smile, he bowed as George made the introduction.

"My lady, may I present the Earl of Wrotham? Late of His Majesty's Navy. Wrotham, this is Lady John Tarkington, widow of the late Major-General Tarkington." Abernathy beamed at her. "I am so pleased this special light of the *ton* has re-emerged."

"Delighted, my lord." The widow's low-pitched voice managed to convey a touch of the suggestive in just those three words.

"Actually, it's pronounced 'Rut-am,' my lady." He sent George a scathing look that was ignored. "Abernathy here has never said it correctly." He bowed to Lady John. "My pleasure, entirely."

Her eyes narrowed seductively, and an uncomfortable flare of heat touched his face. Well, George had intimated she'd had her share of scandal. So his friend had best beware this woman didn't sink her claws into him, although the man appeared unconcerned. Instead, he continued an avid conversation with her, leaving Nash at sixes and sevens and without an introduction to the intriguing younger woman.

From the corner of his eye he watched her, deep in conversation with two other ladies. She stood out among them, brilliant as a peacock among doves. Her laughter sent a little thrill down his spine. He clenched his fist. Would George never inquire about the blasted introduction?

"Wrotham."

Nash jerked his attention back to his friend.

"I told Lady John you wished an introduction to her friend." Abernathy picked up the quizzing glass once more and gestured toward the lady.

"My cousin, actually, my lord." Lady John's broad smile dimpled her cheeks for the first time.

"I had hoped to ask her for the first dance, my lady."

"Splendid. Charlotte." Lady John stepped toward the entrancing figure in yellow who turned at the sound of her name.

She smiled at her cousin then glanced enquiringly at him. He held his breath.

The face he now saw close at hand confirmed his instincts. A vision of loveliness on the outside, with an energy that pulsed under her skin, making her the most animated person he had ever seen. Her eyes glinted green, sparkling in the candlelight like the sun reflected off the jeweled waters of the Mediterranean. The slight smile on her perfectly bowed lips made her appear both secretive and joyous, filled to the brim with anticipation of something long awaited.

With a rush of desire, Nash wanted to be the one to inspire that feeling in this lovely creature.

"May I introduce the Earl of Wrotham, my dear?" Lady John nodded and stepped back, her gaze darting between the two of them. "A friend of Mr. Abernathy's. My lord, this is Lady Charlotte Cavendish, my cousin."

Lady Cavendish stepped forward quickly, a smile curling her lips. "I am pleased to meet you, my lord." Her eyes widened, her gait faltered, then she pitched forward with a little cry, arms flailing.

Reflexes honed from years in the Navy, Nash stepped in neatly, catching her under her arms. She landed with a thump against his chest, sending a whiff of jasmine all around him and a thrill of lust straight to his loins. He paused, savoring the soft body pressed against him, the shining hair brushing his chin. With regret he got himself under control and reluctantly set her on her feet.

Her neck and face had flushed, turning the color of the deep red roses that adorned the terraces at Wrotham Hall. She kept her eyes downcast and stepped back.

"The pleasure is certainly all mine, my lady." Not the most appropriate response, perhaps, but a heartfelt one surely.

Lady Cavendish gasped and raised her head, her green eyes flashing.

"Are you all right, Charlotte?" Lady John stepped forward, her lips puckered as if trying to hide a smile.

"Yes, I am fine, Jane. I stepped on the hem of my gown is all." She cut her eyes at Nash and her lips thinned to a line. "Thank you, my lord, for coming to my rescue."

Nash smiled. Even angry the woman was a vision to behold. "Not a'tall, my lady. Glad to have been of service."

She seemed to collect herself and returned his smile, albeit tentatively. There would be no better time to make his request. "My lady, I would be honored if you would dance the first set with me."

Her smile widened. "Thank you, my lord. I would enjoy that."

He'd enjoy having her in his arms again too.

"Lady Cavendish?" A blonde young man, in elegant evening dress had approached so stealthily behind her neither he nor the lady had noticed. He touched her elbow and she whirled around.

"Oh, Mr. Garrett. You startled me." The pink had returned to her cheeks.

The buck immediately grasped her hand and had the audacity to kiss it. "My sincere apologies for that, my lady. It is nice to see you again."

"As it is to see you as well." Her voice had a high pitch, but a sweet tone, lilting and light. It suited her down to the ground. "Do you know Lord Wrotham?"

"I have not had the pleasure I believe." Garrett nodded his head briefly, his eyes still on Lady Cavendish.

"Nor I, Mr. Garrett." Nash bowed, then straightened to his full six foot three, pleased to see he looked down on Garrett by a couple of inches.

"It has been several months since we met, I think, Mr. Garrett?" She clutched her fan, but smiled politely.

"March I believe it was. And I am come to claim my dance as promised." His eyes glinted when her jaw dropped.

"Your dance, Mr. Garrett?" Her brows puckered and she tugged on her bottom lip with her teeth. "I don't recall we spoke about a dance." The lady shot Nash a fleeting look, but he was unsure if it was a plea for help or an apology.

"I remember it distinctly, my lady." Garrett claimed her gloved hand and squeezed it gently. "You said you would be glad when you could once again be out in society and that you couldn't wait to dance."

"Well, yes, I may indeed have expressed such a sentiment. But that did not mean—"

"To which I replied that I would be honored to partner you at the first opportunity. Then you smiled and nodded and thanked me." The blackguard raised his eyebrows, affecting an innocent air. "What else was I to assume except that you had given me permission to seek your first dance?"

She fidgeted, almost dancing now. Her eyes had the wild look of a horse ready to bolt.

Well, if she didn't want to dance with the man, he'd make sure she didn't have to. "I'm afraid her ladyship has just engaged herself to me for the first set, Garrett. Perhaps her second is still free." Nash took Lady Cavendish's hand from the man and turned them toward the floor, where the orchestra was tuning up.

"The thing is, my lord," Garrett stayed him with a touch on his wrist, "I have the prior claim."

Nash stared into the insolent blue eyes and forced himself not to call the man out. He'd really like to pummel him into the floor, but such tactics were for the battleship not the ballroom. He shook off the man's hand. "The lady has not acknowledged that, sir. I think I will take her version of the events." Nash glanced at Lady Cavendish, whose face had paled. "Are you all right, my lady?"

She started, as though coming out of a dream. "Yes, I am fine. Something reminded me—"

"That I am supposed to be your partner. There, Wrotham, the lady herself has said it. Are you satisfied?" Garrett nimbly plucked her hand out of Nash's grip and before he could protest, whisked her out to the area where couples were making up the first set.

Stunned, it took Nash a second to register what the rogue had done. He started toward the dance floor, mayhem in his heart. He'd show the scoundrel how they took care of such slights in the Navy.

A hand on his shoulder made him swing around, his own hand coming up to fend off this new menace.

"Steady, Wrotham." George Abernathy held on to him and turned him away from the eyes that were beginning to take notice of him. "He's not worth starting a brawl that will get you banned from Almack's."

Nash exhaled sharply, hot blood still pounding through his veins. Another breath and he was closer to control. His friend was right. He didn't need to start a scandal that would help neither him nor Lady Cavendish. He glanced at Lady John, who had paled, a wan smile pasted on her lips.

"I am certain Lady Cavendish would be very agreeable to partnering you for the second set, my lord." She fluttered her fan and tried to meet his eyes.

"Perhaps I will ask for that dance when this one is concluded." Like hell he would. Nash snapped a bow to Lady John, took his leave of Abernathy, then turned on his heel and strode out of the ballroom.

.

Chapter 3

Drat. How could this have happened? With a sinking heart, Charlotte allowed Mr. Garrett to lead her onto the dance floor.

In less than fifteen minutes her triumphal return to society had dissolved into a dish of scandal-broth. Not only had she tripped and fallen into Lord Wrotham, but she had been unable to stop Mr. Garrett from stealing her away from him. To protest would have created another huge scene. She also resisted the urge to turn and took at Lord Wrotham, the partner she had actually chosen. What must he think of her? Well, she could at least give Mr. Garrett the rough side of her tongue.

"Mr. Garrett, you have taken unfair advantage of the situation." She dropped his hand and turned to face him. "I recall no conversation that would permit you to believe I had promised you the first dance at this or any other ball."

"My dear, Lady Cavendish," he laughed, making his handsome face even more attractive. "I have built my reputation by taking unfair advantage of women. Did you think yourself immune?"

"I thought you a gentleman when we met at your aunt's home. Despite your reputation.". A hum of voices had set off around the room the instant his lips touched her, singling her out. Lord knew what they would make of his stealing her out of the very hands of Lord Wrotham. The *ton* forever whispered about such things, especially when one of the parties enjoyed the reputation of a rakehell the likes of Garrett's.

He grinned and took her hand again. "Oh, I am a gentleman, my lady. However, being a gentleman attracts fewer women than being a rogue. Don't you long to be scandalous after a year of mourning?"

"Certainly not." Oh, the wretch was bad. How could he know she yearned to do something at least a little wild now that she was her own woman?

"You may say 'no,' but a 'yes' lurks in your eyes, my lady."

Charlotte gasped and dropped her gaze. Dratted man. Could he read her thoughts?

Jane had warned her about how wicked the man was. He existed barely within the Pale—Mr. Garrett's reputation for affairs of the heart and ill-considered wagering of large sums at the worst gaming hells made him the bane of every matchmaking mama and the desire of each one of their daughters. His fine physique—broad at the shoulders, narrow at the waist, hard muscled all over—had caused many a maiden's desperate sigh.

Charlotte might have sighed right along with them, for he had made an impression on her in March. He had been gravely respectful of her loss and sweetly attentive—bringing her tea, listening raptly to her banal conversation ranging from the weather to her deceased husband. Yet, when he'd assisted her with her wrap, his fingers had brushed the skin at the back of her neck, lingering just a bit too long. Promising more. And more was what she so desperately wanted.

Jane's revelations, however, had acted like a cold bath to her budding longings for Alan Garrett. She'd had enough threat of scandal held over her head; she wouldn't likely heap more on herself. Now the rake was back, and seemed to have set his sights on her. Well, she would nip that in the bud. One set and she could refuse him the rest of the evening. Hopefully, Lord Wrotham would ask her again.

"Lady Cavendish." Mr. Garrett leaned toward her. His blue eyes deepened and flickered with hunger.

"Yes, Mr. Garrett?" She stepped back, trying to keep a decent distance between them. Was the man trying to compromise her for some perverse reason?

"Are you afraid of me, my lady?" His laugh, utterly charming, gave him an innocent, boyish air. "I promise if you dance with me, I won't bite." He held out his hand.

A wave of heat rose to her face. "I will hold you to that promise, Mr. Garrett." Cautiously, she placed her hand in his.

He leaned toward her slightly, and spoke *sotto voce*. "Very good. Perhaps we will also talk after our dance." He squeezed her hand and drew her closer. Scent of his spicy cologne—bergamot and something with a deep musk—tickled her nose.

Lord, she had to sneeze! Rubbing her nose to prevent the disaster, she stepped back and nodded. "Perhaps we will, Mr. Garrett." *Why did he have to wear so much scent?*

Mr. Garrett straightened and offered his arm. "The musicians are about to commence. Let us take our place in the set."

Charlotte slipped her arm through his, aware that they were causing a stir. She glanced around the room and noted several women darting inquisitive looks their way. Their countenances were anything but kind. The threat of incipient gossip about her made her shudder inside. She would never again dance with a rake.

They had almost reached their places on the dance floor when she caught sight of Jane talking to a young man Charlotte had seen several times at functions her late husband had taken her to. Her cousin stared at her and raised her chin, a summons Charlotte knew all too well.

"Oh, a moment, please Mr. Garrett. I must see my cousin." She steered him around a group of young women and between two sets of young men who seemed to be gathering up the courage to ask them to dance.

Finally, they reached Jane and, as Charlotte feared, her frown and firm lips spoke of her displeasure. What on earth had happened now?

"Lady John, I am sure you remember Mr. Alan Garrett?" Charlotte smiled bravely, although Jane's glare did not waver. What had she done? Certainly Jane could see she had no choice but to dance with the wretch. "As you may remember, we all met at Lady Burrows' house, Mr. Garrett's aunt."

Squeals from instruments being tuned attested the orchestra would be ready shortly. Perhaps they would miss the dance. Of course, the perverse Mr. Garrett would likely try to claim the next one as a forfeit. She might not be able to get rid of him until supper.

"I remember you quite well, Mr. Garrett." Jane said, with icy civility. "How lovely to meet you again."

Lord, judging from that tone, her cousin was in rare form tonight. Jane had the unfortunate habit of causing scenes in public places when trying to protect someone. The embarrassing incident during Charlotte's come-out always came to mind. Lord Reardon had ever after pointedly avoided speaking to her after experiencing Jane's scathing set-down in the middle of the hall. Just because he tried to claim a third dance.

"You are kind, Lady John. To be remembered by you is to gain immortality."

Jane chuckled.

The false tinkle told Charlotte her partner was in for it indeed.

"You have a silver tongue, Mr. Garrett. I trust you will not allow it to tarnish my cousin?"

"Lady Charlotte is in no danger from me, my lady." He patted Charlotte's hand. "Although the reverse may certainly prove true. She could well prove my downfall."

Charlotte cut her eyes toward Jane. What in the world did the man mean by that?

Jane gave her head a slight shake, then fingered her necklace of perfectly matched pearls. "Charlotte, allow me to present a dear friend of mine, Mr. George Abernathy. Mr. Abernathy was friends with Stephen once upon a time. He is also, quite suddenly, the heir to Lord Romney."

Jane's gaze took the man in from head to toe, slow and sensual, all but undressing him as she spoke.

"Jane!" Charlotte whispered, scandalized at her cousin's behavior. She'd never have thought she would do such a thing in public.

"Mr. Abernathy, this is my cousin, Lady Cavendish and Mr. Alan Garrett, with whom I think you are already acquainted?"

George smiled at her, a rather lopsided though charming sight. "My lady. I am so pleased to meet you at last." He then turned and inclined his head almost imperceptibly. "Garrett." The single word did not disguise the animosity in his tone.

"Abernathy. It has been too long." Mr. Garrett seemed amused at the other man's enmity. Charlotte glanced from one to the other, wondering what lay between them.

The music changed, signaling the dance would commence soon. Mr. Garrett took her arm. "If you will excuse us, Lady John?"

They turned to go to the floor. By all means let them get this dance over with.

"Charlotte."

Good Lord. They would never make this dance. "Yes?"

Jane glanced from Charlotte's face to Mr. Garrett's, settling on the latter with a determined stare. "Please return Lady Cavendish to me directly after the dance, Mr. Garrett. Lord Wrotham would like to have her for the second set, if I'm not mistaken." And with a sharp look at Charlotte, "You know he had particularly asked for that introduction, my dear."

Memory of the man's intense eyes, dark and fathomless, coupled with his blatantly sensual mouth caused Charlotte to swallow hard. She recalled vividly being pressed close against him, breathing a clean citrusy scent when her face lay against his jacket front. A riot of butterflies stirred in her stomach. And his voice. There had been something in his voice when he had argued with Mr. Garrett. Something familiar.

Charlotte surreptitiously scanned the area, but no tall, dark man of his description appeared. She hoped he would return at the end of the first dance and ask her for the second.

"It will be as you wish, Lady John, however, we must go now or miss the set." Mr. Garrett peered inquiringly at her. She nodded, and he finally led her onto the ballroom floor. All eyes seemed to fasten on them, though she tried to ignore them and smile.

He grasped her hand as they assumed their places in line. Heat baked her palm and she almost snatched her hand back. This would be the most agonizing set she had ever danced in her life.

"Shall we see if we can be scandalous enough to be banned from the ballroom?" Mr. Garrett spoke lightly, with a twinkle of amusement in his eyes, as the music began.

Good Lord. Was the man mad? Did all rakes act like this? Well, she'd have to brazen it out until the end of the dance. Likely he was all bluster anyway.

"I am certain much more scandalous behavior has occurred within these halls than we could display in this one dance, Mr. Garrett."

He hissed as he tugged her into the correct position for a Scottish reel. "So you wish to play the game with me, Lady Cavendish?"

"And what game would that be, sir?"

"Bait the tiger, my lady. Shall I see just how much scandal it would take for the Ball and Fete committee to demand our removal?" He drew himself up, his spine even straighter than before, his eyes glittering and hard.

He wasn't bluffing. He would destroy both their reputations in the face of such a challenge and think it a great lark. Charlotte's pulse quickened. For the briefest of seconds she imagined herself looking him in the eye and saying, "Do your worst." Then sanity returned. Rash behavior on her part could jeopardize more than her just own reputation merely in the name of exercising her freedom. Besides, she'd already made enough of a spectacle of herself tonight.

"As I have just emerged from a different form of exclusion, perhaps it is best we not undertake that particular experiment." She grasped his hand and stole a glance at him as they marched down an aisle formed by the other dancers.

A knowing smile played about his lips. "As you wish, my lady. However, if you ever care to pursue that particular avenue, please let me know."

When hell freezes over, Mr. Garrett.

"Did you know I would be here tonight?" Had he made inquiries about her? Such attention from him would bode ill indeed.

They spun in a cogwheel, their eyes locked until the pattern of the dance reversed.

"I wasn't sure. But I hoped."

Those words, in his deliciously deep voice, sent chills trickling down her spine. They joined both hands and turned.

"Although you gave me to believe that your obligation to your deceased husband would be strictly observed, I trusted you would return to society as soon as you fulfilled your duty."

He chuckled and they moved into the grand chain.

"I am actually out of mourning a day early," she confessed when they finally met again, staring straight into his sinful blue eyes. "Scandalous, don't you think?" She couldn't help but smile at this, her first rebellion. "My husband did not receive word of his son's death until June 19th then was taken in a fit of apoplexy and so died the day after the battle."

"Then this is a grave breach of protocol, Lady Cavendish." He tried to look scandalized, but the playful twinkles in his eyes said otherwise.

"My marriage was arranged. While he lived, I did my duty to my husband. After his death, I mourned appropriately, as is expected of a devoted wife." She pursed her lips and shuddered. "Now, my life is now my own." And by God she would at last live it as she pleased. "I thought it fitting that I rejoin Polite Society at this ball in particular. If that shocks everyone, so be it."

"I see you wish to become a rebel." Mr. Garrett laughed as Charlotte went into the center for her turn.

She tossed her head as she set and turned first with her partner, then with the other gentlemen in the circle. Much as she hated to admit it, she was enjoying her dance with this rogue. Did that make her wicked? When she finally regained her position next to Mr. Garrett, he resumed their conversation.

"A rather difficult role for a woman, although for a widow it may be more possible. I would certainly wish to be part of your rebellion, my lady. Given my many activities over the years, I am certainly not afraid of public censure. Are you willing to risk your reputation to seize the prize for which you lust?"

His voice deepened on the final word, sending a wave of fear throughout her.

She stopped in the middle of the last ladies' cogwheel, her gaze riveted on his face. Dear God was he about to shock the ton with some public display? Her heart thudded. Had she baited this tiger unknowingly?

He pressed her onward, however, moving into the last grand chain and bowing to her with a flourish when the music stopped.

Relief swept through her, and she valiantly curtsied, then took his arm as he led her from the floor. She actually leaned on him, for that last fright had turned her legs weak. Thank goodness that dance was over, although she must admit Mr. Garrett had proved a good dancer and a very exciting partner. She closed her eyes and breathed a sigh of relief. Jane would no doubt scold her anew for dancing with Mr. Garrett, but she thought she had managed to scotch any scandal brewing.

A shadow crossed her face and Charlotte opened her eyes to find they had entered a dim stairwell, with a flight of dusty stairs leading to the attics. Her mouth dried as though she'd eaten sand.

Before her eyes could adjust, he wrapped his arms around her, squeezing her against his granite hard chest. When his hot mouth found hers, she gasped. Oh, drat. She should have known he would try something like this.

He darted his tongue through her open lips, and she squealed, then quieted. The last thing she wanted was for someone to find them so engaged. His hands cradled her head as he explored every inch of her mouth with a gentle thoroughness she had not known for years. Had anyone ever kissed her thus? With an intensity designed to kindle flames in her soul? Perhaps Edward. But that had been so long ago she'd forgotten how good it felt, except...

That blasted cologne of his. Pressed right up against him, Charlotte couldn't help but breathe in the overpowering scent of bergamot. *Lord, don't let me sneeze.*

That thought broke the spell. She pushed Mr. Garrett away from her.

He panted as if he had run a race. "Devil take it. Are you trying to get us thrown out, Charlotte?"

"Me?" Her voice rose and she stopped and lowered it. "You're the one trying to ruin my reputation. And do not call me Charlotte. I haven't given you permission."

"After that little interlude, I don't need permission." He grinned at her in the faulty light. "You can't deny you enjoyed that."

"I can and do deny it." She pressed her hand to her chest, where he heart still hammered. She hadn't enjoyed it. Not really. But it had been exciting. More exciting than anything in her life for the past six years. Pray God he couldn't see her face. It must be the color of ripe cherries.

"Me thinks the lady doth protest too much. May I call upon you tomorrow?" He grabbed her hand and placed his lips on the palm. The kiss burned even through the glove.

"I don't think that would be wise for either of us." She must hold on to what little sanity was left to her.

His eyes darkened, and he ran his finger over her swollen lips. "Allow me to be the judge of what is wise, my dear. Come, I will escort you to Lady John before we are lost entirely." He took her hand, stuck his head around the doorframe then pulled her quickly into the room.

Blinking in the suddenly bright lights, she stumbled after him as he made his way toward her cousin.

"Here you are, my dear. Safe and sound again." Mr. Garrett bowed, his eyebrows arched in innocence. "Lady John."

Charlotte finally focused on her surrounding enough to find Jane staring at her darkly, through lowered brows. Oh, dear. What on earth must she look like after such an encounter?

Dumbfounded, she stood before them, quite at a loss for words or actions. Dazed by the overwhelming pulse that still throbbed throughout her, she could only glance from one to the other of them, praying one would be her savior.

"I will look forward anxiously to our next meeting, Charlotte." He kissed her fingers, the warmth of his lips like a banked fire. With a final flourished bow, he turned and strode into the crowd.

Stunned, Charlotte simply stood still, the chatter of the ballroom subsiding into one sound—the pounding of blood in her ears.

"Charlotte," her cousin said, grasping her arm until it hurt "we must remove at once to the retiring room."

Distantly thankful that someone had taken charge of her, Charlotte followed docilely as Jane towed her back the way they had come. They descended on an empty corner and her cousin pushed her into a chair.

"Sit there. I must find a footman"

"Whatever for?"

"To send for some lemonade from the refreshment table. I'll go wet my handkerchief to repair your face and see if I can do something with your hair." Jane fired off the strategy as efficiently as any general, then picked up her skirts and hurried away.

Charlotte leaned back against the chair and sighed. She had managed to survive her first encounter with a rake with few people the wiser, than God.

Jane reappeared, clutching a glass of lemonade.

"Tark would be proud of your martial skills, Jane." Charlotte grinned, although Jane seemed not to enjoy her compliment.

"You hold your tongue." She thrust the glass into Charlotte's hands. "Dear lord, he's mussed this whole section on the left side. Here." Jane dug into her own coiffure and produced two pins. "What on earth were you thinking, Charlotte? To be ravished at Almack's on your first night out!"

"I was just congratulating myself that it wasn't worse. At least no one knows what happened."

Jane looked daggers at her, then produced a wet cloth and pressed it to Charlotte's mouth. "Wha ah oo doing?"

"Your lips are swollen, dear. You have that delectable very well-kissed look." Jane's eyes took on a distant aspect and her lips curved into a nostalgic smile. "Excellent after an evening in bed with your husband." The smile vanished, replaced by lips pressed into a thin line. "Disastrous in the public rooms, however. You'll be lucky if it's not being discussed over every breakfast table in the morning." She blotted Charlotte's swollen lips once more. "Now the lemonade. The sugar will guard against shock and the astringent of the lemons may help the swelling."

Jane plucked the glass from Charlotte's hands and shoved it against her full lips. She drank deeply, savoring the cool, sweet liquid. She had no idea being seduced was such thirsty work.

"You must pull yourself back together and return to the ballroom in all haste. You will set the tongues to wagging even worse if you do not." She gave Charlotte a withering look. "As I feared, it is more difficult to secure a partner and hold his attention this evening. Yet you must attempt to do so in order to divert everyone from your unfortunate behavior." Jane pressed the sodden scrap of linen to Charlotte's temple. "I am particularly concerned that Elizabeth and Georgina did not attend tonight."

She shook her head and Charlotte sighed. Two of their friends, also widows, had not quite gotten over their husbands' deaths.

"Where is Fanny? I would have thought she would be here certainly."

"She had a last minute invitation to Lady Beaumont's masquerade. She said it suited her better to make a dramatic unveiling." Jane dropped into the chair next to Charlotte. "I doubt she will lack partners during the night."

Charlotte cut her eyes toward her cousin. Her arch tone spoke for itself. However, she did not doubt it either. Her other friends were another matter. "If we could have the men to ourselves somehow we might have a better chance of Elizabeth and Georgina making an impression on them." Charlotte took another sip of the lemonade, as she turned her mind to the problem of her friends.

"Yes, these gentlemen who are left on the marriage mart have had the most beautiful girls fawning over them all Season. We need to get them alone." Jane paused and grinned. "Not alone *that* way, although I for one would not turn down such a tryst if offered."

"Jane!"

Her cousin had the grace to blush. "You have no right to say anything at the moment, Charlotte. In any case, we need to spend time with these gentlemen and make them see how our sterling qualities surpass those of the younger ladies. As we would at a house party."

"But who of our circle is able to host such a thing?" Charlotte slumped. Their situation seemed more doubtful given the reality of their situations. "Neither Elizabeth's nor Georgie's circumstances will allow it." Upon her husband's death, her best friend Elizabeth and her children had returned to her parents' home. Georgie had fared even worse. Currently she was housed only by the grace and charity of her complaining sister-in-law, Mrs. Reynolds.

"I suppose I might be able to persuade Theale to allow me use of one of his estates," Jane said. "He was quite affected by Tark's death. He and his brother were very close. Of course I couldn't tell him why I need the use of it." She sighed and looked sad for the first time that day. "I do miss Tark, you know." She glanced around the almost empty room. "I will not marry again. He made some canny purchases in real estate. As a result I'd be a fool to relinquish my jointure."

Charlotte tried to fix her cousin with a stern stare. The woman who had been her dearest friend and companion all her life had taught her well that all women were not conventional. Despite Jane's sweet face and soft, womanly body, her heart and soul thrived on breaking society's rules whenever she could. She had done so for most of her thirty years. "Then why do you wish to meet gentlemen again? Surely nothing can come of such attentions, if you have so made up your mind?"

Jane patted her arm. "For the same reason you indulged in Mr. Garrett tonight." She smiled sadly. "Tark is dead, not I. And male companionship is so…stimulating, wouldn't you say?"

Charlotte clamped her hands over her burning cheeks.

"I am not adverse to a little dalliance, if given a quiet, secluded place to dally." Jane's face had taken on a faraway look.

Wishing for something a bit stronger, Charlotte sipped her lemonade and gathered her wits, trying to resolve the problem. A place for a successful house party was the very thing they needed. Such a secluded spot, however, could hardly be attempted here in London under the scrutiny of their families. If they wanted true seclusion, they needed an estate in the country. None of them, however, had such a place to hand...

She sat straighter in her chair as Jane chatted on. An inkling of an idea presented itself as if a gift from the gods. She needed time to think about the organization of it, but yes, this notion just might do.

"Jane, are you free tomorrow morning?"

Her cousin glanced quizzically at her, but nodded.

"Can you please send messages to the ladies of our circle, and ask them to call upon us at ten o'clock. I believe I may have the answer to all our prayers." She stood and looked around the now deserted retiring room, satisfaction welling up in her chest. "We shall have a formal meeting of The Widow's Club and plan our strategy to snare the gentlemen of our choice."

Meet the Author

Jenna Jaxon is the author of Only Scandal Will Do and Only Marriage Will Do, the first two books in her Pleasure House series, as well as the historical romance trilogy Time Enough to Love. She lives in Virginia with her family and a small menagerie of pets. When not reading or writing, she indulges her passion for the theatre, working with local theatres as a director. Visit her at jennajaxon.wordpress.com.

CPSIA information can be obtained
at www.ICGtesting.com
Printed in the USA
BVOW08s0902201217
503308BV00002B/516/P